Replaying the Game

Emily Tudor

For Lexi and Hannah. Thank you for giving me the courage to jump into this crazy dream of mine that started with one text message.

And for anyone afraid to love again. One day someone will prove everything you know about love to be wrong. Be patient. Someone will love every single part of you—of that, I'm sure.

Content Warnings

This book contains references to the loss of a parent off page and sexual touching without consent, and physical violence—not between the main characters.

Some words or phrases used could be triggering. Please protect your mental health.

Playlist

Adore You - Harry Styles
All I Want - Olivia Rodrigo
Bags - Clairo
Better - Gracie Abrams
Big Black Car - Gregory Alan Isakov
The Bottom - Gracie Abrams
ceilings - Lizzy McAlpine
Change (Taylor's Version) - Taylor Swift
Enchanted (Taylor's Version) - Taylor Swift
False Art - Ben Kessler & Lizzy McAlpine
Friends - Chase Atlantic
Green Light - Lorde
Hurt Somebody - Noah Kahan & Julia Michaels
I Don't Wanna Know - Knox

EMILY TUDOR

I Wanna Be Yours - Arctic Monkeys
Jealous - Nick Jonas
Just a Little Bit of Your Heart - Ariana Grande
Like Real People Do - Hozier
Like the Movies - Laufey
Oh No! - Marina and The Diamonds
People Watching - Conan Gray
Pool House - The Backseat Lovers
So High School - Taylor Swift
The Story Of Us (Taylor's Version) - Taylor Swift
Until I Found You - Stephen Sanchez & Em Beihold
The Way I Loved You (Taylor's Version) - Taylor Swift
when the party's over - Billie Eilish
Wildest Dreams (Taylor's Version) - Taylor Swift
You Don't Go To Parties - 5 Seconds of Summer
1 step forward, 3 steps back - Olivia Rodrigo

"Let me tell you something about love. It does not knock often. And when it does you have to let it in."

Brooke Davis, *One Tree Hill*

"And I like large parties. They're so intimate. At small parties there isn't any privacy."

Jordan Baker, *The Great Gatsby*

1

Hadleigh

"Is this book just a how to get away with murder for dummies?"

Ella asks a valid question because it quite literally details how the main character gets away with framing someone else for murder. Finishing this series has been a big highlight for the book club. The first of the trilogy was one of the earliest we all read together, so it will always hold a special place in all our hearts.

One of my favorite parts of the week happens every Wednesday night with the three beautiful people around me—book club. The Grand Mountain Book Club. We meet once a week to talk about the books we read with one another. We all returned to school for the Spring semester about a week ago, and even though we talked every day over break, we still met tonight to discuss the book.

I love what this club has formed into. It used to be only book talk, but since the four of us are all attached at the hip, we chat about any and all things going on in our lives. I don't know why I was so worried about not making friends when I got here—these girls and I fell into a beautiful friendship as soon as I showed up to the first book club meeting last year.

"I honestly think Paige could be the main character in this book. She could one hundred percent get away with framing someone for murder." I smile at the group.

Paige Yarrow is the most sunshiney and adorable human being you will ever meet, but don't let that fool you. Most of the time, her favorite part of the books we read is the murder, arson, or some other thing that makes us question her sanity.

"I am neither going to confirm nor deny that statement." She smiles, her long, dirty blonde hair flowing behind her back. Her light green eyes are beaming—most likely at the thought of framing someone for murder—as she looks around at us. Amelia told us once that Paige woke her up in the middle of the night because she thought she solved a cold case.

She didn't, but she's studying criminal justice, so her love for true crime definitely helps in that aspect of her life.

"Confirm or deny all you want. We all know it's true. I always hear those murder documentaries on your laptop before you go to bed. One time, I walked into the apartment, and you had fallen asleep in the middle of one. I had to turn it off before they started talking about cut-up body parts. Especially before I made a sandwich for dinner. I seriously don't know how you watch those," Amelia says. She and Paige are roommates and have their own apartment on campus for the next two years.

The two are juniors this year and have been inseparable since they were randomly assigned to be each other's roommates when they were freshmen. It was a match made in heaven—or hell. Ella and I have yet to decide.

Amelia has short, curly brown hair and is around 5'9", with eyes the color of the ocean. They stand out against her olive skin and her need to laugh at everyone else's misery.

"I definitely don't want to bail any of you out of jail, but if I had to, I would," Ella tells us. She's the oldest of our group, and I don't even want to think about what will happen when she graduates at the end of the semester.

Her long, reddish-brown hair curls down her back, and her beautiful brown eyes sparkle under the fluorescents of the classroom we're all sitting in. Ella is not only the fiery one in our group, but she's also the mom friend. She's always checking in on us mentally, physically, and emotionally, and I will miss her so much when she goes off into the real world.

She did create the book club, after all—her and Paige, technically. She saw Paige reading one of her favorite books in the library and immediately went up to her to discuss it. They chatted about it for a few hours and decided to make a book club. Only Amelia and Paige showed up to the meeting, and I joined when I was a freshman.

The four of us have been going strong for two years, and nothing can break us apart at this rate.

Grand Mountain College is so much more than a tiny liberal arts college in the middle of Virginia—it's my home away from home. It's a small campus—only around five thousand students and faculty—and is aptly named for the town surrounding the campus.

Grand Mountain, Virginia, is the most adorable college town ever. We get all four seasons here, and that alone is one of the reasons I chose to come. It doesn't snow back home in California, and I've loved being able to see snow fall from the sky since I don't see it back home. It's also wonderful reading and studying weather. There's something so peaceful about studying while snowflakes fall from the sky.

Since we've only been back for two weeks, we've spent most of our Wednesday nights discussing this book, but now that we're finished, we have to pick another book to read.

It's weird to think my sophomore year is almost over. In some ways, it feels like it just started. Though, coming back here after mid-semester break didn't feel as strange as last time—in fact, it felt like coming home, in a way. I'm excited to see what this semester has in store for me, even though I never leave my dorm or go to any of the parties that happen on campus. I care way too much about my grades to bother with dumb parties.

That's me—Hadleigh Baker. I'm not only allergic to going out, but I also put more effort into my academics than most people put into anything. I have short black hair, round brown eyes, and prefer skirts to pants.

"So, what do you guys want to read this month? I could make a chart and Paige could make a pros and cons list about each book so we can discuss," I say to the group.

"A good list is the key to a stable life."

"Paige, when have you ever described yourself as stable? Yesterday you burst into the living room with tears running down your face about that Romeo and Juliette retelling you're reading." Amelia laughs as she remembers. That book is still a sore subject for Paige. I didn't think we would bring it up right now, but Amelia loves to play the emotional warfare game—it's her favorite thing to do with the people she loves.

"Maybe not stable, but organized. At least I get all my assignments done efficiently, and I told you not to bring that book up, or I'll start crying!" She shoots Amelia a glare that's not scary at all.

"Okay, before Paige starts babbling, let's change the subject. Hads, why don't you make a chart with three books and send it to the group chat. We can vote on Friday, or something." Ella grabs her bag and tosses it over her shoulder. "I have to get back to my apartment. I have my stupid internship tomorrow."

"Right." Amelia laughs. "The one with Leo. How's that going so far?"

If I couldn't see the smile already on her face, I could tell just by how she phrased her question.

"Are you guys still at each other's throats?" Paige asks, concern lacing her voice.

Since it's Ella's last semester, she grabbed an internship with a marketing firm around the corner from school. She was one of two people out of hundreds to nab a spot. Unfortunately, the other person who got the second spot is the person she despises the most. None of us knows why she hates him—nobody dares to ask—but all we know is something happened, and now she can't stand him.

"Please do not dare use his first name around me. He is Zimmerman and Zimmerman only. We're not on a first-name basis because he infuriates me with his stupid face and even stupider British accent."

"Ah, yes, the classic enemies-to-lovers trope," Amelia says while standing up.

Ella shoots her a death glare. "That's not what's happening here. Also, enemies to lovers are saved for fantasy books. You don't see me threatening to kill him with a knife to his throat, do you? That's real enemies to lovers. We would be haters to lovers sans lovers because that will never happen!" Her voice gets progressively louder as she exits the room, leaving the three of us behind in silence.

"Like I told you guys before, Zimmerman is a no-go topic right now. We don't even know what's happening with them, but I told you not to bring it up." I stare at Amelia, and she smiles. Damn her and her emotional warfare.

All we know about him is that Leo Zimmerman has a reputation for being an asshole and he tends to sleep around, according to all the rumors that spread across campus. I swear nothing stays hidden at this school. It's impossible not to hear all the whispers that float around.

"I've tried to get Amelia to stop, but she likes how it makes her feel. It is one of her favorite hobbies," Paige states as she grabs her tote bag.

We exit our tiny classroom and catch up with Ella as she walks back to her car. It's a chilly night, but a nice breeze blasts through the air. I'm not too cold because my cardigan and boots keep me warm, even though I'm wearing a skirt and tights.

We all walk in silence for a minute, just listening to the breeze and bustle of the campus around us. It's a friendship like this I never thought I would find—people with whom you can share the silence and not have to fill it with meaningless conversation. Sometimes, their presence is enough—my three non-biological sisters.

"I applied to be a tutor," I say to them before Ella gets in her car.

"Honestly, if any of us were to do that, it would be you. No offense to the rest of us, but Hads is definitely the smartest," Ella says.

"I agree," Paige and Amelia say simultaneously.

"Any specific subject, or a tutor in general?" Paige asks.

"I think in general if the school will let me," I say with slight confidence. Being a tutor is something I've wanted to do, but last year, they told me I couldn't until I took some more classes. Now that I have a few more under my belt, I can at least sign up for it—which I did the day I returned to campus. I'm waiting to hear back, and it's driving me crazy.

Ella strolls across the parking lot to her car and says goodnight to us. "Welcome back, guys. I can't wait for all the books we'll read this semester! Text me when you get home safely, please. Love you all so much!"

We all say goodnight and head toward the apartments and dorms. Grand Mountain College is my unofficial home for the next two years. The campus is tiny, and I'm grateful I live close to my friends and my brother, who also goes to college here.

"Bye, Hads! See you tomorrow!" Paige says as she scurries to catch up with Amelia, who's now unlocking their front door. I wave in her direction and walk back to my dorm.

As I walk through the halls, I can already hear the music my roommate Taylor is playing. We have a corner room on our floor, which is slightly bigger, but it's not soundproof. Taylor only has two volumes—asleep and loud—but I love her regardless. We've lived together for two years, and she helped get me out of my shell when we were new kids on campus.

Taylor also attends most of the parties that are thrown on campus. Ever since we've become friends, she's tried to drag me to one of the crazy parties that happens at the hockey house, the baseball house, or one of the other off-campus houses.

I've told her a thousand times that I hate parties, sports, and have no interest in dating or hooking up with someone, but I'm surprised she hasn't kidnapped me and forced me to go to a party with her.

If anyone could get me to leave the comfort of my dorm, it would be Taylor or Ella.

I open the door, and there she is, sitting at her desk and dancing in her chair. She doesn't even turn around when I come in, and I take this time to scare the crap out of her.

"Boo!"

She jumps and tries to swing her arm around to hit me. "Ah!" When she realizes it's me, she hits me. "You scared the crap out of me!"

I only laugh as she turns her music down. "That'll teach you to turn your music down when you're alone and your back is to the door."

"I like to feel the beat of the music. Sue me," she says. "How was book club?"

"It was good. I have to pick a few choices so we can decide what to read next. Do you want to help before I shower?"

She closes her book immediately. "Absolutely. Hit me with your three best summaries, Hads."

I smile as I grab three radically different books off of my small shelf and stack them on her desk.

"This one is a romantic comedy based on two people who work in publishing."

"Cute, I guess," Taylor says. She's not a big reader, but she loves helping me make decisions for book club. "What about that one?"

I grab the book she pointed at—a pink and purple cover. I quickly read the back. "It's a sapphic romance—"

She cuts me off before I can finish. "Ella would love that one. I like the cover. Let's go with that one."

"I need one more choice, Taylor."

She gets off of her desk chair and walks over to my shelf, pulls out another book and throws it onto my bed.

"We have all read that one already, Tay."

"Perfect, then you can read the other one. Problem solved!" She smiles as she hands me the book.

I scoff before I send a picture to the girls.

Hads: Taylor has chosen our next read.

Ella: Give Taylor a hug for me! This book has been on my shelf forever!

Paige: Yay! I'm so excited!

Amelia: Cute. I can't wait to discuss!

Taylor throws her music on before I head to take a shower, needing to get mentally ready for my classes tomorrow. I'm not much of a morning person, and having a class right at nine a.m. is something I want to smack Hads from last semester for. Why did I make my own schedule like this?

Especially when it's math that I have to learn so early in the morning. Granted, statistics isn't too hard, but it does make my head hurt. At least I have class with Paige and my brother, Oliver, after it. Then, I'm done for the day. Even if I hate getting up early, it's nice I get the rest of the afternoon to myself on Thursdays.

The only thing I want is for this semester to go smoothly. I'm taking as many credits as I can to get ahead, but I'm already exhausted thinking about the amount of assignments I have—and it's only been a week. I don't think I can handle anything else throwing a hitch in my grades, which is why I stay away from most parties and people on campus. I have my friends and I stick to them. I don't need anyone else.

As I step into my lukewarm shower, I silently hope my shower temperature isn't a premonition for how the rest of the year is going to go.

Sophomore year, please be kind to me.

2

Hadleigh

I REACH OVER TO snooze my alarm, but Taylor throws a pillow at me as I do.

"Good morning, sunshine! Please get up or shut your alarm off because it's driving me up the wall."

"Taylor, I'm contemplating my existence right now," I say as I place her pillow over my head. "Please, you know my morning routine."

"Does it involve waking up the entire hallway? Your alarm is louder than a car horn."

"Says you! Do you even remember how loud your music was last night?"

She cracks her neck as she sits up fully. "Fair point."

"That's what I thought," I say as I finally get up.

"Have you talked to your brother since you got here?"

"We flew here separately, but I saw him in class last week. He didn't say much to me, but we did spend the entire summer together, so he's probably sick of me."

Going to the same college as my grumpy older brother wasn't on my life plan, but here we are—both at the same small college in Virginia. He's studying criminal justice, and I'm studying biology. Paige probably sees my brother more than me since they have all the same classes, but that only means she has to deal with his cold stares and quiet demeanor.

Don't get me wrong, I love my brother. He's one of my best friends. He's done all of the typical older brother things like teach me how to drive, threaten any boys that came near me in high school, and always makes fun of my clothes. But never did I imagine going to college with him. Grand Mountain was my safety school, but I might not have met the girls if I had gotten into one of the other schools.

I applied to a few different Ivy League schools but got waitlisted by all of them. When none of them called me when I had to make my final decision, I chose Grand Mountain. Even UCLA rejected me, and it would have been nice to stay in-state for college. But moving across the country got me out of the comfort of the small town we're from in California.

Everything truly happens for a reason, and even though I was heart-broken when I didn't get into the schools of my dreams, it all worked out okay in the end. Now, I get to have class with my brother.

He's only one year older than me, so he will be graduating next year with Paige and Amelia. I'm going to be so bored when they're all gone, and I hope they don't all forget about me when they head off into the real world.

"Are you free for lunch today? I have some time in the middle of the day if you want to grab a bite at the dining hall," Taylor asks me.

"Yeah, I'm free. After eleven, I have all day to get ahead on my homework for this semester. I was planning on going to the library, but we can grab a bite before I do."

She sighs when I finish talking. "Hads, I mean this in the nicest way possible, you're a nerd."

"I care about my grades, Taylor. If that makes me nerdy, then so be it."

"Did you hear about the party this weekend?" she asks me, a sparkle in her eye. "I heard it's going to be huge."

Taylor's a communication major, and she has an on-campus job reporting on everything that happens on campus.

Translation: Taylor loves the gossip that spreads across the campus, and her position at work allows her to know most things before everyone else does. She practically thrives off of rumors.

"No, I didn't," I tell her as I throw on a black skirt, some tights, and a green off-the-shoulder sweater. I lace my boots up and grab my bag. "Are you going to go?"

"It's at the hockey house. Of course I'm going to go."

I hold back my gag. "Sounds fun."

"Can you at least try to be excited? I swear Hads, one of these days, I'll get you to one of these parties if it kills me."

I'm halfway out the door before I turn back to her. "Over my dead body, Tay. I'll see you later."

TRYING TO FIGURE OUT probabilities this early should be a crime. I've never liked math—even though I'm good at it. I much prefer analyzing a book or poem to probabilities and distributions.

Thankfully, my next class is a bit more exciting. This is my first class with one of the girls, and it's so much fun sitting next to Paige in class and seeing her shine as she furiously types notes on her computer. She always saves me a seat, though after the first week, most people stay in the spots they chose on day one.

I head to the third floor of this building, enter the correct room, and immediately spot Paige. She looks up from her book and waves me over. As I sit in my seat, warmth radiates from Paige as if she's had three cups of coffee already. Though I know she hasn't because she doesn't drink it—she gets panic attacks if she does.

As students trickle in, I notice there aren't a lot of female students studying criminal justice. It's us and two others in a class of thirty students. Paige and I look so out of place in this room. My brother walks through the door, and I give him a wave. He shoots one back and sits right behind me like he did last week.

"Has your first week back been okay? Sorry I haven't texted much, but if you want to keep the tradition up, maybe we can go for a walk every Saturday morning like last semester?" Oh yeah, I almost forgot about that.

While I was trying to adjust to campus life and being away from home last year, my brother offered to keep up our tradition of going on walks like we used to do at home. Every Saturday morning, we walk around this park by our house and watch the sunrise.

Oliver and I are from a small city in California. I loved growing up there, but it felt so loud at times. Being on this tiny campus makes the outside noise seem so much quieter. I hate getting up early—especially on the weekend—but it helped me feel more comfortable around campus. I also liked the idea of keeping some traditions from home. Bringing them here made me feel less lonely, as if a piece of home would always be with me.

"That sounds good, and you know how much I like rambling on while you grunt and stare off into space." My brother is a good listener, and he always gives good advice when I ask, but he's not one for small talk.

"Hads, why are you taking this class again?" *Ouch*. Maybe he doesn't like being seen with me.

"I'm trying to become well-rounded in my studies, and criminology interests me. Also, this is a liberal arts college, and being able to dip my toe in different fields will make me more appealing on job applications. I'm not afraid to step out of my comfort zone and try new topics. Boom," I say as I spin back around and face the front as the professor walks in.

Paige leans over to me. "This professor is easy with grading, and there are usually only four chapter tests and a project throughout the year, so I think you'll be alright. Your poor brother just thinks you're trying to steal his thunder." Then she turns around and winks at Oliver. My brother responds with a cold stare at Paige's bright, smiling face.

It's weird to see her interacting with my brother. I knew they have had almost every class together since freshman year, but seeing them interact was like watching a puppy run into a boulder—my brother being the boulder.

"The contrast between you and my brother's personalities is such a dichotomy, I don't even have time to get into it because we'd be here all day."

Paige stares at me for a minute before speaking. "He's one of the only people I like in my classes. Yeah, he's quiet, but he always gets his work done whenever I've had a group project with him. I'd like to call us acquaintances, but sometimes I forget he's your brother. You're both so different."

I turn around and grab my iPad from my bag. We still have some stuff to go over regarding the assignments and such. This class is only once a week for an hour and a half, which is nice in retrospect. I should be able to get ahead on other things and not have to worry about this one.

I spend most of my time worrying about my grades. It's important to me that I keep up my average because I hate the idea of not having perfect grades. I know college is hard and everything, but I know myself.

I'm smart, and I put a lot of pressure on myself to have perfect grades. In high school, it was because I wanted to get into some of the top schools in the country, and since that didn't happen, I feel like I have more to prove to myself. I can be better than I was back then. Maybe if I wasn't so worried about the colleges I wanted to get into, I would've gotten an A instead of an A minus and would have been the top of my class.

I was second in my class in high school, and I cried about that for days.

Now as I start this new semester, I want more than ever to keep my perfect average. Each new start is like a competition with myself, and I always pride myself on beating the voice in my head that says I'm never going to succeed in life if my grades aren't perfect.

"Paige, why was I not aware most people studying criminal justice here are dudes?" I feel so out of place as I sit in this room. I don't know how Paige does it, but big props to her because I would not want to be surrounded by all this testosterone on a daily basis.

"You get used to it. It sucks sometimes having to do the group projects all by myself since I don't trust them to do it right, but you also learn how to stand your ground. I've never been good at that," she says the last part a bit quieter. Paige has always been a ball of positivity, but in the past, she has told me stories where people have treated her like a literal doormat.

The professor starts the lecture, and I open my iPad and start writing my notes down while Paige types aggressively on her computer. I look behind me and my brother writes with terrible handwriting in his notebook. Today's lecture is on the concepts of crime, and I know this class will be a breeze. It's nice knowing I have these two to help me through this class as well. Paige and Oliver are experts at all things crime, and it'll be nice to ask them any questions I might have.

Though, if this class ends up dropping my grade average, I might have to take a page out of the textbook and set something on fire.

I'm sure Paige would help me.

I tuck that idea away for the future as the professor clicks to the next slide.

3

"It's already two weeks into the semester, and you're already failing a class? How is that even possible?"

"Try taking the most boring English class in the world at eight in the morning," I say as I slam my locker shut. I would normally hate how pissy I sound, but I'm too worked up to care. I got my first grade back yesterday, and it was an F—for failure. It's been two weeks of the semester, and I'm already failing one of my classes.

This is officially the worst start to a semester I've had, and if I keep it up, I'm going to be fucked.

Well, I kind of already am since my coach wants to talk with me after practice. I assume it's about the grade because he gets notified if we fail something or if our grades slip below a 2.0 average.

At the beginning of every season, he tells us that if our grades slip, we're automatically benched so we can focus on getting them back up. We're only conditioning because our games don't start for a few weeks, but being benched would ruin my entire life.

Not only am I on a scholarship to play hockey here at Grand Mountain, but I'm normally better at the academic side of being a student-athlete. Apparently, I got too comfortable and the big fat failure grade from my first quiz is all I can see when I shut my eyes.

"You guys ready?" Our captain, Liam Holt, asks us.

We all mutter in agreement and as I head to the gym with my team, my best friend and roommate, Jacks comes over to me, slapping my shoulder.

"Worry about one thing at a time, G. We'll figure out your grades later," he says.

Easy for you to say, I think to myself. He's never failed at fucking anything. And as I lift the weight plates onto the bar, I try to spend today's conditioning session working out all of my annoyed and weird feelings and know it's probably not going to work.

Two hours later, I'm across from my coach in his office as the guys hit the showers and cool down from our workout. He's pretending to filter through some papers, but I know he's doing his usual thing where he waits for you to talk first. It's some sort of psychological power trip or something. After fifteen minutes, I bite the bullet and open my mouth.

"You wanted to see me?"

"I see you're failing a class already."

I practically called it. Not only does word travel fast around this incredibly small campus, but those weekly update emails about all of our grades get sent out as soon as grades are put into the system.

"Your scholarship could be at risk, boy. Get your grades up, or you're off the team." He says nothing else as he stands up and leaves me in his office.

I'm frozen where I sit as his words filter into my brain. *Off the team*. If I don't pass this stupid class, my dreams of playing hockey at a Division two school will be over, and they've barely even started.

I'm such a fucking failure.

I grab my bag and get up, heading toward the locker room so I can get back to my place and study. Studying is all I'm going to be doing until midterms because I cannot afford to lose my scholarship. As the only child of a single mother, she can't afford for me to not have this money to help cover all of my tuition.

I burst through the door, the anger practically fuming off my body as I get to my locker.

"What the hell is going on with you?" my teammate, Ryan, asks. He's a sophomore like me, but his attitude sucks and he goes through women like toilet paper. Typical jock asshole. He's not one of my favorite guys on this team, and hearing his voice after the conversation I had isn't helping.

"Coach threatened to kick me off the team if I didn't get my grade up, so naturally, I'm pissed because I have no idea how to get my grade up." I'm heading toward the shower when Jacks chimes in.

"You could get a tutor."

A tutor? No. No fucking way. That would be like me admitting I'm a huge fucking failure and can't keep my grades up on my own. I've never needed anyone else's help before, and I'm not going to start now.

"I don't need a tutor, Jacks. I need my fucking professor to stop giving weekly chapter tests on the dumb book we're reading." What the fuck is a Gatsby anyway?

"What book did he choose for this semester? We did *The Catcher in the Rye,* and let me tell you, that main character was weird as shit. Honestly, the whole book was strange."

"Why does Professor Collins format his class like that anyway? A semester-long study of one book doesn't make any sense. What is that teaching me?" Nothing. It's teaching me absolutely fucking nothing.

"How to sleep with your eyes open in class?" Holt chimes in.

"How to bullshit your way through life?" Rhodes says as he laughs.

"How to do the bare minimum so you can focus on pulling more chicks?" Ryan says.

"Shut up, Ryan," I scoff and head toward the showers. As I go through my normal routine, the idea of having a tutor doesn't seem like the worst thing ever. Maybe Jacks was right and I should ask around. Though, I've heard through the rumor mill on campus that Collins never gives above a B plus in this class.

I shake it off as quickly as it enters my brain. I don't need anyone's help to pass this class. As long as I put more time and effort into studying for these chapter tests, I'll eventually pass. If I put the work in, I can pass the midterm, and if I pass that, I'll be golden.

I don't need a tutor. I don't need help from someone else. I always admired how my dad seemed to do everything when I was a kid—he was like my own personal superhero. My mom calls the two of us stubborn—well, she did when he was alive. Now, I'm the only one she can call stubborn.

Cancer is the worst word in the English language—at least in my book because it took my dad off of this earth way too fucking soon. Even in his final days all those years ago, he never wanted help changing his socks or doing things around the house.

Asking for help is my greatest fear because why would I need it when I have it myself? I can pass this class as long as I put the work in.

I'm studying physical education with a minor in sports management because I want to become a coach one day. One stupid English class is not going to keep me from my dream of coaching younger kids on the sport I've loved my whole life. Since I had the best coach growing up—my father—my dream career path became clear to me when he passed away. I want to make young athletes feel how my dad did—like anything is possible if you work hard enough, love the game enough, and your dreams can come true.

The pang of missing him hits me in the chest, but I shove that down because I have other things I need to be focusing on. I can't afford to think about how much of my life he's missed out on.

I need a plan. First, I need to figure out what the hell is going on in this book, and then I need to make a study plan so I don't fail the next quiz.

It'll be fine.

The semester has only just begun and I already feel like I need a break. Only a few months until it's over, and then I'll never have to take another English class again.

When I get back to my apartment and settle in for the night, I try to make a game plan for this class, but after twenty different attempts, I give up.

Why the fuck does this book make absolutely no sense? All I've gathered is there's two eggs, some green light this fucker can't stop staring at, and some guy likes to throw parties all the time.

It kind of reminds me of the parties Holt always throws at the hockey house, but that doesn't help me when trying to figure out what all this shit means.

And it doesn't help that Jacks won't stop staring at me. His blond hair looks like it's glowing since he's sitting in front of his lamp. He's got a typical hockey body like me—tall, skinny, and some muscles. But the only place we differ is he's an inch taller than me—which he mentions at least once a week.

"Dude, I can't focus on these fucking eggs while you're staring at me. What's up?"

He's silent for a second before he gets out of his chair, paces across the room, and sits back down. What the fuck is he doing?

"You realize if you confess to a crime right now, we don't have attorney-client privilege, and I would have to marry you to not testify against you. Spit it out, Jacks."

"There's this rumor about a girl who got an A in Collins' class last year. According to Holt, she applied to be a tutor this year." He's looking around as if he's going to get caught telling me this.

"I told you I don't need a tutor. I'm making a game plan." I don't need anybody else's help, but honestly, an A in Collins' class is nearly impossible to do. Maybe I should reconsider?

He lifts my papers up, looks at them, and throws them behind him.

"Dude! What the fuck?"

"Your game plan sucks and you know it. It's okay to need help in something, Grant. Having a tutor isn't admitting you're a failure."

I can only roll my eyes at him—even though he's right in why I don't want one.

But then I think about finding this girl. How would I do that? Holt only heard a rumor about her, but what if it's not true? The rumors that spread around this campus are more often false than they are true, so how can I trust whatever he's heard? And if she was real, how would I get her to help me? I'd have to seek her out—if she exists—and beg her to help me.

Begging is not something I'm used to, and I really don't want to start now.

But if I don't get my grade up and get kicked off the hockey team, I might throw myself off the roof of the student center.

Though, if I had a tutor, I could have spent my Friday night at the bar with the team rather than trying to figure out a plan for how I'm going to pass English.

I'm not a huge fan of going out sometimes. Most of the time, I get hit on by a bunch of girls who want to fuck me, and that's not who I am. Jacks has called me a relationship junkie because I tend to fall hard and fast into girls that catch my eye, but it hasn't worked out in my favor. All three of my last girlfriends have cheated on me, and even though I haven't done anything wrong, it still feels like I have. There's a pattern here, and if three people have deemed me not good enough to be monogamous with, then I *must* be the issue.

I've been single for an entire year, and I've been okay with that. Now that I'm failing a class, having a relationship has moved to the bottom of my list.

Jacks is back at his desk, and I sigh heavily before I speak again.

"So, where can we find this girl?"

Monday Morning

AFTER SPENDING ALL WEEKEND studying and still not being able to understand this confusing book, I've officially decided to track this girl down.

Though, I don't need to track her down because Holt found out her name and Jacks told me he has a biology class with her. He sent her a message yesterday, but she didn't respond, so I'm waiting outside of their class.

Now that I think about it, this could be seen as really fucking creepy. Maybe we should have waited until she answered, but I have another quiz coming up, and time is of the essence.

Am I going to look like a stalker? A creep? Shit.

The class gets out and I try to leave, but I get turned around since I've never been in this building before. I start to weave through the people, but I feel someone's leg get caught on mine, and they fall over. I turn around to help them up, and when I do, I come face to face with one of the most beautiful girls I've ever seen.

Holy shit, has she gone to this school the entire time? And how have I never seen her before? She's looking up at me with the sternest expression, but all I can focus on is how much I want to get to know everything about her so I can figure out how to make her smile at me.

I hold my hand out to her, wanting to feel her touch in mine, but the spell is broken when she swats my hand away.

"Shoo," she says to me as she stands up on her own.

"I—" *Say something! Say literally anything!*

She continues to stare at me as I stand in front of her like a blubbering idiot. I've never had this kind of mental block before. Normally, I can pick up a conversation immediately, but for some reason, my tongue feels dry in my mouth and I forgot every word in the dictionary.

"Did you need something, or are you going to keep staring at me like a wide-eyed puppy all day? Move along, hockey boy."

Well, there goes a good first impression.

While I'm contemplating how to fix this, Jacks comes out of the classroom and walks towards the girl who has made me forget how to speak.

"Grant, this is the girl I was telling you about, the one who can help you pass Intro to Lit this semester." My mouth hangs open a little, shock runs through my body because the girl who I can barely speak properly around is going to be my tutor until midterms.

I feel like I can see steam coming off of her ears, and I know I knocked her over, but that shouldn't have made her *this* upset. I hold out my hand to properly introduce myself, but since she smacked my hand away earlier, I doubt she'll return my handshake.

"I'm Grant, and I would very much appreciate your help. That is if you're available and willing to tutor this hockey boy." I toss her a wink, and she rolls her eyes at me. So much for a second-first impression.

She's silent for a minute, and before I feel like she's going to say nothing, she speaks. "Hadleigh."

Then, she turns and walks away.

Fuck, she's going to make me work for this, isn't she?

4

# Hadleigh

I WOULDN'T CALL WHAT I'm doing running away per se, but when some random guy who's a thousand feet tall knocks you over on a day that has already gone horribly, you tend not to want to stand around and make friends with him.

Oh, and on top of all that, he plays hockey here. *Hockey*.

I've done all I can to distance myself from any and all jocks—well, men in general—and getting tangled up in the web of sports assholes is not something I want to be doing. I have nothing against sports—I find it impressive that one can be a student and an athlete at the same time—but I don't care for them. I don't watch them or have a favorite team from each sport, and it doesn't help that my one and only ex-boyfriend was a football player.

A football player who cheated on me for the entire time we were dating, and I found out about all of his infidelity in front of my entire high school during the biggest pep rally of the year.

It was the single most embarrassing moment of my entire life, and after that, I swore off dating and threw myself into my studies.

But this guy wants me to tutor him? Already? The semester has been going for all of two weeks. There's no way he's failing something at this point, right? I can't help but feel a tiny twinge of guilt and pity wrapped into one.

I don't feel too bad, though. He did run me over, after all.

I walk away from the guy toward the lounge so I can get some studying done before I notice the tower is following me.

"Listen, I understand my first impression wasn't the best, but to be fair, I offered you my hand, and you didn't want to take it."

Is this guy serious? Why would I take his hand when he knocked me over in the first place?

"Are you talking to me, or is there a ghost standing behind me that you can see and I can't?" He's staring at me, and you would think I was speaking another language or something with the amount of silence and stuttering this guy does. He opens his mouth and when nothing comes out, I cut him off. "Look, you seem... okay, but there's no way you're looking for a tutor, so what's the real reason you're harassing me while I'm trying to study?"

"I actually do need a tutor. Professor Collins' class—rumor has it you got an A in his class, which is hard to do, and I'm currently failing. So, I need a tutor, and you seem to be my only option."

It's been two weeks. It takes a special kind of idiot to fail the first quiz, and they get progressively harder as the semester progresses. This guy is right—I am his only option. *Shit.*

"Well, the rumor was right, for once. I also signed up to tutor, but why should I tutor you? You not only knocked me over and dirtied my skirt, but you seem pushy."

"Yeah, we met five minutes ago. Believe it or not, I was there."

I throw a smirk his way. "There's that attitude again."

"There's that joyful spirit I've come to love so much."

"I'm not interested, which you're obviously not used to hearing, so let me say it a bit slower so you catch my drift. I am *not* interested." I turn to sit back at the table, but he still hasn't moved from in front of me. Why is he standing here like a fucking statue?

"Okay, listen, this is exactly like the scene from the book when Nick carried away meets Gatsby. I'm like Nick, and you're Gatsby, right? I'm asking you for help as if I just revealed my identity with a bunch of fireworks in the background."

I don't think I heard him right. "Carried away?"

"Are you getting carried away by denying me so quickly? Yes. Yes, you are."

"No, you said, Nick carried away. Is that what you think his last name is?"

He looks frozen—he might've forgotten how to breathe. *This is worse than I thought.* No wonder he's failing. He can't even get the names of the characters right. I can't even believe I'm going to say the words out of my mouth, but for some reason, they come tumbling out. It's probably the pity talking. "Okay, fine, I'll help you."

His eyes light up, and he looks genuinely shocked. Honestly, I'm shocked I said that, too, but he's worse off than I thought. I said yes out of the good nature of my heart.

"I take it the book you'll be studying all semester is *The Great Gatsby*?"

"You've guessed correctly. I'm all for rich people and parties, but these goddamn metaphors and the fact that Nick and Gatsby are in love just don't make sense to me."

"Wh-What did you say?" I have to hold back my laughter because this guy really needs my help. Just from the last couple minutes of conversation, I can tell he has no idea what's happening in the book.

"The part about metaphors?"

"Okay, never mind. I will help you—it's clear you need it. Out of the kindness of my heart, I won't report you to the dean for stalking me."

"Woah, stalking you?"

"You've been following me for five minutes and won't leave me alone, thus the phrase stalking." I wait a couple of seconds til his pulse starts racing. "Just kidding! Man, this might be fun. After all, you're super gullible."

"This has been one of the weirdest interactions I've had with another person, and I'm starting to rethink asking you to help me."

"Well, it's too late now. You're stuck with me." I give him a condescending smile and open my iPad to look at my notes. He still hasn't left me alone. When did he start sitting across from me? "What are you doing?"

"Well, I have time right now. Let the tutoring commence!"

I shoot him a side-eye. "Okay, pretty boy, listen up. I'm not going to drop everything to help you right now. We can set a scheduled meeting time every week that works for both of our schedules. We can meet for an hour or two, and I can help you then. I have some notes to review now, so please go away."

"Oh, so you think I'm pretty?"

"Wasn't a compliment."

"Doesn't matter. You called me pretty, and that means we're best friends now."

"Nope, considering we aren't even friends and probably never will be."

His hand goes to his chest. "Wow, that hurts, Hades. My pretty boy heart is sad."

What did he call me? "Sorry, what? Hades?"

"You gave me a nickname, and I decided to return the favor. Hades, short for Hadleigh, also known as the God of the underworld."

I stare at him from across the table, and apparently, this interaction is over because he gets up and leaves. As he walks away, he shouts, "I'll email you my schedule with times I'm available, and we can go from there!"

I sit dumbfounded in my chair as I watch him walk away. What the fuck just happened?

"He knocks me over and then demands that I tutor him. Like seriously, what is that about? Have men not heard of decency in the 21st century? This is exactly why I avoid them at all costs!"

Book club started half an hour ago, except we have yet to talk about books. It has consisted of me ranting about my encounter with Grant on Monday. I'm starting to rethink my decision to help him because of two things. Not only do I not want to tangle myself up in a hockey boy, but I also can't stand the fact that one conversation with him has left me this rattled.

Tutoring him is going to be one giant headache and I'm worried about my grade point average because after one conversation with him, I think I lost some brain cells.

I turn to face my friends, who stare at me. "Did I burn a line into the carpet from all the pacing I've been doing?"

"I don't think I've ever seen anyone walk and talk at that speed before. I'm impressed," Amelia says.

"Are you guys even listening? I am in full crisis mode!"

Paige looks between Amelia and Ella. "This is a crisis?"

I let out a frustrated sigh. "Guys, this is the stupidest thing I've ever done. Why would I agree to this? I don't even know this dude! We're not friends, nor will we ever be, yet I still said yes to tutoring him. Now, instead of having my Thursday afternoon free, I have to spend it with Grant who doesn't even know Nick's last name is Carraway and not carried away!"

They're all still staring at me as if I have two heads. "Have you ever considered getting a therapist? They're quite helpful," Paige says as she walks towards me.

"I don't need a therapist when I have friends. You guys are wonderful listeners when I need you to be." Paige guides me back to the table where we usually sit, and I slump in my chair.

"Okay, I know I literally signed up for this, but I thought it would be easier. Maybe some nice girl would need help, and maybe we would become friends in the end. Not some stupid jock I already hate."

"I am still confused about why you hate him and jocks in general." Paige looks at me.

"It's because all the athletes at her high school were major grade-A dickheads, and they used to be mean to her. Not only were they one giant clique, but Hads dated one and he humiliated her in front of the entire school. He cheated on her with multiple people because of that stupid bet," Ella tells the shining twins—Amelia and Paige—and they nod in understanding.

The bet. Yeah, another reason why I hate relationships. Not only was I serially cheated on, but everyone else knew about it because all of the teams had a bet going to see who could sleep around with the most girls at the school. It was *disgusting*, and after that, I had a hard time feeling like I deserved to be loved.

The worst part was that I did love my ex-boyfriend. I *really* loved him. I trusted him and what did he do? He fucked a bunch of girls because I wouldn't put out and he wanted to win the stupid fucking bet. And then he discarded me in front of the entire school and called me a prude. His name was Kyle and that alone should have been red flag number one.

So, yeah, I fucking hate relationships and everything about them. I know something like that probably won't happen again, but when it happens the first time you love someone, you feel like a fool. I still don't trust myself when it comes to people's integrity, and the only people I trust around me are these girls, my roommate, and my brother.

Pathetic, I know, but I don't allow myself to let other people in—especially since I have all the people I need already around me.

"I can't back out now, so I'm officially stuck with Grant. This semester was supposed to go smoothly, and now I'm worried he's going to distract me from my studies or dull my brain cells so I become stupider."

"Hads, you're overthinking this. Think of tutoring as a stepping stone—maybe helping someone else succeed will help you. Try to focus on the good parts. Maybe you and he could eventually become good friends?" Paige smiles at me.

"Yeah, you never know Hads. You guys could be the next Naley," Ella, my fellow *One Tree Hill* lover chimes in. She's laughing at my pain.

"Ella, he's on the hockey team, which means he knows Leo. I bet he was even at that huge party they threw the first weekend back," I say, trying to get her on my side that this isn't a good idea.

"The one where the cops were called?" Ames asks, and I see her brain working to fit all the rumors she heard together.

I nod my head. "Yes."

"Oh, fuck. Maybe this is a bad idea," Ella says, her face falling like it always does when Leo is mentioned.

"Don't judge someone too harshly by the company they keep. Grant and Jacks are best friends and Jacks is so nice! He always asks me about the books we read. Maybe Grant is similar and you guys can become friends or something," Paige smiles at me, trying to put a positive spin on the situation.

"No," I snap. "Shut that down. We'll never be friends."

"Acquaintances?" Paige suggests.

"No."

"Allies?"

"No."

"Work associates?"

"Paige."

She throws her hands up in defeat. "Ok, moving on."

She might be right, though. If I focus enough on the positives, my brain can outweigh the negatives. It'll be fine, right? I need to stop jumping to the worst-case scenario every time something unexpected happens.

"You could just ghost and run away. I find that usually does the trick." It doesn't surprise me Amelia would suggest that. She goes through these periods where she disappears off the face of Earth, but we always know she'll come back.

"Amelia, you can't run away from all your problems. It'll catch up to you eventually," I tell her.

"Watch me," she laughs.

"Okay, can we get back to the book? I have a lot of reactions I want to discuss!" Paige scoots her chair closer to the table.

"Yes, I can't wait to watch Paige scream when the love interest calls the main character a pet name." Ella gives her a look.

"I have a lot of feelings. Sue me."

"Someone might someday, Paige." Amelia grabs her book from her bag, as do the rest of us, and we finally sit down to discuss what we came here to.

5

Hadleigh

As I WALK INTO my class, I wonder in my head for the sixth time today if I should cancel on Grant. I could tell him I'm sick or too tired. Do I feel feverish? Yes, I kind of do. Maybe I need to rest for the remainder of the semester.

It doesn't help that I barely slept last night. My thoughts wouldn't stop racing and all I did all night was toss and turn.

I don't know why this kid gets under my skin so easily. I'd like to think it's because he ran me over the other day, but that's not it. Something about him just sets all the warning signals off in my head, making me want to run in the opposite direction and never look back.

The rumors I've heard about him on campus aren't helping, either. I don't know how I managed to avoid hearing his name for a year and a half, but now that I've bumped into him, all I hear about through the whispers of people is Grant.

Apparently, he's really good at hockey—like insanely good. He's a sophomore, and he's always in the starting lineup. Paige told me that. She also said Grant is a playboy, which didn't surprise me at all. I mean, come on. It makes sense—especially with what he looks like.

Not that I've looked too long at his face or anything. But Paige might have sent me all of his social media accounts and hockey videos last night when she couldn't sleep—the girl loves to cyberstalk people. She sent me a bunch of stuff along with a few hearts and a winky face, which means she thinks this is the start of my own romance novel.

She couldn't be more wrong. I wouldn't say I've lost faith in love completely, but it's not my main focus. Plus, I have perfectly enough love in my heart in the form of platonic relationships. I don't need a romantic one to take over and distract me from my friends or studies. All of the love I could feel for another guy is buried underneath all of the doubt, unease, and anxiety I feel about putting myself back out onto the dating scene.

And maybe if I wasn't so wrapped up in Kyle and his fake love for me, I would have made valedictorian instead of being second in my class. My first real heartbreak kept me from being the best I could be, and for that, I'll never forgive myself.

It's easier to tell my heart how afraid I am that what happened with Kyle could happen again than telling myself how unlovable I truly feel. Plus, nobody has shown much interest here during my time at Grand Mountain, which is fine. I've kept myself low on the totem pole for that reason specifically.

Most people in my classes probably assume I'm cold, bitchy, and way too obsessed with getting good grades. They'd be mostly right. I'm not a warm person—it takes me a while to break out of my shell—but the only people I haven't had that problem with are the girls.

For some reason, they're the exception. It was so easy to slip into a friendship with them—as if we had always known one another. I'm grateful to have found them, especially since I don't make friends too easily.

I take a deep breath as I sit down in my chair for criminology—I'm here early because my class before this got canceled—and notice Paige has barely said a word to me. I think she's waiting for me to mention Grant, but I don't want to talk about it. It's bad enough I'll have to see him later anyway.

It's officially been a week since Grant knocked me over and begged me to tutor him. I emailed him the other day and the two of us found an opening that fit both of our schedules—Thursday afternoons.

So, for now until midterms, Grant and I have a standing study date every single Thursday. Well, not a date. It's *just* tutoring.

What is wrong with me today?

I turn to Paige and am about to start a conversation when someone says my name. When I turn to see who's standing beside my table, confusion comes. Why the hell is this random dude saying my name? How does he *know* my name?

"Hadleigh Baker?"

"Do I know you?"

"Ryan Barnes. I play hockey with Grant." He holds his hand out, and when I don't take it, he speaks again. "I heard through the grapevine you're tutoring Grant. I wanted to see if you were crazy or if he was blackmailing you or something."

I roll my eyes. This is not what I needed today of all days—another teammate of Grant's pestering me and knowing who I am. I should've known the team would talk, but I hoped my name wouldn't be brought up.

"Are you in this class, or do you make it a habit of chasing down your teammates' tutor and harassing them?"

Paige speaks up before he does. "Unfortunately, you've maxed out your talking quota for today, so why don't you get back to your seat and leave us be? Hads doesn't owe you an explanation for why she's tutoring your teammate."

I send Paige a look of thanks before Ryan speaks again.

"Guns down, ladies. I only wanted to introduce myself to the girl who's going to be dealing with Grant. You know, I was the one who suggested he get a tutor in the first place. He can be kind of..."

"Watch it, Ryan," Paige says with a smile. "You wouldn't be talking bad about someone who starts while you sit on the bench, would you?"

He smirks at her. *Damn, she's feisty today.* I like it. "I was only going to say that he's not so book smart, if you know what I mean."

"Well, you'd be right since he has no idea what's going on in *The Great Gatsby.*"

"He's practically allergic to books," Ryan tells me.

"I've never seen you with a book in your hand," Paige tells him. "Not even a textbook."

He must be a criminal justice major since Paige seems familiar with him. I've never heard her talk about him before, and she's all in on the gossip around school.

"I enjoy dabbling in the little spare time I have."

I can feel Paige's eyes roll as he speaks, and I have to stop myself from laughing.

"Do you have a favorite book?"

"I don't want to tell you. It's kind of embarrassing."

"I'm not one to judge what others read." I am, but I'd never tell him that.

"It's *Lord of the Flies.*" Okay, that I was not expecting. I'm assuming he read it in high school like the rest of us and developed a liking to it? It could be the only book he's ever read, so I guess you could call that a favorite.

Something smells fishy here, and my alarm bells are ringing over Ryan. Not only is Paige dismissive of him, but something about him feels off.

"Listen, I would love to continue this conversation when there isn't a classroom full of students filtering in and a professor about to talk to us about blood spatter patterns."

I look around, and sure enough, more people have entered the room. Paige is staring at me like a deer caught in headlights, and my brother just walked in. His stare is drilling holes in the back of Ryan's head.

This isn't good.

"Maybe we could go for coffee sometime? Or maybe you could come to one of my games, and we can go out after? Only if you want to, obviously."

No. "Can I think about it? Your teammate might keep me busy."

"Of course." He smirks before walking away. "Grant can give you my number, or I can be glad I come to class early every week and talk to you then."

Wow, what a line.

I turn to Paige and now Oliver since he got here, and they're both staring at me as if I knifed someone.

"Before your brother grunts loudly and strangles Ryan, can you tell us what in the hell just happened? Was he *flirting* with you?"

"He was not flirting with me, P. He was being a typical asshole. I don't even know why he came over here." The last thing I want is to be on the hockey team's radar, but I might have fucked myself by tutoring Grant.

"I mean, any man would be lucky to have you, Hads, but—"

My brother makes a noise of disgust as she says that.

"Anything to say, Oliver? Or are you going to keep making noises like a broken fan?"

"If any of those hockey fuckers touch you, I get a free punch."

Paige's eyes light up. "I'm not one for violence, but can I be there for that?"

"Nobody's punching anyone unless it's me punching Grant later at our first session."

"You're overthinking it again. Like I said, take five deep breaths and count to ten if he makes you want to rip your hair out." Paige gives me a small smile and turns to the front of the classroom, and for the next hour, I try not to think about what could go wrong later.

"This is it," I say as I set my plate down in the dining hall. Taylor and I are having lunch before I tutor Grant. "The worst is upon me."

"Hads, you're being so dramatic. It's a one-hour tutoring session. Sixty minutes. You'll be alright."

Am I being dramatic? Yes. But how can I tutor Grant when he doesn't know the main character's last name? I know it's my job to teach him all this, but what if he's too far gone, and I can't even help him? What if I'm not good enough to teach him all of this stuff?

And what if my grades start to slip? What am I going to do if by helping Grant, my studies get pushed to the side?

I take a deep breath like Paige said before I spiral too much.

It's just until midterms, Hads. You'll be fine.

"Anyway, you said Ryan Barnes introduced himself to you earlier? What was that about?" I told her briefly about my weird conversation with Ryan, and she practically screamed. She's found him attractive since she saw him at a hockey game last year.

"He strolled right on up to me with a bunch of fake charm and introduced himself."

"I just know he's got a huge—"

"Taylor, stop! Please stop. I do *not* want to imagine anything of that nature."

"You read smut all the time, Hads!"

"Yes, but I don't need to be imagining what a real man's dick looks like!"

She waves her hands around as she grabs her drink. "Fine!" She takes a sip before she continues. "Ryan has a reputation for being a bit of a douche, but despite the rumors, he seems nice, if only I could get a little closer to him."

"If he comes up to me again, I'll send him your direction."

Her eyes light up. "Wonderful. Maybe this will be how I get you out of the house and to hockey games with me."

"Don't get your hopes up," I say as I finish my food, leave the dining hall, and head for the library. It's not a long walk since our campus is so tiny, but I love breathing in the cold winter air as I do. I know most people hate the cold, but I happen to like it. California doesn't usually get below forty degrees, and I always appreciate seeing snow when it falls.

By the time I get to the library, I'm already practicing my breathing exercises, but somehow I always feel more calm when I walk through the rows of books. Each floor gets quieter as you go up, so naturally, I reserved a study room on the third floor. I need things to be as quiet as possible while I deal with Grant once a week.

As I head up the stairs and look around at all the books, my anxiety soothes. I love it here. On days where it all feels like too much, I sit here, listen to music in my headphones and simply exist. Surrounded by so many books and words written on pages, everything will be okay. I get transported to another world here, and I'll never not enjoy escapism when life gets too heavy.

Also, the smell of books is one of my favorite smells ever. I'd bottle it up and spray it on myself if I could.

I head to the third floor, where the study rooms are, and look for the one I rented out each week. I figured I'd have a standing reservation so Grant doesn't get lost. I assume he's never been in here before because I would have seen him.

I'm a few minutes early, and as I get to our room, I notice the door is already open. I assume it's whoever has it before me and not Grant, but when I see him sitting at the table, his back to the door, I pause in the doorway.

It's not too late to make a break for it, is it? I could absolutely run away before he even notices I'm—

"I can hear your heavy breathing from here. Do I make you that stressed out, or is walking up a flight of stairs that hard for you, Hades?"

God, I hate that nickname.

I KNOW SHE HATES that nickname.

That's why I'll be using it for the rest of the semester. It's way too easy to watch her cheeks turn red and her face get all flushed. I have way too much fun pushing her buttons, but I also wish I didn't have to play this stupid game to get her to have a conversation with me.

Even flushed from the cold and her hair blown all over the place, she still looks fucking beautiful.

I'm grateful she agreed to help me, and she's a fiery little thing for how short she is. I could keep her in my locker and still have room for all of my hockey equipment.

Hades is probably around 5'4", and she dresses like one of those academic girls you'd find in an art museum. Black skirt, black boots, and a dark blue sweater.

The more time I spend with her, the more I want to know who the hell Hadleigh Baker is and how I can get her to wear every single pair of sweats I own. She'd look fucking phenomenal in them.

"No, I'm just practicing my deep breathing exercises for when you piss me off, which happened in record time today. Should I catalog that for the future?"

"Aww, you already keep a journal about how dreamy and sweet I am?"

She slams her stuff down across from me before she sits down. "The only entries about you in my journal are the ones detailing how I want to dispose of your body."

At least she's writing about me. "You would never get away with that," I say as I lean forward, my elbows on the table. "I'd be missed too much. You'd be better off disposing of someone who wouldn't be missed."

"Like who?"

I think for a second. "I don't know. Who else annoys the shit out of you like I do?"

"Well, thinking of recently, one of your teammates."

What? Why is Hades talking to my teammates? "Who?"

"Ryan." She rolls her eyes when she says his name, but all I can see is red. Why the *fuck* is Ryan talking to my tutor? For what reason could he have for introducing himself to her?

"What could you two possibly have to talk about?"

"Oh, because I'm incapable of having conversations with other hockey players such as yourself?"

"No, that's not what I—"

"Are you sad you're not the only hockey boy I talk to?" *Kind of.* "I thought so. Now, let's get to what we came here for, shall we?"

I shift in my chair before I nod, opening my copy of the book as she does.

"So, Collins usually does the midterm on the first half of the book and the final on the remaining half, so it's not cumulative."

"Yeah, we only have to know the first five chapters for the midterm. We have a quiz every week on all the chapters we've read before. He randomizes the questions, so I never know which part of the book they'll be from."

"That's usually how quizzes work," she jokes.

God, even when she's sarcastic, she's pretty.

"Your next quiz should be on chapters one and two."

I sneeze as I flip through the pages, and I swear she jumps out of her chair.

"Do you need me to bring Claritin next time, or are you fine with me letting you drop dead due to not liking to read?"

"Why do you think I don't like to read?"

"Besides the fact that you can barely decipher simple metaphors? Or how about the fact that you don't even know the main character's last name? Or how about the fact that I've never seen you step foot in the library before today."

Her mouth turns into a line before she speaks again.

"Sorry. That was a bit harsh. I can be civil for an hour every week, but outside of this bubble right here, don't expect me to smile and hang onto your every word like everyone else does."

Is that what she thinks about me? "People don't hang onto every word I speak, do they?"

Hades nods before she dives back into the book. "I'm thinking we can do a breakdown of each chapter and hit on the main points I think will be on the quiz. The book is short, but there's a lot to unpack in a short amount of time. Does that sound okay?"

"Yeah, that sounds good. I hope you're good at this, so I don't fail the class and have to retake it." Or so I don't get kicked off of the hockey team, but I don't want to tell her that.

"I don't want to oversell myself since you're my first student, but I think you came to the right person. Despite my feelings for you, I love this book. I know it like the back of my hand."

"Well, my life is in your hands. I trust you, Hades."

"Thanks, Grant."

God, the way she says my name—even in that pissed-off tone. It's been a long time since I've had feelings of any kind for someone, and I know if I tell Jacks about this, he'd say I'm doing what I normally do—fall too quickly for the wrong person.

But there's just something about this girl. Every time she speaks, I crave more. Ever since I saw her, I've been in a trance. It's like she woke my body up after years of being frozen. I know I fall easily, and I know my heart could get broken, but Hads doesn't even like me, so it's fine.

She'll tutor me, I'll pass, and that will be the end of it, no matter how much that pisses me off. Maybe she'll want to be friends after this? I could ask her.

I spent all this time thinking about her while she was talking about the book, and I didn't hear a word she said. "Sorry, I didn't catch any of that. Can you–"

I hear a loud thwack, and I look up at her, only to put it together that she hit me with a ruler. Where did she get that?

"Hades, what the fuck? That hurt!"

She laughs. Is she some sort of hidden masochist or something? "Every time you don't pay attention or you get a question wrong, I'm going to hit you with this ruler."

"Why?"

"Well, it's fun for me. It's typical classical conditioning. It'll help you not want to get hurt, and you'll actually pay attention so you don't fail."

Right—not failing the class. Therefore not failing myself and being able to play hockey. The only thing that keeps me going. "Normally, someone slapping me with something comes with some fun after, but hey, whatever works for you, Hades." I throw her a wink, and she rolls her eyes at me.

God, I can't believe I'm doing this. If I told myself weeks ago, I would not only need a tutor but have one that enjoys smacking me with a ruler, I'd have laughed my ass off. But then again, I'd think failing a class would have been complete and utter bullshit, but there's a lot about this semester that has already thrown me for a loop.

All I've been focused on this past year was hockey and making sure my grades were good. Now, I'm failing at one aspect of that which could cause me to lose the only other thing I love most on this planet besides my mom.

In the span of a few weeks, I've become a mess.

Hades smacks me with the ruler again. "Ow! Be careful with the hands. I still need to be able to hold a hockey stick after this!"

"What's your deal? I can tell you're not paying attention because you look constipated."

"Sorry, I'm feeling a bit scattered." I run a hand through my hair. "I swear I'll pay attention this time when you talk about those two eggs or whatever."

"Grant, they're not actually eggs how you think they are."

"What?"

6

Grant

I'VE SPENT THE BETTER part of the past day thinking way too much about the fact that Ryan fucking Barnes has talked to Hades.

The fact that I have to stare at his face for the entirety of conditioning tonight isn't helping, either. I can see his shit-eating grin across the weight room, and all my brain can think about is her smile when I mentioned his name yesterday.

It didn't seem like Hads tolerated him any more than she tolerated me, but the thought of her liking him more than she likes me pisses me off to no end.

And why did Ryan track her down in class? She's *my* tutor, not his. The fact that he chose to find her, seek her out, and talk to her makes me think he has some kind of game at play here, but what? Does he think me getting kicked off the team will increase his chances of playing or something?

I can't give him too much credit. He's not that smart.

Holt whistles, and we all switch stations. Today for conditioning, half of us are in here doing weights, and the other half are doing different cardio workouts on the indoor track. Jacks and I are moving over to the slam balls, but there's all sorts of shit going on. We've got free weights going, deadlifts, and lunges with different weights.

Thank fuck I have a way to get all my weird feelings out, along with the frustrations I've been feeling the past few weeks. Between tutoring and my regular study load—on top of practices and conditioning—I've barely had time to breathe on my own.

But it's fine. In fact, it feels good to never be able to stop and think about how much of a failure I am and could be. Nothing stops unwelcome thoughts like keeping yourself so busy that you can't think.

I notice Jacks staring at me, an odd look on his face, and as I slam the ball down, I ask him about it.

"Can I help you?"

"How was your first tutoring session? It was yesterday, right?"

I should tell him about my feelings for this girl, but I decide not to. Nothing is going to come from Hads and me anyway since she despises me for some reason, and all I need is for her to tutor me so I don't fail. "Yeah, it was. It went okay. We're both still alive, so she decided not to murder me, which I count as a win."

"When is your next quiz?"

"Tuesday."

"Are you ready for it?"

"I think so. She told me the West Egg and East Egg are places and not a new type of breakfast food, so I feel more confident now that I actually know what's going on."

Holt whistles again and we head to the next station. As Jacks and I are walking toward the free weights, Ryan comes over to me.

"If you need help with the slam balls, all you do is pick it up and throw it to the floor," I tell him.

"That right there explains why Hadleigh doesn't like you. Now I have another topic of conversation to use when we eventually go out, other than the fact that I like to read, and you don't."

I roll my eyes. "I've never seen you with a book in your hand. Did you suddenly learn how to read in the past week?"

"Just a little embellishment, but Hadleigh sure enjoyed that fact when I talked to her yesterday." God, he's such an asshole. Why is he fucking around with my tutor? Why is he suddenly so interested in her? I know for a fact he didn't know she existed before this—same as me. I hate that I never knew her, and now that I'm lucky enough to be in her orbit, I don't want to let her go. Ryan over here would fuck her and toss her aside like I've seen him do a dozen times. He's not a good fucking dude.

"Yeah, and why don't you stay the fuck away from her? She isn't your type, Ryan. She actually has a brain."

"Oh, I'm sorry. Have you laid your claim on her, or are you worried she'll pick me in the end?"

"I never said I wanted to date her. I'm only curious as to why you're suddenly interested in her. Have you gone through all the girls at the school and don't want to go back around?"

"She is hot, and it's fun pissing you off. I've never seen you get so defensive over someone you don't like. I thought for sure you lost all your edge, Carter."

I take a step towards him, my weights dangling from my hands. "I'd change your mindset, asshole. I don't think you want to know what my edge looks like."

"She's all yours, at least until I see what's up those skirts of hers. They seem to be getting shorter every day."

I drop the weights I was curling, and Jacks puts a hand against my chest to stop me from being an idiot.

"Ryan, go the fuck away and get back to conditioning," Jacks says. This kid couldn't get worse if he tried. Why is he such a prick? Why does he think it's okay to talk about women like that?

Holt—our team captain who's graduating at the end of this year—signals the end of conditioning, and we all huddle up. Not only is Holt a great guy and player, but he also throws amazing fucking parties. The kind of parties you can barely remember the next day, and where most of the rumors on this campus come from.

As an upperclassman, he lives off-campus in the hockey house. Jacks and I might live there next year, but for now, we're okay with living in an on-campus apartment across from the other sophomores on the team. It's a nice apartment, but I would kill to have an entire house with some guys on the team.

He talks about our practice schedule coming up before he dismisses us. Our first game is in February, and we all get excited about being back on the ice—especially since our first game is at home. There's nothing better than a good crowd when the season starts. God, I can't wait to get back on the ice.

Jacks and I are not only teammates off the ice but on as well. We both play defense—I'm on the right, he's on the left. We work so well together because we're able to know what the other is thinking in those split seconds on the ice, and since we tried out for Grand Mountain together, the two of us fell into a beautiful partnership.

It also helps that Jacks is a fast fucking skater.

Unlike most of the guys on the team, I'm not looking to go pro in the future. All I want is to coach the younger generation of hockey players into wonderful people on and off the ice—just like my dad did. He taught me everything I knew about hockey, and someday, I hope to be half as good of a coach as he was.

Holt and Jacks are talking about the party tonight as we enter the locker room, and I haven't been out as much with the team lately because of my study schedule, but tonight, I need to clear my head. One drink can't hurt, right?

"Are you still throwing a party at the house tonight?"

"Yeah, Carter, I am. Are you finally going to join and get laid for once?" Holt throws a casual smirk my way. I shrug that comment off. I know I act like an ass most of the time, but I'm not into hooking up and getting my dick wet just to get an orgasm. I need to let loose a little, that's all. I've been working hard lately and I think I deserve a night out with the boys.

"I'll be there," I say.

Holt smacks me on the back and heads toward his locker. "Damn, Hadleigh must be doing a number on you. You haven't been to any of my parties this year, dude."

"Does everyone on the team know about Hads?"

"Yup," everyone around me says.

"God, she's just my tutor! And she hates me, so forgive me for not wanting to talk about her when I don't have to."

"Classic haters to lovers. You really don't read, do you?" Jacks asks me.

I can only shake my head. "I need a drink."

"There's vodka at the house, Grant." Holt puts his hand on my bicep. "Let's get you trashed. I think you deserve it."

7

Hadleigh

It's a Friday night and I'm leaving my dorm for once.

Only Ella could get me to stop studying for one night by dragging us all to a party.

We're all at Paige and Amelia's apartment getting ready to go to the hockey house despite my best efforts to tell her how much I don't want to step foot in that place. I'm only going with them because Ella promised to stay by me all night, and the house is so big we might not even see Grant.

And I told her I'd stick by her in case Leo was around—which he probably will be. She told us he tends to hang with the hockey boys, so he's almost always at these parties.

"I have no idea what to wear to a party. I looked through my entire closet and I have nothing." This is my current dilemma. What the hell do you wear to a party when you're not looking to hook up and are being dragged to it against your will? "Can you wear a sweater vest to a party?"

Ella gasps. "Absolutely not, Hads. Let's go raid Amelia's closet for a dress or something."

"Hads, you should really leave your dorm more often. You're worrying me," Ames presses her hand against my head as if I have a fever.

"Coming from you, that's rich," I say as Ella digs through Amelia's closet. "Why can't I wear what I normally do?"

"It's girl's night out, and Ella told us we must dress accordingly. Trust me. I would rather be wearing sweats and a T-shirt right now." Paige does look amazing. It's weird to see her in anything other than comfy clothes. She's wearing ripped black mom jeans, heeled boots, and a brown cropped tank top.

"Guys, I need a night out. My internship has been killing me, and I swear I almost stabbed Zimmerman in the face with a letter opener the other day. We're going out, and we'll all look hot doing it."

Paige, Amelia, and I all share a glance because we still don't know why Ella gets so worked up over Zimmerman. We only know a few things—they both got the same internship, and they hate each other. That's it, and usually, if you're on Ella's shit list, you're there for life. I worry one day she might text the group chat and ask Paige what the best way to get rid of blood is, but that hasn't happened yet.

Yet being the key word, but Paige told us the answer is hydrogen peroxide.

"I think I'll stick with my skirt, but Ames, this top is cute. Can I borrow it for the night?" I pull out this pink, cropped, backless sweater.

"Yeah, go for it. I haven't worn that in forever if you want to keep it. The last time I wore that, I was headed to Monaco for a peace treaty signing."

"When did you go to Monaco?" Ella asks.

"I've never been to Monaco."

"Wait, then why did you just say that?" I stare at her, puzzled.

"Say what?"

"Guys, this is classic Amelia doing one of her bits. Yesterday, when she left the apartment, she said she was off to DC to start a marital affair with a senator. I swear she uses movie plots as exit strategies," Paige says.

Amelia chuckles and sits down on the loveseat. She's wearing a cute floral dress with dark boots and tights.

Paige and Amelia's apartment is very cozy. The front door opens to an open floor plan. The kitchen is off to the right, with a small dining table that can seat four people. We play card games there sometimes or rant about books. To the left is a bookshelf that stands against the wall. Straight ahead is the living area, with a couch and a loveseat, a cute rug in the center, with a TV directly facing the couch. Amelia's room door is to the apartment's right, and Paige's is to the left.

Paige and Amelia are so different, but somehow, their dynamic works. Paige shows off her moods through her tote bags and when Amelia starts showing off her moods, pigs might be flying. Paige prefers the floor most of the time, so her room is carpeted, and Amelia loves how hardwood sounds beneath her feet. They're opposites, but they fit well together.

Ella connected her phone to Amelia's speaker so we could listen to music while getting ready. Most of us are finished getting ready, and a few minutes later when Ella walks out of the bathroom, all of our mouths drop open.

"Damn, girl!" Paige says.

"Holy shit," I say.

"You look hot," Amelia says in the most monotone voice ever.

"I know, I know. No man or woman is going to stand a chance tonight," Ella beams at us. She's wearing black pants, a black crop top that leaves little to the imagination, and black sneakers. Her lips are bright red and her makeup looks phenomenal.

"Now, don't forget to drink water if you're going to drink alcohol tonight. Except you Hads, this doesn't apply to you because you can't legally drink yet."

"Yes, I'm aware. Alcohol is disgusting anyway." I've never been the biggest fan of it. I wasn't much of a rule breaker in high school, and even if I did drink, it was at home with my brother—who doesn't drink alcohol. So, basically never.

"Is everyone ready to go? Let's paint the town red!" Ella yells as we walk out of the front door.

"Wait, red? As in blood?" Paige practically beams. Seriously, you would never think this girl—who's the living embodiment of the sun—likes murder so much. It's a weird dichotomy.

"Never change, Paige. Never change." I throw my arm around her shoulder, and away we go.

WHEN WE GET TO the hockey house and I feel the beat of the music in my body before we're even inside, I mentally curse myself for leaving my dorm.

"This was a terrible idea," I say to them as we shuffle into the house. It's packed in here, but the only thing that's good about it being so busy is that Ella was right—we probably won't see Grant or Leo.

Paige and Ella split off to go find drinks, leaving Amelia and me standing in the entryway of the house. It's... nice, I guess. I can't tell how big it is with all of these people in here, but it doesn't feel or look like a frat house, so that's good right?

As long as I don't get a disease from being in here, I'll take that as a win.

"You're not drinking tonight?" I shout to Ames and she shakes her head.

"Not in the mood, plus someone has to keep an eye on those two in case they wind up doing karaoke again."

The last time we all went out, Paige and Ella started singing *All Too Well* by Taylor Swift—the ten-minute version—in a bar that doesn't do karaoke.

And honestly, they sounded pretty good.

Speaking of the two amateur singers, they find us with drinks in their hands and Ella passes Ames and I cups of water. It's fucking hot in here, and I regret wearing a sweater.

Paige and Ella start giggling as we all find a spot to stand where nobody's making out or dancing. Is this really what happens at these parties? I don't think I'm cut out for this.

"What's so funny?" Amelia asks them.

"Paige and I were betting on if Hads is going to quit tutoring Grant before the next session or after it," Ella says a bit too loud for my taste, but whatever.

"I said before, and Ella said after. We bet twenty bucks." Paige smiles.

"Oh God, I totally forgot that was yesterday. How did it go, Hads?"

"Fine?" I say, but they don't seem too convinced. I vaguely tell them about how we spent the first fifteen minutes insulting each other and how he kept zoning out. I get to the part with the ruler, and Ella practically shrieks.

"Are you telling me you slap him with a ruler every time he zones out or gets a question wrong? Damn, Hads, when did you get so kinky?"

"Ella, it's not like that. It's classical conditioning! I'm teaching his brain to focus so he doesn't want to get hurt. Simple and effective for idiots like Grant."

"Speak of the devil," Amelia says, moving her eyes toward the door.

"Oh, this is about to get real fun," Paige says, already drunk. Man, one drink, that's all it takes.

Sure enough, Grant and a bunch of his hockey friends waltz through the door, and he must sense me staring at him because his eyes catch mine. My heart thrums against my chest—or maybe it's the bass of the music—as I return his stare. Neither of us looks away before he's forced to because one of his friends walks up to him and daps him up. He smiles as his friends walk into the house, but his gaze returns to mine.

He looks confused as if he didn't expect to see me here. To be honest, that's a valid response. I never imagined this is where I'd be on my Friday night, but what Ella wants, Ella usually gets.

Her voice filters into my head. "It's like they're eye-fucking right now."

"Ella! Stop. I will never like Grant. Our entire relationship is based on us either insulting or challenging one another."

"Are you saying you have a relationship?" Amelia raises both her eyebrows and winks. Screw her and her emotional warfare.

I excuse myself and head to the bathroom so I can splash some water on my face, and as I head to where I saw it earlier, someone grabs my wrist before I make it.

Grant's face fills my space as I turn around.

"Can I help you?"

He shakes his head as he lets go of my arm, my wrist now cold and empty. "N-No. I guess I didn't expect to walk in and see you standing in this house. This isn't really your scene, Hades."

"I'm with my friends," I say as I point to the girls. Paige is the only one who notices, and Ella seems to have gone somewhere else because I only see Amelia next to her. Paige waves with a huge smile on her face before Ames smacks her hand down.

"Is that the book club I keep hearing about?"

My face pinches before I can stop it. "Uh, yeah."

"Nice. Well, if you need a drink or someone to dance with, I'll make sure to keep a ruler's distance between the two of us on the dance floor. Just come find me if you need me, okay?"

"I'm not staying too long," I say as I look to the bathroom. "Excuse me."

I don't wait for his response before I shut the door, my heart practically hammering out of my chest. What the fuck is happening to me? I'm blaming all of these weird feelings on the overwhelming environment I'm in at the moment.

Am I insane or did Grant and I just have a nice conversation? Did he offer to dance with me? Why would he do that? What sort of game are we playing here?

I'm warm and uncomfortable, and I feel like my heart is going to explode out of my chest. Is this anxiety? A panic attack? Paige would know. I should ask her. I splash some cold water on my face and step out of the bathroom when I run into someone.

Grant—again.

"Are you stalking me or something?"

"No, I wanted to make sure you were okay. I know these things can be overwhelming when it's your first time."

I cock my head at him. "How do you know it's my first time?" I'm not that obvious, am I?

"Trust me, Hades. I know it's your first time because if I had seen you at one of these before, we would have known one another a lot sooner."

"Is that so?"

He leans down, his hand on the wall next to me as he gets into my personal space. "I never forget a face and the fact that you went under my radar for almost two years is... well, let's just say it's a damn shame."

Thump. Thump. Thump. There goes my fucking heart again. I need to abort this situation as soon as possible, but part of me doesn't want to—the selfish and annoying part. But I won't be another one of his conquests. I know how Grant is, and I have to remain professional if tutoring is going to work between us.

"Hitting on your tutor is low work, Grant. If you're not going to take our professional relationship seriously, then don't bother coming to our next session." I slip under his arm and book it for my friends, not waiting for whatever pretty boy bullshit he was going to spew, only to find Ella still missing.

"Where's Ella?"

Paige's gaze shifts to the corner of the room where Ella and some dude are face to face, screaming at each other. What the hell is going on?

"Who's that?" I ask Paige because she knows everything.

"Leo Zimmerman," Amelia says with a grin. That makes sense. We knew he was going to be here and both of us failed our promises for tonight. Not only did I get corned by Grant, but Ella and Leo are going at it about God knows what.

Leo's tall and towering over Ella, but her rage gives her more height. He's got curly brown hair and lean muscles. He's a specimen. I don't know how Ella resists him because he looks like every girl's fantasy. I don't think words alone could do him justice.

"I ship them."

"Who?"

Paige smiles. "Ella and Leo."

"They look like they're going to claw each other's throats off," I say, not seeing what she does. If sparks exist, those two are going to set each other on fire and laugh as the other burns.

"Oh right, we're supposed to hate him because Ella does too. I hope he loses his favorite pen." Paige makes a face she probably thinks is scary, but I don't think she's capable of that emotion.

"Paige, you're drunk," Amelia says.

"Sorry, I'll stop talking now."

"I might have just told Grant to not come to our next session." The words fall out before I can stop them.

"Why?" Ames asks.

"It's a long story I don't want to get into," I say as I see Grant dancing with some blonde girl that's hanging all over him.

"Someone remind Ella she owes me twenty bucks. I might be too hungover to remind her tomorrow." Paige looks like she's about to burst into tears.

"Why?" I say, and then remember. They bet when I would fold and stop tutoring Grant earlier. Fuck. That's not what happened, but if he doesn't show up next week, I'll have my answer. Maybe I was too harsh in what I said, but we have to remain professional. I can't have my integrity as a tutor be tainted after my first go at it.

"Paige, you've had two drinks. How are you so drunk?" Amelia asks.

"You guys know I'm a lightweight."

Amelia shrugs as she sips her water. "Well, this night has turned into a shitshow."

"I'm having fun," Paige says, but her voice sounds small.

"Paige, are you crying?" Yeah, she is. I don't even know why I asked.

"I just love you guys so much." Oh great, we've hit the kind of drunk where Paige lets out all her sad girl feelings.

While that's happening, Ella storms back over to us and all but drags us out of the house.

WE WALK BACK TOWARDS our places in silence. Paige is blubbering some nonsense about a movie she watched the other day, but nobody's listening or responding. My head is a jumbled mess thinking about what Grant said to me against the wall earlier, and Ella has never been this quiet, so something has her mind tangled.

We get outside Paige and Amelia's apartment. Amelia's practically holding Paige up right now. In fact, she might be asleep—her mouth is wide open and her eyes are closed.

"Do you want help getting her into bed?" I ask as she gets the door open. Ella's staying on their couch tonight since she doesn't want to drive back. She was drinking too, and the four of us are always safe when we go out.

"No, I'll be fine. Paige will curl up in a ball on her floor, most likely. See you Wednesday?"

"Yeah, sounds good." Their door shuts, and Ella goes to head in, but I stop her. "Can we talk?"

"Yeah, what's up?"

"I saw you and Zimmerman going at it tonight. I'm sorry I wasn't there to block him from you." I run a hand through my split ends. "Do you want to talk about it?"

"I saw you and Grant in a pretty interesting situation, so I'll ask you the same question."

I roll my eyes at her. Of course she saw us. "Grant and I aren't anything, but I'm always here to listen if you want to rant about Zimmerman if you need me to."

"Thanks, Hads." She pulls me in for a hug. "Do you really not like Grant? I know high school messed with your head, but he doesn't seem that bad. At least, you looked like you enjoyed where you were against the wall with him..."

"I honestly don't know how I feel about him, Ells. Just something about him pushes my buttons." *And brings my body back to life.* But I shove that thought down as soon as it comes in.

"Hads, sometimes hate and love are close emotions, and the only thing that gets in the way of one or the other is what you put in front of it."

"Are you speaking from personal experience?"

She pauses for a beat before masking her expression. "All I'm saying is, keep yourself open to the possibility of some type of relationship with him. I know you have to remain professional while you tutor him, but there's always after."

"Fine. I'll keep it in the deepest crevice of my mind."

"That's all I ask," she says as she opens their door. "Good night, Hads."

"Good night, Ella."

I turn and head toward my building, pulling out my phone before I swipe to my brother's contact.

> **Hads: Tomorrow morning, 7 a.m. at the usual spot?**

> **Sous Chef: Yup.**

It's always been a running joke between my brother and I that he's my sous chef because of our last name. I like to think of myself as being the better Baker sibling. I called him that once when I was little and it carried into our adult lives. Maybe he can give me some advice about how to go about this new thing with Grant, and the fact that I have two different hockey players who now know who I am.

God, how did I get here? I went from nobody knowing me to one of the most popular guys in school giving me a fucking nickname.

I take a deep breath as I enter my room and hope to God I can get at least one hour of sleep tonight after everything that occurred tonight.

> **Paige: *one attachment***

> **Ella: Is that the noise I heard? I'm too lazy to get up.**

Hads: Is she alright? What is in her hands?

Amelia: She has water and that's her scarlet witch squishmallow. I also heard her fall out of bed, Ella, but she's usually okay.

Paige: I LOVE YOU GUYS!!!!!!!!!!!!

Ella: Yeah, that sounds about right.

Hads: Love you guys! Goodnight!

Amelia: Nighty night xoxo.

Ella: Goodnight cuties! Love you!

Paige: Goodnight!!!! Don't let the serial killers bite!

8

OKAY, SO MAYBE I flirted with Hads earlier. I couldn't help it—she took me by surprise when I walked through the door and saw her standing with her friends.

She looked fucking great, but she was so tense I thought I'd try and loosen her up. Which backfired because I sounded like an asshole, and she basically told me not to show up on Thursday unless I'm serious about getting my grade up—which I am. I've never been so focused on my studies before, and I hate that she thought I wasn't taking my situation seriously.

And then she fucking left. She went back over to her friends, saw me dancing with this random girl who was all over me and left.

Not only did I fuck up in front of Hads, but I made a fool of myself. Hockey and keeping my grades up are all I'm focusing on from here on out. I even thought Hads and I could be friends until she thought I flirted with her.

Fuck this.

I book it off of the dance floor and away from this random girl before I try and find Jacks. After searching for a few minutes, I find him upstairs away from everyone else.

"You good?" I ask him.

"Yeah, fine." He takes a drink. "Are you? I saw Hadleigh here earlier."

Instead of admitting I might have weird feelings surrounding her, I change the subject. "What the fuck is up with the color pink?"

"Sorry, what?"

"Pink. Why is it even a color?"

He tilts his head at me. "Why do you have a bone to pick with a color all of a sudden?"

"I don't! I'm simply making conversation, Jacks."

"About the color pink?"

"Yes!"

He smirks at me, his face beginning to twist as he laughs. "I see what's going on here."

"Oh, do you?"

He nods his head. "Her sweater was pink."

"Whose?" I question, even though her outfit is burned into my memory. She always wears skirts, but tonight, her outfit looked different—*she* looked different. She was out of her comfort zone but she looked more confident. She even threw some flirting back to me, but I don't want to get my hopes up too high. I can't fall for her—not this quickly. Not when she's helping me to stay on the hockey team.

"It's not about her, Jacks. I'm only saying the color pink shouldn't exist." *Because she looked way too damn good in that sweater.* It's all I can fucking think about.

"It *shouldn't* exist?"

"Yeah, but why are you stressing the words like that?"

"Why do you hate the color pink all of a sudden?"

"I don't hate it! It just shouldn't exist!" He stares at me like I have two heads, and fuck, maybe I do. "I'm just saying, pink tries so fucking hard not to be white but it'll never get to the caliber red is at."

He throws his hands up in defeat. "What the fuck is going on?"

"It's only an observation. You're acting like I'm speaking another language, right now."

"Are you?"

"No! I just hate the color pink, Jacks!" I'm yelling now and I'm not sure why.

"So, you're telling me that you happen to declare war on the color pink after Hads wears a pink sweater to the party, but those two things have nothing to do with one another?"

"That's exactly what I'm saying, dude."

"Grant, you're not falling—"

I slap his shoulder with my hand. "Woah! Dude, no. You're jumping a thousand steps, J. She's my tutor! I'm not in love with my tutor."

He only smirks. "I never said you were in love with her."

The two of us are silent as I realize what a colossal error I made. "What the fuck is the point of a sweater if it's going to be backless? Does that not defeat the point of a sweater?"

"Grant, you're doing it again."

"What? I'm not doing anything! These two conversations are unrelated to one another, Jacks. I'm not sure you can keep up."

"I'm pretty sure I'm keeping up just fine, Grant. And you totally have the hots for your tutor. Oh, what have I done?" He shakes his head.

"You know what, you don't get it. I'm going back to the apartment. I hope to see you there when you stop acting like I'm crazy."

I stand and leave him, hoping when he gets back to the apartment later, he's not acting like he can read every thought of mine.

I just don't like the color pink—nothing more and nothing less.

9

 **Hadleigh**

WHEN NO PILLOW GETS thrown at me when I wake up, I remember Taylor went home for the weekend.

I miss her, but I'm glad she didn't see me stumble into our dorm and collapse to the floor after last night's party. If she had taken one look at my outfit, she would've wanted every detail, and my brain was so scrambled last night that I could barely get into bed before I crashed. I'm still wearing Amelia's sweater.

I sigh heavily as I grab my stuff to take a shower and lay out my outfit for the day—leggings, a comfy sweater, and my favorite sneakers. Twenty minutes later, I'm on my way to the bench we always meet at. I yawn a few times while I wait for my brother. I'm not much of a morning person, but the cold morning air works wonders in waking me up.

January in Virginia is no joke; the morning could be thirty degrees, but it's seventy degrees and sunny by the afternoon. It's taken me a bit to get used to the weather here—I even had to buy a jacket.

Something in the distance lifts my head, and as I see my brother jogging towards me wearing his usual all-black running outfit, I smile. This tradition is one of my favorites, and I'm glad we decided to continue it here on campus.

My brother is one of the few people on the planet who enjoys running for fun. I don't share that sentiment in the same way, rather I run from people and my emotions more often than I exercise.

Oliver is not only the taller sibling but also quieter and more active. While he wakes up most mornings to get a run in, I sleep in. He's also taller than me at over six feet tall; his brown eyes look like mine, and his jet-black hair compliments his sharp cheekbones well.

"Are you trying to up your endurance to chase after murderers?"

He slows before me. "That's funny, Hads."

He didn't laugh, though. My brother is a man of few words, but I listen when he speaks. He gives wonderful advice when I ask for it, and I always enjoy his company no matter if we speak or not.

I stand from the bench and we start walking on our usual route. It's only a mile or so—which is nothing to Oliver because he runs multiple miles before seven a.m. This walk is his cool down, according to what he told me before.

"Have you talked to Mom or Dad since you got here?"

Shit. I haven't. I keep meaning to call them back, but I've been so busy I keep forgetting. "No, but I will tonight. What have they said when you've called?"

"Mom wants us to come home soon and celebrate the Lunar New Year. It's in February, so make a note of it on your calendar."

"Ol, it's already on my calendar. Who do you think I am?" That earns a grunt. "Do you think we'll be able to get back?"

"We can try. Maybe for the weekend."

Oliver and I are half-Vietnamese. Our mom is Vietnamese, and our dad is White, but we celebrate most of the holidays and traditions. Mom likes to celebrate as a family, but with school, it's tough. Our schedules often don't match up, and flying to California on the weekend is also difficult. We're going to try this semester, but it might not work out.

"I'll get back to her as soon as I can," I say as I think about my to-do list for the next week.

"Too busy fighting with Carter, huh?" I swear my brother is smirking, right now. *Smirking*.

"How did you hear about that? Please don't tell me this is going around school." I sigh heavily. "That's the last thing I need."

He shakes his head. "Paige told me."

What? "It happened less than twelve hours ago, and Paige was drunk last night. How did she tell you already?"

"She texted me while you guys were at the party."

"I didn't realize you two talked so much, care to comment on that?"

He sends a glare my way. "Look, I know you can handle yourself, but Paige was only looking out for you. Also, who are you and what have you done with my sister? You *actually* went to a party at the hockey house?"

"Yeah, I did."

"Willingly?"

"Believe it or not, Oliver, I am capable of having a social life."

"Could've fooled me," he says before I smack him on the arm.

"Shut up, idiot. You're the one who has no friends."

"And I'm perfectly content as such, Hads."

"Whatever, Ol." If Oliver and I were in competition for which one of us keeps ourselves closed off more, I don't know who would win. We're both distant in different ways—Oliver tends to stay away from any and all human attachment, and I'm more closed off with my heart. I'm very choosy with who I give it to, and Oliver doesn't give any people the time of day.

So, I guess he wins, in retrospect.

We continue walking in silence for a couple of minutes, and I used to think my brother would hate me for following him to college, but I'm glad I have him here with me. It's nice being able to come to him when I need him, and he's still as protective of me as he is at home.

"So, what's the deal with you and Carter anyway?"

Always right to the point he is. "I'm tutoring him," I say, as if he should know this already.

"I know."

"Okay? So?"

"Why do you hate him so much?"

I roll my eyes. "Why does everyone keep asking me that?" We stop walking, and he turns and looks at me. He knows I'm bullshitting him, and he doesn't even have to say it—the look on his face is enough. "I honestly don't know my feelings about him. Any time I'm around him, I get so—"

"Confused? Annoyed?"

"Yeah, I guess. I've never been good at talking to boys or making friends with them. Ever since high school, I've stayed away from them completely."

"Good, I wouldn't want to have to punch any more of them who break your heart. It hurts my knuckles." My brother laughs for about two seconds before it falls from his face.

People often think he doesn't show emotions or feelings, but his shell starts to break when you get close enough to him. He and I laugh all the time. He just has a harder time opening up to people—deep down, he's scared of leaning on people too much only for them to leave in the future.

I don't blame him. His high school girlfriend of three years died in a car crash. It was sudden, and all of us—especially him—were devastated. Since then, he hasn't dated anyone else.

I think he worries it could happen again, so he stays away from it altogether. The two of us are scarily similar, but Oliver's walls are up more than mine. I think one day mine could fall, but I'm not sure if his ever will.

I miss seeing my brother happy. This cold, grumpy version of him is okay, but I miss his real laugh—the one Mia used to bring out of him. If Ol laughed, you couldn't help but laugh along with him. I'm also the only person he lets use that nickname and sometimes I call him Ollie just to mess with him. He doesn't mind Ol, but he hates when I call him Ollie.

"You've only done that for me twice, plus I didn't ask you to, you did it of your own volition."

"You're my family, Hads. Nobody messes with my family."

I smile back at him as we make our way back to the bench. The sun is rising, and we sit and watch it, not wanting to part just yet. I always feel better after I talk with him, but I still feel scrambled over what I said to Grant before I left. "What should I do about this whole thing, Ol?"

"I can't tell you what to do, sis."

I turn to him. "I know, but please give me some advice. I hate that I gave up on him because of one stupid conversation we had. It's unlike me to be so... forward."

"Are you sure about that? You're pretty forward with everyone else. What makes him different?"

I smack him again. "Oliver, I'm serious."

He sighs heavily before he thinks about my question.

"Sometimes something good can be right in front of you, and you don't notice it until it hits you in the face."

"Wow, that's very poetic."

"I'm just saying, Hads. It wouldn't be a terrible thing if you became friends with the guy you're tutoring. It's only a conflict of interest if you make it one—which, judging by your feelings, you won't. Maybe it'll even get you out of your dorm room on the weekends instead of Ella dragging you all out."

I scoff. "I get out of my dorm! The only reason we're talking this morning is because I went to a party last night."

"Please, sis. Your entire life is studying, reading, doing your homework, and slandering Grant."

"I do not *slander* him!"

"The rumors beg to differ," he grins.

"Oliver! What have you heard?"

"Nothing you don't already know."

I pull my knees to my chest and my head falls forward. "This is exactly what I didn't want to happen."

"Hads, it's going to be fine."

I turn to him. "What would you do going forward if you were me?"

He thinks for another moment, and it hits me that next year, we won't be able to do this because he'll be graduating. I'm going to miss these walks of ours, and I hope he doesn't stray far after he leaves Grand Mountain. "Show up."

"What?" I hate when he doesn't elaborate and I have to press him for more. It's like he talks in code sometimes.

"I think you should show up to the tutoring session on Thursday."

"Even if I told him not to bother coming?"

"You two have a standing agreement this semester, and I think Grant is a good enough guy who cares about his grades to show up even after what you said. You just have to show up, too."

"What if he doesn't come?" I know he's a hockey player but one bad grade isn't going to kill him, is it? I wonder why he's so worried about this grade. *I should ask him.* I really don't know much about him besides the rumors I've heard, and maybe I need to be more open to learning about who he is myself.

"Then show up the next week. You hate backing down from a challenge, Hads. I know you won't go down without a fight."

"You make it sound so easy, Oliver."

"It is easy, Hads. Sometimes, all you can do is show up and be there for someone when they need it. Show up, apologize for what you said, and maybe you'll be friends—acquaintances, for God's sake. Don't waste time pushing someone away for no reason. It won't help anything."

"I think that's the most words I've heard you string together in two years," I tell him.

"I know. I sound like a talk show host." He looks at me, and we both burst out laughing.

"Thank you, Ol. I needed this. Believe it or not, you were helpful."

"I'm always helpful." He elbows me in the side before getting up. "Same time next week?"

"You bet."

"Good luck, Hads."

I smile at him, and he runs off back to his apartment. I decide to stay on the bench for a while. I can't sit around and wait for my life to magically work itself out. I have to show up, make decisions, and trust myself that they're what's right for me.

And I think I can do that.

10

 **Hadleigh**

"Now that all of the book talk is out of the way, who wants to start our debrief about last Friday? I need to hear everyone's point of view," Amelia says as she throws her book on the table.

Man, she really gets to the point, doesn't she?

I don't want to continue to rehash this—especially since I don't even know if Grant is going to show up tomorrow—but we haven't really talked about it. The four of us have been so busy with school and work that we've barely talked since Friday night.

"I got drunk and slept on my floor all night!" Paige says a bit too enthusiastically.

"Yes, I know. I was the one who put you there," Amelia says.

"On my floor?"

"On your bed, but you must have fallen off—or crawled off. All your blankets were on the floor with you."

"Oh, that's weird," Paige says.

"Seems like a normal night to me at the Paige and Amelia residence," Ella states.

"Is this book club or group therapy now?" I ask a bit harshly.

"Hads, you were the one who turned it into a therapy session when you were pacing all around about Grant." *Shit.* She's right. "And you can go last. There's a lot to unpack with your situation, but I want to hear about Ella and Leo because the rumors have been swirling around campus."

Amelia then grabs four small popcorn bags from her purse and hands them around as if we're at a community theater.

"Really?" Ella asks, and all Amelia does is shrug, smirk, and toss popcorn into her mouth.

"Go ahead, Ells," Ames says.

"Nothing has happened between us. It's his cocky, holier-than-thou attitude that annoys the shit out of me."

We all wait for her to continue. We know there's more to the story. Ella never hates someone just to hate them—there's always a reason of some sort.

"You guys know I was one of two to get a coveted internship with that marketing firm. What you don't know is how hard it was to get into. I worked my ass off for it. I was one of the only women applying for it, and the interview and intake process was grueling. I had two separate interviews—one with a board of people and another with the head of the firm. I obviously got the position, but I assumed the process was the same for everybody. It wasn't."

She sighs heavily before continuing.

"Zimmerman had one phone call with the head of the company and immediately got the placement. He kept bragging to me about how easy it was getting in here. Meanwhile, I worked my ass off to prove to these people I could do good work for them. During the first week of our internship, I was sent out for coffee while Zimmerman was allowed to sit in on meetings and take notes. It was humiliating, and he won't let me live it down. He also keeps messing with my desk and taking credit for proposals that I did."

"Geez," I say.

"Oh my God," Amelia says.

"Yeah. I work part-time and go to school full-time, and now I have this internship two days a week where I have to eavesdrop to actually learn things. Meanwhile, Zimmerman gets everything handed to him simply because he has a penis. It's not fair. But that's how the world works, and if I have to prove everyone wrong and show them I deserve my spot, then I will. And I'll do it in heels with a goddamn smile."

I take a deep breath. "Ella, I think you might be my hero."

She smiles, but it's not a full one.

"I didn't realize it was like that for you. I'm so sorry." Paige looks like she's about to cry. I love how deeply she cares for us. It's sweet.

"Ella, I'll gladly punch Zimmerman in the dick for you. Just name a time and place," Amelia says with a bright smile.

"Thank you, but I can handle him. I don't think he was expecting me to bite back when he first started this rivalry with me."

"Yeah, I definitely would not want to be on your bad side," I say. Ella as a friend is one of the strongest, most caring people you will ever meet. But if you get on her bad side, don't fuck with her. She might literally bite your head off and not lose any sleep over it—and she'd do the same if someone was rude to us girls.

"On a lighter note, I joined the criminal justice club on campus! I forced Oliver to join me because we get extra credit for a class we are both taking. He grunted at me when I dragged him to the meeting, but I know he has fun while we're there."

"How do you know that?" I ask her.

"Well, he's mostly silent, and he hasn't yelled at anyone yet!" Paige says.

"What exactly does the criminal justice club entail? It sounds like a bunch of you guys sit around and talk about cases, and isn't that what you do in class?" All of us look genuinely confused.

"I'm shocked you got my brother, of all people, to join a club on campus that requires him to be social." I'm a bit stunned. I didn't think my brother was the club type of person, but maybe he joined because I made fun of his social life the other day.

"He barely talks during it, but he did introduce himself and not just grunt. A win is a win." Paige sinks into her chair as she concludes her update.

"Now, moving on to Hads. What the hell is going on with you and Grant?"

"Oh, right," Ella says as she slips Paige twenty dollars.

"Okay, first of all, that bet is null and void because I did not quit being his tutor. I merely told him not to show up if he won't take it seriously. Second of all, I'm going to tomorrow's session, so your bet won't be finalized until tomorrow." I sigh heavily, knowing he might not show up to our session, but at least I can say I tried.

"You're deflecting, and don't say you're not because I'm the queen of deflecting when people ask me questions I don't want to answer. Start talking, or I'll make Paige torture you for information." Amelia points at me with popcorn in her hand.

"I never agreed to that!" Paige jumps out of her seat.

"Fine, Amelia! God, you're infuriating sometimes," I say as I get up and start pacing. "There's no deal with Grant and I. All that happened on Saturday was him flirting with me and me telling him to stop because we have to remain professional. The only reason he knows me is because he needs something from me—my brain. And yeah, sure, he caged me into the wall, and my heart was beating out of my chest, but—"

"He caged you into the wall?" Paige asks.

"Like with his arm?" Ella muses.

"That's the one thing you guys are taking away from all of that? Really?"

"We're just pointing out something obvious."

"And what would that be?" I ask.

"Yes, Paige, please enlighten us!" Amelia giggles. I think we all know where Paige is going with this, and she couldn't be more wrong.

"Your trope is haters to friends to possibly lovers. I can see it all playing out in my head like a romance novel. First, he begs you to tutor him. Then, he spends more time with you. I'm assuming this is a he falls first situation, and maybe you will become friends. Maybe you spend more time with one another, and maybe you fall for him too. Maybe you two will start cooking with gas instead of grease!" Paige looks around as if she had made some grand declaration or new discovery before we all burst out laughing.

"Cooking with gas instead of grease?" Ella asks, as confused as the rest of us are. Paige always has the oddest phrases for certain things, and it makes us all laugh.

"What? It's a phrase people use."

"Maybe old ladies at bingo," Amelia giggles.

"Amelia, this is the most I've heard you laugh, and the fact that it's about everyone else's misery says more about you than me," I tell her, and she merely shrugs.

"What are your next steps, Hads?" Ella steers the conversation back.

"Well, I'm going to show up to tutoring tomorrow, and if he doesn't come, then I guess it's over. If he shows up, we can continue as normal. I'm going to apologize for being so crass, and hopefully, neither of us will bring up the conversation we had." I'm determined to see this agreement through. Oliver was right—I hate backing down from a challenge. And Grant has been the biggest challenge that I never saw coming.

"Well, that's good to know, Hads. We believe in you. Though, keep the banter up between you too. It's fun to see you all flustered over it," Amelia smiles as she stands. "Paige, are you ready to go? I want to finish that documentary before bed tonight."

Her eyes jump out of her head as she leaps out of her seat. "I *knew* you enjoyed it. You kept hovering in the kitchen while I was watching it!"

"The killer murdered a bunch of dudes. Of course I found it interesting."

Paige grabs her tote before they leave the classroom. "Good luck tomorrow, Hads! I bet he shows up!"

After Paige and Amelia leave, Ella and I stay seated for a few moments. "I'm sorry about the internship. I didn't realize it was so difficult for you. I remember how excited you were when you got the spot," I reach over, grab her hand, and squeeze it.

"Part of me wishes I told you guys sooner. Keeping all that bottled up for so long has not been fun."

"I bet."

"I get it, you know."

"What?"

"Hating someone—it can be exhausting."

"I don't hate him—at least I don't think I do. Grant is a puzzle my head can't quite solve. Leo's definitely worse than Grant, though." It is exhausting to keep having to deal with these hockey players. If any more of them come up to me, I might just run away. The two of them are more than I can handle as is.

"It's nice to talk it out sometimes," Ella says as she fixes a table back to its proper place.

"I know. Sometimes it's hard to formulate words about how I am feeling. We got off to a rocky start because of my bias against men and the fact that he knocked me over and thought he was entitled to my time."

"In the future, if your head feels jumbled, you can always come to me. We're in a similar situation, but yours might actually end well." She says that one with a laugh. She could be right. I don't think I could hate Grant forever. That sounds exhausting, and we did have an okay conversation before he started flirting with me. I don't know why he would pretend to be interested in me. Does he think his grades will magically increase if he dates me or something?

"I will, I promise. I've never had an older sister to talk to about boys before, and I'm glad I have you guys now. Oliver's alright but he only threatens to punch any guy that comes near me." I love how protective my brother is, but sometimes, it's nice to be able to rant to the girls.

"Well, now you have three older sisters to come to." She smiles and squeezes my hand. "But I would come to me first. The shining twins are wise, but the two of us could use a bit of comfort from each other."

"I will," I tell her.

"Maybe we could get coffee every week and rant about our problems together? Does that sound okay?" Ella offers.

"Coffee and ranting? Count me the fuck in, Ells. We can also go over our *One Tree Hill* rewatch. Season three is coming, and you know that's the best one."

"Oh my, yes! Things are about to get wild, and my Naley heart will be healed. We can figure out a time to meet next week."

"Sounds good to me! I'm also proud of you. I don't know if I mentioned that." My heart constricts a bit when she says that to me, but I keep my face neutral.

"Proud of me for what?"

"For not quitting and for showing up tomorrow. Your brother might be silent most of the time, but he can give good advice when needed."

"Thanks, Ells."

"Of course, babe. And even if he doesn't show up tomorrow, there's always next week. I think it will work out how it's supposed to. You just have to hope that it does." She heads for the door as I push the last chair in.

"Drive safe and text me when you're home!" I say to her.

"I will. Don't stay up too late doing homework!" she shouts across the empty building.

"No promises!" I smile. I feel a lot better about tomorrow now. Even if he doesn't show up, I won't give up hope. I'll see this through, and maybe there's a small chance we can become friends.

I can only hope that I don't somehow mess this all up. It's my first time tutoring, and if it goes well, I can do it again in the future. One thing at a time, I remind myself.

One thing at a time.

11

Grant

FOR SOME REASON, AT practices lately, I can't fucking focus.

We're supposed to be doing shooting drills right now, but I've missed every single shot I've taken, and I even slipped and fell over on the ice after I missed the puck on one shot. Now, Jacks is making fun of me how I made fun of him when he fell on the ice during freshman year. He says he slipped, but he was totally checking out Claire. The reason I slipped is because I can't stop thinking about a girl.

Apparently, the only thing that can bring Jacks and I to our asses is women.

But I need to be more focused than ever. We have a game coming up, and the team looks good, but I do not. I'm missing shots, missing passes, and worst of all, if this were a real game, the other team would have scored a few times because I'm not doing my job to the best of my ability.

Normally, hockey and skating is where I go to escape the anxiety that follows me around when I'm failing, but now those feelings are seeping into the safe space I used to have on the ice. Something is wrong with me, I'm sure of it. Nothing I've been doing lately has helped me to relax about the impending failure over my head if I don't get my grade up.

I have to get my head out of my ass, and if Hads isn't in the room tomorrow when I go for tutoring, I'm fucked. Even if she hates me, she's damn smart. I need her help and there has to be a way I can prove to her that I'm taking this seriously.

Coach hasn't pulled me aside again, but I have another quiz next week. If Hads isn't there, I'll be fucked. On the bright side, she rented the study room for half of the semester, so at least I'll have a quiet room where I can focus. Maybe I can find one of those videos that will explain the metaphors to me. Do those exist?

The whistle infiltrates my thoughts and I realize it's my turn for the drill again. I look to Jacks and he grabs the puck, avoiding the other players on the ice before he passes it to me. I head towards Holt who's in goal and I try something different and sneak it to Jacks as I skate by the post. He sneaks it in on the other side, and the buzzer goes off.

Huh. I guess Jacks and I really can read each other's minds. And the irony of me passing to him isn't lost on me—sometimes it's okay to need others to help you get to your end result.

It felt good having something work out in my favor—even if it's just at practice.

Coach signals the end of practice and we all circle up around him. He talks about our game next Monday and how we look good but not great. We still have a lot of work to do, and he's changed our Friday conditioning night to an on-ice practice.

We're in the top five in our division here on the East Coast, but the school we're facing at our home opener is above us in the rankings. We're going to have to bust our asses to win this game, and it's not one I want to lose because I'm distracted or benched.

After he's done, we all hit the locker room and shower. I like the fact that the rink is on-campus because it's easier for me to rush back to the apartment when I have a shit ton of homework to do. And it's nice that it's accessible for other students, too. Our crowds are always electric, and nothing beats the feeling of skating at a home game. I can always feel the crowd's excitement; it helps me block everything out and do my job.

Maybe that's why I keep fucking up at practice—it's too quiet and I can hear all of my thoughts.

I open my locker and shove my equipment inside, grabbing the shampoo, conditioner, and my stuff. I'm not the type of guy to use 5-in-1 shit on my hair and body. With hair as nice as mine, you have to keep it well-maintained. Plus, it's weird that some people use the same shit on their hair and body. It seems kind of fucked to me. I change into fresh clothes before I run into Jacks.

"Hey, G. I won't be walking back with you tonight. I'm going over to Brett's for a movie."

"You're going to watch a movie on a Wednesday night after practice?" I ask, skeptical because Jacks usually watches movies by himself, and he hates going out after practice because of how late it is.

"Yeah, so?"

"Will Claire be there?" His face flushes and I have my answer. Jacks has had a crush on her since freshman year when he first laid eyes on her. He's been too scared to do anything about it. It's cute, honestly. "I hope you have fun, dude. Maybe tonight will be the night." I nudge him and he looks embarrassed.

"Shut up."

"Never." I throw a huge smile at him, and he flips me off and walks away. God, I love that kid. I shut my locker and grab my bookbag, heading for the exit.

As I walk across campus, I notice how quiet it is. It's around nine, so that doesn't surprise me—this campus basically shuts down after seven on weeknights. I see a few students walking around, but only one catches my eye. She has short black hair, is wearing a skirt, and is carrying a book. I swear I could spot her from a mile away. It feels like some sort of cosmic sign that I found her on campus when I was just thinking about her.

I smile to myself as I walk next to her, my legs matching the pace that she walks. I break the silence when I notice her eyes stealing glances at me.

I decide to go the banter route because that usually makes her talk to me. "Hades, you're out late for a school night. Shouldn't you be studying down in the underworld?"

"I came up to steal more souls. Are you volunteering? I'll gladly take yours." She turns to look at me as she stops walking. "Oh wait, you don't have one. It looks like you're safe this time."

I grab her arms with mine, wanting to apologize for the other night, when she looks down at where my hands are touching her. I remove them for fear of getting kicked in the balls or something, and now I'm just standing here awkwardly.

What do I do with my hands? I bunch them into fists at my side. Have I always been this awkward? What is wrong with me?

Say something, idiot. She's looking at you like you're insane. "I wanted to apologize properly for all the stuff I said on Friday. I didn't mean to flirt, and I absolutely take our partnership seriously. I never intended to make you think otherwise."

"Okay?"

"So, uh, I'm sorry, Hadleigh. I promise that going forward—if you'll have me—I'll take this thing between us seriously. I need you, after all. You're my only hope of passing this class."

She looks at me for a few seconds and says nothing. I'm worried the ruler is going to come out and she's going to whack me, but she speaks a few seconds later.

"It's okay, Grant. I'm sorry for storming off and not giving you a chance to explain. I ran away instead of talking to you because I can't hold my tongue around you for some reason."

"It's okay. I deserved it."

"No, you didn't." She shakes her head. "Will I see you tomorrow?"

She sounds worried—truly worried that I wouldn't have shown up tomorrow. Does she think one little row with one another would make me not show up? I guess we don't really know one another, so I can't blame her for that.

"You'll see me tomorrow and, if you don't mind, a little more tonight." I motion forward. "Let me walk you back to your place."

She shakes her head before I'm even done speaking. "Grant, it's okay. You probably have somewhere else to be."

"Nowhere else as important as making sure you get back safe. You never know who could be lurking in the shadows, Hades."

With that, she rolls her eyes. "Like you?"

"Well, believe it or not, there are worse people to run into than me."

That earns me a scoff. "I bet there are."

The two of us start walking and I let her guide the way because I don't know what dorm she lives in. We're quiet as we walk, and for once it doesn't feel like an awkward silence that normally fills our sessions before she smacks me with her ruler. It's comfortable and the cold breeze flows between the two of us as our hands dangle beside one anothers.

She has a book in her left arm, and I try to see what the title is so I can ask her about it, but I can't quite tell what it is. Every time I've seen Hads talk about the book she tutors me on, her eyes light up in a certain way. I've never seen them do that when we talk about anything else, and at least I'd get to know her better and see what she loves to read with her book club.

"You know, you need to get out more."

She throws her head back. "Not you, too. You're like the fifth person to say that to me in the span of a week."

"Well, that must mean we're all right."

"No, it means that you're all way too invested in my social life. I've been perfectly comfortable living under the radar on this campus. I can't handle being the center of attention over some big rumor that probably isn't true."

I nudge her with my elbow. "Come on, Hads. Aren't you glad you got out of your shell a bit? After all, it is how we met. You can thank the rumor mill for that one."

"What? Why?"

I smile at her. "The only reason I found you was because my best friend heard a rumor about some girl who got an A in Collins' class."

I can feel her eyes roll without even looking at her. "Damn."

"So, you might as well put yourself out there since the rumor mill has already gotten to you."

We turn left onto the path and I feel her hand brush against mine on accident as we continue walking.

"How do you deal with it?" she asks me as we get closer to what I assume is her dorm.

"With what?"

"All the rumors and stuff. I've heard about a thousand that mention you since we've become acquainted."

"Have you now? And what have they mentioned about me?"

I swear her cheeks turn red, but it's too dark in this area for me to tell. "Nothing I'd care to admit out loud to you, Grant. But you had to have heard about them. You're one of the most popular kids on campus."

I guess I am popular since I'm on the hockey team, but I never hear the rumors that involve me. "I tend not to think too much about what others say about me. I know who I am, and that's all that matters."

She nods, a smile on her face as she goes to pull her ID card out. "I can respect that."

"So, will I see you more than just tutoring or are you not going to listen to the people who are clearly worried about your social life?"

She laughs dryly at me before she adjusts her book to her other arm. "Well, between you and my brother, I might have to listen to one of you. I'm not the biggest fan of partying. I'm way too anal about my grades and academic standing, but I could let loose every once in a while, I guess."

"I won't count you out then, Hades."

"You never should, Grant. I'm full of surprises."

A smile creeps up before I can stop it. "I bet you are."

The two of us stand in front of her building for a few silent moments before she waves at me and swipes into her dorm. "I'll see you tomorrow."

"Cool," is all I manage to say.

"Great."

"Wonderful." *Really, Grant? Wonderful? What's next, exquisite?*

We stand awkwardly looking at one another for a few more seconds before she clears her throat, gives another awkward wave, and heads inside. "Be careful heading back to your place," she tells me. "You never know what's lurking in the shadows."

I wouldn't mind the shadows if you were in them, Hades. "Thanks. I'll be careful." And as I head back to my place, I find myself smiling with more of a pep in my step than before.

It looks like this semester is looking up after all.

To: carter_grant@grandmountain.edu

From: baker_hadleigh@grandmountain.edu

Subject: Alive?

I don't have your phone number, and my friends and I always text one another to make sure we get home safely, so this is me doing that—not that we're friends or anything. I think Ella has just ingrained it in me to always double check, and I'd hate to have sent you off into the night just to get murdered or something.

Please respond if you're alive enough to do so.

At rock bottom,

Hads

To: baker_hadleigh@grandmountain.edu

From: carter_grant@grandmountain.edu

Subject: Unfortunately for you, I'm still kicking!

How nice of you—my friend, Hadleigh Baker—to think of me after our walk tonight. I'm one hundred percent fine and still operating to the best of my abilities. Jacks just got back to our apartment, so if you'd like to confirm with him that I'm in fact still breathing, you can do so.

But I think with this email, your worries should be soothed. You were worried, right? How worried would you say you were on a scale of 1-10? Because I'm thinking you were around the 7 or 8 mark since you emailed me in the middle of the night—on a school night no less! Don't you have studying to do? Or a book to be read? But here you are, emailing your old friend, Grant.

My number is attached in a word document to this email so we can communicate like proper *friends* going forward. I look forward to our regular correspondence.

To infinity and beyond,
Grant

To: carter_grant@grandmountain.edu
From: baker_hadleigh@grandmountain.edu
Subject: Calm down.

I'm not even going to entertain that scale of yours, but know my worry was minimal. I'm glad you're alive. (To whoever kidnapped you and forced you to send that email, tell them they got your cadence and attitude just right! 10/10!)

If I use your phone number, please let it be for normal reasons. I don't need any more GIFs or memes that are backlogged on your phone. You have to *promise* me that you'll be normal. I'll even bring a sheet of paper for you to sign at tutoring tomorrow so I have proof of this deal.

And yes, I am reading, right now. My brain was too tired to do homework after book club tonight, so don't worry, I'll be sharp for our lesson tomorrow. Prepare your brain, and don't zone out because I'm obviously bringing my ruler.

Are you still reading this?
Hads

12

 **Hadleigh**

My brain already feels fried as I walk out of statistics and head to my class upstairs with Paige. Something about me today feels off, and I'm almost certain it has to do with the conversation I had with Grant last night.

The *nice* conversation I had when he walked me back to my dorm. And let's not forget the email conversation we had because when I didn't see him posting anything on social media like he does every night, I assumed he was kidnapped or something.

It's not like my heart sank imagining that or anything, but I was slightly worried about him, so I sent him an email.

Thankfully, he responded, but since I used his number to make sure it was *actually* his, he hasn't stopped texting me as he goes about his day.

My phone buzzes a few times as I walk up the stairs and I roll my eyes at the texts Grant has sent me.

> **Grant: Do you happen to know the square root of sixty four?**

> **Grant: I saw someone else wearing a skirt and I thought it was you so I called your name, and they turned around and looked at me funny.**

> **Grant: I thought this kid was waving at me, so I waved back, but turns out they were waving at the person behind me.**

> **Grant: I think I need to lock myself in a room to save myself more embarrassment.**

I catch myself smiling way too hard at these texts, so I immediately lock my phone and smack myself in the face.

Stop thinking about Grant, his stupid face, and his stupid wet hair from last night that fell in just the right way.

Abort. Abort. Abort!

I walk into class, hoping to see Paige and talk to her about anything else, but she's not here when I walk into the room. That's odd. She's always early to everything. Oliver is here, though, but I'm not sure how much riveting conversation he can be at the moment. I plop down in my seat and all of a sudden, Paige bolts into the room out of breath. Did she sprint here or something?

"Sorry." She takes a few breaths. "I got wrapped up in this mafia book and completely forgot what time it was."

"Paige, you realize you're not late, right? Class starts in ten minutes."

"I know, but my philosophy has always been if you're on time, you're late, and if you're early, you're on time," she says, still catching her breath.

"That doesn't make any sense," Oliver tells us.

"It doesn't have to make sense to you, Ollie. It's my philosophy." Did Paige just call my brother that? And did he let her?

I shift the subject off of another thing my brain doesn't want to think about. "Was that mafia book good?"

"Oh yeah, it's definitely going to be a favorite. It's a *Beauty and the Beast* retelling." She smiles at that.

"You girls and your books." Oliver sounds less than enthused. I turn a bit to say something snarky at him when someone taps me on the shoulder. I turn around, and it's Ryan.

"Hey, Hads."

"Uh, h-hi, Ryan. What's up?" This is only the second time we've interacted, and it still makes me slightly uncomfortable. I'm not used to talking to men this much, let alone a guy who didn't know I existed until Grant started talking to me.

"I just wanted to chat, and I was wondering if you were busy Monday night?"

"Uhm, I think I'm free. Why?" Paige is laughing next to me, and I can feel my brother staring at Ryan.

"Well, I have a hockey game on Monday night—the first one—and I was wondering if you wanted to come watch?"

"Come watch the hockey team with you?" *I'm so confused.*

"I mean, I'll be on the ice, so I can't watch *with* you, but maybe you can bring the book club or something?" He smiles, and he almost looks shy. *What the hell is going on?*

"Right, because you'll be playing. Uh, sure, that sounds fun."

"Maybe after we can grab a bite or something?" I hear Oliver grunt behind me.

"Yeah, that sounds good!" *Why is my voice so high-pitched?*

"Alright, cool." He slides a piece of paper across the table. "There's my number. Text me?"

"Yeah, okay." I doubt I'll use it, but I said that about Grant's number last night, and I used his this morning.

As soon as he walks away, I turn to face Paige and my brother, and when I do, he looks murderous and Paige has a disgusted look on her face. "Why are you both looking at me so weirdly?"

"Uhm," is all she says. Is she speechless? I don't think I've ever heard Paige not have anything to say before. She goes on rants about how some serial killers were stupid and details how they couldn't have been caught, but to *this*, she's speechless.

"I'm going to kill that kid."

"Oliver, calm down. You can't threaten murder in a criminology class." I say to him.

"He asked you out right in front of me! What kind of prick does that?"

"Wait, what? He asked me to watch his hockey game. That's not a date, just an invite to a free hockey game." I look over at Paige, and she doesn't meet my eyes.

Shit, did he ask me out? Did I not pick up on that?

"This all seems fishy. Ryan grinds my gears. My gut says not to trust him," Paige tells me.

"Fuck, did he ask me out?"

"Yes, and now he's going to die." Oliver moves to get up, and Paige shoves him back down.

"I will not be an accomplice to this. Save your murderous tendencies for later. You don't want to go to prison, do you?" Paige asks him.

"I would never go to prison for someone, but for him, I'd think about it." Oliver sounds pissed.

The professor walks into class and we have to drop this conversation for now. Why would Ryan ask me out on a date? It doesn't feel like a date if all I'm doing is watching hockey at his suggestion, is it? The lecture starts, and I can barely think. How did I get roped into this alternate universe where I'm intertwined with not one but two hockey players? None of this makes any sense.

A few minutes into class, I start getting notifications from our group chat.

Paige: Guys! Ryan Barnes just asked Hads out on a date! It was super awkward, and I don't like him. I heard around campus that he dips his cereal in milk rather than putting them in the same bowl!

Hads: Wait, what?

Paige: I know right! Serial killer trait, but Ryan has like fifty of them!

Ella: Ew, what? When did this happen?

Amelia: Who?

Paige: Just now before our class started!

Hads: It's not a big deal. My brother only threatened to kill him twice. But what do I do? Going to a hockey game alone sounds lame, and I don't date? How do you do that? Also dating Ryan sounds disgusting. I barely know the kid!

Ella: Are you guys thinking what I am?

Paige: Ryan said she should invite us, but I still don't like him.

Ella: We're absolutely going. Nothing gets me more excited than hot guys and good beer. Don't worry, Hads, we'll be there with you

Amelia: I'm still confused about who this man is, but sure.

Hads: Thanks, guys! Maybe it won't be too bad?

Ella: Our girls first date in a while. We can all get ready together. I'm so excited!

Amelia: Is hockey the one with a puck?

Hads: Amelia...

I chuckle as the conversation ends. I get another notification. It's from just Ella this time.

Ella: I know you have tutoring later.

Ella: Keep your head up. If he doesn't show, you didn't let him down.

Hads: Thanks, Ells. But I think he'll be there. I have a feeling.

Ella: Proud of you for showing up still.

Ella: Also, does Paige do background checks still? We should ask her to do one on Ryan, just in case...

I look over at Paige and, judging by how vigorously she's typing on her computer, she might already be one step ahead of Ella.

Hads: Don't worry. She's already on the case.

Ella: I love you!

Hads: Love you!

13

Grant

I walk into the library with a smile on my face and for someone who used to never come into this place, I never realized how peaceful it is.

I don't think I ever stopped to take in my surroundings when I was here. The floor-to-ceiling windows, the way each floor gets quieter depending on which one you go to. Peaceful doesn't even begin to cover it, honestly. I never even noticed we have a café in here. I'm starting to question my eyesight after not noticing all these things.

I'm also walking with more pep in my step because I passed the last quiz. Things are looking up immensely since I started tutoring with Hads, and it's weird that I can't wait to dive further into this book.

She was right when she told me she knows this book like the back of her hand. I've never seen someone break down the metaphors and old language of this book like she has.

When I walk into our study room, I notice she isn't here yet. I'm a little early, so that makes sense. I shove my headphones on, pull my phone out, and start watching our best game from last season. Coach always gives us film from the past year to watch and see what we did well—passing, shooting, and all that. He's not impressed with how we've been practicing, so he always makes us watch film before a big game so mistakes aren't repeated.

A few minutes later, I'm too engrossed in my phone to notice that Hads has come in, and she smacks my hand before I can greet her.

"I told you to watch the hands!" I say as I rub the spot on my hand she hit.

"You were the one watching hockey instead of looking at the book I'm tutoring you on."

"This is homework, too. We have our first game coming up."

She sits across from me and drops her bag on the floor. "It's on Monday, right?"

My eyebrows pinch in confusion at her. "Yeah... how did you know that?" I lean forward on my elbows. "Are you keeping tabs on me, Hades?"

"Just because I'm oblivious about sports, that doesn't mean I don't see all your social media updates about your game schedule." She looks down at her lap before she talks again. "Ryan invited me to it."

At the mention of his name, I tense up. God, that kid is the worst. "Are my eyes deceiving me or is Hadleigh Baker thinking about going to a hockey game?"

She rolls her eyes at me. "I might stop by. That only means you're going to have to win, Carter. Do you think you can handle that?"

"I think so." I smirk at her. "Wanna bet?"

She cocks her head at me. "What do you want?"

"If we win, you have to hang out with me outside of tutoring." I throw my hand out to her.

"And if you lose the game, I get five hits on you from my ruler any time—not just at tutoring. I'm talking any time and any day." She holds out her hand in front of her.

"You're definitely a masochist, Hads, but deal." We shake on it before Hads starts to dive into chapter three of Gatsby. Now more than ever am I excited to win this first game of the season. Not only will the team be off to a great start, but then Hads has to hang out with me for one night whenever I want her to. It's a fucking win-win.

"Now, sign this before we start," she says as she slaps a piece of paper in front of me.

"Seriously?" I thought she was kidding when I woke up and saw that email, but I also had a message from her this morning testing if it was actually my number—as if she didn't think I'd give her my real one. "You haven't enjoyed my—"

She cuts me off. "No, I haven't enjoyed your hour-to-hour updates. Sign the paper."

It's literally a sheet with one sentence on it and a highlighted line. I sigh heavily before I scratch my name down, and she folds it up and puts it in her bag.

"Wonderful. Now, to the book," she says as she opens to the proper chapter. "This is the chapter where Gatsby is finally introduced, and—"

"Finally! The book is literally named after him and I'm astonished that he's not even the main character." She tilts her head at me, probably annoyed that I cut her off. "Sorry. Please continue, you genius."

Her face flushes as she continues. "There's a lot of mystery sounding him on purpose, and this introduction is important to knowing who Gatsby is as a character. Now, Gatsby is well known to many as this guy who throws lavish parties that last all night, but no invitations are ever sent out—people just tend to show up through word of mouth."

That reminds me of the parties we always throw at the hockey house. All Holt has to do is tell the right people and word about it spreads like wildfire. Huh. Maybe this book does have connections to the world around me.

"Nick Carraway is the only person who has ever received an invitation, and they live next door to one another, so Nick decides to go to the party. He hears all these rumors about who Gatsby could be, but none of them are true because Gatsby himself is sitting down at a table that Jordan and Nick are at and he introduces himself. He looks like any normal guy and not at all what Nick imagined him to look like due to the rumors that swirl about him."

"And Nick is attracted to Jordan—the golfer that cheats?" I ask, wondering if I read that part of the book correctly.

Hads nods her head. "Yes. Gatsby calls everyone old sport, the party rages on all night, and Gatsby seems to separate himself from the party and his persona because Nick sees him watching everyone else all night."

"And you're sure Nick and Gatsby aren't in love? All it feels like Nick does is watch Gatsby and try to unpack who he is."

She laughs at me. "No, they're not in love. Their relationship is more admiration than anything. Nick admires Gatsby for who he is, and Gatsby uses Nick because of his connection to Daisy—the girl Gatsby loves."

"Whatever you say, Hads, but I think those two are in love. Isn't that what's so cool about books? People interpret the same one differently."

"Yes, I guess that's part of it. I'm glad you're starting to dive more into this book, Grant. It seems like you're enjoying yourself a little more than before."

I nod my head. "I am. And I passed the last quiz, so at least we know this partnership is working. Aren't you proud of me?" I bat my eyelashes at her so she knows I'm joking. I know she'd never say that.

"I'm proud of myself. You seemed like a lost cause before you had me." She tilts her head. "I guess I'm proud of you through association."

"How nice of you to say, Hades."

We spend the next forty-five minutes talking about the metaphors in this chapter and how Fitzy—F. Scott Fitzgerald—up until this point, has made the reader see Gatsby from a distance, but now we see him closer but he still remains a mystery. I only got slapped with the ruler two more times, and somehow Hades always manages to hit a different spot on my hand.

We're just about finished when the most random question slips out of my mouth. "Why do you like to read romance books?"

I feel like I stepped over a line because she stares at me, dumbfounded. "How do you know I read romance?"

"The one in your arm last night had a bunch of lipstick kisses on the cover, so I assumed romance." And I looked it up last night, but couldn't find out what it was about.

She chuckles a bit and shakes her head. "That's our book club pick this month, and it actually was a romance, so one point for you, creeper."

"You never answered my question. Why do you like romance so much?"

She ponders it for a minute before she answers. I like watching the gears turn in her head. "I enjoy watching two people fall in love. It's nice when you open a book and know the two people will have found their way to each other when it's over. I have never really believed it could happen for me after—"

She pauses, and she cuts herself off from saying something. I wish she kept going, though. I want to know why she doesn't believe she could have what they do in books. Plus, why would people write about romance if it didn't exist in real life?

"I have a pretty messed up view of love and romance too, but it still exists out there. Somewhere, hopefully," I say with a slight chuckle. I don't talk about the fact that the first time I saw Hads I never wanted to stop looking at her. In a way, I think I remind myself of Nick from this fucking book.

Hads is Gatsby because I can only see her from a distance. I can't reach her because I barely know who she is outside of these sessions we do once a week. If I were able to, I'd pick her brain about anything and everything. I want to get closer, but I know she doesn't see the two of us ending up as anything after we're done here.

But the last thing I want to do is fall more and more in Hads if she doesn't feel the same way. It wouldn't end great for me because my heart would be broken again, and Hads would probably be embarrassed, or something. Plus, I wouldn't want rumors to spread about her. I'd hate for her to get dragged into something and have her credibility get shot for no reason.

She deserves better than that. She deserves better than me, but damn, that hurts.

I wish I saw her more up close, but if I win the game on Monday, maybe I'll be able to have normal conversations with her like the one we're having now. God, I've never been more determined to get a win than I am now. I'm going to have to hit the ice this weekend to make sure I'm at my best for Monday.

Because as the timer goes off, signaling the end of our session, I stop her before she can run away from me and leave the library.

"I'll walk you back to your dorm," I say.

"No, Grant, it's—"

"It wasn't a question, Hads," I say as I open the library doors for her.

And I swear I see her smile as she walks past me and out the doors. *Huh*, I think to myself. Maybe she does feel something other than annoyance for me...

14

Hadleigh

I'm finally out taking pictures on campus this morning before I meet Ella for coffee. I've barely had time for my hobbies on my schedule, but ever since I started tutoring Grant, I've wanted to spend more time doing what I love, rather than studying all the time.

Plus, I finished all of my homework on Friday, and the only things I could study for are quizzes coming up where I haven't learned the material.

It's early in the morning, so there aren't a lot of people out who could mess my shots up. I normally take pictures of whatever calls to me, and right now, it's these flowers that are beginning to bloom. It's still pretty cool out, so I'm surprised I found some small buds peeking out of the ground.

Ella and I have our first-ever coffee date in half an hour, and I'm not only excited for the coffee, but also the company. I know Ella has a difficult time talking about things like I do, but maybe I can get more out of her about Zimmerman. I know I can barely talk about my feelings toward Grant—whatever they are—but at least it's not pure and utter hatred like it is for her. Maybe mine started out that way, but the more time I spend with him, the more my guard comes down.

Which is terrifying in and of itself, but I try not to think too hard about that as I take a few pictures of the fountain on campus. I hear someone call my name, and when I look around and the only person I see is Jacks—who's walking toward me—I assume it was him.

Jacks Moore is *another* hockey player, and he happens to be Grant's best friend. I've known him for longer since we have some similar classes together, and he's actually the one who told me Grant needed a tutor.

"Jacks Moore," I say as I put my lens cap on. "What's up?"

He only smiles at me before he sits on the side of the fountain. "Not the full name, Hads. Don't make me nervous."

"Am I that scary?"

"No, not at all." He runs a hand through his blond hair. "I had a few questions about the biology homework that's due tomorrow. Have you started it?"

"I finished it on Friday. Did you need help with it? We can go over the answers later, if you want." Who am I and what have I done with myself? Did I really offer myself up to help another hockey player? If I keep this up, I'm going to have the entire team on speed dial.

"No, that's okay. I think Grant would be mad if I tried to poach you from him."

"Yeah, that sounds like him, but it doesn't matter. I can handle him, Jacks."

He only laughs. "Oh, I'm aware. I didn't think you knew that, but if he pisses you off, it's only because he likes you."

I can only roll my eyes.

"He's just misunderstood, that's all. Most people think of him as a typical asshole because of all the rumors, but he isn't like that. He wants real connection over some fling. And believe it or not, his worst fear is failing himself or the people he loves."

I pinch my brows together, unaware of why he's telling me all this.

"He falls quickly and usually for the wrong people, Hads. His last three girlfriends have cheated on him, so go easy on him. He's trying his best and tends to use humor as a deflection."

I believe that. He's always way too fucking smiley, and I figured there was more to him that met my eyes, but I never wanted to open him up. If I did, I was worried I would make a stupid mistake, and I will *never* do what I did in high school again. "Why are you telling me all this?"

He only smirks. "I'm just making conversation about my friend to another person who's probably heard about him around campus. Don't believe the rumor mill, Hads. He's like a giant puppy dog when you get to know him."

"If I throw a stick, will he fetch it?" I joke.

"You never know, but I can assume if you're the one throwing it, he'll bring it back unharmed."

I can only laugh at his insinuation. "Then consider my help with your homework as a thank you for the clarity you're giving me."

"Nah, it's okay." He shakes his head. "I give clarity free of charge. And this might give me a chance to talk to Claire instead."

"Claire Canes? The girl who sits two rows in front of you in our lecture?"

"That's her." His cheeks get all red, and I think he's got a huge crush on her. How adorable. "Grant keeps making fun of me because I'm too much of a wuss to talk to her and ask her out—which he's right, I am. I wish it were that easy."

"Jacks, that's adorable, and I can't believe I'm saying this, but I agree with Grant. You should just talk to her. Girls like it when you can be direct with your feelings."

"Noted." He smiles at me, but before he leaves my personal space, he stops. "This might be too direct, but fuck it. Grant's the type of person who cares aggressively about the people in his circle. It's his nature, so go easy on him if he says some douchey shit. He just... cares about you, that's all."

Well, I couldn't be more confused. Is he insinuating what I think he is? No. Grant and I may have flirted a few times—him more than me—but it never means anything. It's a joke—a stupid thing Grant does with most people around him, I assume.

"Okay." I laugh awkwardly. "Thank you for this enlightening talk. I'll see you in class tomorrow," I say as I throw my camera in my bag and head for the library. I'm determined to escape my weird feelings and whatever Jacks was insinuating.

There's no way he meant it in a relationship way—maybe he meant Grant cares about me in a professional sort of way. That's got to be it, right? Because that's the only relationship Grant and I have ever had. Nothing more and nothing less.

I rush into the library cafe and see Ella sitting in one of the booths reading on her Kindle. My mind is a mess, and my face probably shows that because Ella looks wide-eyed at me when I sit down across from her.

"Why does your face look like that?"

"No reason, just a friendly conversation with Jacks about how Grant has confusing and caring feelings for me. Another normal day for me over here." I say all that too fast and screechy for my liking, but Ella understands me anyway.

"Wait, what? Jacks talked to you about Grant?"

I go over every detail from the past half hour, explaining everything he said to me, and when I'm done, she has no words.

"Wow, that's a lot to unpack this early when you're hungover." She presses a hand to her head.

"Well, imagine being me, Ella! But I can't wrap my head around how he thinks Grant cares about me. I barely know him!" In the span of a month, I've gone from someone who hated sports, men, and everything about relationships, to having a conversation involving all three of those things.

"This is why women are better. They're less confusing about things more than men are," Ella sips her coffee and takes her sunglasses off. She's pansexual, and I'm glad she's here and not Paige or Ames because neither of them have had many romantic relationships. Ella's had the most out of all of us.

"My brain is a mess. I didn't even like Grant at the beginning of the semester, and now I think he's tolerable?"

She slides a coffee over to me. "Drink this, it'll help."

"You ordered my coffee for me?"

"Triple shot latte with a pump of liquid sweetener. I figured you might need it." It is truly the little things in life. I love Ella so much.

"Thank you."

"I have some advice for you if you want to hear it."

I take a large sip of my coffee. "Yes, please, I'll take anything."

"You have to figure out how you feel about Grant without all of the noise. I know you're tutoring him, but that doesn't mean you can't have a friendship outside of that. There's no rules stating you can't, so it's all up to you. As soon as you figure that out, your brain will be less scrambled."

"I guess, but I'd rather stay far away from romantic relationships for the time being. I not only have to focus on my grades, but I want to make time for myself this semester and maybe get out of my dorm a little bit. I forgot how nice it felt to have an actual social life."

"Ugh, I'm so glad you said that. Going out with you guys was so much fun. We have to do it more often."

I smile, knowing Ella has waited a long time for all of us to be as extroverted as she is. "What if I don't know what I want with Grant? What if I don't want to be friends with him?"

"Then tell him that, but I think you do, Hads. Or, I think you could eventually be friends with him. I know you prefer keeping most people at a distance, but it's okay to let new people in. That's the point of college—you find the people you're meant to spend your life with."

"What about Ryan?"

She makes a weird face. "What about that creep?"

"Well, he's taken an interest in me. He's the reason we're going to the game tomorrow night. But I agree with Paige, something about him feels off. He only started talking to me after he knew I was tutoring Grant."

"Could you see yourself being friends with Ryan?" she asks me, and I take another sip of coffee because I hate that I'm even having this conversation.

"I guess? He hasn't been too much of an asshole, but I barely know him too. God, this is so frustrating."

"Fine, then you're good, Hads."

I don't know if good is the word I would use, but I guess. "You make everything seem so easy, Ells."

She winks at me and sips her coffee. "I know, and that's why you guys love me so much. I'm the level-headed one in this group. It brings a nice balance."

"Do you think if I entangle myself with these two guys that rumors will start to circulate about me on campus?"

She shrugs her shoulders. "This campus is notorious for those, Hads. Nobody is immune. The other day, someone asked me if I had ever pegged someone before, and my response was a middle finger as I kept walking to class."

"What the hell? Someone came up to you and asked you that?" God, when does this end? "Who would say that about you?"

She tilts her head at me, already assuming I should know.

"Zimmerman? He wouldn't do that, would he?"

"He would," she says as she pinches the bridge of her nose. "He absolutely would. But I've been thinking about how to spread one about him."

"Oh, I'm dying to hear these, Ells." I smirk as she leans closer to me. And for the next hour, we brainstorm which rumor could have the same effect as the one he spread about Ella. As we're leaving, I ask her something. "Do you want to make this an every Sunday activity?"

"Absolutely, I do."

15

Hadleigh

"Okay, so that thing flying on the ice is called a puck?" Amelia asks because she has no clue about sports, and it shows.

Neither do I, but I can at least follow certain things. I know there's a puck, a goal, and they use sticks, or whatever.

"Yes, and Grant's on defense, which means he's trying to prevent the other team from scoring!" Paige shines as she explains this to us. She's the most athletic one out of all of us, which basically means she goes to baseball, hockey and a bunch of other games when she can. The rest of us wouldn't be caught dead watching sports in our free time.

"I can somewhat understand what's going on, and I have to admit, I'm intrigued," I say as I watch them zoom around the ice. I wish I could skate, but I'd definitely fall on my ass.

"Does anyone want a drink? This seems like it would be really fun watching while drunk." Ella makes a point. However, I don't drink and hockey is hard enough to follow sober.

"Do you guys see Ryan? I don't know what position he plays," I ask. He is the reason I came to this in the first place, but we've spent the entire time talking about Grant.

"Ryan is benched, but Grant's on the ice. He's number eleven! Look, he just hip-checked that guy!" Paige says a bit too excitedly.

"Hip what? Is that illegal?" Amelia asks.

"No, it's when you slam the other guy up on the glass," I say.

"Doesn't that hurt? I'd feel all out of sorts after getting smashed against the glass," Amelia asks.

"That's the point. It throws the other person off their game so you can swoop in and steal the puck." Paige knows way more about hockey than I thought.

"P, why is Ryan benched? I assumed he would be playing if Grant is."

"He's a goalie, but Holt starts in goal every game. Normally, he stays in the entire time unless we are up by a lot, then they switch so the newbies get more playing time."

"Oh, I guess that makes sense, but why is Grant on the ice then? He's only a sophomore. I didn't think he would be a starter."

"Grant's really good. He starts most games." Ella shares that piece of information.

"How did you know that?" I say.

"He who shall not be named talks about hockey all the time. He thinks Grant and Jacks are the perfect pair or whatever. Plus, he's friends with a bunch of people on the team, so he goes out with them all the time."

I'm kind of loving the fact that we've gone from using his full name to not even wanting to mention it. What the hell is going on with those two?

We've all heard the rumors about Leo on campus, but I doubt the entire reason Ella hates him is because he fucks like a God and gives more than he takes, if you know what I mean.

"He was right!" Paige exclaims. "Grant and Jacks are the best defenders on the team, and they both took over after the seniors graduated last year. They work well together and I feel like you can see what great chemistry they have!"

It's safe to say Paige likes Grant—she has not stopped talking about him the entire game.

"I know what you're doing, P," I tell her.

"If what I'm doing is hyping up our hockey team, then yes, that's what I'm doing. Anything else is pure conjecture, Hads."

I roll my eyes before I focus back on the game. We're winning three to one.

"Okay, but why are the sticks shaped like that? They seem awkward to hold." Amelia's trying her best, I'll give her that.

"I feel like they would be too. I've seen people break their sticks from slamming them too hard. They look really limber," Paige tells us.

"I could make a thousand jokes about the male species right now, but I'll refrain." Ella smirks as she takes a sip of her beer.

"Hads, what's the plan for after? Are you going out with Ryan?" Paige asks me.

"No. I asked for a rain check because I'm exhausted and I don't want to hang out with Ryan one-on-one."

Ella nudges my body with a smile on her face, and I know she's excited I seem to be making decisions on my own feelings for once. It's not that I dislike Ryan, but I barely know him, and I don't have the brain capacity to learn more about him at the moment.

I already have a hard enough time keeping up with Grant. I don't need another hockey player fogging up my mind.

The buzzer signals the end of the second period and there's a small break before the last one. All the players gather around the bench, and I spot Ryan from here. He looks at me and waves his glove. I send a small one back, my smirk toward him feeling forced before I see Grant take his helmet off and look right at me.

He shakes his head, his brown curls falling all over the place—even over his eyes. I don't even know how he found me between those and his helmet. His eyes pierce mine from all the way down on the ice and my body shivers underneath his stare, but I'm not cold.

It's freezing in here, but suddenly under the heat of his stare, I'm warmed from the inside out.

I can see a small smirk forming as he brushes his hair out of his face, his gaze still on my seat as Jacks brings him back into the huddle they're having, but he can't focus. His eyes keep coming back to mine, as if I'm the light and he's in a dark tunnel trying to escape.

"Oh, they're definitely eye-fucking this time."

Ella's joke gets me out of my trance before I excuse myself to go to the bathroom. I need to get as far away from Grant's gaze as I can. It's messing me up, and I practically trip up the stairs but Amelia's following me and she helps me get back on my feet.

We get into the bathroom and she tries to follow me into the stall.

"Amelia, what are you doing? I know you know how bathrooms work, which is one aspect in life I don't need help in."

"I don't have to pee. I just wanted to talk to you."

"About what?" I ask as I shuffle out of the stall.

"Hads, you can't play this game with me. I'm the queen of deflecting and changing topics about things I don't want to discuss."

"I can't change the subject if I don't even know what we are talking about." I absolutely know what she wants to talk about, but I can't relive the past fifteen minutes.

"Hads."

"What?"

"You guys were staring at each other, and I could feel the tension coming off of you."

"It has been a very busy semester so far! I have a lot of tension around my neck area. That's what you must have felt."

She rolls her eyes at me. "You like him."

"I tolerate him."

"That stare looked locked and loaded with about a thousand different emotions—none of them being just tolerable. Why are you so freaked about this?"

I sigh heavily as someone tries to enter the bathroom, but Amelia shoves the door closed and lets me speak. "I don't want to get too involved with him and have the entire campus know who I am. I'm worried about the rumors. I've done all I can to stay under the radar and out of trouble, but this would open up a new can of worms that I don't like." My high school thrived under cliques, rumors, and everyone was in everyone else's business.

Yet nobody bothered to tell me I was being cheated on a thousand different times. Nobody would have *dared* to threaten the football team—the highest of the hierarchy at my high school.

"It's okay for people to know you, Hads. You're a great person and anyone would be lucky to know you." She steps closer to me. "But you can't deny your feelings for him—whatever they happen to be. It's okay to run towards scary things sometimes."

I roll my eyes at her. "Coming from you, that's rich."

"Well, yes, but that's part of my brand, so I'm allowed to. I do want my friends to be happy, though," she says with a soft smile. "Now, splash some water on your face or whatever, and I'll be waiting outside."

"Thank you, Ames. I appreciate it."

"Of course."

I calm my running thoughts and meet Amelia by the stairs, and we return to our seats in time for the third period to start.

And twenty minutes later, Grand Mountain wins and Grant points at me from the ice with his stick.

I know what he's trying to say—he won the bet we made. Now, I have to hang out with him outside of tutoring. Great. I wonder what that is going to look like.

The four of us exit the stadium and by the time we get outside Ella starts yelling about how our school is the best. She's one hundred percent drunk right now, and Amelia is trying to grab her so she doesn't run into traffic and get hit by a car.

"Grant played well tonight, don't you think?" Paige asks me.

"He did," I say, my cheeks heating as I remember how he looked at me after the win.

"So, it's like soccer on ice?" Amelia's still very confused about hockey.

"I guess, Ames." Paige interlocks our arms as we walk.

"P, you know my memory sucks, and—" She cuts herself off as Ella runs from her again. "Ella, get out of the parking lot, I'm not saving you if a car is coming!" Ames chases after her.

"Hads, do you want us to drive you back to your dorm or do you want to walk?" Paige asks me.

"I can walk. You guys get her home safe, okay?"

"We will." Paige slips off towards where Ames and Ella are sitting on the sidewalk. "Text us when you're home! We love you, Hads!"

I smile, thankful for these three girls more than anything else. "I love you guys, too."

I walk back to my dorm, away from all the loud noise from the rink. The atmosphere there tonight was incredible, and I had more fun than I thought I was going to. The girls can make anything fun, but I actually enjoyed watching the game. It fulfilled my sports romance loving heart, and now I have the urge to go download a hockey romance onto my Kindle.

I breathe in the cool air, and as I walk into my dorm building, I grab my phone and open my text thread with Grant.

> **Hads: Congrats on keeping all of your teeth intact.**

He answers as I get back to my room. I thought for sure he'd be out celebrating his win tonight, but it's nice to hear back from him.

> **Grant: Uh, thanks? I think?**

> **Hads: Congrats on the win tonight, it was more interesting to watch than I thought it would be.**

> **Grant: Well I'm glad tonight has made you a future hockey fan.**

> **Hads: I'm not buying season tickets, calm down.**

> **Grant: It was nice seeing you in the stands. Hopefully you can catch another game before the season ends?**

> **Hads: Maybe.**

Grant: Don't forget about our bet... Who won again?

Hads: You did. What are we doing, then? I'd like to prepare for the worst.

Grant: I'm not telling you—not yet, at least.

Hads: Ugh, fine.

Grant: See you Thursday?

Hads: Sounds good.

Grant: Goodnight, Hades.

Hads: Goodnight, hockey boy.

16

Grant

I'M ABOUT TO HEAD out for my next tutoring session with Hades when Jacks walks into our apartment. He drops his bag, looks at me funny, and proceeds to the kitchen to grab a drink. He's been acting weird since our game on Monday, and I haven't had time to ask him why.

I open the door and get halfway out of it before he finally says something to me.

"Are you off to tutoring?" he asks me with a smirk on his face.

"Why have you been so weird lately? Did you get lucky with Claire recently or what?"

He squints at me. "When have you ever used that phrase in a sentence? And don't talk about Claire. We're in a bit of a rut." His face falls, and I feel like a shitty friend. I've been so busy trying to keep my grades up that I've let our relationship slip.

"You're right, and I'm sorry. What's going on with you and Claire?"

"It doesn't matter." He shakes his head. "I came here to catch you before tutoring, not to talk about my life." He's deflecting, but I don't press.

"Okay, what did you want to talk about?"

"You."

"Me?" I ask.

"And Hadleigh."

"Me and Hads?"

"Yup."

"What about us?"

He shrugs his shoulders as if it should be the most obvious thing in the world. "Oh, you know, just about how you fell for her and are trying to convince me you're not falling too quickly."

I try to think of a way to deny it, but I can't. He saw how I looked at her at the game on Monday. He saw my smile the entire time in the locker room when we celebrated our win—and he knew it wasn't about our win. It was because Hads was in the stands watching, and when the final buzzer went off and I pointed my stick at her in the stands, she smiled at me.

"You're right."

"I know, dumbass." I let go of our door and let it close behind me as I walk towards him. "Are you going to listen to me this time and not fall so hard so quickly or are you too far gone already?"

"I don't really know how to answer that," I tell him.

"Can I give you some advice?"

I cock my head at him. "Always, dude. You know that."

He throws a smile my way. "Take your time with this girl. This time feels different, and I know you feel it, too. I've watched you fall hard and fast and I don't want to see it end like it did before. Hads feels different. Hell, even you look different than you normally do."

"What does that mean?"

"It means that I think it could work out with you two, but Hads isn't quite where you are yet." He gets up and grabs his book bag. "Just take it a little slower this time and don't come on too strong. Let her drive the bus a little if that makes sense."

"Thanks, dude."

"No problem. It's what I'm here for."

He's about to head into his room when I say something else. "Hads wouldn't use me for my popularity on campus. That's why she feels different—why I feel different. She doesn't care about any of that."

"I know, Grant. But that's what makes this a slippery slope. You have to find a balance and not scare her off too easily. Think you can handle it?"

I scoff as I grab my stuff. I'm going to be a little late to the library, and I see a ruler smack in my future. "I think so. Can we talk about you and Claire at some point? Maybe I can give you some advice on that if you're open to it."

"No offense, but Claire and I are more complicated than you and Hads. But if I need help, you'll be the first one I ask."

"That's all I ask." I smile at him before I leave. "I'll see you later."

My walk to the library is slow, even though I'm already running late to meet Hads. I knew as soon as I ran into her that I felt something for her, but Jacks telling me he could feel it when I looked at her only solidifies that I've yet again fallen hard and fast for someone.

It's my thing, you know? Some people think love at first sight is real, others don't believe in love at all. I'm a guy who has fallen so in love or lust or like with every single girlfriend I've had—including the one here during freshman year. And I did—love her, anyway. Until I found out the only reason she was with me was to brag about it and use me to become more talked about on campus.

It hurt for a few weeks, and then I never felt that rush of feelings again—not until Hads. Jacks is right; maybe I need to tone myself down a bit if I am going to go down this path with Hads, but I don't even know if I will.

It's just fun watching her cheeks get all red when I look at her. And it's fun pissing her off because I don't know if anyone else can make her as annoyed as I can.

I finally make it to the library, shuffle up the stairs, and make my way over the room. She's obviously inside, and as I softly open the door, my apology coming off my lips.

"I'm so—"

"Were you too busy putting gel in your hair and forgot what time it was?"

How does she know I have gel in my hair? She didn't even look up at me when I came in. "No, but Jacks needed my help with a crisis, and I already know it's coming, so do it and get it over with." I hold my hand out and wait for the sting to come from her ruler, but it never does.

"Are you actually that scared of me?" she says as I open my eyes. She's still sitting down in her usual spot, so I take my seat and get my stuff out.

"I mean... yeah."

She only smiles, a small laugh coming from her lips. "Good."

And then she starts talking about chapter four and how in this chapter we dive further into who Gatsby is as a person and how he's madly in love with Daisy Buchanan. Apparently, they knew one another before he went off to war, but when he got back, Daisy was married to Tom, and the letter Gatsby sent made her want to call off her wedding.

"I never understood why people write letters to one another," I say.

"I think it's beautiful," Hads says quietly.

"Why?"

"I think it's far more personal than a text message. Plus, there's the added touch of someone sitting down, thinking of you, and sending you something that shows they thought about you."

God, I wish I could crawl inside of her mind and go through every filing cabinet inside of her head. She has this way of speaking about the simplest of things, and I can't help but turn to her and listen. She's like a siren in the sea, and I'm the pirate being lured to my eventual death.

It would be worth it just being able to see her up close.

She switches back to the book. "Anyways, this chapter also highlights the metaphor of the green light at the end of Daisy's dock and how Nick saw him reaching out to it one night. This represents the hope that Gatsby still feels about Daisy." She pauses and looks up at me, making sure it's clicking in my brain. "Gatsby's love for Daisy is the source of his romantic hopefulness and the meaning of his yearning for the green light in Chapter One. The light that was once so mysterious to us in the beginning becomes the symbol of Gatsby's dream, his love for Daisy, and his attempt to make that love real. Does that make sense?"

"Yeah, it actually does. The green light is what keeps him hoping. It's what keeps him clinging onto the fact that he might be able to have her again one day," I say, hoping I finally understand something about this book.

"Exactly. It can be argued that this metaphor could also be interpreted as the American dream, but I prefer the romance of it all. Gatsby really did want to be with her, but in the end—well, best not to spoil it." She sighs and sits at the table rather silently.

I prefer the romance of it all too, because I've never felt so connected to a book and a metaphor before.

I think Hads is my green light.

It all makes sense if I think about it in terms of the book. Hads is Daisy and I'm Gatsby. She represents this thing I keep reaching out for—the hope that if I fall for someone, they'll eventually fall for me too. With no reason other than that they love me for who I am and not for all of the things I have.

If I reach for her and not just her light, will she welcome me in? Will she push me away? I have no way of knowing unless I try, but I can't try until tutoring is over because I need to show her I'm capable of taking this seriously. And I need to prove to myself that instead of falling into people and not getting to know them first, that I'm capable of taking it slow.

"Is that all for today?" I ask her because she's suddenly become very quiet, and she didn't even notice I zoned out for a few minutes.

She shakes out of her fog. "Yeah, that's all." She opens her mouth to say something else but she ends up shaking her head.

"Something else to say, Hades?"

"I'm building up the courage to ask."

I cock my head at her. "You can ask me anything, and if you didn't know that before, then you do now."

"Is there any truth to the things I've heard around campus?"

"The ones about me sleeping around?" They're everywhere, and I'm surprised this is the first time she's bringing it up. She nods at me. "No, they're all fake. I mostly fall hard for girls who don't even like me back."

"You?"

"Mhm. My track record isn't great, and most of it is my fault. Well, besides the cheating and using me for my social status."

Her eyes bug out of her head. "I'm sorry that happened to you."

"I'm the only one to blame," I say as I shrug my shoulders. It's in the past. There's nothing I can do to fix it now. I want to ask her about the only rumor I've heard about her on campus—the one I've only heard in whispers this semester. "Can I ask you something?"

"Sure."

"Have you never had a boyfriend?"

She rolls her eyes at me. "I have no idea who started that, but it's false."

"So, you've heard about it?"

Another nod. "Of course I have." She throws her books in her bag as she stands up. "I've had a whopping total of one former boyfriend and that was humiliating. So, I've sworn to myself that my studies and academics come before everything, and romance has moved to the back burner—which I'm fine with. Nobody has shown much interest here at Grand Mountain anyway."

Nobody has shown much interest? Is this entire fucking campus blind? I sure as hell thought I was when I first ran into her. It's like everything around me before I saw her for the first time was black and white, and as soon as I looked at her, colors reappeared.

That's the only way I can describe what she made me feel in that moment.

"I'll see you next week, Grant." And as she rushes out of the room, I realize I'm way too far gone.

I'm reaching for her and the hope that one day we can be together. I'm at the end of the dock and she's the green light flashing across the water. I want her to hit me with that ruler all day long as long as it means she's mine.

Shit.

17

 **Hadleigh**

It's a Tuesday night, and I've spent most of my time sitting in the library after my classes. Only this time, I'm reading for pleasure and not for an assignment.

Well, I'm taking a reading break from my biochemistry paper. I had been working on it for so long that my hands started cramping from how fast I was typing. But my timer went off, and now I have to get back to it. Usually, when I have long homework sessions, I like to split them up into increments so I don't get too tired.

Paige and Amelia are meeting me here in half an hour, and I can definitely get some words in on my criminology paper, so I switch over to that because if I have to write about the structure of cells for another second, I might go crazy.

After twenty minutes, I feel someone slide into the booth I'm in, and when I look up expecting Paige and Amelia, I'm met with someone else.

"Ryan."

"What's with the cold shoulder, Hads? Did I do something to you?" he asks me.

"Well, you sat down in my booth uninvited when I'm waiting for my friends." Why do some men have this huge audacity and think they can do whatever they want? It pisses me off to no end.

"Apologies, Hads."

He says nothing else and keeps on staring at me. "Did you need something?"

"No, not really. I was wondering why you haven't used my phone number yet. I bet the paper I gave you is burning a hole in your pocket."

I have to stop my eyes from rolling to the back of my head. Again, with the fucking audacity. Why do guys think just because they give their number out that girls will use it? I also definitely lost his number—I had never planned on using it in the first place.

"I've been busy, Ryan. I don't have a lot of time for extracurriculars with my class schedule and things I've committed myself to. And I don't want to date you, if that's why you gave me your number. I'm not interested and I'm not looking for anything."

"Woah, that's not the message I wanted to send. Hads, all I wanted was to be your friend."

Oh. I guess that makes sense but from what I've heard around school, Ryan isn't friends with many girls. But then again, I can't trust the whispers. They were wrong about Grant and they could absolutely be wrong about Ryan too.

I look to the side, and Paige and Amelia walk in. They make eye contact with me and sit at a different table—one with a direct eye line to where I am. Paige immediately takes out her phone, and I know what she's doing when my phone buzzes. I prop it against my laptop screen so I can see the messages, and so Ryan can't.

Paige: SOS!

Amelia: Paige, I'm right next to you.

Paige: The SOS is for Ella.

Ella: What's going on? Is someone hurt? Did Amelia trip someone again?

Amelia: That happened once and it was an accident!

Paige: Partially.

Amelia: He couldn't find Asia on a map—the biggest continent! I think tripping him might have added more brain cells. I was doing him a favor!

Ella: Is this what the SOS was about?

Paige: No! Ryan's sitting in a booth in the library cafe talking to Hads! He took our spot.

Ella: That sounds bad.

The messages keep coming, and my phone buzzes, but I don't answer yet. Ryan's talking about the game from the other night, and I'm zoning out. I now understand why Grant seems to do it so much. Maybe I need to rethink my ruler method...

"Do you think you'll go to any more hockey games?"

"I might. You guys did pretty well the other day, and I'll admit it was fun to watch."

"Yeah, you showed up with Paige and two other girls."

I nod, knowing that he stared at me the entire game from the bench and I felt nothing but when Grant pointed at me after the win, I thought I was going to fall through the floor. "Yup, my friends Amelia and Ella came too."

"How did you all become friends?"

"Ella and Paige started a book club, and I joined it when I was a freshman. We meet every Wednesday night." My phone buzzes a few more times.

> **Paige: Did he say our names?**

> **Amelia: What's he asking you, Hads?**

> **Ella: If he says some shit, let me know. I'll be at the campus in two minutes.**

> **Paige: If he repeats my name, I'm coming over there.**

> **Hads: Please don't. I'm trying to get rid of him.**

I speak before he can keep blabbering. "Ryan, it was nice talking about hockey and stuff, but I'm waiting for some friends to study with and they're on their way here."

"Oh yeah, no problem." He starts to slide out of the booth but pauses before walking away. "Hads, we're friends, right?"

"Um, I guess. Why?"

> **Amelia:** Why isn't he leaving? Did he forget his manual on how to dress appropriately? His shirt is ugly.

> **Paige:** Do I need to come over and kick his ass for you, Hads?

> **Ella:** Paige, your punches feel like a feather hitting the ground—soft and delicate.

> **Paige:** At any given time, I have twelve murder scenarios in my head. Try me!

> **Amelia:** Oh my…

> **Ella:** Girl, what? You need to stop watching those true crime docs. You worry me.

> **Amelia:** It's weird how someone so cheerful could be so murderous. Yesterday she told me she was feeling stabby, so I migrated to my room and stayed there.

"I just wanted to tell you I think what you're doing for Grant is nice. Tutoring and helping him even though he talks bad about you at practice."

His words catch me off guard. "I'm sorry, what did you say?"

Amelia: Hads, why are you making that face? Did he say something stupid?

Paige: Amelia, remove your hand from holding me back, or I'll bite it.

Ella: Do I need to come to campus right now?

Paige: Amelia won't let me go over there!

Amelia: P, enough with the empty threats.

Ella: Seriously, I will speed over to campus. Zimmerman made me furious today, so I have a lot of pent-up anger.

Amelia: Any threats of murder today?

Ella: Only four.

Paige: That's good!

Hads: I am going to murder all of you. Please stop for a second.

"Yeah, he says some stuff about you when we practice. Something about being easy and how he just wants to befriend you to get up your skirt."

That sounds nothing like him—especially after our talk the other day at tutoring. Grant told me point blank that he doesn't sleep around, but instead falls fast and hard for people. I don't trust this. My gut is screaming at me that something isn't right, so I try to make it seem like I believe Ryan so he goes away.

"Wow, really? And has anyone else heard him say this stuff?"

"Not that I know of."

Exactly. "Thanks for telling me, but I can handle Grant myself. I'll see you in class, okay?"

He winks at me before he leaves and as soon as he's out of view, Paige and Amelia scurry over to the booth.

"What did he say to you before he left? Your face turned as soon as his mouth opened," Amelia asks as she shuts my laptop. We all know the scholarly part of the night is over after my interaction with Ryan. If there's one thing I know about us, it's that we'll talk about the same interaction a thousand different times before we get sick of bringing it up.

Us girls love to debrief every small, medium, and large interaction we have. It's like a reward for dealing with whatever stupidity is thrown our way.

I tell them what Ryan mentioned about Grant and by the time I'm done, Amelia looks giddy and Paige looks as pissed as she can.

"He's lying," she tells me. "I bet if anything, it's the other way around. Ryan's the one who's known to hump and dump."

Amelia almost spits out her water and I can't help my laughter from coming out.

> **Ella: Guys, is everything and everyone okay? I haven't gotten an update in a while and I'm worried!**

"Hump and dump? Paige, you sound like an 85-year-old grandmother," Amelia laughs.

> **Hads: Paige just said the words hump and dump, and Ames and I are dying.**

> **Ella: Oh God, another Paige phrase to make her sound like an old lady. I love her so much.**

"Okay, whatever! My point is that Ryan's a liar, and I'm still on Grant's side," Paige states.

"There are no sides, Paige. Unless, you're on my side," I tell her.

She throws her arm around me. "We're always on your side, Hads."

Amelia lifts her water bottle at me. "Always."

18

Hadleigh

"I KNEW SHE WASN'T coming. She had articles sprawled all over her floor and her laptop in the center of it. Hurricane Paige strikes again," Amelia says.

"I don't understand why she loves the floor so much," I say. Ever since I've known her, she's loved being on the floor more than a desk chair or couch.

"Paige told me she likes to get different perspectives on things and calls it organized chaos. I'm not even going to lie, the carpet in her room is super comfy. I've laid on it before and I may have fallen asleep," Amelia tells us. I can confirm that, too. One time after a night out, I walked into her room and they were both asleep on the floor. It was hilarious and adorable.

We talk a little more about the book, and all of us agreed it was a solid four star read. This one has a love triangle and we're all discussing which person we like for the main character. I chose the goofier brother—as did Ella—and Amelia chose the more serious one.

After half an hour, we switch topics.

"Ella, how's Zimmerman been lately?" I ask her.

She throws her head back in response. *This can't be good.* "I met his sister the other day."

"How did that happen?" I'm shocked. I didn't know Leo even had a sister, but I'm guessing Ella didn't either.

"She was waiting for him outside the office."

"Ells, why do you sound so monotone? Did something happen with her?" Ames asks her.

"She's nice."

Amelia and I look at each other, both confused as fuck. "And why is that bad?"

"I'm not supposed to like her—she's related to my nemesis! I honestly don't know how their mother birthed one evil spawn and one super nice, gorgeous, and funny spawn!"

"What's her name?" I ask.

"Alissa."

"Does she go to school here?"

"No, she graduated before us. I think we're becoming friends. She gave me her number and asked if I ever needed to rant about her brother to come to her and we could go for drinks."

"She sounds fun. Does she like to read?" Of course Amelia asks that. Books are very important for a friendship—especially with us.

"Yes. She's sassy and sarcastic, and I was basically flirting with her before I knew she was related to him. I was a bit embarrassed, but she didn't mind."

"Are you going to text her?" I ask her curiously. I don't know how Ella could manage being friends with one good sibling and one person she can barely stand.

"I already did. We're going out Friday night for drinks. She's only a year older than me, and she's British and funny, and ugh!" She sulks back.

"She sounds fun, and let's be honest, we're a bit too chill for you. I think becoming friends with her will be good for you. You'll have someone to go out with when the rest of us don't feel like it."

"Good point, Hads. Don't get me wrong, I love you guys, but sometimes I need to go out and let loose without worrying about what you guys are getting into." The three of us laugh. I think this could be good for Ella. Paige, Amelia, and I only go out when she drags us all out to the bar near campus, or some party. She's the most extroverted one in our group, and I think Alissa is the partner Ella needs for going out on the town.

"Ames, what have you been up to lately?" Ella asks her.

"Homework and a whole bunch of nothing."

"Are you planning your next trip yet?" Amelia is studying journalism and she loves to travel. I think she wants to be a traveling journalist one day, though I'm not sure. She always shares pictures from her travels with us, and it's always fun seeing the world through her lens.

"I have a few places in mind, but haven't narrowed it down yet." That's all you'll get out of Amelia. She's about as open as a closed door.

"Hads, how's everything with you?" Ella looks over at me with a sympathetic smile. I should have known this was coming. Since Ryan crashed our study date yesterday, Ella has been dying to hear about it.

"Well, I definitely don't trust Ryan—he feels like a weird red herring—and Grant and I are pretty much the same. There's not much going on with me for once." Though, it has felt like my thoughts have been playing tug of war for some reason, and I keep waiting for Grant to text me about the bet we made, but he hasn't yet.

"Just try to focus on tutoring and you'll be okay. I know you get overwhelmed when there's too much on your plate," Ella says, and she's right. I'm not good at keeping track of my life when it's chaotic—like it has been this semester so far. That's why I love charts so much. I can organize my thoughts coherently and it helps to keep me centered in the things I have to accomplish.

I check my phone and note the time. "I'm gonna head out. Taylor wants to do a movie night."

"Movie night sounds fun," Ella says as she gets up. "We'll head out too."

"Are you plotting out more ways to threaten Zimmerman tomorrow?" Amelia asks.

"Yes, but I also have to figure out what to wear on Friday night," Ella tells us. "I might send outfit pictures in the group chat later."

"Sounds good to me," I say as we exit the classroom.

Parting ways, I shift my bag to my other shoulder while I carry my book in my other hand. It's a fairly chilly night out and I didn't bring my sweatshirt since it's a decently short walk back to my dorm. I notice someone walking the opposite direction from me, so I move out of the middle of the sidewalk while they walk by.

Only they don't walk all the way by, but they stop as I pass them.

"How nice of you to make room for me on the sidewalk, Hades," Grant says, because who else would I run into on a campus with five thousand people on it?

"I made room for your giant head to go by. I don't know if that predicament is because of your ego, your hair, or if you're just an airhead." I smile, and I know he can tell I'm joking because he smiles at me.

"There she is."

What does that mean? I shake that off because now that he's in front of me, I have a question I need him to answer.

"I have a question, and I need you to be honest with me," I say to him.

"Hit me," he says as he throws his arms out. The two of us are still standing where we stopped on the sidewalk.

"If you wait long enough, I might."

He smirks at me. "Hades, stop stalling and ask me."

"Do you like Ryan?" I don't know why I need to know, but I do. Ever since Ryan crashed my booth in the library, I've thought back to all my conversations with the two of them. Ryan always brings Grant up and talks shit about him, but Grant couldn't care less about Ryan. It's just odd, and maybe if he tells me a straight answer, I could understand why Ryan is trying to talk badly about him.

He makes a weird face. I don't think he was expecting that question. "Do I *like* Ryan?"

"Yes, it's a fairly simple question. Do you need me to sound it out phonetically?"

"No, I don't need you to do that. The question just threw me off. I'm not his biggest fan but he is my teammate. If you want a straight answer, I tolerate him." He runs a hand through his hair. "Why do you ask?"

"He's told me some things about you and they didn't make sense at the time, so I wanted to know how you felt about him."

"What did he tell you?"

"A bunch of things, but they seemed like bullshit to me," I say and as I'm about to turn and walk away, he grabs my wrist.

"Does he make you uncomfortable? Do you want me to say something to him?"

I shake my head. "I can fight my own battles, Grant, but no. He crashed my study date with my friends at the library the other day. It was weird and he caught me off guard."

"Hads, I don't mind saying something to him for you. It's not cool of him to keep bugging you and saying stuff about me to you."

I put my free hand on his bicep. "It's fine, Grant."

"Can I ask you something?" He drops his hand from around my wrist, and goosebumps cover my body as the wind blows through the air.

"It's only fair," I say to him.

"Has he tried to kiss you, Hadleigh? Has he made a move on you?"

The question catches me off guard. "What? No, but why do you care?"

"I-I don't care," he says, his voice getting higher. "I was only wondering."

"Jealous?" The word slips out before I can stop it. Why do I even care if he is? I don't, right?

"If he had, I would've been."

Is he serious? No... no he's joking, right? We've been joking around all night! There's no way he's being serious. "But he hasn't, so you have no reason to be."

"Right, of course. Of course," he repeats.

Is it hot in here all of a sudden? And by here, I mean on the planet because as I go to walk away from whatever tension-filled conversation we're having, he grabs my wrist and pulls me back to him.

And his lips meet mine.

I should pull away. In fact, that's normally my first reaction when someone gets an inch too close to me, but with Grant, my head fell right into place as he turned my body around and grabbed my neck—his hand guiding me the entire way.

My favorite book falls to the ground as he deepens the kiss, and my mind starts to float away as I think about how gentle his lips feel against mine, and how much I missed feeling so connected to someone as I do to Grant right now.

Wait. The admittance of that in my mind snaps me out of whatever trance I'm in from the kiss. Did I just say I feel connected to Grant? I feel something for the guy I'm tutoring and one of the most popular dudes on campus?

What's happening to me? Am I coming down with something?

I pull away—his smile beaming at me—and out of reflex, I slap him.

"Oh my God, I-I'm so sorry." I didn't mean to slap him. The first kiss I've had in a few years ends with me hitting the guy who kissed me. *I am such an idiot.*

Though, he surprised me with his stupid soft lips!

I turn around and practically run away, leaving him standing there on the sidewalk.

19

TUTORING TODAY HAS BEEN the most awkward session of my life and it's all my fault. Even the first one wasn't as tense as this and Hads literally despised me.

I kissed her last night. I *kissed* Hadleigh fucking Baker—my tutor and the girl I can't stop thinking about. I promised myself I wouldn't fall fast and I'd let her come to terms with if she had feelings for me on her own, but I fucked up again.

I couldn't help myself. I ran into her last night, and she looked so perfect standing there in front of me, with those brown eyes challenging me how they always do. She was in front of me practically sparkling under the moonlight and I wanted to kiss her, so I did. Then she slapped me and ran away as I tried to digest what just happened, but for a moment, she kissed me back.

Hadleigh Baker kissed me back.

I could jump around the room just thinking about it.

I've been fighting the urge to ask her about yesterday and see how she feels, but I can't. Her head is probably a mess—typical Hads behavior—and she has barely looked me in the eye the entire session. She's super closed off, and I don't want to make it worse. I know she's on guard again. I can practically feel the walls I've slowly broken down the past few weeks being built back up and reinforced.

She slaps me with the ruler. "Fuck, sorry, I got lost in my thoughts for a second."

"It's fine, but make sure you listen because I don't like repeating myself."

"Yes, ma'am." She stares at me for too long and then continues to talk about the book. We have around fifteen minutes left of today's session, and I need to break the ice about the kiss. I can't have every session going forward be as weird as this one is.

I take a chance when she pauses. "Listen, Hades–"

"No," is all she says.

"You don't even know what I'm going to say."

"Yes I do, and I don't want to talk about it."

"Isn't saying that talking about it, technically?"

"Grant. I'm serious. It was a mistake, and if I'm going to keep helping you, we have to remain professional. What you did yesterday was anything but." She throws me a glare while I think about what to say back.

She's right—like always. We have to remain professional, but all I've been able to think about for the past twenty-four hours was that kiss. Don't even get me started on how her flowery perfume is all I've smelled around me since yesterday.

It smells nice, and I wouldn't mind it around me and all over my clothes in the future.

"Okay, professional it is. That doesn't have to stop us from being friends, does it?"

"I guess not."

Perfect. "Is that all for today?"

"Yeah, I hit everything I wanted to talk about. We only have one more session until the midterm."

I check what time it is on my phone. "We still have ten minutes of this room reserved."

"So?"

"Why do you never wear sweatpants?" I ask her, my question throwing her off guard.

"Why do I what?"

"I've never seen you in sweatpants—like ever. You're the weirdest college student I've ever met."

She tilts her head at me. "I happen to like my style, thank you very much."

"I never said I didn't like your style. It's very... academic or whatever. I was just wondering why you never wear sweats. You always look like you're on your way to an art museum, and not a college lecture." Her style is one of my favorite things about her. This girl is one-of-a-kind in more ways than one, but I've never met anyone who can throw an outfit together like she can.

"It's what I like to wear. I always feel like I'm drowning in sweatpants; they make them too long, and I have short legs. Happy?"

"The happiest, actually." I throw a smile in her direction.

"If we're going to do this, then why do you always wear that chain?"

I hesitate for a second before the words spill out of my mouth. "My dad gave it to me before he died. I wear it to always carry him with me, and it has my hockey number on it." My voice breaks a bit at the end as I look down at the gold chain around my neck. The chain is brand new because it broke last year and my mom had to get me a new one. I couldn't bear to part with the one my dad had last touched, so it's still at home hidden under my dad's old journal.

I didn't think she noticed the chain. It's usually hidden under my shirts and stuff. "I'm sorry. I didn't mean to make fun of it."

"I didn't think you were, but thanks."

Our eyes lock for the first time all day, and I have a flashback to when we were like this at my hockey game the other day. The room feels charged all of a sudden, and it's taking everything in me not to reach over the table, grab that cute sweater of hers, and kiss her until she falls over.

I can't.

I want to. God, I want to, but I can't.

And then a crazy idea pops into my head, and before I brush it off as a stupid idea, I smile to myself. This could be the way I see Hads outside of tutoring. After all, she did say we only had one more session before this is all over, and if I play my cards right, my plan could work.

AFTER TUTORING, I WALK into my apartment and bypass Jacks on the couch, probably texting Claire before I say nothing and head straight for my room.

I go right underneath my covers and I hear him walk into my room and he pulls them off of me. He stares down at where I'm lying in my bed and just sighs.

"That was mean. I'm cold now," I say to him.

"What's your deal?"

"My deal? What are you talking about? My only deal right now is that I'm cold!" I say as I try to grab my sheets back from him, to which he stretches them further from my reach. "Rude."

"Dude, you're sulking," he tells me.

"I'm not sulking. Sulking is for sad people, and I'm not sad." After I say that, he rips my sheets clean off my bed and throws them in a pile in the corner of the room.

"That was for lying to me."

"Dude! I just put those back on my bed!" I run a hand down my face. "I'm making you put those back on."

"No, not until you tell me what your deal is," he says, still holding my sheets hostage.

There's no point in lying or saying nothing. Jacks always finds things out one way or another. "Hypothetically, I may have kissed Hadleigh, and she may or may not have slapped me for it."

"You did what?"

"This is all hypothetical, of course."

"So, you didn't kiss Hadleigh and she didn't slap you?"

"Well, no, those things did happen, but the situation I'm talking about is hypothetical." He pauses for a beat before he leaves my room. "Where are you going?"

"To sign up for therapy! Just hearing about your life is making me want to speak to someone," he says as he walks out of our apartment.

"You're totally putting my sheets back on for me later!" I yell to him, and I can see him shake his head as he walks out of our door.

I grab my phone from my pocket and text Hads, wanting to talk to her even though I saw her twenty minutes ago.

> **Grant: Do you know the fastest way to put sheets back on a bed?**

> **Hads: Is this some sort of pickup line?**

Grant: No, I have some better ones though, if you want to hear them.

Hads: I would rather stick my hand in a blender.

Grant: Do you believe in love at first sight, or should I walk by again?

Hads: Keep walking, preferably to Canada.

Grant: It's a good thing I have my library card, because I am totally checking you out.

Hads: Is the fact that you know what a library card is supposed to impress me?

Grant: Okay, I'm done. But seriously, any tips?

Hads: Google is your friend Grant.

Grant: You're like my own personal Google.

Hads: Goodbye.

Hadleigh

As my eyes roll of their own volition, my phone buzzes again where I set it down on my table, and just as I'm about to curse past Hads for using Grant's number, it's not his name that pops up on my phone.

It's another number—a strange one I've never seen before.

Unknown: Thank you for subscribing to alerts from: HOCKEY HOUSE. This is an automated message to let you know the next party is: THIS SATURDAY NIGHT. We hope to see you there. REPLY STOP TO UNSUBSCRIBE.

I don't know how I can go to one party at that house and suddenly get subscribed to whatever system they use to invite people. I will never step foot in that house again after Grant and I are done with tutoring—I'm sure of it.

Hads: STOP.

I send my reply, delete the message, and grab my book to get some reading done before I have to start my homework.

20

THE PARTY HAS BEEN going for an hour and I'm running around trying to find the girl I invited.

I can't find her, and I'm starting to think she's not coming.

I've been at the hockey house all day preparing everything for this party with Holt. When I asked him if I could throw a party at his house, he looked at me weird and agreed. Holt's usually the one who throws them and gets the word out, but I told him I would handle this one. He's definitely curious as to why all of a sudden I want to be involved in these things when I usually show up, get hammered, and dance all night. This time, I'm in full host mode and making sure everyone is having a good time, though I can't hear most people when they yell back to me.

But the one person I specifically invited through an unknown message hasn't shown up. She's nowhere to be found—none of her friends are either.

I should have just asked her to come, but that felt way too straightforward. I was sure she would laugh in my face if I asked her, so I went a different route and decided to be more on the down low about this.

She came to one party with her friends, and I thought if I gave her another little push, she would maybe come to this one. I guess my hopes were too high, but the night is still young. I'm not giving up all hope she might show up. Hads is full of surprises—at least she has been since I've known her.

A few people smile at me as I make my way over to Jacks and some of the guys—who are currently playing beer pong. Jacks' duo seems to be winning because he has a huge smile on his face as he launches a ball into the cups across from him. I lift up my hand for him to high-five as I finally make it to him, and he's definitely a little drunk already.

The two of us pre-gamed a bit before everyone showed up here tonight. It was the only way I could calm my nerves about seeing if Hads would come, and Jacks was also acting super weird earlier, but he appears to be fine now. I don't see Claire around here either, but she also isn't the type to come to these things.

Maybe Jacks and I will both get surprised tonight, but there's a sinking feeling in my gut that knows Hads probably isn't going to show up. Maybe if this party is big and rowdy enough, she'll hear about it and want to come? Or maybe I should take the low route and tone it down a bit because that's more her style.

I'm so fucked in the head over Hads, and she doesn't even know it. She doesn't even know the only reason I pulled a Gatsby and threw this party was so I could see her outside of tutoring and behind the wall she put back up. If I got her here, I think we could've talked more, danced a little, and maybe I could have shown her the real me.

The real me is a lot tamer than the rumors she's heard. I don't sleep around—in fact, I don't fuck at all unless I feel a real and genuine connection—and I might be one of the most popular guys on campus, but I want someone I can look up at in the stands and have the whole rink turn to muffled sounds. All I want to see is the person I love cheering me on in the stands.

That's all I've ever wanted if I think about it, but I keep giving my heart to people who don't deserve it. This time with Hads, I want to do it right because my heart has already decided on her, I just have to make sure hers is able to decide on me, too.

"Wanna play?" Jacks asks me as Hanson goes elsewhere. "I need a better partner than him."

"You guys won, didn't you?" I smirk.

"Yeah." He jabs me with his elbow. "But you'd never let the other team get as close to winning as he did."

"Count me in," I say as I steal a drink from one of the cups the guys refilled and Jacks and I start playing.

You know what I never understood about the book? Gatsby never drank and never got involved with party activities when he threw the big, extravagant parties to see if Daisy would come.

But me? I'm all in on these fucking parties.

Okay, so maybe I'm a little drunk. Jacks and I played a few rounds of beer pong which quickly turned into smaller cups filled with shots of vodka. Or maybe it was tequila? No, vodka. It was vodka.

Now I'm fucking trashed, and trying to walk up the stairs so I can get to the bathroom. It's been hours since it started, and Hads officially hasn't shown up. It's fine, I guess. It was a long shot anyway, but I had the smallest sliver of hope she would magically appear.

God, Hads. Hadleigh Baker. Hades my fucking tutor. I never realized how gorgeous her full name flows off of my mouth. And don't even get me started on those lips of hers. They were so soft when I touched them against mine for the first time—and hopefully not the last.

I wish she was here.

I stumble up the stairs and knock into a few people, all of them smile at me because everyone knows me on the surface but nobody knows me beneath all of the bullshit.

I open up a few doors wanting to find a room to myself so I can calm down, but every room I open, there's either people making out or about to fuck. I hope nobody fucks in Holt's room because he would kill me and force me to wash his entire house from top to bottom.

I head into his room at the end of the hall and sure enough, there are two people about to fuck laying on his floor.

Jesus. This party got very out of hand very quickly. Music blares from downstairs and even when I opened the door, they didn't stop.

"Get out!" I yell so they can hear, and the two of them scramble out of the room, the girl throws a smile at me on the way out. It's not the right one. It's not the one I want smiling back at me.

I lock the door as soon as they leave, and as soon as I hobble into his bathroom and look at myself in the mirror, I can only think of one word—pathetic. Not only do I look pathetic with my stupid hair and lazy smile, but I feel pathetic as I wonder why I thought this tactic would work.

Of course it worked in a book that's like a million years old, but why did I think it would work in real life? Although, if certain things like love, romance, and friendship didn't exist, people wouldn't be writing about them, right? Am I even making sense?

I've felt romance, love, and all the things that come with giving your heart to someone. But one of these times I want it to last long enough and not peter out like it always does when people get what they need from me.

I splash some water on my face after I piss and wash my hands. I need to get my head on straight, but for some reason, I don't feel like going back to the party. It seems insignificant going down there when I know Hads isn't here.

My hands move to my pocket before I can stop them.

Grant: Is it possible to cry underwater?

I send it without thinking, and as I slump against Holt's door, the music playing making the door move against my back, I wait for her to answer.

I'm so fucked in the head over this girl, I'd rather leave a party I threw to text her and wait for a message back. And until Jacks comes to find me two hours later after most people have left, she still hasn't responded.

21

Hadleigh

"HE DID WHAT?!" ELLA asks me, her voice rising as our conversation continues.

"Yeah," I say, my eyes widening as I soak in what I told her. Grant fucking Carter kissed me after book club on Wednesday, and it's all I've been able to think about since it happened—and that's terrifying.

"I need every minuscule detail again."

"Ella, I just gave you every detail! I can't tell it again. Please don't make me tell it again."

"Please, Hads?"

I sigh heavily before I take a sip of my coffee. Ella and I are back at the library for our weekly date, and I'm finally telling her about the kiss. I haven't told anyone else because it fucked with my head so much that I needed to figure out my own feelings about it—which has been unsuccessful.

And then, on Thursday at our tutoring session, he brought it up, and I could barely look at him without my cheeks turning red. I could feel my face getting hot every time I looked at him to explain something about the book.

"We were talking about how he was jealous of Ryan but had no reason to be, and when I tried to walk away, he grabbed my wrist, spun me around, and kissed me until I was breathless."

"And then you slapped him?" Ella questions, unsure if I actually did that or not.

My cardigan sleeves cover my eyes. "Yes."

"Why did you do that?"

"I don't know, Ells! It was a reflex!" I slump further down in the booth. I've never been more confused about a single kiss in my life. To be fair, I've only ever kissed one other guy, and when I had my first kiss, I stalled for thirty minutes because I was afraid.

Grant just kissed the living daylights out of me in the middle of the sidewalk. He caught me off guard, and that's not something that happens often. I have to applaud him on that, at least.

And the fact that it was the best kiss of my life. But with only one other thing to compare it to, I might not be able to count it as such. If you run an experiment once, it's usually luck. If you run it twice with the same result, it could be a coincidence. But if you run it multiple times and you get the same result, your test is accurate.

It was only one kiss. One stupid, amazing, and enchanting kiss.

"So, what do you think?"

Was she talking? "About what?"

"Do I need to get your ruler out? I've been talking for five minutes and you didn't hear a word I said!"

I throw my hands up in defeat. "I'm sorry! What were you talking about?"

"The party at the hockey house last night," she says as if it's supposed to ring a bell. "I heard through the grapevine that Grant was pretty trashed last night."

"And I care because?" I ask her.

"What time did he send that text to you?"

Fuck. I forgot I told her about that. "Uhh," I say as I swipe to his contact. "A little after midnight."

She only cocks her head at me.

"What?"

"He was at a huge party and he decided to text you while he was there? That means he was thinking about you while he was drunk. He's got it bad for you, girl."

"Can we please stop talking about this? I need a subject change." I only told her about the one text. I don't know how Ella would react to finding out that I got a message straight to my phone telling me that the party was last night and that I was invited. I don't think she's ever gotten one of those, so I file that information away for later.

"We absolutely can, but I'll be bringing this up on Wednesday in front of the two psychos, so be prepared to talk about it again while Paige screams."

"Yeah, I know," I say. The two of us giggle about Paige and how she wants us all to be the happiest we can be. I love her, but her assumption that Grant and I are going to become more after tutoring is over is crazy.

Although, it was crazy before he kissed me. Now, I'm not so sure.

"So, what's been going on with you?" Ella asks. "You know, besides kissing a hot hockey player in your free time."

I roll my eyes. "In academic news, I have to work with Ryan on a criminology project. Our professor assigned partners and we have to do a case study. I have no idea where to start, so I guess it's good I have a partner who majors in this stuff to help."

Ella's face twists. "Yeah, but it sucks that it's Ryan of all people. Why wasn't Paige your partner?"

"The professor has had Paige and Oliver before, so they're partners."

"This case study isn't going to interfere with book club, is it?"

I take a sip of coffee. "Book club? No. But my Tuesday nights are now filled every week." I'm excited to get out of my comfort zone and research a serial killer. This is all more of Paige's purview and I'm intrigued to see what I think of all these weirdos Paige seems to be infatuated with. Our study is due at the end of the semester, and it's our final project besides another chapter test.

"Does Grant know about this partnership?" Ella asks me.

"It's for a class, so no. Why do you ask?"

"Well, he kissed you after admitting he's jealous of Ryan spending time with you, and it seems like he hates the guy. Just tread carefully. I know you're not involved with Ryan, but if people see you guys spending a lot of time together, it might get around."

I didn't even think about that. I've heard very minimal whispers of Ryan across campus since he's not as popular as Grant, but again, how the hell did I get here?

"Have you finished your season three rewatch yet?" Ella and I are doing a rewatch of one of our favorite shows, and we're almost caught up with one another.

"Almost," Ella replies. "This semester has been insane, but this part of the season always gets me deep in my feelings."

"I haven't finished either, but our favorite couple is coming back, so it'll be worth it in the end."

"Exactly." And for another hour, we talk about all of our favorite things about the show and reminisce about our favorite parts ahead. As she gets up to leave, I stop her.

"Ella?"

She turns to face me. "Yeah?"

"How do you hear about the parties at the hockey house? Do you get invited or what happens to get the word out?"

Her brows pinch as she thinks about why I asked the question. "Uhh, usually I hear about it through friends of friends. I don't think anyone has ever sent out specific invitations to people."

"Oh," I say to her. "Cool, I guess."

"Why do you ask?"

"Just wondering." I throw her a smirk and I can tell she's looking straight through me. "See you Wednesday."

"Unless I'm in prison for murdering Zimmerman, then yes, I'll see you then."

"I thought you two were okay? Don't you like his sister more than him?"

"Yes, and it will stay that way." She throws me a smile as she turns to leave. "Next time he kisses you, let me know immediately! I want every sexy detail, including if there's tongue used!"

I roll my eyes, and she blows me an air kiss as she walks out of the library.

22

As I MAKE A clean pass to Jacks while we're working on drills, I smile to myself. I remember not even a few weeks ago my head wasn't in the game and I was struggling.

Now, I feel more confident—I guess—as I skate across the ice while we're doing drills. Though Hads never answered my stupid drunk text, the time I've seen her around at school she's smiled at me instead of pretending I don't exist. I've decided to count that as a win for now because I'm playing the long game instead of jumping head-first into things like I always do.

Half of us are working on defense while the other half does offense. Our first game went well, but our offense definitely needs some work. We did a scrimmage at practice the other day and it was a giant shitshow. Coach yelled at us for like fifteen minutes before he let us leave and shower. We deserved it for sure, but he's scary when he yells. The vein in his neck protrudes, and that's all I can focus on.

Our puck gets away from us, and I go to retrieve it when Ryan bumps into my shoulder. "Watch it, Carter."

I roll my eyes because I know he can't see me through my helmet too well. "You're the one who ran into me. I just need my puck, that's all." It's really hard to remain composed around him at practice sometimes because he goes out of his way to be an asshole towards me.

"Your sweet tutor will be getting my puck soon." He jabs my shoulder again as he passes by, so I reach out and trip him with my stick.

"Sorry, dude! Totally an accident," I say as I reach my hand out to him. "I'm just not used to seeing you on the ice this much!"

He swats my hand away as the whistle blows and practice is over.

"Good work today. On Wednesday, we'll continue doing what we have been doing except switching groups, so be prepared. Barnes and Holt, you guys will be doing one-on-one goalie drills. Dismissed." The team murmurs, and we all skate towards the locker room.

As soon as I get in there, I rip my skates off and shove my practice gear into my locker. I'm about to grab my stuff for the showers when I overhear Ryan talking to some other guys.

"I swear her skirts keep getting shorter. Do you think she wants me or not?"

"She'll be an easy pull for you, Ry. Why haven't you sealed the deal yet?"

"I'm taking my time with this one," I hear him say. I have to fight the urge to round the corner and punch him if he keeps talking about Hads like he is. "I've got the long game going, and it's going to be so sweet when it all works out how I want it to."

I clench my fists together as I turn the corner and walk into their conversation. I could have gone a different way, but I want Ryan to know I just heard everything he said.

I don't say a word as I pass him and the other pricks dealing with him. They murmur some phrases to me and one of them even smiles at me and slaps my back like we're buddies. I get into the shower and hope this will help ease the emotion filling my body if Ryan ever gets his hands on Hads. He's literally the worst but I can't do anything to keep him away from her.

Just when I started to think I was doing better, the world always seemed to come crashing down around me. Failure is a one-letter word but it carries the weight of forty tons of pressure.

I sigh heavily as my arm reaches out to steady me against the shower as I try not to fall into the rabbit hole of feeling like nothing I do will ever be good enough.

It doesn't work, and I can feel my head spinning as I get out of the shower and head for my apartment.

By the time I get back, I'm in full panic mode. All of a sudden, I'm going to fail the midterm coming up, I'm going to fail Hads in some way, and I'm going to fail at hockey and be kicked off of the team.

Before this goes any further, I decide to call the one person who I know can help me come out of this. She picks up almost immediately.

"Hi, sweetie! How are you? How's school? Is Jacks okay?" I missed hearing her voice, and even the thousand questions she always asks me when we chat. It's nice to hear when I'm feeling this shitty.

"Hey, Mom. It's good to hear your voice and don't worry, your other son is fine."

She sighs over the phone. "Oh, good. But how is my actual son doing? I haven't heard your voice in a bit and I know hockey probably has you busy."

"Are you going to get down here for a game this season?"

I can hear her smile through the phone. One of the biggest adjustments for us was me going to college so far away—far enough that she isn't able to be down here for every game. My mom always prides herself on having never missed a single sports game my entire life—which is true, she never did—but since I moved so far away from her, she's missed most of them.

She got to a few last year, and I'm sure she'll do the same this year, but I know she streams the games online when we have them. Even if she's not physically present, I know she's watching replays or live on the school website.

My dad never missed a game either, but now he's missed hundreds. That ache never really goes away.

"You guys are coming up to Pennsylvania and I might get down for that one. It's a bit closer, and I can take a long weekend from work."

I smile. My mom is a realtor in Vermont, and I know how much she loves her job. "Did you get that big promotion?"

I know she had a huge showing last week for some house that nobody else has been able to sell. And one thing about my mom is that she loves a challenge. She told me that the head of her firm said there was a promotion in someone's future if they could sell the house.

"I did. The house had four offers on it by the time I was done with it. It went to a lovely couple with two kids and an even cuter dog."

"Congrats. I'm glad at least one of us is having success in their career." It slips out before I can stop it.

"What's going on, honey?"

"I'm failing a class and I had to get a tutor to help me because if I can't get my grade up, I'm off the hockey team."

"A tutor? Wow, well, I'm proud of you for taking the steps to get your grade up. Has it been working?"

I nod but remember she can't see me. "Yeah, it has been. She's great—really smart. You'd like her. She's snarky and has basically used psychology to get me to pay attention to what she's saying."

"Well, that's good. Is your grade going up? Hockey is your life, honey. I know you'd hate to lose it because of a grade."

I would. It pains me to even think about not playing hockey for the remainder of my time at Grand Mountain. It's also the only connection I have left to my father, and I can't lose that piece of him. "I won't know until midterms if my grade is actually passing. My professor is the weirdest one on campus, but I've passed a few of the quizzes. The midterm counts more, so if I pass that, I should be in good academic standing again."

"Good," she says. "Well, I won't hinder any more of your study time. Just make sure to rest that brain of yours. Don't work it too hard and make sure you're eating well, too."

"I know, Mom. I am—trust me. I'll call you again soon, okay?"

"You *and* Jacks better call me again soon. It's not enough seeing you two on the ice together. I want to actually talk to you both and hear about your lives."

"We will. I love you."

"I love you too, sweetie. I'm proud of you, and I know your dad would be, too. Just remember that."

I subconsciously touch the chain that hangs from my neck. "I will," I say, my voice quiet as I hang up the phone, throwing it onto my bed.

I feel a bit better than before—talking with my mom always helps the weight come off of my shoulders for a bit. I worry sometimes that I'm not a good enough son. I'm all my mom has left and I want to make her proud. She's all I have left too, in terms of a family. I have a few friends back home, but both of my parents were only children like me, so our family unit has always been tiny.

My phone buzzes, and I feel something sprout in my chest. When I retrieve my phone, I can't help the smile that comes to my face.

Hads: You can cry in the shower, but underwater I'm not too sure of.

Hads: Were you up late staring at your ceiling thinking of this? Why did you think I'd have an answer?

Grant: You're my own personal search engine, Hades.

Hads: I regret texting your number all those weeks ago.

Grant: Aw, come on. I'm not that bad am I?

Hads: I plead the fifth.

If Hads could see the smile blossoming on my face, she'd probably run the other direction, but I can't help it. I want her smiles, her eye rolls, and everything that comes with her, and maybe one day she'll want the same from me.

She already has my smile and my heart wrapped up. Now, all she has to do is want those from me, but I can't force a connection if she ends up feeling nothing for me.

But that kiss said differently, and I'll bet deep down somewhere in her heart, there's a feeling for me—what feeling, I'm not sure. There's definitely something, though.

23

Hadleigh

ALL OF US GIRLS met up for lunch yesterday, and in the middle of the dining hall, Ella told Paige and Amelia about Grant kissing me. Paige screamed and almost fainted, and Amelia laughed like a maniac. I thought she was going to wait until we were in a closed and secure location like the classroom at book club, but she said she couldn't hold it in any longer.

I just hope nobody heard us all talking loudly because if that were to spread around campus, I would have to go off the grid and hide forever.

"Paige, I'm late to meet Ryan. What do you need from me?"

I hear her sigh heavily across the phone as I rush around my dorm and try to grab all the stuff I'm bringing to the library. Ryan and I are meeting up this afternoon to work on our project, and I'm running late. My class went long and I had to ask my professor a question, so it took even longer.

"Are you sure you don't want Amelia or I to come to the library and make sure Ryan doesn't pull anything? I don't trust him, Hads. He creeps me out."

"I appreciate your willingness to stalk me while I'm with Ryan, but I think it'll be fine. I promise I'll call you or SOS if anything weird happens."

"Okay, fine. I guess that's okay. Just try to stay five feet from him at all times."

A laugh comes out—I can't help it. Paige makes it seem like Ryan has some sort of contagious disease.

"I will. Now, I have to go or he's going to think I'm not coming."

"Love you!"

"I love you too, P."

Then I grab my bag and walk swiftly to the library. I don't need to rush too much because Ryan can wait.

As I speed toward the building, my mind goes back to my messages with Grant this past weekend. Not only did he drunk text me in the middle of the night, but it was also in the middle of a party at the hockey house.

I hate to admit I've been thinking about the kiss nonstop, and part of me is nervous about this week being our last session. Is he absolutely sure he's not going to need my help to pass the final exam? I remember it being pretty difficult when I took this class but maybe he doesn't care as much because hockey season is over in the middle of April.

Ugh, whatever. I need to calm down and focus on what I'm doing today. My last session with Grant isn't for two days. It'll be fine.

Right now I need to focus on this stupid project with Ryan. I've never done anything like this before—especially not on a serial killer—and I have no idea where to start. I pulled a Paige and spent last night doing some typical research on the guy we have, but other than that, I don't know what other points we need to hit.

Ryan might annoy me, but I hope he's a decent partner. I hate when I'm always the one doing the most in every group project, but sometimes it's better that way when you know your group members are idiots. Sometimes, it's best I'm doing the entire thing—at least I know I'll probably get an A.

I turn into the library doors and immediately stop in my tracks when I see Ryan standing in the middle of the café with a radio blasting a song I don't know and flowers in his hand. What makes it a thousand times worse is the four hockey players behind him with letters that spell out my name.

What the hell is going on?

Embarrassment creeps up my body as I take in what looks like a promposal for something, but confusion sets in because school formal isn't until the end of the semester and we're barely at midterms.

My mind flashes back to the pep rally in high school when Kyle broke my heart in front of the entire school and I thought nothing could compare to the humiliation of that moment. This is coming in at a very close second.

Kyle dragged me on for months trying to sleep with me while also fucking girls on the side—at least twenty others, though I never confirmed that. And then, in front of the entire school at the pep rally, the football team came out, and in front of the entire school, he made fun of me, called me a prude, and everyone laughed.

I was laughed at by my entire high school because I was in love with someone who only wanted me for my body. And I was the one who blamed myself for all of it. There were so many signs and red flags, but I was dumb enough not to open my eyes and see what was happening.

My brother ended up punching Kyle after he did all of that, but I never got to say my peace with him. I never got closure with why he did all that. I assumed it was because he's an asshole who likes to take advantage of women, but I never got to yell, scream, or make him feel as bad as he made me feel.

Then I threw all my energy into my grades and now I let those define my worth instead of a man.

But now, as Ryan does whatever he's doing, all those feelings I shoved away three years ago are bubbling back up. I feel like I'm caught in the middle of something I shouldn't be.

Ryan smiles at me as he steps toward me, my feet rooted to my spot in the ground. My body is frozen with a mixture of embarrassment and confusion, and I want so badly to reach into the pocket of my skirt and text the girls an SOS, but I can't move.

The fact that he chose to do whatever this is in public where everyone can see it, is making my skin crawl. When my head gets back to reality, I see his lips moving, but I haven't heard a single thing he's said to me. My ears are ringing so much because my body is shutting down or something.

Or maybe I'm dead because anything seems better than the actual situation I'm in right now.

Ryan's face comes dangerously close to my personal space, and that seems to pop me out of my haze.

"Sorry, what?"

He throws a smile my way. "I asked you if you would accompany me to the hockey banquet at the end of the year."

"I—" My heart starts to beat faster, my palms are sweaty all of a sudden, and it feels like the library has shrunk in size since I stepped in here. The last time I was speechless was that day back in high school. I always have some sort of snarky comment to say back to people, but nothing comes to mind as I stand in front of Ryan.

Why does he even need a date for this banquet thing anyway? It's not like it's a school dance. Why is he making a huge fuss about this?

"Will you?" He holds the flowers out to me, and it's almost like he's making this decision for me. People have crowded around the spectacle from all sides, and if I tried to run away, I would have to go through crowds of people no matter what door I run out.

I'm trapped in this moment, and even if I wanted to run, I couldn't. My legs don't work anymore because I can't make them move.

And since there are all these people here, some of their phones up as they record Ryan and I's interaction, my breathing gets worse. I don't like being in the spotlight. I don't like hearing rumors spread about me like they were in high school, but this is going to change everything about my dynamic here at Grand Mountain.

I used to fly under the radar and all it took was one semester for that to change completely. This is going to be all over campus by tonight, and by tomorrow, more people will probably know who I am.

I can't decide what's worse. If I say no, I'll probably get dragged through the mud since I turned down someone on the hockey team or something. If I say no, people will whisper and stare at me all across campus—I'm sure of it. It's what happened to me in high school and I didn't have any friends that stuck by me after the pep rally. They faded away because they didn't want to deal with all my drama.

If I say yes, people might assume Ryan and I are together, but that seems easier to squash than the stares and weird looks. I promised myself I wouldn't fall in love with someone that doesn't deserve it and Ryan definitely doesn't deserve anything from me, but we could go as friends, right? That's not illegal to do.

But that might be hard to explain to the entire campus. Ryan might be able to understand we're just friends, but these videos say differently. I might have to ask Ella to help me spread that around campus after this dies down.

I'm stuck between a rock and a hard place, and I already know in my gut which one is the lesser of two evils. I have to say yes, no matter how much I want to run away, change my name, and live off the grid.

"What do you say?" Ryan nudges me with the flowers, and the words fall out of my mouth before I can stop them.

"Sure, but just as friends, okay?" I make sure to say it as loud as I can, but Ryan has a different idea.

"She said yes!"

Applause ensues all around us and I want to sink into the floor and never come out. Public displays of anything are bad enough when you witness them as a bystander, but being at the center of one is the worst thing I've ever experienced—twice, now.

The hockey guys who were holding the signs with my name on it smack his shoulder a few times, and a few people I don't know come over to congratulate me. I've officially entered an alternate universe or something. This is my nightmare scenario, and maybe if I pinch my skin enough, I'll wake up.

I smile as best I can to all these people and eventually as the crowd disperses, I make my way over to an open booth and sit myself down, throwing my laptop open as Ryan thanks his friends for helping him.

As I look up from my screen, I see Grant looking back at me, his face twisted up. And then something shakes him out of his stare because he looks down at the floor and practically runs out of the library.

As soon as Ryan sits down, I know I'm not going to be able to focus because of everything that's happened today.

24

Hadleigh

THIS WEEK HAS BEEN the weirdest week of my entire life, and as I walk out of my math class and see Paige's bright and shining face, I somehow feel a little better. I don't know how she does it, but her positivity has this way of seeping into your body when you're around her. I think she knows I need it—especially after I spent all of book club yesterday talking through what Ryan did on Tuesday.

It was nice a venting session with the girls, but I wish I could go back in time and not have put myself in that situation with Ryan. Though, Ella did say if I managed to avoid him yesterday, he might have just done it somewhere else, and she's right.

Paige threads her arm through mine as we walk upstairs to our next class.

"How are you today, Hads?" I know she's asking because I left first last night, and I think the girls have devised some sort of plan to check up on me because of all the shit going on. Amelia has texted me a million memes since last night, and now Paige is waiting outside my class so we can walk together.

I appreciate these girls like no other. Back in high school, when all the drama started, the loose friendships I had stopped talking to me almost immediately. But with Ella, Paige, and Ames, they spent last night jokingly thinking of ways to get me out of this banquet thing with Ryan.

Paige and I are halfway up the stairs when my brother comes up next to us.

"Do you ever announce yourself, or do you always go up next to girls and stand there wordlessly?" I glance in his direction. He's straight-faced as usual, and then he walks faster so he can pass by us.

"I don't know how you get him to talk more than three words when doing projects," I tell her.

"Honestly, he doesn't. But I can speak the language of Oliver Baker. One grunt means yes, and a scowl usually means no."

Paige and I get to our seats and I pull out my iPad and get ready for the lecture. I've been dreading this class since Tuesday because I have to see Ryan again. I've successfully avoided him the past two days, but I know he's going to talk to me. I was out of focus during our session on Tuesday, and he could tell.

Speaking of him, he walks through the door and sits down, throwing a smile in my direction that I return. I hear Paige gag as she sees him, and I try my best to keep my laughter down.

"Paige, it's fine. I've come to terms with my jail sentence at the end of hockey season."

She shakes her head at me. "I don't trust him, and I don't like him. I hate that he embarrassed you like he did the other day. I *knew* I should've gone with you. I might have been able to cause some sort of distraction so you could have run away."

"If I was there, I would have punched him and his stupid hockey friends in the face for making you uncomfortable," my brother chimes in, and of course he heard about this. I bet Paige told him last night, or maybe he heard it from the whispers across campus. I've heard my name whispered through the halls and people won't stop staring at me when I go places.

I might start hiding in my dorm again. It has everything I need, after all.

"In fact, why don't you stay away from the entire male population for the foreseeable future," Oliver says.

"Even you?"

He nods. "Yup."

"Fine, but if you didn't steal Paige from me, I would have been working with her on this project and I wouldn't be in this mess. She was my friend first, and you can't have her."

"I don't want her, so fuck off," he snaps at me in his usual Oliver tone.

"Okay, before this sibling spat gets out of hand, I'll intervene. Oliver, calm down and go for a run tonight, or something." Paige turns to me. "And Hads, keep your head up. I'm sure the rumors will stop when some other crazy thing happens. Be careful, too. I overheard Ryan say once that he doesn't like animated movies!"

"Easy, Paige. Not everyone looks and acts like Rapunzel from *Tangled* like you do." Oliver says while still looking at his phone. *Has he seen that movie?*

"I just don't understand how you don't like animated movies. It's an underrated genre but most people recognize how amazing those films are! That's definitely his serial killer trait."

"Sorry, what?" I ask.

"His serial killer trait!" Paige smiles and when she realizes I don't understand her analogy, she continues. "When it turns out he's a serial killer, people will say it makes sense because what kind of monster doesn't enjoy animated movies?" Oliver and I look at Paige, confused but not surprised.

"Does everyone have one?" I ask her.

"Yup! Oliver's is that he has feelings but never shows them and yours might be how you hit people with the ruler."

"I have feelings," Oliver tells us. "I smiled the other day, isn't that enough?"

And as our professor comes into class and starts the lecture, Paige and I shake our heads and turn to the front.

Class ends at the usual time and as I pack up my stuff, Paige turns to my brother.

"Oliver, you must have found that lecture enlightening since you threaten murder all of the time. That would be a homicide, and you would go down for it unless you have someone like me who knows how to cover your tracks."

"Paige, I would never actually do it. Plus, who's to say you wouldn't be the person I was murdering?" he says to her.

"Aww, you would do that for me? How nice." She smiles at him.

Oliver scowls and leaves class. He's been acting weirder than normal for him lately. He canceled our last Saturday morning walk because he was too busy, but something else seems to be bugging him. I doubt he'll tell me—the Baker family is not fond of sharing our feelings.

Somehow, I managed to avoid an interaction with Ryan after criminology, and Paige and I walk toward the dining hall to grab lunch before I have to tutor Grant. Today's our last session, and since I know he saw what Ryan did the other day, I know it's going to be as awkward as the one after Grant kissed me.

My brain is way too full for me to keep track of all of this going on with these two wildly different hockey players.

"Amelia and Ella are meeting us at the dining hall."

I turn to her as we walk. "I know what you guys are doing, and I appreciate it, but I don't need you guys to make sure I'm okay in shifts. I've had people stare and whisper about me before, at this point, I'm used to it."

Paige's arm caresses mine. "That isn't something you should be used to, Hads. We just want you to know we're here for you through all this."

I smile at her, thankful for my beautiful friends around me. "And that alone is why this time is better than the last."

Since this is the last session before the midterm, I've spent the entire time going over all of the chapters and the key points I think the professor will hit in each. This book is short, but it's packed full of a bunch of different metaphors, analogies, and most of them have multiple meanings and not one solid thing.

It's not as awkward as I thought it was going to be, but I feel like I should bring up what he saw on Tuesday. I'm scared to mention it because he might not want to talk about it, but I feel like we need to clear the air for some reason.

I feel the need to explain what he saw. I want to make sure he knows the situation Ryan put me in and how it felt impossible to say no in the moment. I want to explain that Ryan and I will only ever be friends—if that. We're more group partners than anything because I don't know much about him and he doesn't know anything about me.

Something smacking my hand brings me out of my spiral. When I look up, Grant has my ruler in his hand. "Hades, I've been talking to you for five minutes, and you haven't said a word."

I swipe my ruler back from him. "You're not allowed to smack me with the ruler. Only I can do that."

"Now that you know how much it hurts, can you please stop hitting me with it?"

I pretend to mull it over. "No, and this is our last session, so after this, you won't have to deal with it anymore."

He cocks his head at me. "Unless you smack me with it outside of this room, or did you forget about our bet?"

"How could I forget about it when you remind me of it every time I see you?" I roll my eyes.

"I'm just reminding you I can cash it in at any time." He smirks at me as he flips his notebook to a new page. "I can't say I didn't enjoy the ruler smacking sometimes."

"I know you'll miss it after you pass the midterm because of me and my methods. You're welcome, by the way." I look up from my notes, and he's already looking at me. There's something about his stare when it's directed at me—it always sends shivers down my spine.

His voice and tone get more serious as he speaks. "Hades, I can't thank you enough. You saved my ass, and I'm grateful you chose to do this with me."

He seems genuinely thankful and the only other time I've heard that tone of voice was when he begged me to do this in the first place. "It was no problem, Grant. Really, it wasn't as bad as I thought it would be at the beginning of the semester."

He's looking at me with the same expression I saw on Tuesday, and I change the subject so I don't have to mention Ryan because my thoughts have been too clouded with him lately, and I hate it. I dig around in my bag for what I'm looking for and when I find them, I hold my hand out to Grant.

"I made you some flashcards to help you study before the exam in case you need a last-minute refresh on certain things." He continues to stare at me. This silent treatment he's giving me is odd because Grant always has something to say—at least when he's around me. "What? I can be nice sometimes and if you fail, that means I failed as a tutor." I'm blabbering, but he still hasn't taken the cards from my hand.

He blinks a couple of times before he grabs my hand. "Thank you, you didn't have to do that. I think I'll be alright."

I shove them at him again. "Take them anyway—for my peace of mind."

"I didn't hear a please, Hades."

I roll my eyes. I'm glad to know he's back to his usual annoying self. "Please take the damn flashcards, Grant."

He smiles. "I know that was hard for you, but I appreciate it."

"Whatever. Just don't fail. Got it?"

"I'll try my best not to. I don't want to be kicked off the team, so a lot is riding on this stupid test." He closes his eyes aggressively as if he didn't mean for that to slip out of his mouth.

"That's why you needed a tutor? I thought it was because you were failing two weeks into the semester, not that you would get kicked off the team." It all makes sense now—why he begged me to do this as if his life would be over if I declined. I thought it was weird because nobody usually cares too much about grades at the beginning of a new semester, but I guess he has to always keep his grades up to still be able to play.

"Yeah, my coach threatened to do that if I didn't get my grade up, and now here we are."

"I guess that makes sense. Would you really miss ice skating and slapping the puck that much?"

"Yeah, I would. It feels like it's the only thing I'm good at."

I relate a bit too much to that statement. I've put all of my worth into my academics and if I get a bad grade on something, my entire week is ruined and I do as much extra credit as I can to get it to even out. Getting straight A's is all I'm good at because nothing else fills the ache of not wanting to open myself up to anyone.

I don't need people if I have good grades. If I get good grades, my future will be secure and all the people I meet in college will fade away when I graduate.

"I don't think that's true," I tell him. I've seen him play, and he was pretty impressive. "You're already better at skating than me. Congrats, you've officially beat me at something."

"Oh, just one thing?"

"Yup, and that's all you get."

"You can't be that bad, Hads. You walk around as if you're not bad at anything. I'll believe it when I see it."

All I do is fake it until I make it—to what? I don't know. I don't know what waits for me at the end of the finish line I've created for myself. "I've never been ice skating, so you'll probably never see it."

"Never?" he questions.

"Never." I've always preferred watching Oliver surf while I take pictures and read my book on the beach. I'm not too sporty of a person and I never felt connected to anything like that. Photography, school, and books are all I feel drawn to, and those are all I'll ever need.

"Can I ask you a question?"

"About the book or personal?" I don't know why any time someone says that my stomach drops.

"Personal." He leans forward on the table on his elbows. "Why did you hate me when we first met?"

"I didn't hate you," I say. And it's the truth. Hate is a strong word for what I felt about him—he was only annoying more than anything. "But you did knock me over and not apologize."

His cheeks start to change color as he thinks about the moment we first met. Is he embarrassed? "I guess I didn't apologize, but I did offer my hand and you shooed me away."

I laugh at the memory. I did in fact do that, but only because he didn't say anything when he reached out for me on the ground. He looked like he was in some sort of trance and at that point, he was pissing me off.

It didn't help that he reminded me of Kyle—similar hair, same colored eyes, and they're probably about the same height. Along with the fact that he was wearing hockey apparel, it felt like a recipe for annoyance. It definitely started out like that, but Grant couldn't be more different from Kyle.

"I hated you at first glance because you reminded me of someone from my past." I don't know why I blurted that out to him when we're supposed to be reviewing for his midterm. It's been three years since everything went down with Kyle, but the ache that I'll never truly be loved still sits on my chest most days. I know I have the girls to fill some of it, but I spend most of my time reading romance novels where despite everything, love persists.

It just feels like I'm one of those people who's destined to never feel the things I read about.

Not only did I trust and love him, but it turned out to be a lie the entire time. I never understood how people did that—lie to someone you're supposed to love.

"Someone bad, I assume?"

"The worst," I tell him. Kyle is the worst person I've met in my whole life and I think it will always stay that way.

"Does Hadleigh Baker have an ex that I need to take care of? Or do I need to get plastic surgery so I no longer remind you of him? I'll do whatever you need me to, just say the word, Hads."

I smile as he suggests all these things. This conversation alone is why I don't need him to do all of that. He'll never be like him, but Grant and I will never be anything besides almost-friends anyway. "No, you don't need to go that far. He was a football player—"

"Ah, I get it. He played football and I play hockey. You know our sports aren't actually that similar right? Mine is played on ice. Football is on—"

"Okay, I'm not that stupid. I know the basics of each, Grant." I reach my hand over to him. "Now you know. Congrats, our feud is over."

"I'm not shaking your hand. In fact, I wouldn't mind if this continued for the rest of our time here at Grand Mountain."

"Why?"

BECAUSE IF IT'S THE only way I can get you to talk to me, then I'd be an idiot to end this between us.

"I have fun pretending to argue with you," I throw her a smirk. "Don't you enjoy whatever this is between us?"

Say yes, Hads. Confirm what I already know. "I do."

"Exactly, so what do I have to do to this ex so you stop letting him win even after your breakup?" I can tell it was something bad. Hads is a strong and confident person. Nothing knocks her down without her fighting back. I should know—she likes to fight me at every turn.

"Nothing, Grant. It wasn't a big deal anyway." She pulls on her sweater vest and that's how I know she's lying. "He cheated on me and I was in love with him until I found out and he embarrassed me in front of our entire high school. It was my fault, in the end. I chose not to look at all the red flags which were right in front of my face."

Why does she talk about this as if it doesn't mean anything? That sounds horrible, and if that happened to me, I'd close myself off worse than she has. "I'm sorry on behalf of all men in general, Hads. And stop acting so nonchalant about what happened to you. It's his fault he lost the best thing to ever happen to him."

Another tug on her vest. "Jacks told me once that you've had a hard time with relationships, too. I didn't believe him because well, you're you."

When have Jacks and Hads ever spoken to one another, and why were they talking about me? This new information makes me nervous because I don't know what he would say. "When have you and Jacks talked about me?"

"A couple of weeks ago, he found me while I was taking photographs outside. He came and talked to me and told me a lot of enlightening things." She looks at my eyes, back down at the table, and then back to me. "I shared my biggest secret, and now you owe me one—if you're comfortable, that is."

She did, didn't she? Although, that's not what I wanted to talk to her about. I really want to ask about what happened with her and Ryan on Tuesday in the library but the whispers I've heard around campus are not helping.

A few people have said he asked her to be his girlfriend—which I know is bullshit. Another one I heard is that he asked her to formal in May, and that feels plausible, but why would he do it in such a huge way? Hads isn't the big and flashy type, in fact, she prefers not being known to most people on campus.

If Ryan really knew her, he would know that.

But whatever happened, I'm pretty sure she said yes, and I saw how she looked after it happened—deeply uncomfortable and embarrassed. But I couldn't do anything about it then and I probably can't now.

"All three of my girlfriends have cheated on me and the last one only dated me to up her social standing here at Grand Mountain." It feels good to talk this out with someone besides my mom or Jacks. "It's all my fault, though. I tend to fall too fast and ignore the signs that these people aren't right for me." *Which is what I'm trying not to do with you, Hads.*

"You didn't deserve that, Grant. Nobody deserves to be cheated on and used. It's the worst feeling in the world."

I shrug it off because there's nothing I can do to go back and change what happened. "It's alright, I only have trust issues and I may never feel those emotions again, but it's not a big deal."

She tries to smack me with the ruler, but I dodge it. "Too slow."

"You shouldn't say that. It's a big deal that you gave your heart to someone and they abused it. That's not on you, Grant. It's on them."

I cock my head. "I could say the same to you, but you wouldn't believe me."

I stare at her like we always do because I know she knows I'm right. I also know there will always be a hole that can't be filled because she was left feeling like a fool back then.

God, I want to kiss her again. I want to kiss her and give her all my love so I can show her how easy it is to love her.

The door opens to our study room and it startles the both of us.

"I'm sorry, guys, but I think I have this study room reserved for now...."

"Right! I'm sorry we were just leaving!" I say as I practically jump out of my seat.

"Apologies, we'll get out of your hair." Hads shoves all her stuff into her bag without organizing it like she usually does, and the two of us book it out of the room and into the library.

She walks ahead of me and I race to catch up to her, wanting to continue our conversation but she changes the subject.

"Well, good luck tomorrow, and let me know when you pass."

"When I pass? Do you have that much faith in me, Hades?"

She stabs me in the arm. "Faith in myself, yes. Plus, those flashcards are next level, so you better use them."

"You made them for me. Of course I'm going to use them."

She swallows hard before she speeds up again, and by the time she's out of sight, I feel another idea forming in my head and I grab my phone from my pocket.

"What's up, Carter?"

"Can I throw another party at the house this weekend?" Not only do I need to get my mind off of the test I'm taking next week, but this was our last session between Hads and I. I'm worried I'll never see her again, but if I throw a party and she shows up this time, maybe all hope isn't lost.

25

 Hadleigh

I PULL MY SKIRT down as the four of us walk to the hockey house for this stupid party. Ella heard about it through Alissa—Leo's sister—but she couldn't make it tonight, so Ella dragged the rest of us.

I was adamant about not coming because midterms are next week and I've only studied for a few days. I really needed tonight to test my knowledge on the things I'm iffy about for my classes.

I obviously didn't win, and now we're at the stupid party that already feels too loud even though we're not inside yet.

"Hads, stop messing with your outfit. You look wonderful." Ella smacks my hand away from where I adjust my skirt. It's a lot shorter than I'm used to, but Ella picked out all of our outfits for tonight, and this one was buried in the back of my closet.

"I feel like I can't breathe."

"It's the corset!" Paige tells me. "I'm wearing one too and it's not that comfortable, but I've never had cleavage before!"

Amelia laughs as Paige says that. Her dress highlights her curves a bit more than her usual ones do, and Ella looks hot as usual. We all look great, I just feel like my outfit is wearing me, rather than me wearing the outfit.

"Last time we came to one of these, it ended terribly. How is tonight going to be any different?" Amelia asks Ella.

"Because we look hot and it's been a busy ass semester and we deserve to have one night of fun, so at least *try* to have fun. Please and thank you," Ella says as we get inside, the music blaring, but this is one of our favorite songs. The four of us have absolutely screamed this in the car before.

Paige smiles as she recognizes the song. "Let's go dance!"

I don't have time for her to answer because she drags Amelia and I onto the dance floor as Ella talks to another friend.

I can't help but smile as the three of us dance. I can feel my body getting less tight as I move with the music and try not to think about all the stuff I have to go over before my first exam on Tuesday.

But I'm listening to Ella's instructions, and I'm going to attempt to have fun. I'm not much of a party person, but with the four of us, I'd go anywhere with them. As long as we're together, I know I'll be having fun.

When the song switches and another song I love comes on, I smile. Normally I don't know a single song at these parties—not that I've been to many—but it's refreshing to at least know the words.

When I see Paige's smile widen and feel a hand on the small of my back, I don't even have to turn around to know who it is. We are in the *hockey* house after all.

I tilt my head back to meet his head and sure enough, blue eyes the color of the sky on a clear day look back at me.

"Hads, how nice of you to join the normal population of college students and actually come to a party for once."

I roll my eyes at him, and I'm about to say something when Amelia hits me in the arm.

"Grant, these are my friends. Paige," I say as I point at her.

"It's nice to finally meet the guy who Hads won't stop talking about!" Paige says, a smile on her face. I know she knows what she's doing but I don't have the capacity to care about it at the moment.

"And the one who hit me is Amelia."

"I hear you're used to being smacked by this one over here," Ames says as she side eyes me.

To that, he laughs. "I am, and don't tell her this, but I'm going to miss that damn ruler."

"I bet you will," I joke.

"Isn't there another one of you book club girls? I thought I saw the four of you walk in?"

"You saw us come in?" I ask because I didn't see him.

"Of course I did, but Paige dragged you to the dance floor before I could." He smirks at me.

Someone else comes by him and whispers something in his ear. I recognize Jacks and give him a smile. "Hi, Jacks!" It's so loud in here that I have to scream so anyone can hear me.

When he recognizes me, he smiles. "Hello, Hads and company. It's nice to see the book club out and about." The one thing I like about the rumor mill is that most people recognize the four of us as the book club. It's cute. "So, you want me to keep the playlist as is or change it?"

Grant shakes his head. "Keep it as is. It's a special playlist for tonight."

"Special, huh?" I ask him as Ella finds us on the dance floor.

"Wow, it's a party over here." She smiles as she hands all the girls drinks. "You must be Grant, I'm Ella."

"In the flesh," he says. "It's nice to meet you. I recognize you all from the game you came to."

I take a huge sip of water because it's already hot as fuck in here, only to realize it's vodka. Amelia chokes on her drink before she covers her mouth.

"Ella, you have to warn us it's alcohol! I thought it was water," I tell her as Grant takes my cup and sniffs it.

"No, that's definitely vodka," he says as he hands it back to me. "Do you want water? I can grab you some."

"I'll come with you," I say, needing a minute to collect myself. I'm not used to this atmosphere and it's overwhelming me.

As if it's the most natural thing in the world, Grant grabs my hand and leads me off of the dance floor and through the crowd of people. We get to the back of the kitchen, and I already feel better. There's less people in here and the noise is a bit more bearable. Though, I haven't minded the music. Most of my favorite songs are playing.

"Overwhelmed?" Grant asks me as I watch him pour me a water. "These things can be a lot if you're not used to them."

"Yeah, a little bit. It's not too bad yet. I'm having fun." I did just get here but it's the thought that counts, right?

"Good, and you're enjoying the music?" He eyes me curiously.

"Yes..." I sense a double meaning there. "Why?"

"Well, hypothetically, it may be your playlist that I found online. It's good, Hads. And people seem to be enjoying it too."

My eyes widen because there's no way he said what he did. "You're playing my music? Why?"

"Well at first it was because I liked most of the songs on your playlist, but now that you're here, it feels like I summoned you," he says as he hands me my water.

I don't know what to make of that, but luckily Jacks finds us again before I can fully dive into what he just told me.

"If Grant annoys you too much tonight, come and find me, Hads. I'll drag his ass away from you."

"Or maybe I could just throw a stick?" I say, noting our conversation that day on campus.

He smiles, catching my reference. "I'm sure that would work, too."

Grant looks between the two of us and his face is pinched together. "Do you guys have an inside joke? How is it that you two of all people have one before Hads and I do?" Grant turns to me. "We need an inside joke, so what should it be?"

I roll my eyes at him. "In due time, Grant. Though, I could argue the ruler is a good inside joke."

Grant only smiles wide and Jacks dismisses himself from our conversation. "I don't wanna know, but at least she's not wearing pink this time! I'd hate to go through another conversation like that, Grant."

"What does that mean?"

He waves it off. "Oh, nothing. Don't worry about it."

I take a few sips of water as Grant stares at me, and I want to ask him why he's playing one of my playlists at this party, but I refrain. If I find that answer, it might not be the one I'm hoping for—though, I'm not sure what I want him to say.

Grant pulls out his phone when I'm done with my drink and changes the song to one of my favorite songs. *Green Light* by Lorde blasts through the speakers and doesn't give me time to laugh because he drags me back to the dance floor and we find my friends. Another guy seems to have joined our circle, and my breath catches in my throat as I realize who it is.

Leo Zimmerman is dancing chest to chest with Ella and the two look like they're about to claw each other's faces off, or they're going to makeout or something.

She raises her wrist to slap him, but he catches it before she can, and then he leaves as soon as Grant and I get back.

"Was that Leo?" Grant shouts.

Ella only rolls her eyes.

Grant then spins me around and the two of us dance as if we're the only two people in the house. The beat helps me let loose and the way Grant is looking at me heats my entire body. I like the way his stare makes me feel. It's not weird and gross like most guys on this campus, but I swear I see his eyes sparkle when he looks in my direction, but that could just be the lights in here.

I'm not sure if I'm good at dancing, but I do what feels right—especially to this song. It makes me feel like I'm floating or driving with all of the windows down on a cool California night. It's nostalgia and hope for the future wrapped in a song.

Sometimes, when life gets to be too much, you have to dance it out, and this song is perfect for that. Things have felt so messy and overwhelming lately, and it's nice to be able to dance it out with my friends and have fun for once.

Paige comes over to me and grabs my hand, twirling me around because it's what we always do when this song comes on when we're cooking dinner at her place.

My guard is down the most it's ever been, and I laugh my ass off because for the first time in years, I feel like this is exactly where I'm meant to be. Gone are the feelings I don't deserve love. Gone is every bad thing I've ever thought about myself and in its place is love and excitement for what's to come.

"Are you feeling okay? Do you need more water?" Grant leans down to my ear.

I shake my head at him. "I'm wonderful, but thank you."

"I like seeing your real smile. I never knew you had dimples on both of your cheeks," Grant winks at me and I feel my knees get weak. "Does this convince you to come to more parties in the future or am I going to have to summon you with your music again?"

I run a hand through his hair, feeling bolder than I've ever been, and his neck falls as I do it. I tell him to come closer and he listens.

"I guess you'll have to find out."

26

Two Weeks Later

I'M SITTING IN MY room when I hear the front door slam open, and Jacks runs into my room a few seconds later.

"Dude, the midterm grades are in! Check your email!"

"Shit!" I say as I scramble off of my bed and rush to my computer. I log in and all of my stuff autofills, yet it still feels like it takes forever to load.

"Did you pass?" Jacks asks me over my shoulder.

"It's loading!"

He throws his arm out in front of him. "Well, make it load faster."

"I'll refresh it. Hold on."

"Grant, did you fucking pass or not?" he yells at me.

"I'm looking! Be patient, asshole."

"Look faster!"

I scoff as my screen finally loads and I navigate over to my grades, my breath catching in my throat as I wait to see if my life is over.

It's not. "I passed! Holy fuck, I passed." I swipe my hand through my hair before I jump up and Jacks throws his arms around me. He pats me on the back a few times, and I've never felt so much relief in my life.

"Thank God, you being kicked off would have killed our season. Not that I was worried about it. Hads is a miracle worker." I can tell he's lying and was definitely worried, but as her name enters my ears, she's the only one I want to tell.

"Do you know where she is? I want to tell her I passed."

Jacks shakes his head. "I would try her dorm or the library. But her dorm is closer to us. It's across the quad."

"Thank you," I say as I grab my phone. "I'll see you later?"

"Sounds good, loverboy." I throw him the finger as I close the door and run towards her dorm. I don't know which building she's in, so I guess and hope for the best. I knock on the first door I see and it opens after a few seconds.

"Hi," the girl says as she straightens her hair with her fingers. "How can I help you?"

She's clearly flirting, but I don't have time for this. "Do you know where Hadleigh Baker's room is? It's an emergency."

The girl smiles at me and motions to one down the hall. I rush to that room and knock, trying to appear less winded and crazy than I am, but Hads doesn't open the door.

"Is this Hadleigh Baker's room?" I ask her.

She eyes me curiously. "Grant Carter," she smiles. "I was wondering when I'd meet you officially."

"Are you Hads' roommate?"

"I am." She smirks. "Hads is at the library."

"That was my next stop. Thank you..." I trail off because I didn't catch her name.

"Taylor."

"Thank you, Taylor," I say as I speed out of her building and head for the library. I'm fully sprinting at this point. I'm way too excited to tell Hads I passed. I can't wait to see the look on her face because I couldn't have done this without her.

Part of me is upset that I have no reason for her to tutor me anymore, but ever since she came to the party I threw, I think it'll be easier to get her out and about more often. I didn't even have to invite her this time, she simply showed up with her friends.

And she had fun. I could tell because I've never seen her smile as much as she did that night a few weeks ago. It was refreshing—seeing her actually enjoy herself and let loose. She's always so wound up and tense. It was beautiful to see that other side of her.

The library inches up on me and I push the door when it's really a pull door, but I finally get inside and spot her immediately. Her black hair and skirt are so easy to spot, and she's at a table with the book club I met at the party. These four seem to not go anywhere without one another, and I think it's cute how close they all are.

As I sneak up on Hads, Paige's eyes widen and she smiles at me as I get next to them.

"Hades!" I whisper yell as soon as I get close to her ear. I don't want to yell since this is the library, but I have to show my excitement in some way.

"Grant, what are you doing h—" I pick her up and spin her around before she can finish her sentence. She wraps her legs around me and hugs me back. My heart is beating so fast. *I wonder if she can feel it.*

"I passed! We did it! We passed!" I'm still whispering in her ear while spinning her around. I could do this all day and it kills me when I have to set her down. I feel her smile on her face before I set it down, but when she aims it at my face, my heart beats even faster than it was.

"You did it! You really passed?" She smiles excitedly. "I knew you would!"

Ella smirks before she speaks up. "Hads, you said five minutes ago you were worried he wouldn't pass."

"She's kidding. Hads had total faith in you, Grant! Great job!" Paige throws her fist out for me and I bump it.

"Thanks, Paige," I tell her. I've never felt this much support from people I barely know, but it feels good.

Hads pats the seat next to her. "Sit down and tell me how it went. Did you use my flashcards like I told you to?"

"Of course I did. I would be an idiot not to have used them. They were helpful, so thank you again."

"She made you flashcards?" Amelia asks, her face shocked at this information.

"Ames, shut it. I was his tutor, of course I made him flashcards," Hads tells her.

"Sorry, you don't often make people study materials. Color me surprised, that's all." She smirks.

"We did it!" I reiterate to her, excited that all this work paid off. "We passed and I can keep playing hockey."

"Grant, why do you keep saying we? You're the one who took the test. I didn't do anything." She's selling herself short. I can tell she feels awkward about it, but this is all thanks to her.

"Hades, I couldn't have done this without you. Therefore, *we* did it—together. I mean it when I say that." She looks down and smiles. Her face turns red, too. God, she's so fucking cute. I would kiss her if we were alone, but I stop myself from doing that. It would be way too fast, and after the last kiss, I want her to kiss me this time. Then I'll at least know that she wants to kiss me as much as I want to feel her lips on mine again.

"Thank you for saying that. I'm glad I could help."

"Let me teach you to ice skate as a thank you." Oh fuck, what am I doing? Did those words just come out of my mouth? "You owe me after the bet we made." I use that as a cover because I didn't mean to blurt that out.

"What?"

"At one of our sessions, you said you had never learned how, and I'm using our bet to teach you. I'm good at skating and besides the bet, let me teach you something for once. After all, you basically taught me an entire class."

"Grant, I don't know. I'm not great at being a student when I don't know how to do something."

"Did you really just say that? Hads, you're the most disciplined student I know, you psycho," Amelia tells her before Ella chimes in.

"She's only nervous, but she'll let you teach her. That way we can all go in the future, and you can skate with us rather than sit on the benches and watch."

"It's cold in there and I'm always fine watching."

"Grant, she would love for you to teach her!" Paige tells me.

"Guys, stop," Hads snaps at her, clearly annoyed.

"What do you say, Hades? Please? I hate that I feel like I'm trying to convince you when you owe me after our bet. I'm teaching you, and that's final," I say as I smack my hand on the table as if it's a gavel.

"Fine. Text me like a normal person and we can figure out when we can go. How does that sound?"

"I can make any time work for you, Hades." Paige squeals but she tries to cover it with a cough. These girls are fucking hilarious. "But maybe I'll send you a formal email like we used to do. You know, for old time's sake."

Her cheeks turn red again, and I love being able to do that to her. I can tell she feels weird about all this, but all I feel is excitement because I'll have Hads all to myself and it'll be on my turf.

"Whatever mode of communication works best for you, hockey boy."

I stand up from my seat and ruffle her hair a bit. "Make sure to wear gloves and a jacket because it's colder down on the ice than in the stands." I throw her a wink before I look up at the rest of the girls. "Thank you for letting me crash your book club meeting or whatever this is. I appreciate it."

"Oh, he's the cutest," I hear Paige say as I leave the library.

27

 **Hadleigh**

"Guys, I can't wear a tight dress to go ice skating!"

Ella's trying to get me into one of the tight dresses she normally wears to go out, but there's no way I'm wearing that around blades on ice skates.

"Ella, it's a bit too cheeky for skating." That would be Alissa—Zimmerman's sister and Ella's new friend. We might be in an alternate reality since Ella officially likes a member of the Zimmerman family.

"What about leggings and a crewneck? That's simple and warm enough for the rink!" Paige pipes in. We're all crammed into my tiny dorm room and they're all helping me get ready.

"Hads, I can get an Uber here for you in minutes, just say the word," Amelia says as she scrolls on her phone. She's sitting on my bed with Paige.

Ella shoots her a death glare as she hands me my leggings and a cute bookish crewneck. "Amelia, stop. She's going and that's final."

"Guys, don't overwhelm her. Hadleigh, babes, I think you're going to look adorable." Alissa's presence is oddly comforting even though this is the first night all of us girls are meeting her. She's absolutely adorable at five foot two, her long brown hair has balayage, and according to Paige, she loves neutral colors.

Paige did some internet stalking on the Zimmerman family because Ella is so tight-lipped about them, and the stuff we found was crazy. Apparently, their family is pretty well known back in England, meaning they're super rich.

She looks a lot like her brother—which is just painfully attractive. I have not stopped staring at her since she came in. She's freaking beautiful.

I slip on the crew neck and leggings, put some thick socks on, and throw my boots by my bag. "Alissa's right. I think comfort over style is what will work today. I'll be uncomfortable as it is trying to learn how to ice skate."

"Ah! I'm so excited! I feel like a proud sister watching you get ready for a date, Hads. Someone take some pictures and document this moment," Paige says to us.

"Paige, don't overwhelm yourself or you'll start crying again," Amelia tells her, grabbing the tissue box in case she needs it.

"I just love you guys and these little moments together. Ella's graduating this year and it feels like this era is coming to an end." Paige is tearing up—I can tell by her voice.

"Does Paige crying happen often?" Alissa looks around the room, and we all nod.

"Thank you for helping me get ready. I really appreciate it," I say to the room.

"Of course! We wouldn't miss this milestone for the world." Ella sweeps some brown matte eyeshadow on my lids and smiles at me.

"Ells, I'm ready to go out whenever you're done, so I'll meet you at the car?"

"Sounds good, Liss. I'll be five minutes max. I'm almost done."

Alissa stops in my doorway before leaving. "Good luck on the skating, Hads. Don't be too nervous. It's quite easy once you get the hang of it."

"Thank you for your help, Alissa. I hope to see you soon! Make sure Ella doesn't get too wild tonight!" I shoot Ella a look, and she smirks again.

"Don't worry, we both fire each other up. I'm the one she has to worry about." She closes my door and leaves.

"I like her. She's so nice," Paige says to the room.

"Same, and I love the accent. I would love to listen to her narrate audiobooks," Amelia says.

"Her presence is so comforting. Are you sure she's Zimmerman's sister?" I ask. "She might be adopted if he really is as bad as you say, Ells."

"I don't want to talk about him. But they're blood siblings, and she's the better one." Ella finishes applying the last of my makeup and picks up the mirror to show me. "All done! I spruced up your original routine with simple eyeshadow and eyeliner. What do you think?"

"I love it, Ells. Thank you." Seeing myself in the mirror isn't calming my nerves for tonight, but the girls being here have. I don't know why my stomach feels so weird. I've been on dates before, but it's been a while—I feel like I'm out of practice.

Can you be out of practice from dating? I don't know. I think deep down I'm scared to put myself out there again. Honestly, I'm not even sure this is a date. To me, I'm honoring our bet from way back when and I'm only doing this because Grant wanted to teach me something for once. As of right now, it's just a regular Saturday night skate session—nothing more and nothing less.

The fact that I trust him enough near sharp skates and cold, hard ice says enough.

"Hads, did Oliver say anything this morning on your walk?"

"No, because he doesn't know I'm even going out with Grant. It's bad enough he wants to murder Ryan every time he glances in my direction in class, Grant shouldn't be on his radar, too."

"Hads, your brother may be grumpy, but he would never actually do it," Paige tells me, and she's probably right, but I don't want to take that chance.

"Paige, please enlighten us more about what Oliver would do. Grunt? Stare? Ella and I have had a bet to see if he can speak more than three sentences at once," Amelia says.

"Really, guys?" I say to them. "Oliver's very talkative when he needs to be."

Three knocks on the door startle all of us, and as I get out of my chair, my stomach drops.

"Is that him?" Paige's eyes light up.

"Shit, you guys were supposed to be gone before he got here. He's early."

"Maybe he thought you would slap him with that ruler if he was late again," Amelia giggles.

"Can you guys shut up?" I say as I swing the door open and see Grant standing in front of my door with flowers.

"Telling me to shut up already? We haven't even done anything yet." He smirks at me as he hands me the flowers. "These are for you. I didn't know what kind was your favorite, so I got black roses to match your skirts."

That last sentence is going to send me into a coma. "Thank you. I'll put them in a vase later. Let me just grab my boots and we can go to the rink." He leans against my door frame, looking me up and down before I hand the flowers to Paige.

"Can you find my vase?"

She looks at me confused. "You don't have a vase, Hads."

"We'll go buy one," Ames whispers to me.

"Now, Grant, what are your intentions with my girl Hads tonight?" Ella asks him.

"Ella," I threaten.

Grant is smiling ear to ear as he answers her question. "I intend to teach Miss Hades to skate and nothing more. But if she wants to make weekly lessons a thing, I'll gladly oblige."

"Good. Just make sure she doesn't get hurt," Ella says as she heads out. "I'll talk to you tomorrow if I'm not too hungover, Hads."

"Sounds good," I say as I grab my bag. I turn to Paige and Ames. "You guys can let yourselves out?"

They both nod at me as I lace my boots up. When I look at Grant, he's watching me with that same look he always is.

"You ready?"

"Ready as I'll ever be," I say.

"Alright, then let's get skating."

Grant

I THINK I MIGHT have overstepped a little by getting her flowers, but I don't give a shit. Neither of us has said this is officially a date, but I wanted to show her in a less obvious way that she means something to me—and flowers seemed like a decent way to do that.

She didn't throw them back at me, so that feels like a good sign.

As the two of us walk to the rink, I start to feel nervous. Never in my life have I felt so scared walking into the arena before, but I'm determined to make this night perfect and to get her out of her comfort zone a little.

But holy hell, I need to calm down. When she opened the door and I saw her in leggings and a crewneck, I almost fell over—I had to lean against the doorway to steady myself. It's the first time I've seen her in something other than a skirt and while it threw me off, I had to remind myself to slow the fuck down.

I open the door for her and go to grab her some skates while she looks around. I have my hockey skates with me, but Hades doesn't have any, so we have to fit her in some before we start. I wish I could just skate around with her in my arms, but I don't think she'd be open to that.

I also made sure to have the rink cleared because the school does open skates sometimes on the weekends, but tonight wasn't one, thankfully. I told the guys who run the rink that Jacks and I wanted some on-ice time to prepare for our upcoming away games, and they told us we could use it. What the school doesn't know won't kill them, right?

Plus, I'd do more than lie to make sure Hads is comfortable.

"So, this is the arena from down here. What do you think?" I open my arms out wide as if I'm showing off my new house.

"It's nice. It definitely looks a lot bigger from down here."

I let her take it all in as I grab her a pair of skates. "Let me guess, a size seven and a half?"

She eyes me curiously. "How did you know that?"

"It's not that hard to guess. I'm basically an expert," I say as I hand her the skates.

I can feel her eyes roll as I lace my skates up on the bench next to her. I take a look at the ice and sure enough, Bobby—the guy who drives the

Zamboni for the school—resurfaced the ice for me like I asked him to. I slipped him a fifty and he pulled through.

I look over at Hads and she's struggling to lace her skates up. "Do you need help?"

"No, I've got it. The strings are tangled."

"Hades, let me help you."

"Grant, it's fine. I got it."

"Asking for help is not a weakness. Let me help you before you strain that big brain of yours." I tell her.

She looks at me for a moment. "Fine."

I hobble over to her on my skates and I kneel down, the height difference between us even worse than it normally is. I'm on both knees in front of her—careful not to catch myself on my blades—and look at her laces. I carefully untangle them and look up at her. "What are you thinking about, Hads?"

"I'm trying to figure out if I can reach your throat with my skates."

"A simple thank you will suffice."

She whispers something I can't hear before standing up and almost falling back over. I steady her and help her walk over to the small door that leads out to the ice. I let her take her time as I glide onto the rink and get my footing while she still stands firmly at the door.

"It looks slippery. What if I fall and break my head open?" she asks me.

"It's ice, so it is slippery—that's the point. You're more likely to fall if there are cracks in the ice. This is fresh thanks to yours truly. And do you think I'd let you fall and break your head open? What kind of teacher would I be if I let that happen?"

"A worse teacher than me," she smirks.

"Exactly! And that's not what I want," I say as I glide over to her. "Even if you break your head open—which you won't—your intelligence will still be intact, Hads. Come on, grab my hand. I'll steady you." I reach my hand out to her but she doesn't budge.

"Promise you won't let me fall."

I smile at her. "I promise, Hadleigh. You're safe with me." My arm is still stretched out to her. "Come on. We don't have all night."

She looks down at my hand, back up at me, and finally takes my hand. The contact is electric, and I know she felt it too because she jolts as we grasp hands.

"First things first, if you feel yourself losing your balance, bend your knees and try to recenter yourself. If you fall, try not to use your hands to break it. I don't want to end tonight with you having a broken wrist. Got it?"

"Got it." She smiles, and it hits me right in the chest. I should know this girl would never do anything halfway. She'll probably be a professional skater by the end of tonight.

"To stop yourself, stand with your feet together and stick one skate out sideways. It's a bit weird initially, but you'll get the hang of it."

"I'm more of a visual learner. I like charts and stuff, so maybe you could demonstrate it, and I could try and copy what you do."

"Will you be okay standing on your own?" I ask her, just to make sure she's comfortable.

"Don't underestimate me, Mr. Carter. I can do anything I put my mind to."

"I would never dream of doing that, Miss Baker. Okay, watch me." I show her some beginner moves while I feel her eyes on me. She's taking in what I'm doing without my stick and a puck on the rink. It always feels a little weird skating without it in my hand, but her eyes on me are making me put my best foot forward.

"Do you want to try gliding on your own? All you have to remember is to switch feet and lift one and then the other."

"Alright, I got this." Watching her hype herself up is cute. God, I can't get enough of this girl. I'm glad we made that bet in the beginning of the semester or else tonight wouldn't even exist.

She tries and it's like she's a natural at skating. She looks up at me when she stops and smiles. "I did it! That wasn't so bad."

"It's not that hard, I told you. That was good." I skate over beside her, and her cheeks get all red. "I know your turf is more academic and book-related, but this one is mine. We complement one another quite nicely, don't we?"

She tries to push me over but she wobbles a bit. "I guess we do."

We take a few laps around the rink. On the first lap, I skate backward and hold onto her hands. By the third lap, I let go and let her try adjusting to skating by herself.

"Okay, try doing some swizzles."

"Swizzles? That's an actual word?"

"Little Miss Dictionary doesn't know what something means? Wow. This is truly breaking news!" I yell, and it echoes in the rink.

"Grant, shut up." She laughs at me. "This skating terminology is new to me."

"Let me show you." I demonstrate how to put her heels out and in, and she copies me perfectly. Why did I expect anything less from little Miss 4.0 over here?

"Oh my God, I'm so good at this! Look at me go—"

I smile as I watch her get a bit too cocky and fall over. "Hades!"

"Ow," I hear her say as she lies on the ice.

I quickly skate over to where she is and lean down to look at her. "Where are you hurt?" I ask her as I run my hands over her to check for bumps.

"I don't think I'm injured. I feel okay, just sore."

"Maybe we should stop for the night," I say, a bit panicked. I hope she didn't hurt herself too badly. Should I get a medic in here? Or maybe I should take her to the health center?

"Grant, I'm fine. Let's keep going."

"Hades, you don't have to perfect ice skating in one night. Skills like this take time. Let's go before you hurt yourself more." I stand up and look down at her.

"No."

I groan. This girl is really fucking stubborn and I was worried she hit her head or something, but if she's still talking back to me, I don't think she did. "Listen, I'm not getting my ass kicked by Ella after you hurt yourself more. I promised I would keep you safe. Come on." I offer her my hand, and she crosses her arms at me. Always a fucking challenge with this one. "Hads, get up."

"No."

"Hadleigh."

She cocks her head at me. "You don't scare me, Grant."

"Good, I don't want to scare you, I want to sweep you off your feet." I skate around her in circles. "How am I doing?"

"Considering I'm on my ass on the ice, not very well." She tilts her head down.

That won't do. I need her to look at me, so I kneel down next to her on the ice and lift her chin. Her eyes connect with mine in an instant, and I don't know what possesses me to lean down and press a kiss to her lips, but I do.

I think it was the way she looked up at me—as if I hold all the secrets to the universe in the palm of my hand. She holds everything of mine in her hands—my heart, my sanity, and every single beat of my heart is hers.

She freezes for a second before she kisses me back, her hands grab my hoodie as she pulls me as close as I can get, but this position won't do for long, so I pull back for a second and speak against her lips.

"How am I doing now?"

"You're doing much better but there's always room for improvement."

"Do you want me to keep going?" I want her to say yes so badly. I think I might die if I spend another second not kissing her while she wants me—while she wants this as much as I do. But I need to hear it from her. I need her to tell me she wants me to kiss her again.

"If you don't kiss me again, I'm going to smack you." She smiles at me, her face lighting up as her gaze lingers on my lips. If putting a smile on this girl's face was a full-time job, I would apply for it immediately. "Please, Grant."

As soon as my name leaves her lips, I get her on her feet but she almost loses her balance. I can't have that, so I decide on something even better. "If I pick you up, can you put your legs around my waist, baby?"

The term of endearment makes her smile up at me, her eyes sparkling under the lights on the rink.

"I don't want to nick you with my skates."

Aw. Once upon a time, she would have threatened me with that. "I'll take them off for you if you hold onto my shoulders, okay?"

She nods at me and I kneel on the ice, carefully slipping her skates off and throwing them to the side. It's not like she needs them anymore. She doesn't need skates if I have her in my arms. I'll be her own personal chauffeur while we're on the ice tonight.

The second they're off, I pick her up into my arms and she wraps her legs around me like she did when I picked her up in the library the other day.

"This can't be safe, Grant," she whispers against my neck. "What if we fall?"

I rub my hand up and down her back. "I've got you, baby. Do you trust me?"

"I do," she doesn't hesitate to say and I could scream just from that. Hads trusts me and that's all I could ever hope for. This girl is going to be my undoing if she keeps being fucking perfect in every goddamn way.

"Good because all I want tonight is to kiss you until you can't breathe." I press a small peck to her cheek. "Does that sound good?"

"That sounds perfect," she says as I capture her mouth in a kiss, my tongue tangling with hers as we skate around. As soon as I get a little scared we're going to run into the sides, I press her against the boards and kiss her harder than I was, needing more from her. I want to get lost in her all night, and being able to memorize every small noise and reaction from her is all I need.

"God, Hads, do you realize what you do to me?" I say as I kiss down her neck, her hands tangle in my hair as she pulls it and my face goes back to hers.

"What do I do to you?"

I grab her ass and hoist her up so I have a better grip, and while one hand holds her up, the other caresses her face as I look into her eyes. "You make me fucking crazy, Hads. You make me want to say fuck everything and if I wasn't such a gentleman, I'd take you against these boards right now."

Her breath catches in her throat. "But you're a gentleman."

My mouth comes to her neck and I bite it, not hard enough to leave a mark, but enough for a small sound to leave her lips. "I am, but the things I'm thinking about doing to you are anything but."

I can't get enough of her. Even after this is over tonight, it's all I'm going to think about. If she clouded my thoughts before, there's no telling what it's going to be like after this.

If it wasn't too fast, I'd get on my knees and worship her on this rink for hours. I can't do that, but I'll gladly kiss her until we both can't breathe.

"Just let me feel your lips on mine, Hads," I say as I press my lips against hers again. Nothing has ever felt so perfect as her mouth on mine. I take the lead as she runs her hands through my hair, down my back, and over my arms. One of her hands lingers on my arm while the other caresses my face, guiding me as we find a rhythm while we kiss.

She tastes and smells like vanilla and suddenly I've found my new favorite scent in the entire world.

God, the feeling of her against me is unlike any other. There are way too many thoughts running through my mind, and I have to keep reminding myself to go slow, but my hand lingers against her throat as I kiss her.

"Looks like I finally found a way to get you out of that head of yours," I say to her. "Does this feel okay?" I say as I keep her in the spot I want her.

She nods at me, her face flushed with desire as she smiles lazily at me. "Kiss me."

Who am I to deny this girl what she politely asks me for? I thread my tongue into her mouth before I lean my forehead against hers, feeling a swirl of too many emotions running through my body.

It's all too much. I can't handle everything this girl in my arms is making me feel. Tonight feels like some sort of dream I don't want to ever wake up from.

"Can I hold you and take a few laps? I need to calm down a bit before we walk back."

She smiles as a small laugh bubbles up. "I know. I can feel how crazy I make you."

"It's your fault, Hads," I say as I adjust her in my arms and skate around the rink. She nestles her face in the crook of my neck, and as my arms are around her and I feel the cool air against my face as I skate, all feels right with the world.

I'm not thinking about Ryan and her in the library. I'm not thinking about how this could end horribly like the rest of my relationships do. The only thing clouding my mind is the girl in my arms, and I wouldn't have it any other way.

Because the way she looked at me tonight? The way she fell apart in the palm of my hands as I kissed her against the boards? Yeah, there's nothing that could erase that from my mind. I have a feeling that my hand and I will get very well acquainted after tonight. The echoes of her are going to bounce around in my head.

I got hard as a rock from kissing her—from just touching her for the first time. Nobody has affected me as much as her, and the thought should scare me, but it doesn't.

Ten or fifteen laps later, I set her down outside of the rink while I grab her skates from where I tossed them on the ice and I bring them out and put them back behind the counter.

She's sitting on the bench, so I sit next to her as I unlace my skates and throw them back in my bag.

"So, how did I do?" she asks me.

I pull her closer to me and press a kiss to her forehead. "If there was anything higher than a 4.0, I'd give it to you."

"I appreciate that."

"How did I do?" I ask her, and to my surprise, she threads her hand in mine and places our joined hands on her lap.

"You did okay, but there's always room for improvement."

I playfully shove her off of me and before she can say anything else, I pick her up, throw her over my shoulder, and she laughs as I carry her out of the arena.

28

Three Weeks Later

I'm sitting in the library sipping my coffee as I type out a report for one of my classes. It's not due for a few weeks but if my brain stops moving about my academics, I'll start to think about a bunch of other things I don't want to be thinking about.

Spring break came and went, and I went home with my brother to California. It was nice to be home and have a change of scenery. Paige and Amelia stayed on campus, opting not to go home, and Ella went home to visit her dad and sister who are only a half hour away from campus. None of us had much to discuss since we were only gone for a week and the four of us stay attached at the hip even from different states.

But despite all that, I've slowly pulled away from Grant. I was fine after our ice skating date—or whatever it was—but as time went on, my head started to fill with a bunch of thoughts that were very unpleasant to deal with.

You know those paintings that look beautiful when they're hanging up and everyone comes and takes pictures of them because of how they look? It's surface level—those people take the pictures because they can only see what's hanging in front of them. But if you read the plaque underneath most of them or go home and research the meaning behind the paintings, it's completely different than what you thought it would be. Maybe it's darker or more vulnerable than what's on the surface.

That's what I'm afraid of. On the surface, Grant is wonderful. He's sweet and he cares about my feelings and was so respectful on our date, or not date, or whatever. But what if underneath all of that as we start to get to know one another, he decides I'm not what he wants? What if we get involved and I realize he's completely different after he gets what he wants from me?

Deep down I know that likely isn't the case, but my brain won't let it go. I don't want to throw myself into the first guy who has shown me attention since Kyle and have the two of us become art that on the surface looks perfect, but the real meaning is hiding and waiting to be discovered.

And the worst part is that he made me feel again. It's been a long time since I've felt anything, and having all these butterflies again makes me want to retreat like I always do.

Grant is the first person in three years to show any speck of anything toward me, and I knew it would happen at some point, but it feels too soon for me for some reason.

Or I'm making excuses to try and avoid feeling anything—which is most likely what my brain is doing. I don't know what to do with all this. I'm simultaneously terrified but a small, miniscule part of me wants to give in and jump into something with him.

But something is holding me back—something is keeping me from knocking down all of my walls with a sledgehammer. That's another thing Grant was able to do. When we were skating around, I was out of my head. I wasn't thinking about anything else but being in the moment with him and nobody has ever been able to do that. Even when I'm with the girls, I'm usually thinking about the assignments I have to do or whatever else is on my to-do list that week.

Not with him. With him, all the clutter in my mind cleared and I was only focused on how he looked at me when I skated around.

I slam my laptop closed and sigh heavily as I rest my hands on my face. I hate being alone with all of these stupid emotions and I don't have a plan for how to get them out of my mind.

"Taking out your frustrations on your laptop? I didn't know this semester was going so terribly for you, Hads."

Shit. When I remove my hands from my face and see the person who's been clouding all of my thoughts, I smile. He looks good—like always. His hair is a little messy, but all that does is remind me of how I ran my hands through his hair at the rink.

"I can't hit you with a ruler anymore, so I have to find something to fill that void."

"Got it." He puts his hands in his pockets. "Can I sit or are you waiting for someone?"

"You can sit. It's just me." It's good to see him. Usually, when he's around, my thoughts are clear. But whenever I'm by myself, the bad ones sink in again and make me think I'm not cut out for relationships that end happily.

As soon as he slides into the booth, he smirks. "You're avoiding me."

"No, I'm not." I absolutely have been. I should've known he'd bring it at some point. It's been weeks, and he hasn't even messaged me about it.

"Yes, you are, Hades." He reaches across the table and doesn't touch my hand that lies on top of it, but he's close enough so I can feel the heat coming off of his body. "Are you running from me or the possibilities of me?"

"The latter, I think." There's no use lying. "I'm sorry."

He shakes his head at me. "Don't apologize, Hads. If anything, I should be. I came on too strong again."

I grab his hand in mine, feeling more confident. "No, you didn't."

"Yes, I did. I kissed you and I took it too—"

"Don't make me get my ruler out," I joke. "Grant, I had a great time at the rink. It's my own insecurities and weird feelings that have made me pull away the past few weeks. It wasn't you, I promise."

"Are you sure?"

I nod. "Believe it or not, I enjoy talking to you."

"Do you?"

My eyes roll before I can stop them. "Don't let that go to your head."

"I won't." He rubs his thumb over my hand. "But next time you're having big feelings, tell me about them. I'm not a huge fan of the silent treatment."

"I'll try my best. I'm not the best at talking about things that are bugging me." It's my fatal flaw. Oliver does the exact same thing, too. Our family isn't big on discussing things that involve feelings, so we tend to steer clear of those topics if something is bugging us. "Would you call us friends?"

He's surprised by my question. "I'll call us whatever you want me to. If you want us to be friends, we can be friends. If you want me to be your sworn enemy, I'll oblige as well."

"I mean, I don't really think we're friends. I definitely don't go around and kiss my friends like that night at the rink. But we're not exactly anything either."

He squeezes my hand. "Hads, I don't think we need a label. How about you're just Hads and I'm just Grant."

I nod at him, and of course he found a solution to one of my brain's problems without even trying. I can be myself, and he can just be Grant.

"How was spring break? Did you go back to Vermont?" I ask him.

"I did. I got to see my mom and hanging around with her for a bit was good." He runs his free hand through his already messy hair. "I saw you went to the beach a few times. Who were you photographing on the surfboard?"

"My brother. He loves to surf, and I'm more of a watcher than a participant."

"That's cool. Those pictures looked great, and before you ask, I did stalk you online to see what you were up to."

"I see," I giggle. I know Paige is a fan of cyberstalking us when we're apart, but now I know that Grant likes to do it, too. And why does the fact that he kept up with my life over break make me feel so giddy?

Another person slides into the booth next to Grant, and as soon as I see Jacks, I smile at him and Grant and I stop holding hands.

"Hi, Hads."

"Hey, Jacks. What are you doing here?"

"Well, Grant and I were supposed to be in a study room, but when I came down to get a coffee, I saw him talking to you."

I eyeball Grant and he plays dumb. "So, I got a little distracted on the way in. How about I buy you a coffee to make up for it?"

"That sounds perfect, actually," Jacks says as he moves out of the way for Grant to get out. "Hads, do you want anything?"

"Triple shot latte with a pump of liquid sweetener, please?"

"Coming right up," he says as he heads for the counter. It's just Jacks and I in the booth, and before I can ask him how Claire is, he beats me to it.

"You know, that kid is the most hopeful person I've ever met."

"Grant?"

He nods. "He tells me most things, and he was worried when he hadn't heard from you in a few weeks, but when I asked him about it, he smiled and told me it was going to be okay."

"For someone so afraid of failure, he sure has a lot of hope that things will work out," I say. "I'm not like that. I tend to know things will work out because of my hard work."

"You two are different, but I'm glad you're at least talking again. I can't stand mopey Grant. I'd rather have you deal with him."

"Well, if it all works out in the end, we can figure out a schedule or something."

Grant returns to the table with our drinks, and Jacks gets out of the booth. "I'll cheers to that." He holds his cup out to me, and I clink his.

"Deal."

As they walk away from me, I hear Grant say something to Jacks. "Do you guys really have another inside joke together? It's not fucking fair."

I smile as I take my phone out and text my brother.

> **Hads: Are we still on for Saturday morning?**

> **Sous Chef: Yeah.**

> **Hads: See you then.**

> **Sous Chef: Okay.**

And when I get up from the table, a small slip of paper catches my eye. It's addressed to me, and when I open it, an invitation to another hockey party sits in the envelope for this Saturday.

I assume Grant left this here, and if he is specifically inviting me, then I wonder what he has in store for Saturday night.

But the only question that remains is if I'm going to go or not.

29

 **Hadleigh**

I'M AT THE BENCH under the tree in record time today. I barely slept last night because I kept thinking about the party tonight and I still have no idea if I'm going to go. The girls are all busy, so if I did, I'd be going by myself. I'm sitting down and shivering when Oliver jogs up to me and throws me his hoodie without saying a word.

"Thanks." I smile at him while he takes his headphones out. Oliver still uses headphones that aren't Bluetooth enabled because he thinks the ones with strings stay on better. We start our usual route and neither of us speaks for the first fifteen minutes.

He breaks the ice in usual Oliver fashion—harsh and direct. "Why are you being so quiet?"

I chuckle. "Isn't that what I'm supposed to say to you, Ol?"

"Yeah, but you always have something to say. I don't."

"That's true."

"What's going on Hads?"

"Nothing! It's just been a weird few weeks!"

He stops walking and turns to me. "So, tell me about it. Isn't that what these walks are for?"

I continue forward. "I don't want to!"

"Why not? Are you scared I'm going to threaten Grant?" I finally stop walking and sigh heavily. Paige must have told him about all this. I thought she was good at keeping secrets—she's practically a damn CIA officer. "No, she didn't tell me. I figured it out on my own. I'm not stupid, Hads."

I didn't realize I said that out loud. "I never said you were. How did you know if Paige didn't tell you?"

"You've been really closed off for a few weeks. Before break, I was on a night run when I saw you walking with Grant to the rink. I later found out from Paige that he taught you how to ice skate that night—cute, by the way."

"First of all, you're the only person I know who goes for night runs. You're weird, by the way. And why do you and Paige text so much? Your conversations can't be that interesting. You either send me one word responses or an emoji."

"Stop changing the subject and tell me what's been going on."

I look back at him as I meet him where he stopped. "How did you know you were ready to start dating after what happened?" I ask, being as vague as possible. None of us say her name, just in case.

"After Mia?" He looks at me with sad eyes. Damn, I hate that I brought this up. I know it still hurts to talk about, but I need some help weeding through my own fears.

"Yeah, and after what happened."

"Hads, you can say her name. I won't be offended."

"Sorry, I was being respectful."

"And I love you for that, but it's okay. I can talk about it."

"Okay." Oliver's first girlfriend—her name was Mia. She was super nice—pretty, too. She and my brother dated from sophomore year until the accident senior year.

One of her friends was speeding down a busy road, racing this other car when they lost control and crashed into a tree. The driver—Mia's best friend—was in a coma for months, while Mia was pronounced dead on the scene. It was horrible. Our community mourned for months.

My brother was a wreck after. He wouldn't come out of his room, and I barely saw him for weeks after it happened. He saw a therapist after, and eventually, things got better. It took a while, but then he went to college, and that was that.

"Well, Hads, I haven't dated since then."

"You haven't?"

"I thought you knew that."

"I don't keep a chart of your dating habits, Ol." He lightly laughs at that.

"Good."

"So, how do you know when you'll be ready to put yourself back out there?"

He ponders the question for a moment. "I think I've been ready for a while, if I'm being honest. Don't get me wrong, I loved Mia. I think part of me always will, but I can't change what happened. She's gone, and I know being sad she's gone is the way love manifests after bad things happen. Grief and sadness remind you that what you once had was beautiful. I wouldn't change anything about what Mia and I had, but life continues. It has to go on, or else you're stuck." I didn't realize my brother could be so poetic. "Hads, I know you're scared because of what happened with Kyle—I would be, too. But don't run away from something good because you're scared."

"I don't know how to feel any other way except scared. I can't seem to take that leap into the unknown. It scares me that I might not be cut out for love like normal people are, and I don't know how to stop the thoughts that swirl when I think about what I could have."

Oliver cocks his head at me. "Grant isn't Kyle, you know."

"Was that a compliment?" I ask.

"No," he snaps. "Call it an observation."

"What do you mean?"

"Grant taught you how to ice skate, Hads. He offered to do something for you, and according to Paige, he got you flowers before your little date. Kyle never even offered to drive you to school, let alone do something specifically for you."

I'm never telling Paige anything ever again.

"He invited me to a party."

"Who? Grant?"

I nod. "Yeah. It's tonight."

"Are you going to go?"

"I have no idea," I say as I mess with my hoodie strings. "I went to the last one and had fun, but the girls were with me. I'd be going to this one alone."

"So? Go anyway, Hads. Step out of your comfort zone and do something that scares you. You know you're doing the right thing if you're a little scared when you're doing it."

I let what he's saying sink in. He's right in more ways than one.

Grant offered to teach me something on his own time—he did it *for* me. It never really clicked until now. I can't remember the last time someone did something just because they wanted to help me.

"Don't close yourself off like you always do, Hads. You deserve to be happy with someone who will treat you well."

I hit him with my elbow. "You deserve to be happy too, Ol. Have you thought about getting back out there?"

He shrugs. "With the right person, maybe."

"And who might that be?"

"Not sure. When I know, you will too."

I laugh, knowing it could be years before Oliver finds someone to spend his life with. "Good. I'm sorry I kept this from you. I know we usually tell each other things, but I was confused and didn't know what to do."

"It's okay. I get why you did it. Just don't make any rash decisions. Being friends first is usually the best thing you can do. That way, you have time to figure out your feelings, and it puts less pressure on things."

We're almost back at the bench again, and I didn't realize how much I needed to hear this from my brother. I know our family doesn't talk much about this stuff, but we try to do the best we can.

"Damn, I owe Ella and Amelia twenty bucks," I say out loud.

"What?"

"You spoke more than three sentences today, and they had a bet going. It's not important. Thank you for being the best brother I could ask for, Ol."

"You're welcome, Hads. I told you I can be wise when I want to be."

"Yeah, whatever. I'm going to sit on the bench for a bit, so feel free to go."

"Sounds good. Just remember what I said, and don't be afraid to text me if you need anything. I mean it, Sis. That's what I'm here for."

"And here I thought it was your job to bully me as a kid."

"Yeah, well, I already accomplished that." He smirks at me.

"You sure did," I say back at him as he starts to jog away.

"I love you, idiot," he says while running away.

"I love you too," I say under my breath.

I sit down on the bench and listen to the sound of the leaves rustling on the trees. Spring is almost here and I couldn't be more thankful for that. It's my favorite season—a season of new beginnings.

I hope that still reigns true because I could use a fresh start, or a new beginning of some sort. I wish there was a way to erase my mind of all the bad things that happened to me in the past so I could move forward with nothing holding me back.

But life doesn't work that way. Us humans carry everything that's happened to us through the rest of our lives. You can forget the details after a while, but the ache still lingers to remind you what it felt like when you hurt the first time.

Life continues is what my brother said earlier.

He's right. I feel like I've been so stuck in the past that I never had time to move on. I've been stuck right where Kyle left me—in that feeling of humiliation and regret.

I have to continue on before it eats me alive. I will not remain shackled to someone who never deserved me in the first place. I bet he lost no sleep after what he did to me, while I was up late at night questioning whether or not I'm capable of love.

I'm deciding right now to let him and the past go. I release it into the wind and watch it float away. I have to move on and starting now, I'm going to try and move in that direction.

I smile and let the wind carry me away as I get up and walk back to my dorm—feeling lighter with every step I take.

30

THE PARTY HAS BEEN going for about forty five minutes, and Holt has control of the music for now. I have yet to see any sign of Hads or her friends, and I know it was a little forward to leave her an invitation, but I didn't know what else to do.

I was surprised she even let me sit down considering she hadn't spoken to me in weeks, but after we talked, I felt like her walls were slowly coming down.

But I don't know if they're down enough to come to another one of these parties I'm throwing. I know she was overwhelmed last time she was here, and I don't blame her. These things can get rowdy very quickly.

I haven't moved from my spot in the front hallway because I want to keep my eye on the door in case she does show up. The party is raging around me, the music as loud as ever, and the only thing I'm focused on is the front door.

Jacks makes his way over to me and hands me a drink. "Your leg is shaking the floor more than the music is."

"I'm a little nervous she won't show up," I tell him. "It was a long shot, anyway."

"Just take a drink and relax." Jacks pats me on the back. "The night is still young, Grant."

"I know, but—"

Jacks surprises me by grabbing my head and turning it toward the front door where the prettiest girl in the world walks through it and into the house. She's all on her own because I don't see her friends trail in behind her and that makes my pulse race even more.

Not only did she accept my invitation to come to the party, but she also trusted me enough to show up on her own.

She looks uncomfortable and I can tell she feels out of place as she steps in and moves her head around until she sees me and her face lights up. I never thought having her look at me like she just did could mean so much. But knowing she feels relief seeing me at this party is making hope bloom in my chest.

She came. She actually came when I invited her.

She walks right over to Jacks and I, and my mouth is still dropped open because I can't believe she's in front of me.

"Glad you made it!" Jacks shouts to her.

"I have no idea what I'm doing here, but yeah, I made it."

"What?" Jacks says. Holt must have turned the music even louder because I can barely hear what Hads is saying.

I lean down to her ear so she can hear me better. "Do you wanna go somewhere quieter?"

She nods at me, and I knew she'd prefer it. The only reason I threw all these parties was so I could hang out with her and I can't do that if I can't hear her.

"Follow me," I say as I grab her hand in mine and Jacks salutes us as we leave. He's probably going to go find the guys and play beer pong or something, but all I want is to be able to hear Hads when she talks to me.

I head up to the second floor and head to the guest room Holt keeps for any of us guys who want to stay over after these parties.

"I already feel better," Hads tells me as she stands awkwardly in the doorway. I close the door, the sound of the music now muffled. "Thank you."

"Well, I left you that invitation for a reason, Hades. I'm just glad you showed up."

"I almost didn't," she says as she steps more into the room. She looks fucking phenomenal. She's wearing one of her usual skirts, but instead of her usual sweater vests, she's optioned for a backless long sleeve shirt. It's black with rhinestones scattered all over it. "These parties terrify me, and you scare the crap out of me, too."

"Me? Scary?" I press my hand to my chest. "Why are you scared of me?" I ask as I pat the ground next to me. I opted for the floor over the bed because I don't want her to think all I wanted when I invited her was to fuck. I just want to talk away from all the noise.

"Because you make me feel things, Grant. That's terrifying," she tells me.

I'm not sure what to make of that, but I think it's good. "Well, then let's just hang out."

"What does that entail?"

Has she never just hung out with a guy or someone while at a party? She sits down next to me, her legs tucked underneath her knees, and looks at me as if she's awaiting instructions.

"Okay, how about we play some stupid party games."

"Like what?"

I think for a moment before I speak again. "Okay, are you ready?"

"I guess." She eyes me with confusion.

"Kiss, marry, and kill: charts, books, and your ruler."

Her face drops, clearly not expecting me to say what I did and I laugh as I try to think about what she's going to choose.

"I hate you."

"Oh, come on. You can ask me one after, but I'm dying to hear your answer to this."

She pats her hands on her knees as she thinks. I knew it was going to be hard. I took three of her favorite things and pit them all against one another. "Okay, I would kiss books because I read books about kissing."

"Obviously."

She giggles when I agree. "I would marry my charts because I don't think I could survive without them, and I'd kill my ruler."

"That thing is practically attached to your hip. Care to explain that answer?" And then she smacks me.

"My hand is just as effective as my ruler."

I roll my eyes. I should have known that was coming.

She turns to face me more, and I smile knowing she feels comfortable enough to invade my space on her own. "Kiss, marry, and kill: hockey, the color pink, skating."

Damn, she's good. "I would kiss skating because it helps me clear my head when I think too much." This is almost too easy. "I would marry hockey, duh. And I would kill the color pink."

"And you still won't tell me why you hate it so much?" She tries to push me over, but fails.

"I'm taking that to my grave, Hads."

She rolls her eyes at me. "Fine, but I thought this was supposed to be us getting to know one another."

"Fine, then let's play a different party game. How about would you rather?" I ask her. "Have you played that before?"

"I have," she smirks. "You go first."

"Okay," I say as I start to think. "Would you rather never wear skirts again or every time you raise your hand in class, you get the answer wrong."

"Grant! That's impossible to answer!"

"That's why it's a hypothetical, Hads!" I smile as she scooches even closer to where I'm leaning against the end of the bed.

She throws her head back in annoyance. "I would…" she trails off, trying to think.

I like seeing her like this—unguarded, carefree, and having fun just sitting with me on the floor while the actual party rages underneath us. I couldn't care less about the actual party. The only place I want to be is right next to her, and no matter where we are, I'll be perfectly content.

My only goal for tonight if she showed up was to keep her out of her head and make sure she has a good time. I think I'm doing okay, and I guess if she pulls away after this, I'll have my answer. It's what she did last time I started to chip her walls down piece by piece.

"I think I'd have to go with the class one."

"And why is that?" I'm shocked. This girl cares more about her grades than anyone else I've ever met.

"Because I wouldn't raise my hand. Problem solved."

"How are you always finding loopholes for everything?"

"I'm a genius, Grant," she reminds me. "I can do anything."

"It's your turn, Hads," I tell her as I reach over and grab her hand. She takes it and puts both of our conjoined hands on her lap. It was so natural the exchange that just happened. It's as if we've done it a million times before.

The next words out of her mouth stun me so much that I think I misheard her.

"Would you rather kiss me or make out with me?"

Hadleigh

I CANNOT BELIEVE I just said that.

I mean, I was thinking about it, but I didn't think it was going to come out of my mouth. I haven't stopped staring at his face, mouth, and hands since I sat down next to him.

I've never felt like this before—never been so drawn to someone as much as I am to him. Normally, it would terrify me. I think the atmosphere of the party booming below, and the fact that Grant and I are alone in this room is making the normal fog on my brain disappear.

All I can think about is him. Him and the kisses we shared that night on the rink and all I want is to feel that way with Grant again. My guard isn't fully down and destroyed, but I know for a fact I want to kiss him.

And I think he wants to kiss me again. His eyes are sparkling like they always do when he looks at me, and his blue eyes are staring right into mine as if he wants to know every thought running through my head at the moment.

"What?" he whispers.

"You heard me." Last time, he kissed me. But this time, I want him to know I'm thinking about kissing him again. He may have surprised me last time, but this time, it was my turn.

"Hads, I didn't bring you up here for this," he tells me as he gets up and paces around the room, stopping so he can lean against the wall.

"I know," I tell him as I stand up from my spot. I don't move toward him because I can tell he needs to pace out his anxiety or something. I caught him way off guard, and seeing Grant all flustered is hilarious. "But I want you to kiss me again, Grant."

"Hads—"

I cut him off. "Grant, look at me." He complies, his hair falling all over his face. "You have to pick an answer. You have to follow the rules of the game."

He shakes his head. "We're not playing the game anymore, Hads."

"Humor me then," I say to him.

He's quiet for a few seconds and as soon as he locks eyes with me, he takes a few steps closer.

"Well, one leads to another," he tells me, still walking towards me.

"That is how it works most of the time."

He invades my personal space and I have to crane my neck to look up at him. "It only feels appropriate to start with a kiss, doesn't it?"

He reaches down and his hands go around my thighs before he lifts me up and my legs instinctually go around him like last time. "It does," I whisper, my heart beating fast as if it's going to fall out of my chest.

And then he lays me down on the bed, his hand braces my head for when it hits the mattress, and his lips connect with mine. I suddenly understand what all the romance books mean when they talk about their bodies coming alive at a simple kiss.

But there's nothing simple or plain about this kiss. Grant is caging me in with his body, and I can feel the heat coming off of him as he presses into me. My arms are around his neck and I try to get him as close to me as I possibly can while he deepens the kiss, a moan coming up his throat as his hands run all over my legs.

"You're perfect, Hads." He presses a kiss to my neck, softly biting it before he gets to my ear. "God, you're so fucking perfect."

"Grant," I breathe out and my hands fall from his neck. He grabs both of my hands in one swift motion and pins me to the bed.

"Let me make you feel good, Hads. Stay out of that pretty head of yours and be in this moment with me, okay?" He looks down at me as if I'm a new painting in a museum that was just hung up. "Please don't retreat from me. Just for tonight, don't run away and let me make you feel again."

Every part of me is screaming at me to leave to make sure I don't get hurt. But for the first time in a long time, I want to feel everything. And what Grant is making me feel right now is something I don't think I'll ever have words to describe. "Okay."

Then his hands are in my hair, tracing down my body, sweeping over my boobs and down my legs and I feel everything. Every small touch, every place his hands graze lights a fire underneath my skin, and it feels so damn good.

Grant flips us so now I'm on top of him, straddling his body as he keeps kissing me. His hands find my neck as he caresses a spot on it right below my carotid artery. "Does that hurt?"

"No, why?"

His cheeks flush as I look down at him. "I may have accidentally left a mark." He brings his hands up to his face as I go to smack him.

"Grant! What the hell?"

He only laughs, which causes me to laugh and the two of us spend the rest of the night chatting in between kisses before he eventually walks me back to my dorm, and kisses me goodnight.

31

 Hadleigh

I CAN BARELY FOCUS on this project I'm doing with Ryan because I'm convinced the cover up job I did on the bruise on my neck is horrible.

I've never had to hide a hickey before, and thankfully, Taylor let me borrow her color corrector when I came back to the dorm with it very visible on my neck.

I've been staring at my laptop looking over a source for our project but none of the words I'm reading are making sense in my brain. I seriously hope Ryan is doing something productive because I don't want to fail this project because of my distracted behavior.

Ryan and I got assigned to research the infamous Ted Bundy for our criminology project, and thankfully there's a lot to find about him and what he did, but I'm not sure how we're going to create a twenty page long report about him. According to our project guidelines, we have to have twenty five unbiased sources, but most of the things I've found have some sort of bias in them.

There are also way too many people out there who think Ted was framed, but that's a whole other thing.

"Hads, can we talk?" Ryan asks me from across the table.

"Yeah, I'm having a hard time finding credible sources—"

He laughs at me. "I don't want to talk about the project, Hads. I'm not worried about our grade, I think we'll be okay."

Now that's something I've never said. I worry about my grades for things I haven't even started. "What's up?"

He almost looks shy as he gains the courage to speak again. "We have another home game next Monday and I was wondering if you wanted to come?" I'm about to open my mouth and decline, but he beats me to it. "And before you say no, the team does this thing once a season where the players invite someone to wear their jerseys. I was wondering if you wanted to come and wear mine?"

Oh. That's interesting. I'm not a big sports person so I had no idea they do things like that, but it's cute, I guess. I'm still not too sure about it because I feel like Grant would have said something about it, but he never did. Maybe he asked someone else, like his mom or something?

"Ryan, I—"

He cuts me off again. "I get it. You're probably already wearing Grant's, right? I should have known." He smirks at me before he looks back at his computer.

"I'm not, but I wasn't aware this was a thing you guys did. It just caught me off guard, that's all."

He looks up at me, his face full of... pity? "Oh, Grant never asked you to wear his?"

"No, he didn't."

"So, you could wear mine, then?"

I could, but I don't know if I want to. "In theory, yes, but—"

"Perfect! Then it's settled," he says as he throws his laptop in his bag. "I'll drop it off to you in class Thursday."

I don't remember ever actually saying yes, but in typical male fashion, Ryan has assumed I'll do it just because he asked me. And before I can say no, he walks out of the library. I wasn't aware we were done talking about our project, but it's probably for the best since I was barely focused anyway.

I wonder why Grant would never mention this jersey thing to me. I haven't seen him since Saturday because the two of us have been busy with classes and he's been practicing a bunch. Plus, Grant and I aren't dating, so it's not like we're in constant communication all of the time. We've just kissed a few times and that's it. We're taking it slow, or maybe we're not going anywhere at all because I don't think my walls can ever fully come down.

I want to be all in with him, but the voice in the back of my mind is shouting at me that it's going to end terribly and no matter how many times he proves he cares about me, I still can't make myself believe it's all going to be okay.

I shake my head out of those thoughts and since I don't want to go this game alone, I pull my phone out.

Hads: Are you guys free for a hockey game on Monday night?

Ella: Absolutely! I'm bringing my own drinks this time.

Ella: Can Alissa come?

Hads: The more the merrier!

Paige: I'm totally in!

Amelia: If I say no, Paige will drag me anyway. So, no.

Paige: Ames, you're going and that's final!

Amelia: Fine, then I'm off to a country with no extradition laws. That way you can't make me go.

Paige: Which one?

Hads: I'm disregarding the entire back half of this conversation.

Ella: If our messages ever got leaked, people would commit us to an asylum or something.

Paige: Amelia is the one who makes jokes that I can't tell are jokes over text messages!

Ella: You guys together should be considered a state of emergency sometimes…

Hads: We can figure out a plan for Monday at book club.

Ella: Sounds good!

32

 **Hadleigh**

"WHAT THE HELL ARE you wearing?" Ella asks me as she walks up to where I stand outside of the arena.

"So, I may or may not have forgotten to mention why we're here in the first place."

"That's not Grant's last name," Paige says, a concerned look in her eyes. Amelia only giggles and Alissa definitely has no idea what the issue is with me wearing Ryan's jersey.

"Hads, what's going on?"

"There's this thing tonight where the players invite a friend to wear their jersey and Ryan asked me," I explain. "Don't make it a big deal because it's not."

"I've never heard of that being a thing," Paige tells me. "If it was, Grant would have asked you to wear his."

Ella moves her head around at all the people heading in around us. "Most of these people are wearing Grand Mountain apparel. I don't see anyone else wearing a jersey."

I look around, and sure enough, a sea of green, black, and white is around me. But I don't see any other jerseys from players being worn into the stadium—at least by any students.

"Whatever, let's just head in," I tell them.

The five of us start to walk into the arena and when we find our seats, they're closer to the ice than I thought they were. Ryan gave me these tickets, but I told him to get ones where we were last time. It looks like he didn't listen.

Ella excuses herself to go get some drinks before the game starts in a few minutes. The players from our team are gathered around the bench in some sort of huddle, and Ryan keeps making eye contact with me while he smiles. After the fifth stare, I ignore him.

"So, remind me again why you're wearing his jersey? I don't see many other people wearing a team member's jersey in the rink," Alissa asks me. "I'm very confused about all this."

"By the way he keeps staring at her, Ryan definitely has an ulterior motive," Amelia says.

"Amelia, you're wrong." But is she? I never actually answered Ryan about wearing this tonight, and when I tried to backtrack in class Thursday, he made me feel horrible if I were to say no. He told me he had nobody else to ask and he was thankful I agreed to do this for him.

I move my gaze to Alissa. "He asked me to wear it because it's a tradition or something. He didn't give me much of an explanation, but I agreed."

"Oh, that seems a bit odd." Alissa smiles and Ella hands her a drink as she comes back to sit down. "Thanks, babes. I don't think I could watch this without being at least tipsy."

"I said that last time too!" Ella is practically screeching. Who knew the sister of your rival could turn out to be a good friend? I certainly didn't.

I'm looking down at my phone when Paige starts nudging my arm, and I turn to ask her to stop when she points down at the team. In the huddle, looking right back at me, is Grant. I've never seen his face like that. My stomach drops because I know he noticed the number of the jersey I'm wearing, and my gut tells me something is very wrong by the way his face falls before he puts his helmet on.

"Is Grant mad at you or is he constipated?" Paige asks me, but all I can focus on is how tense his body just became. I see his helmet move between me and Ryan a few times, and it's now when I realize Ryan tricked me. He did all of this just to mess with Grant's head and probably mine, too.

"Oh, I'm so glad I came out of the apartment tonight. I do not want to miss the show that's about to happen when Grant beats the shit out of Ryan." Amelia chuckles and grabs a snack from her bag. Seriously? Does she walk around with snacks at the ready?

"This is like a jealousy scene from a romance novel come to life. I'm actually a little bit obsessed. Sorry, Hads." Alissa pats me on the shoulder.

"Ryan tricked me," I say to nobody in particular.

"You think?" Paige smacks Amelia as she says that. "Sorry, I mean, of course he did. Ryan's the worst."

"Grant and I are just friends, but why do I feel like the worst person in the world right now?" I not only feel like an idiot for falling into Ryan's trap, but I feel like I betrayed Grant in the worst possible way.

"I don't think someone you're friends with looks at you the way Grant is now," Alissa says to me.

"Do you often make out with your friends at parties you're directly invited to?" Ella asks, a smirk on her face. *She makes a decent point.*

"He looks like he wants to rip that jersey off of you and give you his instead," Paige says and I stare at her. "What? It happens in all the hockey romance novels we read! It could definitely happen in real life."

"No, he's just mad I'm wearing Ryan's." That's all it has to be. It's not like Grant is in love with me or anything. He's told me he falls fast but besides a few kisses, we haven't talked about whatever's going on. We don't have a label—that's our thing. We're Hads and Grant, two people who happen to know what the others' mouths taste like.

Even when I say it in my mind, I sound like a fool.

"Babes, you're insane if you think the way he looks at you is only friendly," Alissa tells me.

"Have Grant and I kissed before? Yes. Have we kissed on this very rink? Yes. Is he in love with me? No. Am I in love with him? No. Case closed."

"I've always been team HadsGrant in this love triangle," Paige says, smiling at me.

"This is not a love triangle! It's not love anything! There are no shapes, no love, nothing!" I say, my breath catching in my throat as the buzzer goes off to signal the start of the game. "Let's just watch the game."

"Ah, deflection. I've taught you well, Hads. My work here is done." Amelia puts her hand on her chest and hugs me from behind. She and Paige are sitting behind me, and I'm on the end seat next to Ella, who's between Alissa and me.

The team gets on the ice. Ryan's benched, but Grant is playing like usual. The face-off happens, and Grant isn't moving. He's stuck in his spot—staring at me. His trance seems to break after a few seconds because he suddenly bursts into action as the game unfolds.

I suddenly can't breathe, and thankfully, I'm wearing Grand Mountain merch underneath this because this jersey is officially coming off. I don't know why I've kept it on this long, anyway. I rip it off and throw it over the back of my chair and I want to smack myself for falling for this stupid trick.

I'm barely paying attention to the game before I hear Paige yell, her arm coming out in front of her. "Look!"

I look at where she's pointing—the other team has the puck and it looks like they're going to score. Jacks misses the interception, and Grant swoops in to try and protect the goalie from being scored on—I saw him do that hundreds of times at the last game I went to. This time, he misses, and the other player soars by him, and they score. The buzzer goes off and the other team celebrates the fact that they scored in the first three minutes of the game. It's now 1-0.

"Oof." Paige slumps in her seat.

"This is going to be a rough game," Ella says.

"What? It's only the first period!" I say. There's plenty more time for them to come back.

"This is an easy team to beat and Grant just fucked the play up. Even Jacks seemed confused, and normally they work well together."

Alissa smiles, trying to lighten the mood. "I'm sure it's just a rough start. There's still a lot of the game left." She stands up and cups her hands on her mouth. "Let's go Grand Mountain!" Ella joins her in cheering as she stands up and sips her drink.

Paige leans to my ear. "It might be an off night for him, but I think you had a bigger effect on him than you think."

"All athletes have off days. I'm sure it's not because of me," I lie. I know it is. Grant is a great player, and all I can see in my mind is the face he made when he saw me wearing Ryan's jersey. I wish I could go back in time and say no to Ryan before he talked over me and assumed I'd wear his stupid jersey.

Wanting to banish all my thoughts from my head, I grab Ella's drink and take a long sip before handing it back to her.

"Oh, absolutely." She smiles at me, and I wince.

"Who puts straight tequila in a flask?" She only shrugs and smiles. It's going to be a long night.

Grant

I GOT PULLED IN the final minute of the first period—I'm benched for the rest of the game. My head is not in it tonight, and I know why. A certain black-haired girl sitting in the stands wearing Ryan's jersey has fucked with my head. She took it off a little while ago, but I still can't get the image of it out of my head.

Ryan's fucking jersey.

There's no way she would do that just to piss me off. I bet he pulled some typical Ryan bullshit to get her to wear it and when I find out what, I'm going to beat the shit out of him. I don't care that he's my teammate. He's been nothing but an asshole the entire time I've known him.

My heart feels like it was run through the shredder, but I know there's something deeper going on. Hads and I have been connecting more and more the past week, and I'm trying not to jump to any more conclusions without talking to her first.

But Ryan is meddling and playing some sort of game with her, and I'm going to find out what he's doing. The only reason he's targeted Hads is because he hates me and wants to fuck with me.

Jacks skates up to the bench and stares at me. "What?"

"What the fuck is up with you? You're playing like shit." The one thing I like about our relationship is that I know he's not saying this to be rude. He's genuinely concerned because being benched is something that hasn't happened to me since junior league.

"I'm having an off night," I say what he already knows.

"Grant, you don't have off nights. You have a few misses here and there, but you always come back stronger. Something is clearly wrong." I flash my eyes to where she's sitting out of habit, and Jacks follows my gaze.

"Oh," he says.

"Yeah."

"And she's distracting you? What?"

"Look behind her," I tell him, noting that she took off the jersey and put it behind her where she's sitting. *At least she took it off.*

His eyes pinch together before he finally makes out the number behind Hads. "Why does she have Ryan's jersey?"

"I don't know, and I don't want to talk about it."

"Fine, just don't do anything too stupid."

"No promises," I tell him, my tone of voice indicative that I'll probably do something stupid.

The second period starts and we're tied one to one. This team is so fucking easy to beat—it should be a landslide—but it's not because Ryan decided to fuck it all up. Normally nothing could rattle me as much as this has, but for some goddamn reason, anything involving Hads always gets me worked up.

Hockey was the one thing that if I failed at, I could always put more work in and focus on bettering my skills. But being benched has put my mood down even further.

I've never been this in my head about a girl and it's fucking scary how fast she's been able to get underneath my skin.

She's directly across from our bench, and my eyes are like magnets—so fucking attached to where she's sitting. I keep stealing glances hoping she'll catch my eyes like she always does, but no matter how hard I try, her eyes are following the game. I can't read what she's feeling, and there must have been a reason as to why she took it off. I wonder what it was.

"Hey, Carter, fancy seeing you here." Ryan slides over to me on the bench.

"Yeah, I'm usually not here because I'm normally on the ice playing. No wonder we don't see each other often." I'm being short with him, and I know I'm probably adding fuel to the fire, but I don't fucking care.

I hate to sound like a petulant child, but he started it by messing with the girl I can't stop thinking about.

"That's low even for you, Grant. We made the same team, didn't we?"

I nod my head at him as I follow the puck on the ice. "I guess we did, but the only difference between you and me is that I care about my teammates. You couldn't give a shit who you fuck over as long as you win in the end."

"Oh, I'll win alright. In fact, I've already won, haven't I?" He slides a little closer to me. "She was wearing *my* jersey, wasn't she?"

I want to slam his head into the side of the rink. "And then she took it off because she realized this stupid game you were playing."

"Who says I'm playing a game with her?"

"Anyone could see it from a mile away. Stay the fuck away from her. She deserves better than you."

"Oh, and by better, do you mean you? Is that what you're getting at?"

Yes, actually. That's what I'm getting at. She deserves someone who loves making her talk just so he can listen. She deserves someone like me who only wants one thing—to make her happy. Ryan could never and would never do that. She's just another conquest to him.

"Boys, watch the game. Barnes, you might be going in soon!" Our coach yells from the other end of the bench.

"Got it, Coach!"

I shuffle away from him. "Just go away, Ryan. I don't have time for this."

"Fine. I'll leave you alone." He slaps me on the shoulder and returns to his original spot.

I've never wanted a game to be over as much as I do now. God, I can't stand this feeling. What would my dad say if he saw me? I look pathetic. He would probably tell me it's a minor setback and always to look ahead but all I feel stagnant. I'm a fucking mess.

One girl has collapsed me in a few months, and I wouldn't change a single thing about it. Sure, this could be another case of me falling too quickly and I could end up hurt, but something in my gut is telling me that this isn't going to end like the other ones.

Something in my body—whether its misguided hope or a gut feeling—is telling me that this girl could be the one. *The* one that everyone is always talking about.

But I can't push it with her. She's been hurt before and her walls are still up, but I think I could break them down. I want to break them down, but she has to let me in a little more first. I know she's scared, and all I can do is ease her mind and let her know she's safe with me. As I look up at her in the stands, she smiles as Paige points out something to her.

Maybe if it all works out, she could be a regular at these games—wearing my jersey instead. Fuck, that would be the best case scenario.

Grand Mountain scores again which brings me out of my haze, and I really need to pay better attention.

Get your head in the game, Grant.

As TERRIBLE AS THE game started, Grand Mountain came back and won two to one. Thank fucking God because if we lost, I would have blamed it all on me and my inability to focus.

I sat on the bench for basically the entire game, which allowed me to clear my head a little, but I still feel like shit. Today officially sucks, and

I need a shower. Coach gave us a pep talk—part of it about players not being distracted—and I know that shit is aimed at me. I'm a giant failure since I can't even do the one thing the team counts on me for. I sigh heavily as I slam my locker shut, grabbing my shit from the bench. I hear a voice as I grab my stuff.

"I can't wait to see her in only my jersey later. I know her pussy is tight." Ryan and the guys around him laugh.

"Who the fuck are you talking about, Barnes? Because if I remember correctly, she wore your jersey for about five seconds before she took it off for the rest of the game." I don't remember turning the corner, but it's too late now.

"That sweet little thing showed up wearing *my* jersey tonight, Carter. I bet I can get her to put it back on while she begs me to keep going."

I'm going to kill this motherfucker. "Say one more thing about Hads and you won't like where this goes."

The fucker smiles before he looks away from me. "Do you think that bitch can suck and fuck?"

I lose it. All I see is red before my fist connects to his face. I punch him square in the jaw, and fuck, it feels good. He deserves it after all he's said about her. Ryan Barnes is a piece of shit, and I'm surprised I haven't punched him sooner than this. All the fucker does is mess with people and make most girls uncomfortable.

How dare he call my girl a bitch? Ryan's the bitch. He's the one playing games with someone who clearly doesn't want him.

Jacks pulls me off of him and pushes me back. "Take a walk, Grant!"

"Stay the fuck away from her! If you even breathe in her direction, I'll kill you. Consider that punch your only warning." I don't wait for him to respond as I grab my stuff and get changed. Fuck the showers. I need to get out of here because if I don't, I'll be kicked off of the team on account of beating the crap out of my teammate.

And I didn't do all the work I did this semester to be kicked off of the team because of my own stupidity. Ryan deserves a lot worse than what I gave him, but I know Coach is going to hear about this.

Whatever he decides to do with me will be deserved. If I didn't put Ryan in his place while he was talking about Hads, I would have regretted it.

After I'm changed, I exit the locker room only to find the reason for me punching Ryan walking away from the doors. I notice Ryan's jersey folded by the entrance.

Was she waiting for him or me?

"Hi," is all she says. Her voice sounds defeated, and I can sense her walls being built up brick-by-brick again.

"Hey," I say, my voice gruff and strained. It's been a long night, and all I want is to sleep all my emotions off. But all I can see when I close my eyes is her wearing his fucking number on her back.

"I want to explain something," she tells me. "Can I walk you back to your apartment and we can talk?"

I nod, needing to get the fuck out of here. "Sure, but I'm walking *you* back."

"Got it." She smiles, and suddenly the world feels right again. The two of us are quiet as we walk before she finally speaks. "Ryan tricked me into wearing his jersey tonight. I'm eighty percent sure he did it to get inside your head, and I'm sorry."

"What did he tell you?"

And then she explains the bullshit Ryan told her about some fake tradition we do at one home game a year. I roll my eyes. He's such a fucking idiot, but I guess it worked out how he wanted it to.

"He has this way of making me feel bad if I were to back out. I should've just done it, but I was a coward. I'm sorry, Grant. I didn't mean to mess you up during the game, and I—"

I cut her off. "Hads, it's not your fault. It's Ryan's. We're both his stupid victims in whatever game he's playing."

She shakes her head. "I was naive and I let him walk all over me. It's my fault, so let me take some of the blame. You're the only one innocent here."

This time I shake my head. "Believe me, I'm not innocent. The things I thought about doing to him and you when I saw you wearing that jersey were borderline homicidal."

"What did you think about doing?"

I sigh heavily, wondering if I should tell her about what happened in the locker room, and decide the truth is always better. "Well, I thought about killing him but I ended up only landing one punch."

"He's not worth hurting yourself, Grant. And you once told me you needed your pretty hands to play hockey," she smirks at me.

"I do, but unlike me, Ryan deserved it." I adjust my bag on my shoulder as the cold breeze hits me in the face. It's a fairly nice night and walking back with Hads is the perfect end to this absolutely horrible day. Somehow, she makes everything better without even trying.

The rest of the way back to her dorm, the two of us are quiet, just enjoying each other's company. I can tell she still feels horrible about what Ryan did, and I wish I could tell her it's not her fault and she'd believe me, but I know that won't work.

By the time we stop in front of her building, all of my anxious thoughts have stopped.

"Thanks for walking me back, and I'm sorry again." She tugs on her long-sleeved shirt.

"Stop apologizing, Hads. You didn't do anything wrong."

"I fucked with your game, Grant. You were benched, and I—"

"Stop. Just promise me something," I tell her and she looks up at me. "Promise me you'll realize I'm right in front of you, and if you ever want to come to another game and wear someone's jersey, ask me. I'll happily hand you a clean jersey with my last name on the back."

"And your number?"

"Number eleven, Hads. It would be perfect on you, I think."

She tilts her head at me. "You think?"

"Well, I haven't seen you in it, so I can't know for sure," I joke with her. "But the only one you'll wear from now on is mine. Got it?"

"Understood, hockey boy." She looks down at my knuckles. "Is your hand okay? Do you need an ice pack or anything?"

I shake my head. "I'll be fine. The pain was worth it, in the end." I want to ask her so bad about if she's still going to go with Ryan to formal or whatever he asked her that day in the library, but I refrain. I don't want to fuck her head up more than it already has been tonight.

Before she goes into her dorm, she gets up on her toes and presses a kiss to my cheek.

"One bad game doesn't mean you're a failure," she tells me. "Just remember that."

I look down at her, suddenly having the urge to kiss her, but I stop myself. *Slow.* I'm supposed to be taking this slower than normal. "I will. Good night, Hads."

"Good night, Grant."

33

Hadleigh

Paige and Amelia are arguing about something in the book we read this month, and I'm completely zoned out. Ever since the game on Monday, I've had a thousand different emotions. I thought I was confused before, but nothing compares to what my brain sounds like now.

My brain sounds like a busy city, a sold out concert, and a car alarm all at once.

I canceled Ryan and I's study session last night under the guise of having too much to do, but I didn't want to see him. After the stunt he pulled on Grant and I, I loathe the fact that I have to do this stupid project with him from now until the end of the semester.

Don't even get me started on the stupid moment in the middle of the library. I'm kind of hoping he forgot all about that because the rumor mill on campus has, but I don't think he has. I'll probably end up backing out of the banquet if he asks me about it. I'm sure I could come up with some excuse that he probably won't hear anyway.

And then when I think about Grant and I's conversation after the game, my head spins even more. I would love some calm vibes going forward for the rest of the semester, but something tells me I'm not going to get what I wish for.

"Hads?" Ella gently touches my shoulder and brings me back into the conversation.

"Sorry, I got lost in my thoughts for a second." I grab my book and open it up. "What are we talking about?"

"Don't make me get the ruler. I'm not afraid to use it..." Amelia chuckles.

I roll my eyes. "I should have never told you guys about that."

"It's not a bad thing. I thought I was the kinkiest in this group but you might give me a run for my money." Ella's trying to lighten my sour mood, and it's working, I guess. We're all silent for a minute until Paige breaks it.

"Can we please talk about the elephant in the room? It's been killing me not to bring it up, and Ella I know you said not to, but I have to!" Paige turns to me. "Hads, what the hell is going on with Grant and Ryan?"

"Paige!" Ella shoots her a death glare. I love my friends for not wanting to provoke me, but I really need to talk this out and there's nobody better to do that with than my girls.

"I don't even know where to start."

So, I tell them everything. I tell them about Ryan and all the things he's been doing to mess with Grant this semester. I tell them what Grant said on our walk back to my dorm about me wearing his jersey and how if I ever need someone, he's always in front of me and willing to talk. I spare no details and when I look up, Paige is on the floor, and Amelia and Ella are speechless.

"This is the best day ever!"

"Is Paige having some sort of cardiac event? What is she doing?"

"He loves you, Hads. Or he likes you a lot. Either way, this is amazing!" I've never seen Paige on drugs, but if I had to imagine it, it would look a lot like this.

"Okay but wait, why did he punch Ryan? Did he ever tell you?" Ella asks me.

"He only told me that Ryan deserved it. I didn't ask for specifics." I've never known Grant to be a violent person, so whatever he said to make Grant punch him, he probably deserved it.

"Grant isn't normally the punching type." Amelia reiterates what I was thinking. "That's more reserved for Oliver and Paige—who threatens it but never follows through."

"Hey! One day it might happen. You never know." Paige gets off the floor and sits in her chair. "I think this proves he likes you. He wouldn't have punched Ryan unless he had a good reason and he walked you home again!"

"Yeah, I guess, but what do I do about my hesitation to fully get involved with Grant? Can you guys like untangle my brain, or something?" I slump down in my chair, hating that I keep going back and forth about this and can't make up my mind.

I have straight fucking A's—perfect grades—and I can't even understand my own brain.

"We can't untangle your thoughts, Hads. Sorry babe, but you have to do that yourself," Ella tells me.

I change the subject so I can chill the fuck out. "Can we please talk about this book because I truly believe these two characters are soulmates and nobody can tell me otherwise."

"I agree!" Paige shouts, and that stumbles into a long-winded conversation about the book. In my head, I kick myself for not mentioning one little detail about something Grant said yesterday—the thing that hasn't left my mind since he said it.

Promise me you'll realize I'm right in front of you.

I swear I stopped breathing for a second. I know he's right in front of me. In my bones, I know that, and if I were less terrified, I'd run full speed into Grant and I know he'd catch me.

I'm trying my hardest to do what my brother said, but it won't happen overnight. Time is everything—it heals all wounds or whatever—and I need to focus on moving forward. It's hard to do that when my head is pulling me in a different direction.

I zone back into the conversation and look at the girls around me. Even when we're passionately arguing about the books we read, I adore them. I smile and join the conversation, trying to dissolve the thoughts swirling around in my head when my phone buzzes, and the girls all look at me.

"What?"

"Is it him?" Ella asks me.

"It can't be the three of us because we're all sitting in front of you right now." Amelia makes a good point. I take my phone out and look at it.

"It's Ryan."

"Ugh," Paige says as I swipe my phone open and read what he said.

> **Ryan: Hey! Do you want to get coffee on Saturday? At the cafe in the library?**

> **Hads: Okay. We can work on the project since I canceled on Tuesday.**

> **Ryan: Yeah, that sounds good.**

"He wanted to work on the project on Saturday. I said sure."

"Why?"

"Because even though he pisses me off, I'm not going to let my grades slip." I did that once, and never again will I have a man be the reason I kill my grade point average.

And as we spend the rest of the night talking about books, our lives, and everything in between, the one thing I know for sure is that these girls are my favorite people to talk to when my mind feels like it's a dumpster on fire.

Thank goodness these girls exist.

34

MY HEAD HAS BEEN a mess for weeks, but this is a real low point for me. Right now, I'm doing what I usually do when things feel too loud—skating around the ice trying to clear my head.

It's not working.

This semester has been a shitstorm, and I should have known it would have been one when I was failing a class weeks into the semester. I feel like a giant failure in every aspect of my life. This season for hockey has been subpar at best. The team isn't meshing like we normally are and we're not ranked as high as we want to be in our league.

I have no idea what to do about Hads. We kissed and made out a few times, but after those things happened, she pulled away. If I could attach her to my hip so she stops overthinking when she's not with me, I would.

But I can't. So, I guess I'm stuck in this weird waiting period. I'm not giving up on her, though. I hope that this will all work out, whether it be this semester or at some point in the future. If I have to throw endless parties just to see her one more time, I will. I'll do whatever the fuck it takes to have her in my life.

I can't believe I never knew her before this semester. I can't believe she was on this campus and I never knew about her.

It's so crazy if I think about it too long. Hads existed on this campus long before I knew her, and now she's a person I can't imagine not knowing. I can't imagine floating through life while she lived hers, unaware that one another existed. I'm sure at one point or another our paths would have crossed, but I'm glad they decided to now instead of later.

I speed up my skating, needing to feel a bit more wind on my face as I take out the rest of my energy and try to drain it. I find comfort when I'm on the ice, but lately, it's been hard to regain my confidence—especially after being benched.

I should call my mom or something. I'm sure she'd make me feel better.

I do a few more laps, knowing I have to get back to my place soon to start studying, and as soon as I start to slow down, a flash of color catches my eyes.

Someone else is in here, and when I see Hads sitting up against the glass watching me with a small smile on her face, I wonder if I have telepathic powers or something. Every time I seem to think about her, she appears in front of me.

Maybe manifestation *is* real.

"You didn't want to join me?" I ask, my question echoing around the rink.

"Didn't want to fall and break my brain. I need it, you know."

"I'd like to think I'm a better teacher than that," I say as I leave the ice and head over to my bag. I feel her presence come up on me and it's taking everything in me not to think about what happened last time the two of us were alone in the rink like we are now.

"How did you know I was here?"

She looks down at her boots as she answers. "Well, I went to your place to see if you wanted to go on a walk or something, but Jacks opened the door. He told me you were here."

She went out of her way to find me so she could talk to me? I shouldn't be so excited about this, but I am. Normally, it's been me chasing her the entire semester.

But for once, she chased me. God, I feel like I could fly.

"How did you know where I lived?"

"My brother is in the same building as you. I had dinner with him tonight." She smiles.

"Your brother goes here?"

She nods. "You've probably never seen or noticed him because he's more reclusive than I am."

"Ah," I say as I throw my skates in my bag. I pat the bench next to me, and Hads sits down. "So, what can I help you with, Hades? I'm all yours."

She takes a big, deep breath before she speaks. "I know we've been kind of back and forth all semester and I feel like I owe you an explanation as to why."

"You don't owe me anything, Hads."

"But I do." She smiles at me. "You know about my ex-boyfriend, but what you don't know is how much I loved him and how much he humiliated me after things went down like it did."

"Hads, really—"

She reaches over and grabs my hand. "I have to say it, Grant. Once I say it out loud, I can release it into the air and it'll hopefully go away."

I motion for her to continue and she does.

"He was the first person I ever loved. I've been reading romance novels for my entire teenage and adult life, and when I met Kyle, I felt the feelings they describe in the books. I felt the butterflies, the sparks—all of it. I convinced myself that he was the one for me and when he asked me to be his girlfriend, I was ecstatic. I had never felt that way before and after watching my friends fall in love throughout high school, it was finally my turn."

"I know the feeling. It's even more special the first time." Everyone can remember the way you feel when someone turns into something more for you. It happens to every human on the planet at one point or another. Love is a universal experience, much like grief. Everyone feels it and sometimes it can swallow you whole.

"It started off okay, but towards the end, he wouldn't talk to me in school, he would only text me late at night, and he would blow off our dates. I was so confused."

Who in their right mind would stand up Hadleigh Baker? God, I'd kick their ass if I wasn't so happy she was here with me now.

"And then I confronted him before the big pep rally at our school. I had to work up the courage for a week until I finally exploded. I asked him in front of the entire football team why he didn't want to be seen with me and why he was treating his girlfriend like he was."

"What happened then?" I ask, not sure if I really want to hear the answer.

"He laughed at me—so did the entire football team. And then they all told me about this bet the team had about seeing who could fuck the most girls during the school year."

This is horrifying. What kind of sick fucking people are they? It's not cool at all to play with people's feelings like that.

"Kyle—my ex—was winning. And apparently, the team had a bet to see who could deflower me first. My high school was a lot like Grand Mountain in terms of the rumor mill. Rumors that were true and false spread through it like wildfire and the sports teams basically ran the school."

"I'm sorry, Hads."

She takes another deep breath. "It's okay, Grant. But I owed you an explanation as to why I've been pushing and pulling away from you. It's hard for me to trust anybody—even myself. I know I trust you, but the small voice in my head is holding me back."

"Hads, I know me saying this isn't going to help, but I would never do that to you. All I would want is to make you happy." I squeeze her hand in mine and she smiles.

She nods. "I know, but be patient with me, okay? This semester has been eye-opening, to say the least, but in a way, I'm thankful for these past few months. I've grown and I'm on the way to healing from the past and I'm proud of myself for that."

I smile, unable to stop it from shining through my face. "I'm proud of you too, baby." I press a small kiss to the top of her head as she leans into my arm. "Does this mean you see a future with me?"

She shrugs. "I don't know, but this is the first time I've thought about their being a possibility of one."

When I get back to my apartment, I'm going to run laps around it. "One of these days, I'll break down those walls of yours, Hads."

"I'm not totally sure how to get them down yet, but if anyone can break them down, it's you."

I grab her chin with my free hand. "Are you giving me permission to pursue you officially?"

She purses her lips together before she smiles. "I guess I am."

I release her chin from my hand and she nuzzles back into my side. "One day I'll tell you about all my relationship demons and then you'll realize we're not so different."

"Is that so?" She rubs her hands together in her lap. "How do you still hope love exists when you've been burned so many times?"

I take a second to think because I have a few answers to this question. "Well, lots of reasons. My parents showed me growing up what real love looked like, and when my dad died, it was hard for my mom to recover. Hell, it was hard for both of us, but when I got older, I don't know how she did it. She lost the love of her life and still had to raise me. And then I started to think about how I'm a culmination of the love they shared. I literally wouldn't exist if my parents never loved one another."

"That was beautiful."

"So, yeah, I've been used, cheated on, and fucked over so many times by love. But I exist because of that emotion, not in spite of it, and that's all I ever need to know going forward if love truly exists."

The two of us stay on the bench for a few more minutes, just taking in the weight of all we talked about tonight and letting it digest in our brains. I walk her back to her dorm, kiss her goodnight with a peck on her cheek before I jog back to my apartment.

On the way, I text Jacks and our other friend Brendan to meet me at our place. I have a plan to start concocting.

> **Jacks: Did you forget I lived here? I'm already here.**

> **Brendan: Is Grant having a mental breakdown? If so, I'm on the way.**

> **Grant: Guys, just shut up. I need your help. Hurry.**

I shove my phone back into my pocket and open the door to my building. Jacks is by the stairs with a sly look on his face.

"What's wrong with you? Are you having an allergic reaction?" I ask him.

"No, just excited. Your text seemed urgent, so I assume it has something to do with the visitor I had asking about you earlier."

Shit, I forgot he saw Hads tonight. So much for making this a surprise. "Maybe it does. Where's Brendan?"

"On his way." Jacks puts his hand on my shoulder. "I'm proud of you, buddy. I know it's been a hard semester for you, and I'm glad that something good will come out of it."

"Thanks, man. I appreciate it. It has been a difficult year, but Hads is the light at the end of the tunnel."

"Are you guys about to kiss? Should I give you the room or something?" Brendan walks in and stops next to us. He's not on the hockey team, but we all sat together at orientation and have been friends ever since. His wavy blond hair is all over the place—probably because he ran here. He sounds a bit out of breath.

"No, we're not. Let's go," I say as we all file into the apartment. Jacks immediately goes over to the couch and sits down, while Brendan opts for the small chair we have at the desk in the living area.

"So, what's going on? Why did you need us here so late?"

"I need help with Hads." Brendan is all caught up on what's been going on this semester between Hads and I, so he's another head I can use to figure some shit out. "I need to do something to help prove to her that I'm boyfriend material and that she won't regret being my girlfriend. Ideas, people. What do you got?"

Jacks takes a sip of water and points at me. "You know there's a Taylor Swift song for this. It's literally called *How You Get the Girl.* Maybe listen to that a few hundred times and you'll be set."

"Yeah, that's a good idea. Plus, I'm not an expert at relationships like Jacks is. He has Claire and I have nobody. I would listen to him." They both high-five each other. Seriously? This has not been helpful at all.

"You guys are terrible at this," I tell them.

"Maybe just be there," Brendan says.

"Be where?"

"Wherever she is. That forced proximity bullshit in romance books that people love so much." Jacks and I both stare at him. "What? I have a sister! She goes on and on about this shit during dinner. That and the one-bed trope, or whatever. She goes crazy over those two. It's funny." Brendan commutes from about fifteen minutes away. I've met his family a few times, and they're all hilarious.

"What about a flash mob?" Brendan asks.

"No."

"Hold up a stereo in front of her dorm?" Jacks says.

"Absolutely not."

"Cover her room with flowers?" Brendan says.

"Maybe? Flowers die super quickly, so that's not ideal."

"Buy her like a hundred new books?"

"Something more like getting her to trust me that doesn't break my bank account. Also, not something from a rom-com I've never seen." The two of them go silent.

"Well, clearly you have seen them if you know those suggestions are from rom-coms." Jacks counters.

I sigh heavily and slump down on the chairs. "This is not going to work."

"Come on. We have all night. Let's go to the whiteboard and draw up some ideas that aren't from Brendan's little sister."

"Fine, but we're ordering pizza," Jacks says.

There's nothing like a night spent with your best friends trying to figure out how to get a girl to fall in love with you, but I guess there's a first time for everything.

35

Hadleigh

"Paige, I'm not going to get murdered in a public place during the day. You and Amelia can stay in your apartment." I just got back from my morning walk with Oliver when Paige called me saying I should cancel my project session with Ryan. I offered to do this because we missed a session, and I do not want to get behind on this. We've got about two months left of the semester, and I can't afford to be behind, especially with final exams creeping up on me.

"What if he slips something into your drink? I don't trust him!" She's shouting through the phone, and I have to pull it away from my ear. I hear Amelia in the background telling her to chill out.

"Paige, it's going to be fine. Stop worrying so much about me. I can handle myself."

"I know, I know. Don't tell Ames, but I had a small latte this morning." She's whispering now. Shit. Paige having coffee equals a panic attack. "Okay, I have to go. Text us if you need us!"

"Sounds good. Please don't show up in the library with wigs and—" She hung up.

> **Hads: Just wanted to give you a heads up… Paige had coffee this morning.**

> **Ames: That explains a lot.**

> **Ames: Thanks, and be careful today. Paige might be hopped up, but she is right. Be careful.**

> **Hads: I will. Promise.**

I do my usual morning routine, and I'm packing my bag to leave when Taylor walks in.

"Hey, girl. Where are you headed? Do you want to grab some breakfast?"

I notice she's in the same outfit as last night. Good for her. "I'm off to the library cafe to work on a project. Rain check? I could probably do dinner tonight."

"That sounds good. The project with Ryan right?" She's eyeing me curiously as she waits for my answer.

"Uh, yeah." I shift my bag on my shoulder. "Why are you looking at me like that?"

"Come sit," she says as she pats her bed next to her. I comply and plop onto her soft blanket. "I know you never really knew about most of the sports guys on campus, and I'm sure people have told you about Ryan by now, but he and I are friends, I guess."

My eyebrows raise. "No, I didn't know you were friends with Ryan, I thought you just wanted to fuck him?"

"Well, yeah, but that's only because I've heard whispers about him and apparently the sex is good." She nudges my shoulder with hers. "He's a natural flirt, and he's not a relationship guy. I don't know what he's told you, but he never has real relationships and he never sleeps with someone more than once."

"Ew," is all I can say.

"Exactly. Just be careful if he's flirty with you. He's probably only thinking about one thing and one thing only. And because you're hanging with his teammate so much, he probably has something else in play, too."

"I will be," I say as I lean my head on her shoulder. "I'm not Ryan's biggest fan anyway. Especially after what he did in the library in front of a ton of people."

"I guarantee that was part of his plan the entire time. You know you don't have to go with him if you don't want to, right?"

I nod. "I know. I'll probably tell him at some point because I don't want to go to that stupid banquet or whatever." I'm not saying I'd rather go with Grant, but the bullshit of Ryan needing a date to an end-of-the-year hockey banquet seems phony as fuck.

"Good." She smiles as she gets up and grabs her shower caddy. "I'll text you later so we can have dinner, but I need a shower."

"See you, Tay."

She throws me a wave as she heads into the showers and I head off to the library.

Ryan's already in a booth when I walk through the doors, a coffee already on the table in front of him. "Hey, I'll go order mine, I'm going to need it. Can you watch my laptop?"

"Of course. Does it do tricks?"

"Sorry, what?" I look at him, confused about what he said.

"I was trying to make a joke." He runs his hand through his hair. "Guess it didn't land how I wanted it to. My bad."

I give him a weird look and go up to the counter to order. There aren't many people around, so it's pretty quiet here. I'm glad because all I'm trying to do today is get further on our project and leave so I can get started on the rest of my homework.

Our project is simple, but it's a lot of work. Researching and putting together all the information we find has been the most challenging part. Each group was assigned a different serial killer. Paige and Oliver got the Unabomber—someone Paige was very excited to get. Ryan and I got Ted Bundy. Paige laughed when I told her because she'd compared Ryan to him a few times before.

"So, I made this chart and put together all the things we have on Ted if you want to look at it."

"Damn, Hads. You really do like making charts."

"Don't knock the charts, dude. They're helpful." He looks like he's judging me, but I wave it off. We've been working on the project separately for fifteen minutes before he changes the subject. "So, what has been your favorite book you have read this year?"

"Difficult question but I think we should—" I'm about to say we should focus on the project but he cuts me off.

"But if you had to pick a favorite, which one would you pick?"

"I would probably say—"

Another voice cuts me off, but it's not Ryan. "The one with all those kisses on the cover. I saw her holding it the most."

Grant stands at the end of the booth, staring down at me with a huge smile on his face as if he knows he's right.

Which he is, of course. That *was* my favorite book so far this year.

"Grant, nice to see you," Ryan says, clearly trying to get him to go away.

"So, Hades, my favorite book this year—thank you for asking, by the way—has been Gatsby."

I roll my eyes but I can't help my smile. It was probably the only book he read this year, but the fact that he chose the one that I tutored him on definitely isn't a coincidence. "That's a good one," I say to him.

"Actually, the reason I wanted to find you was because I'm trying to branch out a little. Do you have any other recommendations for me? Besides your favorite, because I already rented that one out from the local library, but I need more." He smiles at me before sliding himself into the booth. I shuffle over, wanting to give him enough room. I'm sandwiched between Grant and Ryan, and I'm definitely more comfortable being next to Grant.

"Grant, leave," Ryan snaps, trying to be nice but it doesn't come across that way.

"Why do you want me to leave? Am I intruding on this date or something?" Grant asks.

"It's not a—"

"Yes, you are," Ryan cuts me off, but I know Grant heard me over him.

"Uh, uh." He holds up his finger to shush Ryan. "Can you let Hads speak? I want to hear it from her."

"We're working on a project together," I say as I look into Grant's eyes. "It's not a date."

"Great! Now, Hades, I have a few questions about chapter seven of Gatsby."

"Grant, leave. We're working on a project and you're distracting us," Ryan insists this time.

"Ryan, she was my tutor and I have a couple of questions. You'll get your time, okay?" Grant turns back to me. "May I?"

"Ask away," I say to him, and I can feel Ryan tense next to me. He's probably pissed, but I don't give a shit. He made me uncomfortable in the worst way possible. He can handle this small intrusion that nobody is paying attention to.

"Are you sure Gatsby and Nick aren't in love?"

"Grant, you've got to be kidding me. You really think—" Grant cuts Ryan off again.

"Yes, I really do think they are in love. Hadleigh? Confirm or deny."

"As I've said before, the book is about Gatsby's relationship with all these people, but Nick and Gatsby's relationship is at the center. Though many online users would say otherwise—they're not in love." I think it's funny how he's latched onto this small detail. I'm sure there's fanfiction I could send him about Gatsby and Nick.

"I knew it! I knew there was at least a chance. Like I said before, love always wins."

"Okay, Grant, is that all? We have more work to do." I can tell Ryan is mad at the situation, so I might as well diffuse it before it gets too out of hand.

"Yes, that is all. Apologies for the intrusion." He gets up from the booth and stops before he leaves.

"Actually, one more thing, Hades. I'm wondering where I could get some good pens and sticky notes."

"Uh, I usually get mine online or in any supply store. Why?"

"No reason. I just figured you know where the best ones are. Thank you!" He slaps the table before walking away, a pep in his step that makes me giggle.

"Why does he call you that?" Ryan asks after a few seconds of silence.

"Call me what?"

"Hades. That seems kind of rude."

"Oh, it's just a nickname he has for me." I didn't even catch Grant using it. He must use it so much that it's ingrained in my brain now. It almost feels weird when he uses my full name. "When I first met him, I called him a hockey boy, so he returned the favor by calling me Hades. We only used to do it during our sessions, but it kind of seeped out. So, back to good old Ted, okay?" I change the subject because I don't want to talk about Grant with Ryan anymore. That's not what we're here for.

Ryan and I work for another hour and then call it. Thankfully, he wasn't untoward in any way, just a bit awkward and annoying.

It looks to me like Grant is really coming after me, and I'm sure he has a few tricks up his sleeve to break my walls down. I can already feel my defenses weakening, and every interaction we have only seals our fate more and more.

I can see myself falling for him, and that scares the crap out of me.

36

"Great practice tonight, boys. We have playoffs next week, so get some sleep and keep those grades up!" Our coach dismisses us, and as I'm headed into the locker room, Jacks stops me before I can grab all my shit.

"Have you had a chance to do what we talked about? Brendan keeps asking me, and I'm curious as well." He eyes me and I nod.

"I've started, but I still need to get some things."

"Dude." He smacks my shoulder. "It's Wednesday. Maybe go to book club and walk her back to her room or something. They meet in the same classroom every week."

"That sounds creepy," I tell him.

"Or ask the other girls for help. Do whatever you want, Grant, but make sure it gets done." He slams his locker and grabs his shit. "Do you want me to grab shit for our party coming up?"

I knew I forgot to do something. "Yes, please because I forgot we were throwing one at our place soon."

He smirks at me before he walks away. "I figured."

Ten minutes later, I find the classroom Jacks told me they meet in, and take a deep breath before I walk into the room. The door is already open, but I'm going to knock so I don't scare them into thinking I'm someone randomly walking in on them.

Brendan's sister helped me get this thing started. She told me all about where I could get Hads' favorite book and explained all of the shit to me about highlighting, tabbing, and all that shit. It was *very* confusing, but I'm sort of coming around to understanding what all of this lingo is. She made me buy certain kinds of tabs and highlighters, but I need to see exactly what she uses so it all matches.

And that's how the book girls come in. I think they could either help me and steal the supplies, or they could tell me what to do.

I knock, but I don't see Hads so I assume she left already. Knowing her, she probably left early to go study, which is good for me. When I first met Hads, I wasn't one for begging. Now, I'd get on my fucking knees if it made her happy. Oh, how the times have changed.

"Hello, book club. How's the reading going?" I ask as I take a look around. All of their faces are equally surprised and... giddy, I think?

"It's going," Paige says, a giggle falling from her mouth.

"Oh, this ought to be good," Amelia says, pulling out some crackers from her bag.

"It's nice to see you again, Grant," Ella says as she walks over to me. "What can we do for you?"

"Are you looking for Hads?" Paige asks me, a smile beaming off of her face still.

I smirk as I sit down. "I am, actually, but I'm kind of glad I didn't find her."

"Why?" Amelia asks me.

"I need your help. I'm doing this thing for Hads, and I need you guys to help me verify a few things."

They all lean forward towards me, intrigued at my vague ass question. When I start to explain my plan and basically swear them all to secrecy, they agree to help me. I sigh with relief because all this book stuff confuses my brain, but I'd do anything for Hads.

"That's the cutest thing I've ever heard!" Paige says.

"I think Hads is going to love that," Amelia agrees.

Ella smiles at me. "We can get you what you need."

"Thank goodness. I thought I was going to have to sneak into her room and steal a bunch of stuff."

"We can distract her if you still need to do that! Ah! I'm a pro at sneaking into places!" Paige claps her hands, excited at the possibility of breaking and entering. *Is that normal?*

"Forgive her excitement. She's really into true crime," Amelia says.

"Paige has never even hurt a fly. Don't let her scare you," Ella tells me.

"I won't," I smirk. "But where's Hads? I assume she left to go study or something." My gut is telling me something is wrong, and since I haven't heard from her in a few days, the worry picks up even more.

"She has been down and out for a few days," Ella tells me. "She thought it was allergies with spring coming but she's barely gotten out of bed."

"She's sick?"

"Seems that way," Amelia tells me.

"Have you guys seen her? Is someone taking care of her or are you guys taking shifts because I would love to help—" I stop because they're all laughing at me. "What?"

"Hads would bite one of our hands off if we tried to take care of her. We tried to go to her room, but she wouldn't let us in. She doesn't want us to get sick, but that's an excuse because she hates when people do things for her." Ella grabs her bag as she stands up. "I can already see your brain working, and if you go over there and she turns you away, don't be surprised."

Paige's eyes light up as she stands, too. "Or bring her some tea!"

"Well, thank you for your help. I appreciate it." I smile as I stand up and speed walk for the door. "See you guys around, I'm sure!"

I shove out the doors and down the steps. I'm heading to the store, and then I'm heading to a certain stubborn girl's dorm room to nurse her back to health.

I STOPPED AT A nearby pharmacy to grab a bunch of different things. I've never nursed someone back to health, but my mom has done it for me a hundred different times growing up, so I think I have everything I need.

I bought a bunch of different crackers because those used to be all I could keep down when I had the flu. A bunch of tea because Paige never told me which she liked best, and even some honey in case her throat hurts. Along with a bunch of medicine, I'm sure Hads will feel better after no time.

If she lets me in, that is.

I head into the building, and her door is unlocked. I texted her roommate and she's staying with a friend so she doesn't catch whatever Hads has, so it should just be her in here. I slip in, and when I don't immediately get yelled at, I assume she's sleeping.

I quietly set all the bags on her desk, trying not to make too much noise. I turn her tea kettle on and look around at the small tea station she has. I recognize the box and it's empty, but thankfully, I bought some more at the store. This has all been way too easy, and if she wakes up and sees me here, she's definitely going to throw something at me or probably murder me.

I head to her book cart and grab a few tabs off of it, not enough to make her notice they're gone, but enough so I can start my side project for her. The kettle starts making a noise, and I see her stirring on her bed. Fuck. I am *so* busted.

Hadleigh

I'VE SURVIVED ALMOST TWO years on campus without getting sick, but one goddamn virus going around campus like wildfire is what finally gets me.

Not only have I missed multiple classes and assignments, but I don't see an end to this in sight. My body still feels weak even though I've been sleeping all day. The only good thing is that I can finally keep water down, but I ran out of crackers yesterday and didn't want to ask anyone to get them for me.

I'm running on water, remnants of flu medicine, and sweat even though my body is freezing fifty percent of the time.

I woke up because I heard a noise, and since I think it's Wednesday, I assume the girls are coming over after book club. I told them a thousand times I don't need anyone to take care of me, and I even told Oliver to go away earlier. Paige probably told him I was sick, but he came into my room for two seconds to bring me some juice.

I hear movement and my eyes have yet to adjust to the darkness, but someone comes and sits on my bed, holding a glass of something up to my face.

"Ella, I said you don't have to take care of me. I'll be fine in a few days." I groan as I sit up fully.

"While Ella does seem like the one to take care of all you girls, it's just me." I know that voice. Why do I know that voice? "Drink this, baby. It'll help your stomach."

"Grant?" I ask. "What are you doing here?"

"I stopped by the book club to ask you something after practice, but you weren't there." He sets the glass down. "The girls told me you were sick, so I stopped at the pharmacy and grabbed some stuff."

"I don't need you to do this, Grant."

"Too bad." He smiles at me as his face comes into focus. God, he's so pretty. I was right all those months ago to call him a pretty boy. "They told me you were going to be stubborn about this. I figured if I showed up here you would be too sick to turn me away when all I want to do is help you."

"Grant—"

"Please just let me help you, Hads," he says, his voice low and tender. I look around my room and notice bags all over my floor and the drink was warm when he put it up to my face, and I can smell tea in the air—my favorite kind.

Did he do all of this for me?

"Can I have the cup?" I ask and he hands it to me. I take a sip and it's perfect. Of course he made it just the way I like it. "I didn't want anyone else to get sick, so I sent them all away."

It's a lie. I hate when people make a big fuss over me, but I'm nowhere close to feeling better. I'm weak and I have no energy to fight against anyone at the moment. Plus, Grant looks like he actually wants to help me.

"I don't care if I get sick," he says as he holds my cup for me. "As long as you get better, I'll succumb to the plague for all I care."

"The plague? Do I really look that sickly?" I joke.

"You know I always think you look beautiful, Hads." He tucks a spare stand of my hair behind my ear. "How's the tea? Did I make it right?"

"It's perfect, Grant. Just like you—always so freaking perfect." I hear him shuffling around at my desk and wonder when he got over there. I didn't feel my bed move when he got up. "What are you doing? Did you ask Paige how to build a bomb and this whole ruse was to blow me up?"

"I'm glad being sick has not changed that damn attitude of yours. Nobody on this campus can joke with me as much as you do. Nobody's quite like you, Hads." More shuffling. "Hades, what's your favorite type of cracker?"

"My favorite what?"

"Cracker," he states plainly. I feel like my brain has become a lot smoother since I got sick.

"Usually saltines. I've kept a few down, but I ran out yesterday." He returns to my bed and hands me a box of them.

"Thank God I bought every variety because I'd hate to have come here empty-handed." He smirks as he opens the box for me, handing me a sleeve of them.

Oh. I feel nauseous again, but it's not from my stomach bug. He bought every single kind of cracker for me. This has got to be some sort of fever dream or something.

"Thank you for the tea and the crackers, but you can leave now. I'll be okay." I try to flip over, but I know he's not going to listen to me and leave.

"What kind of person would I be if I left you here like this?" he says as he holds out a hoodie or some sort of clothing to me. "Take these."

"What is it?"

He cocks his head at me. "Seriously? Miss 4.0 doesn't know what sweatpants are?"

"I know what they are, but why are you giving them to me?"

"Hades, you're wearing jeans while you're sick with the flu. How have you been sleeping in these? That's definitely your serial killer trait."

"You've talked to Paige, then." I grab the sweatpants because I won't admit this out loud, but I have been uncomfortable. When I first came down with the flu, I fell asleep in the clothes I wore to my classes that day, and I haven't been back up since. He's got a point, I guess. "Turn around. I don't want you getting any ideas."

"You can blindfold me if you want. I don't mind." He turns and faces my closet as I take my jeans off and throw them on the ground.

"Gross," I say as I realize his double meaning.

"I'm kidding, Hades. Just put the pants on, please."

"I am! Give me a second!" I'm pulling them up my body when I realize it says Grand Mountain hockey down the side of it. "Are these your sweatpants?"

"Yes, but now they're yours. They look much better on you than they do me. They belong on you, Hads." I don't know how he knows that since he's facing the other way, but whatever.

I crawl back into bed and get under my covers. "You can turn around."

He complies and as he cleans up the mess he made, I think he's going to leave, but he doesn't. He plops onto my twin bed with my laptop in his hands.

"What are you doing?"

"We're going to watch a show, and hopefully, you'll fall asleep."

"I've been sleeping for days," I tell him.

"And you need rest. Your body is purging a sickness," Grant tells me, handing me some medicine. "Take this and it should help."

I grab the medicine from him, and normally, I hate being doted on, but this isn't bad. He's fighting me at every turn, and I find myself enjoying his company even through my sick haze.

I hear the familiar tune of my favorite show's opening credits as Grant settles into my bed.

"This is my favorite show, but I'm assuming you already knew that."

"I'm aware," he says, not elaborating on how he knew that.

The show plays for a few minutes, and I feel overcome with a sense of peace as I sit here with Grant and watch my favorite show with him. I guess I never liked someone taking care of me before, but when Grant is the one to do it, it makes me feel good knowing someone cares about me enough to go through all this trouble.

I never felt like I was worth it before, but with him, he makes me feel like I deserve it. Like I'm worth all the hassle he went through tonight.

"Hads, you're supposed to be sleeping."

"I love this show," I say as I yawn. "It's hard to sleep when I'm having such a good time."

"Sleep, baby. I'll be here in case you need anything."

Before I can think of something snappy to say, my eyes start to close, and I feel my head on Grant's shoulder as I fall asleep.

I STARTLE AWAKE FROM the fever-induced dream I had of Grant coming to take care of me, only to swing my legs over my bed and step on something on my floor.

But it's not something, it's someone. Grant is asleep on my floor, and I'm having flashbacks to when Paige fell asleep on my floor one time when we were hanging out in my dorm room. She said my floor was really comfortable, but she says that about every floor she falls asleep on.

I softly kick him to wake him up, and he yawns awake as he stretches his body out on my floor.

"Hey." He smiles as he notices me. "How are you feeling?" He stands up, still wearing the same clothes as yesterday.

"Well, I can stand up." I pause because I want to ask him for something, but I can't quite get the words out.

"Do you want to try taking a shower while I make you some tea?"

I nod. "And you'll be here in case I need you?"

"Anything you need me to do for you, Hads, I'll do it. Just say the word."

That's the hardest part about being me, though. I hate outright asking people to help me. I've always had the mentality I can do everything myself. "Okay."

He presses a kiss to the top of my head. "I know asking is the hardest part, but I'll try to read your mind until you understand that doing things for you isn't a chore for me. It's a privilege."

A privilege. "Thank you," I say with a whisper.

"Any time, baby."

<h1 style="text-align:center">37</h1>

<h1 style="text-align:center">Grant</h1>

It's been a few days since I nursed Hads back to health, and all I've been able to think about is her. I've heard from her a few times because I've been checking in on her every hour of every day, hoping that she's feeling better. I saw her at the dining hall yesterday, and she looked less pale and sweaty, so I know she's feeling a lot better.

I was going to invite her to the party Jacks and I are throwing at our apartment tonight, but I don't want to risk her slipping back into her sickness, so I've let her be. Plus, this is only for the sophomore guys on the hockey team who live in our building, and it's less of a party and more of a get-together.

My phone buzzes and as soon as I see who it's from, I can't help the smile on my face.

> **Hads:** Just checking in. You don't feel sick, do you?

> **Grant:** Nope. Your sick germs stayed with you, Hades.

> **Hads:** Good.

> **Grant:** I'd take all of your germs if it meant you were giving something to me.

> **Hads:** I don't think that sounds how you wanted it to.

> **Grant:** It didn't. Please disregard.

I'm annotating Hads' favorite book when Jacks comes in and drops all of his shit in our living area.

I—the guy who used to hate the library—am now reading a book because the girl I like said it was her favorite. And the only reason I'm doing this is to put a smile on her face and prove to her I'm in this for the long haul.

"Dude, people are going to be here soon! Why haven't you set anything up yet?"

I close the book and set my highlighter down. "Slow your roll there, Moore. The drinks are cooling in the fridge, all the snacks we bought are in the pantry, and the karaoke machine is charging."

"What? Karaoke?"

"I never said karaoke."

"What is your weird obsession with karaoke?"

I throw my hands up. "It's fun and it lifts people's spirits up!"

Jacks only groans as he heads into his room, and I don't know why he's so freaked out. It's only a small gathering. It's not like it's going to get too out of hand.

So, it's officially gotten out of hand.

I don't know how this happened—really, I don't. It was only supposed to be a few of us doing some team bonding since we were going to be together for two more years on the hockey team.

But instead of there being only a few people in our apartment, it's now filled with a bunch of other random people, the music blaring like it does at the hockey house. It's going to get out of hand soon, and I'm worried we're going to get a noise complaint filed on us. I really don't want to get kicked out of our place because someone opened up the invite to the rest of the fucking school.

Jacks runs up to me, his eyes popping out of his head. "Dude, where the hell did all of these people come from?"

"I don't know! I didn't invite them!" Erikson—another sophomore on the team—passes by me and I grab his arm. "Do you know anything about this?"

He's drunk, his body swaying from side to side. "Ryan spread it around the school. He said this party was going to be the biggest one of the year, and he was right!" He smacks my chest. "This is sick, dude. You guys should do this more often."

No, we absolutely shouldn't. "Ryan did what?" I practically scream. I should have known he would fuck this up somehow. The guy has it out for me for some goddamn reason, and it can't just be over Hads because he never had her on his radar before she started talking to me. What the hell is he doing with all of this meddling? Is he bored? Is his life so uninteresting that he has to fuck with other people and their lives to get some excitement?

"Grant, let me talk to him," Jacks says.

I don't even say anything before I search the party for him. As soon as I find him, I grab him by the collar of his shirt and drag him outside so nobody hears me say what I have to say to him.

He only smiles as I throw him on the grass and start to yell at him. "What the hell are you doing? Why are you so obsessed with making my life harder than it needs to be?"

"And what makes you think I care so much about you? I didn't think your ego was that big," Ryan smirks. "What exactly did I do?"

Where the fuck do I even begin? "Tonight was supposed to be small, but Erikson said you told the entire school. Why, Ryan? Why would you do that?"

He wipes off his jeans as he stands up, coming closer to me. I look down at him, wanting to punch the goddamn smirk off of his face.

"It's way too fun seeing you worked up, Grant." He steps closer to me. "Tell me something, did you think about punching me when you saw me that day in the library with Hads?"

"You two were studying for your project. So, no. Because you were the one who wanted me to leave, but Hads is the one who invited me to sit down."

He only shakes his head as he laughs. "That's not the day I'm talking about."

What?

"I know you saw it. I timed it just right. And she said yes, by the way. I don't know if she told you that, but you'll see her on my arm at the banquet. And I can't wait to see what kind of short, slutty, and easy-access skirt she wears so I can—"

I raise my fist to shut him up, but I don't swing on him. The rage that I'm feeling in my body at the fact that he said all that about her makes me want to hit him, but it would only cause more harm than good. And I've already hit him once. This time he would surely tell our coach what I did.

Then I'd get kicked off of the team because there's a zero-tolerance policy for fighting with one another. He's getting inside my head, and he knows it. He clearly wants me off of the team and he'll push as many buttons as he can to achieve it.

"That's what I thought. You don't care what I say about you, but she's your weakness, Grant."

Of course she is. I'll protect Hads with everything I've got, especially from assholes like Ryan.

"Leave, Ryan. You're no longer welcome in my apartment." I turn to head inside when he speaks again.

"Have you guys fucked? I bet Hads—"

I whip around, wanting him to stop saying all of these things about Hads. "Keep her fucking name out of your mouth."

He only rolls his eyes at me.

"Eventually more people will realize how much of a disease you are, Ryan. People will see what I see and they'll hate you for it. You'll lose everyone who cares about you, and you'll be all alone to finally think about how your own actions have affected the people around you. Be a goddamn adult and grow the fuck up. Stop fucking around with other people's lives when yours needs some fixing, too."

"You'll never have her, Grant. She'll never care about you because she can't fucking trust you."

I throw my head back and laugh. "You don't know my relationship with her, Ryan. I'd rip my heart out for her if she asked me to do it. That's the difference between you and me. You're all talk, but I actually follow through on the things I say I'm going to do."

He shakes his head at me. "We'll see you at the banquet, Grant. Unless of course, you don't want to see her drooling all over me."

I take a big, deep breath before I head back into my building, but I suddenly don't feel like going back into the party. Someone I shouldn't even be listening to has officially killed my mood, but he made some good points. I hate that he was able to get under my skin so much, so as I sit on the bench outside of my building, I look up at the sky and wonder.

I wish I could tell Hads how shitty Ryan is, but I don't want to do anything to make her not trust me. She already knows I don't like Ryan, but when he asked her to the banquet, it was way before where we're at in our relationship now. That was when she still disliked me and with the way he asked her, there was peer pressure to say yes.

He's been playing games the entire semester, and it pisses me off that I can't do anything to stop him.

"I can practically feel how bad you wanted to punch him," a voice says. "But it's better you didn't."

I look over and see another guy sitting on the opposite side of the bench. He's wearing all black, and I feel like I'm in the start of some sort of spy thriller, right now. Who the hell is this guy and did he hear my conversation with Ryan?

"What?" is all I can manage.

"He'll get what he deserves eventually, but a little verbal assault doesn't hurt."

This conversation is way too vague and it's kind of creeping me out. Is he about to kill me or something? He looks like he'd be into slow and painful death for his victims.

"Don't kill me if this comes out wrong, but who are you and how much of that conversation did you hear?"

"Oliver," he says as he holds his hand out. "I'm Hads' brother, and I heard all of it."

Oh. That explains a lot. I grab his hand and shake it—his hand is fucking freezing.

"Hads told me you went here. It's nice to finally meet you." Unless he kills me, then it's really not that nice to meet him.

He's silent for a few moments after he answers, and I would leave, but he must have sat here for a reason. I assume he wants to talk to me, but I'm not sure about what.

"You're a criminal justice major like Paige, right?" I say, trying to move this conversation forward.

"How do you know Paige?" He looks murderous. I'm so fucked.

"I-I met her when I went to the library once to find your sister. They were all sitting at a table together," I stammer. This guy is making me so nervous. "Did you need something from me?"

"I heard what you said to Ryan. All of it."

Yeah, I'm fucked. "Okay..."

"You're a good guy, Grant." That's not where I thought this was going, but he continues. "I know all about what's been going on with you and my sister, and at first, I was pissed."

"You seem protective of her, so that makes sense," I tell him.

"I am. She's a great person and deserves to be happy after all she's been through."

"She does," I agree.

"Before tonight, I thought nobody would ever be good enough for her—especially when I heard about this Ryan nonsense. I hate that kid. He gives me bad vibes."

"I don't like him either. He's a dick."

"Yeah, he is." At that, he smiles, or I think it's a smile. It's more like his lips turn up and that's about it. "I want to caution you on a few things about my sister, if I may."

"Yeah, go ahead. I'm all ears."

"Do you like her?"

I pause, not expecting the question. "I do."

"Good. I like you, I think you'd be good for her. She needs someone like you to soften her a little bit. Don't force her to open up to you. She'll retreat if you try to force her to do anything." He pauses to take a breath. "She's a thinker, always leading with her head and not her heart. But in time, I think her heart will win over. Just don't push it, and you'll be fine."

I don't think he blinked that entire sentence.

"Thanks. I know she has a hard time trusting people, but I'm going to try my best to prove I'm in this with her. My biggest fear is failing her, and well anyone, I guess. I don't want to fail her." I don't know why I'm laying out my issues to Hadleigh's brother in the darkness, right now, but this night hasn't gone how I thought it would anyway.

"Failure is part of life. It happens, unfortunately. I know about failing people too and it's not easy to forgive yourself. It took me a while to realize how you get back up from it matters more. I failed someone once by not being there for them, not protecting them." He pauses. "The fact that you said all that to Ryan proves to me that you're a good man. Even if you fail—which you won't—but if you did, what matters the most is how you pick yourself up and promise to do better next time. Actions, not just words. My sister deserves that. Someone who will always get back up and be with her—someone who cares about her."

I really digest what he's saying, and he's right. "Thank you for telling me all that. I promise I will always get back up for Hads. Nothing on this Earth could stop me from standing up for her. I want her to be the happiest she can be, even if it's not with me. Her happiness is all I care about."

He's quiet for a minute, then he looks at me. "You're a good man, Grant. Believe in that and yourself for once." Then he gets up and walks into my building.

Has he lived here the entire time and I've never seen him? I'm barely in my room because of classes, studying, and practice, but I'd like to think I would have seen him in passing once or twice.

Huh.

This conversation brings me back to all those years ago when I heard my Dad tell the story of how he knew he was ready to settle down and be the man for my mom. I think that's how I feel now. I want to be the kind of guy she deserves—the kind of guy she could love.

Because I know for a fact I'm already falling into the idea of us being together, I just need her to catch up.

38

Hadleigh

It's Friday night and I'm currently in Paige's car headed to Ella's house for her birthday dinner and a sleepover. Amelia's playing super depressing songs as she sits in the passenger seat, and I wonder which of the twenty sad playlists this one is.

I'm not sure why we let Paige drive because she's the slowest driver ever. I swear she's actually a grandma hidden in a twenty-year-olds body.

"Paige, the speed you're driving combined with the music is making time stand still back here." I'm in the backseat with my eyes half closed from how tired I feel. I'm still getting back to my full self after being sick for two weeks.

"I told Paige I could drive but she threatened to put sugar in her own gas tank so she could. You know she hates when other people are behind the wheel," Amelia reminds me.

"I don't hate it, I just prefer to be the one driving. Plus, I'm a safe driver, so both of you hush. We're here," she tells us as she parks in Ella's lot.

We all filter out of the car and grab the snacks we brought. Ella insisted on making dinner, but since it's her birthday, we compromised and all made side dishes. I made Pho—which is a noodle soup with beef broth, ginger, onions, and fish sauce. My mom usually makes the broth herself, but I had to improvise since the kitchen in my dorm is terrible. I used to eat this all the time at home and was excited to make it again. Paige made homemade mac and cheese and Amelia brought snacks for the movies we're going to watch.

We walk up to the second floor of the building to Ella's apartment. She doesn't live far from campus—about fifteen minutes.

As soon as we step into her apartment, the smell of tacos hits us all in the face and my mouth starts to water. Ella loves hosting things, and she's gone all out this time by making an entire taco bar. With those tacos, she's made margaritas. I see the glasses on the counter and I silently curse myself for not hydrating before I came. I should have known alcohol was going to be involved tonight.

Ella's apartment is very on-brand for her. It's an open floor plan, and neutral toned for total tranquility. There are pops of color here and there with certain accents, and she has a few plants scattered all around her place.

Her birthday is technically April 4th, so we missed it by a few days, but she and Alissa went out for a night on the town since the rest of us were busy. Ella wanted to do something more lowkey for the four of us, so we decided on dinner and getting drunk in the comfort of her apartment. I'm excited for a night of just us since we won't get to have many of these get-togethers next year.

All three of us put our stuff on the counter as she hugs us all. "I'm so happy you're here!" She pulls back and sways a bit. The girl is absolutely already a little tipsy.

"Happy birthday, Miss Ella," Amelia says.

"Yes, happy birthday! I was going to bring balloons that said twenty-two on them, but I was forbidden," Paige says.

"Happy birthday!" I say, making myself comfortable at the dining room table.

"The taco bar is all ready for us! But before we eat, I need to see margaritas in your hands! We are getting fucked up tonight," she declares. Whatever Ella wants to do tonight is what we'll do. It is her birthday party, after all.

"I think Paige is going to be drunk after half of this," Amelia says. I might be, too. I haven't had alcohol in a while.

"That's fine. You guys know I only drink around you guys," Paige says while sipping her drink and sitting at the table. We all grab our plates and make our tacos, and as we sit down at the table together, the four of us chatting away, I smile.

I love nights like these.

By the time we're done eating, we're all drunk and giggly, and the three of us clean up while Ella tries to help because she's the host and apparently she wants to do everything.

After that, we all take a spot in Ella's living room, blankets covering all of us as we sit and decide on a movie to watch. Ella and I are on one couch and Paige and Amelia are on the other.

"I think we should watch a horror movie!" Paige says, and nobody is surprised at her suggestion.

"Paige, you watch horror movies alone at night in the dark like a psycho. You know I won't watch them with you and tonight is no different. I say we watch a travel documentary!" Amelia says, slightly slurring the last few words.

"No, no, no. It's Ella's birthday. She should pick what we watch," I say to them.

"Okay! I'll pick...." She pauses for a second, taking another sip of her margarita. "*John Tucker Must Die*!" Amelia groans.

"We watched that one last time, but it's fun, I guess." She takes a sip from the bottle of prosecco she brought. She doesn't even have a glass anymore.

"I love this one! It's got so many good cliches in it. Plus, I'm feeling sleepy, so I won't feel bad if I doze off since I've seen it before," Paige says, yawning at the end of her sentence.

"Nobody's allowed to fall asleep on my birthday! We're staying up all night!" Ella yells at us as she queues up the movie. It's only ten in the evening, but alcohol makes all of us tired, so I guarantee we're not going to watch movies all night.

Though, Amelia doesn't ever sleep most nights because she's always sending us all memes in the middle of the night. So, she'll probably be up later than all of us—unless the prosecco knocks her out.

Around halfway through the movie, we get up to get snacks that we pass back and forth. By the end of it, Paige is asleep and sprawled across Amelia while Ames plays with her hair. I don't know when or how it happens, but eventually, we all fall asleep against each other while more movies I can't name play in the background.

I WAKE UP SPRAWLED on Ella's couch while she sleeps soundly next to me. I take a poll of the other two and notice Amelia's curly hair underneath a blanket on the other couch, but I don't see Paige.

I hear some noise, so I get up to investigate only to find Paige sitting on the floor of Ella's kitchen eating snacks in the dark. I turn the light on, and she flinches, but her smile returns to her face when she notices it's me. I sit next to her, and she mindlessly passes me the bag of my favorite chips that are on the counter above us.

"What are you doing in here? It's five in the morning, P."

"I couldn't sleep, so I came here to have a snack. Did I wake you? I'm sorry, I wasn't trying to," she says, a bit sadder. She might still be drunk, but I think I am, too.

"No, you didn't wake me. Why couldn't you sleep?" I ask as I put my hand over her shoulder.

"I had a nightmare, but it's no big deal. It happens a lot, and I'm usually hungry after. Amelia sometimes meets me in our kitchen and snacks with me at home. It's sort of a routine we have."

"What was your nightmare about?" I hear footsteps coming towards us, which I assume are Ella and Amelia. They enter our field of vision and look about as good as I feel. Ella's curly hair is all over the place, and Amelia looks relatively normal. This is probably around the time she goes to bed every night.

"What are you guys doing?" Ella asks as Amelia sits down, having done this before.

"Paige and I couldn't sleep, so we decided to snack on the floor. Come join us," I say as I pat the spot next to me, and she sits right down and grabs for the chips. We snack in silence for a bit when Ella finally talks.

"Leo stood up for me at work the other day, and I realized that maybe he's a human being and not a demon inside a skin suit." I don't think she realized she called him Leo, but I'm not going to be the one to mention it. She never calls him by his first name—apparently, neither does he to her—and it must have been a slip of the tongue.

"What?" Amelia says as her eyes get wide. Paige's eyes light up, being the only one in the group who likes to ship people together. It's funny that Paige loves relationships, but since I've known her, she has never been in a serious one. I'm sure she'll find someone someday—we all will. And if not, then we'll always have one another.

"I was having a rough day. There were some things going on with my sister and he helped me out. I was stressed, and he took the blame for a mistake I had made. It made me realize he might not be as shitty of a person as I thought he was." All of us are stunned. Ella complimenting Leo is something I thought I'd never hear—not in this lifetime at least.

"I thought you hated him?" I ask.

"I didn't say I changed my mind about him—he's still a little bitch—but he might have more human DNA in his body than I originally thought," she says.

"How is he a little bitch when he's taller than you?" Paige asks under her breath.

"Someone please change the subject off of Zimmerman or I'm going to need more alcohol," Ella says to the room.

"Paige, what was your nightmare about?" I ask her straight up and Amelia nudges me with her elbow—shooting me a harsh look.

"It was nothing—just a memory I'd rather not relive." She's talking quietly, and I feel bad for bringing it up. "I know I say it all the time, but you guys mean a lot to me. My home life was never great, and I always felt left behind as a kid. When I came here and met all of you guys, that changed. Just the fact that you guys will sit on the floor with me and eat snacks makes me want to burst into tears. I used to do this alone when I was younger, but now I'm not alone, so thank you." She says, some tears running down her face. All of us are silent, letting those words sink in.

Ella reaches out to her and holds her hand. "I know the feeling, P. I have a shitty parental situation too. I'm always here for you if you want to talk about it. Ask Hads. I'm a very good listener."

"She really is. Ells gives great advice, too," I say.

Paige looks up at Ella and smiles, her eyes still wet with tears. "Thank you." Ella simply smiles at her and a look of understanding crosses each of their features.

"On a lighter note, my next trip has officially been booked! I'm heading to Crater Lake in Oregon. It has one of the deepest lakes in the United States and is on top of the Cascade Mountain Range. I'm very excited about it." She smiles, and I don't think I've ever seen Amelia smile more than when she talks about her travels.

"That sounds fun, Ames. When are you going?" Paige asks her.

"This summer, probably in July," she tells us.

I sway where I sit, still feeling a bit drunk from last night, and as soon as Amelia said the word lake, my mind flashed to Grant's eyes when they were close to me while he took care of me. His entire face is beautiful, but I could get lost in his eyes any damn day of the week. It's hard because my first instinct is to run from him, but as soon as those eyes capture mine, it's like they pull me towards him and I can't let him go.

"Grant's eyes are blue like a lake." I clamp my hand over my mouth, wondering why that came tumbling out. The girls all look at me like I confessed my love for him.

"Are they now?" Amelia asks me.

"I've never noticed that. Please tell us more, Hads." Ella obviously wants me to spill my guts, but I'm not going to budge.

"It was an observation I had. I blame Amelia. She was the one who was talking about lakes!" I say, yelling at her, and then we all start overlapping with our shouts and arguing. We stay on the kitchen floor until the morning, talking and gossiping about all sorts of things.

As soon as we're all strong enough, we start to make breakfast. Ella makes mimosas as we all groan because more alcohol this early doesn't sound good.

"I cannot handle any more alcohol. I have to drive," Paige says.

"That's fine, but for you two, the only cure for a hangover is more booze. Trust me," Ella says, throwing a kitchen towel at me. I try to throw it back but I fail miserably and it misses her completely.

Ella continues to make the French toast while I scramble the eggs. Paige is sipping water while quietly mouthing along to the song Amelia put on for us.

When breakfast is over, we all sit on the living room floor and play board games until Ella politely kicks us out because she needs to take a nap before going out with Alissa tonight. They're going to a concert not too far from campus.

"That works for me. I have plans with Oliver tonight to work on our project for criminology, and I'd rather not be drunk still when we meet," Paige says to us.

"I have plans to blackmail a U.S. Senator tonight, so I should be going as well." We all stare at Amelia as she gathers her stuff. Paige throws her clothes and things in her tote bag and we all gather in a group hug before we head out.

"Thank you guys so much for coming over to celebrate with me. You're the best friends a bitch like me could ask for." We all smile at that and shuffle out her door and into Paige's car.

"Paige, please go over the speed limit this time, or I'm grabbing your wheel and running us into a telephone pole," Amelia says while hooking her phone into Paige's car cord.

"Amelia, I'll delete all the music off your phone! Let me drive how I want!"

Ames puts both her hands up, conceding, and I sit in the back seat and laugh at them.

That was one of my favorite nights we have had together this year. I wish it never ended. In the future, I'm not sure where we'll all be, and I don't know how many more nights we'll have like that one. Is it odd to miss something that isn't truly gone yet?

It might be, but the four of us could never be gone from the rest of us for too long. I think it would upset the timeline or something.

And on the quiet drive back to campus, I try not to cry as I think about the future coming for the four of us and how I wish it would slow down.

39

Hadleigh

I'M WALKING INTO THE library cafe for Ella and I's weekly Sunday sit down when I realize she's not here yet. I find that odd because she's always here before me, so I go to order our drinks. When she doesn't show up for another ten minutes, I send her a message. She could have overslept or something.

She texted me yesterday to double check we were still on for today, and I agreed. I know she went out with Alissa last night to the Hidden Bear, so maybe she's hungover and moving a bit slower than usual.

I sip my coffee as I read through my book and twenty minutes later, she sulks into our booth.

"Is everything okay?" I ask, a bit worried because of the look on her face.

"Yes. No. I don't know," she says. I've never seen her look so... off before.

I slide her coffee over to her and she takes a huge sip of it. "Do you want to talk about it?"

"No."

"Okay, that's fine. I'm always here if you want to talk about anything. Just because you're like my older sister doesn't mean you can't come to me with stuff, too."

"I might've had a regretful hookup last night. I wish I could erase my memory, but it doesn't work like that," she tells me quietly.

"Yikes, that doesn't sound fun. Female, male, or nonbinary?"

"Unfortunately, male."

"That sounds about right. I'm sorry."

"It's okay. Alissa and I got super fucked up last night, so it was kind of my fault. I had fun until I woke up this morning next to someone I shouldn't have, but it's fine. I'm fine. How are you?"

Before I can answer, Amelia plops down in our booth.

"Hey, guys. What's up?" She makes herself comfortable and looks at us both. "You look like shit."

"She had a rough night," I say.

She raises her eyebrows. "Clearly."

"Amelia, I can't deal with your emotional warfare shit this morning. What are you doing here?" Ella asks her.

"Paige is working on this project for her investigations class and she's taken over the apartment. She's playing detective and I was scared of the energy she was giving off, so I left the apartment. I stopped by here to grab some food and a coffee. She tried to trick me into getting her some, but I'm not handing her a guaranteed panic attack in a cup."

"That's valid."

"Yeah, that makes sense," I agree with them.

"That girl is the last person I ever expected to be into murder so much. She has literally turned our apartment into a crime scene she has to investigate. Apparently, she set up some famous murder scene and is trying to figure out what the police could've done better for this project. It's scary how good at this she is."

"I agree. That girl could solve anything if you give her enough time. She scares me sometimes." Ella says that, and I laugh along with Amelia. Paige is the sunniest person we know, but she has this other side to her that she doesn't show many people. I'd trust that girl handling my murder case—if it comes to that.

"I need help with something, so I'm glad you're both here. I was going to bring it up on Wednesday but now is better," I say, and they both listen intently as I speak. "The banquet is coming up and I don't know how to approach Ryan and tell him I don't want to go with him."

"And you don't want to go because…" Amelia is smiling because she already knows what she's goading me into saying.

"Because not only did he embarrass me in front of half of the school when he asked me, but I don't want to go with him." I'd rather go with Grant, but I don't want to admit that out loud quite yet.

I'm falling for him, or I already have. I'm not sure where I'm at but when I think about all he's done for me in the past few months, all he's said, and how I feel when I'm with him, one thing always remains the same.

I trust him, and I want to be with him. I want to call him my boyfriend and stare at his eyes all day because I'm allowed to. I want to skate with him, watch him play hockey, and jump into this scary next chapter together.

I would scream it out loud if I wasn't worried about it backfiring. I'm still nervous and cautious of all of this, but as soon as I'm with Grant, all my fears are eased, and I've never had anyone do that for me.

"I would just be straight up with him. Explain it all and be done. A clean break is usually best," Ella tells me.

"If I were you, I'd change your name, go off the grid, and disappear!" Amelia says a bit too cheerfully.

"Don't listen to her," Ella reminds me.

"I wasn't planning on it," I say.

"Guys, you have to be prepared at all times. You never know when you'll need to suddenly disappear."

I don't want to dive too deep into that, but it actually makes sense now why Paige and Amelia get along so well—they're both extremely insane.

"So, what's new with you, Ames?" I ask, trying to change the subject.

"Not much, just the usual. My major change went through and on paper, I'm no longer a medical student. I'm expecting a passive-aggressive message from my parents any minute now!"

Ella and I stare at her for a few seconds because it is not only too early to unpack all of this, but Ella is hungover, so her brain is working overtime.

"You officially told them about your major change?" I ask.

"Yup," she says. "It's a better fit for me, but they're going to be upset I'm straying from the path they set up for me. It's not a big deal, so why do you want to bail on Ryan? Did he finally creep you out enough?"

Ella only rolls her eyes as she finishes her coffee. "It's too early for this. My vagina is sore."

"Fun night, Ella?" Ames asks her.

"No."

"What happened?"

"That's a secret that will stay with me until my grave." She groans as she puts her head down on the table. Amelia and I look at each other before we start to laugh, and Paige blows up all of our phones with a bunch of messages because all of our phones buzz at the same time.

Paige: Guys, I think I've done it.

Paige: Someone needs to call the news because I've done it!

Paige: I solved it, guys! Oh my gosh!

Amelia: I really didn't want to bury another body this morning.

Hads: What did you do, P?

Ella: Did you finally discover decaf coffee? It would be a gamechanger for you.

Paige: No, I solved the case! I know how the killer did it!

The three of us laugh as we slide out of the booth, knowing Paige is going to want to walk us through it in person.

As we walk toward Amelia's place, I start to imagine what my life would look like without them, and my heart starts to ache. I can't imagine not having them in my life.

My brother is a great sibling, but I've never had sisters before. Paige, Ella, and Amelia are my non-biological ones now. I can't imagine not joining the book club during my freshman year. My life would look so different, and that thought scares me—the fact that one or two decisions could have altered my life so drastically.

"Thank you, by the way," I say to Ella as we walk.

"For what?"

"For dealing with me and helping me through some tough spots this year. I don't think I ever told you how much I appreciated these weekly coffee dates."

"Hads, I'm your friend. You're not someone I have to deal with. You're someone I truly love spending time with—all of us do. We love you for who you are, and you shouldn't have to change anything about yourself to be with someone else. You're perfect and worthy of everything as you are."

Her saying that to me is making me a bit glassy-eyed. I don't normally cry—especially in front of others—but I let one tear fall before I push them back.

Who knew books could bring these amazing people into my life? I had no idea how powerful something as simple as literature could be.

But damn, I got lucky with these three girls around me, and I'll never forget how fortunate I am for walking into that meeting last year.

40

Hadleigh

RYAN AND I HAVE been working on our project in the lobby of my dorm building for two hours. I got sick of always meeting at the library and needed a public change of scenery, but this project has to be completed and turned in whether I like working with my partner or not.

We've been working for about two hours and since we're almost done, I take a deep breath before I figure out how to bring this up. The banquet is next week and I hate that I feel like shit for doing this to him, but I can't go with him.

It sucks that he's the one who asked me yet I feel like a bad person for backing out like this.

I can't go, though. I can't go with Ryan to this stupid banquet thing only to see Grant sitting in the same room and know I can't speak to him. Well, I could, but I'm sure Ryan will be attached to my hip at all times.

Plus, I don't want Grant to see me with Ryan. Especially since I know how I feel now—about Grant, at least. I know I want to be with him. I know he cares about me, that I trust him, and I know I wish I was going to this with him. If all goes well, that might be the case.

Leave it to me to have all my walls finally come down when I'm still tangled up with Ryan. This freaking sucks.

I take a deep breath to calm the nerves I'm feeling before I finally speak up.

"So, about the banquet next week," I say and his face lights up.

"I'm super excited to go with you, Hads. I think it's going to be a fun night."

My saliva catches in my throat. "I wanted to talk to you about that."

His face pulls together. "What's going on?"

"I don't think it would be appropriate for me to go with you any-more," I say, my heart rate picking up for some reason. "I'm sorry to back out so close to it but—"

"You're not backing out, Hads. You're not."

"I am, though. I can't go with you, Ryan, and I'm sorry if this isn't what you wanted to hear, but I cannot go with you. I don't want to go with you."

I swear I see his lips turn up, a smirk crossing his face as he looks down at the table. "Hads, you're going with me." It sounds more like a statement than a question. What the hell is he trying to say?

"I'm trying to tell you I'm not—"

He cuts me off again. "You're going with me because if you don't, I'll spread, oh about a thousand different rumors around campus about you. I know how much you hate the attention and the whispers, but I can make your life hell for the next two years with stares in your direction everywhere you go."

Is this a threat? Is Ryan seriously threatening me to go with him to a stupid banquet, right now? "Are you serious, Ryan? Petty threats?"

"I'm not threatening you, Hads. I'm just pointing out something that might happen if you back out of this on me."

Oh, is that all he's doing? "Do whatever you want, but I'm not going with you. Spread all the misinformation you want about me. I don't care."

I do care a little, but he doesn't need to know that. I'm sure he's bluffing and this is some sort of sick joke he's playing on me that I don't find funny.

"Well, it's good you don't care. That's really good, Hads."

"I hope you can understand."

He nods at me. "I completely understand. It's because of Grant, isn't it? God, it's always him."

"No, this was my decision, Ryan. I can't go—"

"You're going with me, and we'll dance, have a good time, the whole nine yards, Hads."

"I don't know who you think you are, but you cannot make me—"

"I'll get Grant kicked off of the hockey team, and I'll make this campus think he did a thousand different things for it to happen and all of them will be horrible."

I shake my head, my stomach dropping down to my feet. "You can't—"

He shrugs his shoulders. "Think about it, Hads. Grant's already punched me once, combine that with his previous failing grade and some made-up story from me and a few of the other guys, I could do it. And you wouldn't want that to happen, would you? You wouldn't want to ruin his life like that would you?"

I can't believe he's actually doing this. I can't believe he's gone from threatening me and my hatred of the whispers on campus, but now he's moved onto Grant. I hate that it's working, though. I don't want Grant to lose his spot on the hockey team because Ryan did something stupid.

But then again, it would be my fault. I could stop him from doing this if I just go with him to the banquet.

And if I have to grin and bear it with Ryan for one night so he doesn't do something stupid to fuck up Grant's life, then I'll do it. One night of suffering, and hopefully, I'll never have to deal with Ryan ever again.

"Fine."

He smiles at me before collecting his stuff. "You made the right decision, Hads. I'll pick you up at seven?"

I nod as he walks away, feeling worse than I ever have before.

Ryan is a piece of shit, and if I only have to deal with him for one more night, then one more night is all he'll ever get from me. After that, I'm sure Grant would beat the shit out of him for coming anywhere near me.

I should have known he would pull something like this—especially after everything people have told me about him. But the one thing I can't wrap my head around is why he's still playing this game with me.

Why me of all people? What do I have to offer Ryan? Why has he latched onto me like a parasite this semester?

One night, Hads. It's just one night. But the feeling in my gut won't go away, and I have a feeling I'm going to regret this decision when all is said and done. At least Grant will be at the banquet. Maybe I can pull him aside and tell him what's going on. Or maybe before then, I can—

My phone buzzes, and as soon as I see Ryan's name, I hold back a gag.

> **Ryan: Oh, and don't tell Grant about any of this. I'd hate for him to do something stupid.**

> **Ryan: I'll make it a night to remember, don't worry, Hads. Soon you'll realize you don't need him anymore.**

Hads: Fuck. You.

Ryan: That's the spirit!

41

Hadleigh

TODAY IS THE DAY I've been dreading and waiting for at the same time. I'm nervous and excited for tonight to be over because then I'll never have to talk to Ryan ever again. Not only did he basically force me to go with him tonight, but he's also blackmailing me.

I don't understand what his game is here, but since I haven't been able to talk to Grant all week, I'm worried he's going to think I'm pulling away again. I've been texting him back and stuff, and I even typed out a message about Ryan a few times, but I never sent any of them. I'm a goddamn coward.

Grant has been busy with hockey season ending, and I've been too busy studying and trying to get ready for finals, so I haven't seen him in a while.

Tonight could either backfire or work out in my favor, and I really hope it works out in my favor for once.

I'm taking deep breaths as my friends surround me, helping me to get ready even though their faces mirror mine. When I told them about what Ryan said, they were all ready to head to his dorm and give him a piece of their mind.

But I told them there was nothing I could do. I don't know what else Ryan has up his sleeve when it comes to getting Grant kicked off of the hockey team, and I can't risk it.

"Hads, can you stop moving so much? I can't get this piece to stay curled," Alissa tells me. Ella's working on my makeup and her face looks as pissed off as I feel.

I have my dress on already, and all that's left is to put my shoes on and grab my purse before Ryan gets here. He's driving us to where it's being held and I really want to bring something so I can stab his eyes out for doing this to me—for putting me in this position.

He not only used my feelings for Grant against me, but he's also forcing me to be on his arm for this stupid thing tonight. It's all bullshit and I'm not going to look happy being on his arm tonight—he can't fucking force me to have fun.

"All done, babes," Alissa tells me as Ella sweeps some blush onto my face.

I stand up, my black belted mini dress flowing down my body. The mesh sleeves cover my arms because I don't want Ryan touching the skin on my arms when he tries to lead me into the room.

"So, how do I look?" I ask my friends.

"Like you're headed to a funeral," Amelia says.

"It feels like I am," I tell them, adjusting the bow Alissa put in my hair. "I need this night to be over."

"It's only three hours, okay? I'll start a countdown!" Paige says, trying to lift the spirits in the room. It's not working, but I appreciate it anyway.

Ella comes over to me and smooths my dress out. "Text us if he does something stupid."

"Is there anything more stupid than blackmail, Ells?" Alissa asks her. "I could drain his bank accounts in two seconds if he does something. Just let me know."

Alissa is a technological genius, and she works for some fancy company that does software analysis or something to that effect. It all sounded like gibberish when she explained it, but she hacks and fucks with things in her spare time. She's a badass and Paige already wants her to teach her how to stalk more efficiently online.

"Thanks, Liss. I'll let you know." A few knocks on the door make my stomach drop. "I'll text you guys if I need you. I promise."

I feel like I'm going to throw up, or that I'm being led to my death.

My friends all envelop me in a hug, and as soon as we're apart, Ella hands me my bag.

"Take a breath, and keep your phone in the pocket of your dress at all times, okay?"

I nod, taking another huge breath before I open the door and see Ryan's smug face looking back at me. I want to spit on him or kick him in the balls so hard that he keels over and never gets back up.

"Ready to go, Hads?" Not even a greeting, he just jumps right to the chase.

"Just let me put my shoes on," I say as I turn around and step into them. They give me a few inches, and it's going to take all night to get used to walking in them. I would have worn my boots, but they don't go with my dress.

"Ryan, so you're aware, I have three perfectly planned murder scenarios in my head. If you try anything funny tonight, I will be using them on you," Paige tells him, and I think that's the scariest she's ever sounded.

"Good to know, Paige. Are you all going to threaten me, or can Hads and I leave?" he asks the room.

Asshole. He's such an asshole. "Let's get this over with."

I'm trying to keep my spirits up tonight, but knowing Ryan is going to show up here with Hads is making me want to run into traffic.

She's been distant lately. We've been talking and texting like normal but something feels off. I think she's pulling away again—just when I thought I had her, I lost her again. It also doesn't help that this time of the semester has been ridiculously busy. I wanted to have a few study dates with her, but she had an excuse every time I brought it up. Or maybe she was busy, but I don't know.

Did I fail her in some way? Did I scare her off? Did I move too fast?

I don't know, and since she won't talk to me, I'm not sure if I will ever find out what happened. I could corner her tonight, but if what made her pull away was me being too clingy and too much, that wouldn't help.

Now I'm here by myself. Well, I'm with Jacks and Claire, officially third-wheeling the two of them. I'd never dream of asking someone else to come to this, but knowing I'll have to see Ryan with Hads is making my head hurt.

And my heart hurt, but that's been beating irregularly since I laid my eyes on Hads in the first place.

The fact that we ended our season not where we wanted to be hasn't helped. We lost our last game in the playoffs to a team we easily could have beaten. It was an off day for all of us, but we're still celebrating another completed season in the top ten of our division, so I guess that's a win.

The banquet is held in the same ballroom every year, and the three of us got here early so we could leave early. I'm not in the mood for celebrating and Jacks knows that. Thank God for him being by my side—Claire, too. They practically forced me to get dressed and leave the apartment tonight.

I'm wearing my all-black suit, my jacket around my chair because it's really warm in this room for some reason. The three of us are at one of the sophomore tables, sitting down and getting ready for dinner to be served. Coach groups all the class levels together for some reason, and there are two tables of sophomores. I don't have to deal with being at the same table as Ryan and Hads and for that I'm thankful. Jacks and I are next to each other, and Claire smiles at me from next to him.

"How are you doing, Grant?" Claire and Jacks make a cute couple. Claire has long blonde hair—curly tonight—and a bunch of freckles on her face. She's wearing this cute pink dress that reminds me of the sweater Hadleigh had worn one night.

Fuck, don't go there. "I just want to get tonight over with."

"Well, if you want someone to dance with for a song or two, I'll dance with you unless Jacks steals me first. I don't want to see you sulking all night. You deserve to have fun after the season you had." She pats my hand, and I smile at her. She's one of the photographers for the team, so she's at every home game snapping photos from the sidelines.

"Thanks, Claire, I appreciate it." I'm sitting facing the door, which I regret because I see Ryan walk in first, and then I see her.

Her.

She looks fucking perfect and it's killing me she's here with him. She doesn't look too happy about it, and I wonder why she's glaring at Ryan like she used to glare at me.

Is there something else going on? Why is she with him if she hates him—at least that's what the look on her face is telling me right now. I thought if she showed up here, smiling and happy next to Ryan, I'd be able to move on.

I should have known something bigger was in play, at least that's what my gut is currently telling me.

As if she senses I'm looking at her, she turns to me. Her eyes connect with mine and I swear I can feel a silent prayer pass between us. The entire world fades away as we look at one another, and I swear she feels it, too. She wouldn't be looking at me the way she is if she didn't feel a fraction of what I do every time we do this.

But I can't do anything about it because she's here with him instead of me.

Ryan looks over at me and flashes me a middle finger, and I feel like I'm going to be sick. I excuse myself and find the bathroom, needing to splash some water on my face so I don't make a huge scene in front of the entire team and administrators.

I feel Jacks follow me in. "Are you okay?"

I'm fisting the sink so hard my knuckles turn white. "Fine."

"I know it's killing you to watch her with him. That doesn't mean it's over for you, though. I saw how you looked at each other—neither of you wanted to look away. There's still hope."

"I don't want to give myself hope, Jacks. I might end up disappointed." I lean my head down. "It's fine. I'm fine."

I'm not fine at all. All the memories of our study sessions, ice skating, and those damn stolen moments when I had her are flashing through my mind. All those parties I threw just to see her one more time... God, I thought they meant something to the both of us. I thought she was dropping her walls when she told me I was the only one who could demolish them.

Something else is going on here. Another game is being played, and I'm assuming Ryan thinks he's the smartest motherfucker on the planet doing whatever he's doing.

"Let's go back, okay? Dinner's starting soon."

I take a deep breath. "Okay."

We head back to the table, and dinner flies by. I spend the entire time trying not to look at where they're sitting, and I fail. Yet another thing I've failed at—I can't stop looking at her.

Coach makes a speech after dinner and I don't listen but at the end, he tells us to have a great night of dancing and fun.

I don't feel like dancing or doing anything. I'd rather be in my dorm than watch them dance together. Jacks and Claire excuse themselves from the table so they can dance. A slow song just came on, and everyone is flocking to the dance floor. I stay back at the table, trying to understand what's going on.

I need to get the hell out of here, but I can't stop staring at Hads where she is on the dance floor. She has no clue how to slow dance, and it reminds me of the night we danced together at the second party I threw. I remember how her body felt against mine, how she smiled as we danced around together, the two of us uncaring of what we looked like.

I remember how carefree and relaxed she looked that night. Now, she looks uncomfortable as Ryan leads and does a terrible job at it.

Then her eyes find mine again. She's looking at me while dancing with him. She should know I've been watching her the entire time. I know she can feel my gaze on her, but her eyes look regretful as she stares back at me.

If I could speak to her with only my eyes, I'd be saying a number of different things.

Drop his hand and dance with me instead. He wants you, but I need you.

I'm halfway to grabbing you off the dance floor, sweeping you off your feet, and making you mine.

I want to be yours. Please give me a chance to be yours. Because never in my wildest dreams did I see you coming, but I'm so glad you're here.

I love you. Let me love you how you deserve. Please.

The song ends, and Ryan pulls her off the dance floor and they get lost in the crowd just as Claire comes over and offers to dance with me. As we get onto the floor, another slow song comes on and the lyrics describe the exact state of my life at the moment.

"We can wait for another song, Grant. I'm going to grab some water. Do you want one?" she asks me, trying to distract my swirling thoughts.

"Uh, sure. That sounds good."

"Babe, do you want one?"

Jacks lifts his head and smiles. "I'll take whatever you want to get me." He turns to me as soon as she leaves. "How does it feel getting the top defensive player for the team this year?"

Right. Before dinner, Coach gave out awards. Nothing too fancy, he just likes to highlight the team and our accomplishments. I got the top defensive player, and Jacks got the one for top blocks this season. We make a good team. I'm glad to have him by my side—on and off the ice.

"It felt good, I guess. I'm proud of how I played this year and I'm thankful I'm still on the team, but it all feels kind of pointless if I have nobody to celebrate it with."

"You've got me, buddy. And Claire. Your mom, too," he reminds me.

"Thanks, dude. I appreciate it, I—" I cut myself off because the only person I want by my side more than ever is bolting for the door. Is she leaving? What's going on? "Jacks, I'll be right back." I excuse myself and follow her out where she went. I think she's headed for the parking lot, but she looks flustered as fuck. What happened in the ten minutes after I lost her in the crowd?

Hadleigh

THE SONG ENDS AND Ryan all but drags me off of the dance floor. He asked for one dance, and I complied because if I hadn't, he would have done something stupid.

I think it pissed him off that I stared at Grant the entire time we were dancing, but I couldn't care less. It's hard not to look at Grant—my eyes can always find his, even in a crowded room.

Tonight is weird. There's so much I want to say to Grant, but we're standing alone in this huge room filled with people and I can't speak to him. I can't say a word because Ryan is the worst person on the planet, and I can't risk him doing anything tonight.

Grant has been faking smiles the whole night, and every time I look at him, his face looks more melancholy than before. I want to show him this is all a facade, a game, a fucking sick manipulation by Ryan to hurt him, but I can't. All I can do is hope he forgives me when I tell him everything that's going on.

Ryan leads me into a small hallway and pushes me against the wall.

"If you look at him one more time, I'll tell my coach everything. And I mean it, Hads. You're here tonight with me, not him. Act like it."

I roll my eyes, officially done playing this stupid part he wants me to play. "You'll never be him, Ryan. You're a liar, a manipulator, and I hope you rot in hell."

And then he slaps me. He slaps me so hard that I feel blood rush to my cheek. I go to knee him, but he lifts my dress up instead and he runs his hands all over my body.

"You'll listen to me, Hads. Even if I have to force you to listen, you'll understand sooner or later. All those short skirts you wear, you're a fucking tease, but you wanted him. Everyone always wants him." He spins me around and pushes me into the wall, grabs my hands, and puts them behind my back so I can barely move.

This isn't happening. I knew he was horrible, but I didn't know he was this horrible.

"Ryan, stop. Get off of me." I try to wiggle against his hands, but my mind is going ten thousand miles a minute. I need him off of me. I need to get the hell out of here. This entire night was a mistake, and I was an idiot to think all Ryan wanted was to parade me around and make Grant jealous.

"No. You're such a whore, Hads. Wait until I tell Grant how you're going to be passed around the hockey team but he'll never have you like I'm going to."

Absolutely not. "Stop, Ryan. Please stop." My voice is muffled against the wall, and I know he can't hear me. "Get off. Now."

I squirm against him, and as he tries to pull my underwear to the side, I get my arm free, elbow him in the face, and get the hell out of this place. God, I'm such an idiot. How could I be so stupid? Why didn't I just tell Grant about all this in the first place?

I have to get out of here. I can't risk Ryan chasing after me, and thankfully, the hallway isn't too far from the ballroom, but I don't even stop to grab my purse because I'm already pulling my phone out to text the girls.

I get out of the building and I step into the parking lot, still crying because all of the emotions from the past few weeks are hitting me in the face. I take a few breaths as I try to calm down, the weight of what could have happened if I didn't elbow Ryan is going through my mind like a bullet train.

A hand touches my shoulder and I step back immediately, thinking it's Ryan, but the guy I should have been here with tonight stares back at me, his face sorrowful and confused. He notices the tears on my face and tries to wipe them off, but I back away from him.

I don't want to be touched right now, not by anyone. It's not him I'm afraid of, but I need some space. I need a minute.

"Did he hurt you?" is all Grant asks me, but I'm sure he already knows the answer.

"I'm sorry," is all I can say. I don't even know why I'm apologizing. I just can't think of anything else to say.

"Hads, did he hurt you?" He searches my face for the answer and he must find it because he turns to go back inside, his fists already clenched when I stop him.

"Please don't leave me alone." I trust him, and I'm worried he'll go in there and Ryan will find me out here before he can find him. My breathing starts to pick up and more tears fall. "I'm sorry, I just need someone I trust here with me."

He shakes his head, starting to reach out to me but then he stops. "Baby, please don't apologize. You didn't do anything wrong." He holds out his jacket for me, and I realize I'm shaking, but I don't feel cold. I take his jacket and put it on, hoping to stop the shaking.

"I-I need a minute. So, say I told you so about Ryan, and go back to the party." I'm ruining his night even more than I already have.

"I'm not going to do that, Hads. What did he make you do? What did he say to you when he pulled you off of the dance floor?"

And then I can't stop the words from tumbling out, but I tell him everything about Ryan and how he manipulated me to come with him tonight. I tell him about the threats he made toward me and him, about how he would spread rumors all over campus and get him kicked off of the hockey team.

"I was scared he'd follow through and get you kicked off because everything he said made sense in my mind. I'm sorry I didn't tell you."

"Stop apologizing, Hads. He's the one who manipulated you and forced you to do something you didn't want to do. It's his fucking fault," he says through gritted teeth.

"That's not all he tried to force me to do," I whisper, more tears falling. "Please, just leave. I can't bear to look at you after all I kept from you. I should have come to you in the beginning but Ryan made me feel like I couldn't."

"Hads, I'm not going anywhere. Why do you want to push me away so badly? You know I'm always going to be here for you."

I shake my head, my head swirling as I take in tonight. "I feel like a fool, Grant. I knew I was falling for you, but I played Ryan's game anyway. I let him play me while I knew I was in love with you, and now it's all ruined. I ruined everything."

He shakes his head and steps closer, his presence making me feel safe instead of scared. I don't move back as he grabs my hands in his. "You fell for me?"

"It was hard not to, Grant," I admit, and his head falls to my forehead, and I feel my body shake as more tears fall. This isn't the time I wanted to admit all of this, but I might as well put everything on the table. Especially since I have no damn idea how he's going to react, and I have no idea what the future holds.

I wanted this night to mark the end of the chapter of my life when I stopped playing into other people's games. I wanted to move forward and start a new chapter with Grant. One full of happiness, laughter, and stupid jokes that I laugh at because everything he says is funny to me.

I'm not sure if that's possible anymore. Tonight has fucked with my head so much, and my stomach drops as he finally opens his mouth to speak.

42

I CAN'T BELIEVE THIS conversation is happening now considering the state of how I found her, but if she wants to talk about it, I'm all for it.

"I think I love you, Hads."

Her breath hitches as another tear falls from her eye, and I reach up and wipe it away. She looks so goddamn vulnerable in front of me, and when I find out what else Ryan did, I'm going to kill him.

Not only did he manipulate my girl, but he also fucked with the wrong guy. I'm done being nice. I'm done being the bigger person, and he's going to be the one suffering when all is said and done. I'm going to triple the pain Hads is feeling at the moment and give every bit of it to him.

"What did you say?"

"I said I love you," I admit. She's standing in front of me wearing my jacket bearing her soul to me and I can't take all the pain she's feeling away. I can't physically do anything except let her know that I love her, and I'm not going anywhere.

"Why? I'm a mess, Grant. I pushed you away. I ignored you and I—"

I cut off her anxious rambling because none of that matters. I know she did it because she felt like she had to, but it's not her fault, and I need her to know that I don't care about all that.

All I give a shit about is that she's okay.

"Because when I'm with you, it stops. You're like…" I choose my words carefully because I'm really bad with metaphors and shit, but I need her to know how much I am in this with her. I need her to know how much she's fucked up my head and how I don't ever want to go back to who I was before I met her.

"You're like the spring. Before you, I was stuck in this never-ending winter. I was so cold and didn't know if I would ever get out of it. Then you came along. Our banter, the games we played, the conversations we had at the parties I threw—it melted every bad thing around me until all I saw was you."

She's crying more now. I don't know if that's good or bad, but I keep going.

"I wanted anything I could get from you. I know I fell quickly just like every other girl I've cared for, but you were different. I knew it from the moment I saw you. You made me feel all these new things, and I know I pissed you off but I didn't care. I didn't care because if I had just a little bit of your attention, that was good enough for me."

"I should've come here with you tonight. It should've been you and I, Grant, and it wasn't because I—"

"Because someone played with you and your feelings for me, and they took advantage of you. You came with him to protect me, Hads, and that tells me all I need to know."

She looks rooted to the ground, and I know tonight has been a lot for her, but she needs to know I'm in this for the long haul. I'm in this with her even if she has some pieces to sift through in her mind first.

"Hads, I know this was a terrible time to say all this, but I couldn't hold it in any longer. I *love* you, and it scares me because I feel like I've already failed you in so many ways. Hell, I'll probably fail you a few times if we decide to give this a shot."

"I need time, Grant."

"And I'll give you as much as you need." I drag my hand through my hair, and another thing pops into my mind. "You're my green light. I've been reaching for you this whole time, unable to get to you. But now I have all these pieces of you in my mind, ones I never want to let go of. I want to be yours, Hads."

Hadleigh

MY FEET WON'T MOVE. Roots from the nearby trees have grown around them, and I need an axe to get them out.

He wants to be mine? Even after all I told him about Ryan and how I kept it all from him, he still wants to be mine? Is he crazy? I'm not worth all of this. I'm not worth the struggle, especially since all I seem to do when Grant gets close is pull away. How does he still want me?

"You're lying."

"I'm not." He shakes his head. "I'd never lie to you, Hads. Never."

I know, but I still can't wrap my mind around all this. He reaches his hand out to me and I take it. He leads me over to a nearby bench and he sits me down on it while he kneels in front of me, unstrapping my heels.

It reminds me of when he undid my skates for me after he taught me how to ice skate.

"What are you doing?"

"I'm taking your shoes off because they look uncomfortable." He removes my shoes and sets them off to the side before he takes a seat on the bench next to me. "Did you know I threw three different parties this semester hoping you'd come?"

"What?" I say, and then it hits me. "You were the one who texted me about it the first time."

He only smiles, confirming the truth in my statement.

"Why?"

He shrugs. "I wanted to see you outside of tutoring and that was the only way I knew to maybe have a chance of seeing you. I know you're not the party type, but I am thankful you came."

"The third one was my favorite. That was when I realized I trusted you for the first time."

His eyes soften when they look at me, and we sit quietly on the bench for a few more minutes before I break the silence.

"You love me," I say, my stomach somersaulting as the confession he made hits me.

"I do. So damn much," he admits in a low whisper.

"That scares me."

Why lie? It does scare me, especially after the night I've had, but I know he'll take care of my heart. I just have to patch some parts of it up before I let him.

"I know, baby. It's okay." He starts rubbing my back, comforting me, and confirming that I trust his hands to be on me. I've never felt safer in anyone else's embrace like I do in his.

"Hads, you don't have to say anything back. I know your mind is going crazy at the moment."

I take a deep breath—that validation comforts me. I know I've fallen for him, but the only love I've ever felt has been a lie. I don't want to say it—not tonight, anyway. I have to get my mind straight before I can even begin to think about my feelings for Grant.

I trust him, but do I love him? Not yet.

I could, though—love him. I really think I could.

"I'm not going anywhere, baby. And if you need me anytime after tonight, call me. I'll drop everything for you, Hads. One message. One call. Hell, even an email."

I chuckle as I hear three car doors shut, and when I look up, I see Ella, Paige, and Amelia running toward me. I stand up as Paige reaches me, her arms coming around me and squeezing me tight.

"Are you okay?" she asks me, her face searching mine for an answer. I've never been so happy for her presence. She can make everything brighter just by being around. Amelia stands by her and catches my hand, squeezing it. Ella bypasses me and goes up to Grant.

"Where is he?" Her voice is cold and distant.

"Inside."

"Thank you." She nods and tries to get by him, but Grant puts his arm out in front of her.

"I'll take care of him," he promises her. "Just make sure Hads is okay. She needs you right now."

Ella nods before she reaches out, touches his arm, and then turns around to look at me. "Are you okay? Are you ready to go?" she whispers in my ear.

"I'm okay, I think. Just a bit shaky." I tell her, tears still falling because I'm grateful they're here. I sent one message and they all showed up for me. I love these girls so much.

"Did you leave anything inside? I can go grab it," Amelia offers.

"My purse, but I can't go back inside, Ames. I can't," I say as I shake my head.

"I'll be in and out," she tells me as she jogs inside.

Paige looks at Grant standing awkwardly by the bench. "You'll take care of him for us?"

He nods. "I will."

"Good. If you need help burying his body, I'm always available."

He laughs, but the rest of us know she's not joking.

Amelia gets back and they start for the car but I hang back with Grant. I take his jacket off of my shoulders and hold it out to him.

"Keep it."

"I'm not cold anymore. Take it, please," I tell him, my voice breaking.

"No. It looks better on you, Hads. I'll be fine." He smiles at me, but it's not his normal one. "Get back to campus safely, okay?"

I nod, and I turn around and head for Ella's car, the girls standing outside of it as they wait for me to come over. Amelia opens the door for me, and I shuffle into the back seat, Paige following behind me.

"Are you okay?" Paige asks me again and I don't know if it's the heightened emotions or what, but I burst into tears. Paige shuffles over, holds me in her embrace, and lets me cry. They don't judge me for crying the entire way home. I cry into Paige's lap until my body calms down and I can finally speak.

"Thank you for coming to get me." I sniffle.

"Anytime you need us, we're there, Hads. It's what friends are for. Do you want me to call Oliver?" Paige asks.

"No, I'll talk to him at some point." I don't need his cold stares. Just these three people's warmth around me.

"Hads, you don't have to tell us what happened yet. Just feel what you're feeling and tell us when you're ready," Ella says, and I nod. I slouch back into Paige's embrace and cry more.

As long as I have them, I'll never be alone again.

43

Hadleigh

It's been a few weeks since the banquet and I've been ghosting through my life.

I've stayed on my normal routine, and it's been really fucking hard. All I think about is that night and what could have happened if I hadn't elbowed Ryan in the face.

After I finished crying in the back of Ella's car, I stayed the night at Paige and Amelia's apartment. Paige brought out a bunch of blankets, and we all had a sleepover in their living room. We stayed up all night. They made me laugh, we ate snacks and watched movies, and I passed out in Ella's lap as she combed my hair and took off my makeup for me.

They didn't ask me what happened, and I didn't tell them because I didn't want to say it out loud. I couldn't.

Ella asked on the way home if I needed to go to the hospital, and I said no. I didn't need to, but I might have ended up there if I hadn't stopped it when I did—that fucking terrified me.

I thought my emotions would lessen as time went on, but they haven't. If anything, I've become more secluded and closed off than I was before. All the progress I made getting out of my dorm and being more social has faded after one night.

I even got my first A-minus while being at college. My grades have started to slip and I don't even care. If this happened weeks ago, I'd have had a full-on mental breakdown, but now one grade slip doesn't even matter to me.

I talked to my brother yesterday and when I say talked, I mean I said a few sentences and he barely said anything. I think he could tell somethings been off with me, but he hasn't pressed me about it. We just did our normal walk and spent some time together, not needing words. I only needed the comfort of my big brother yesterday.

It's Sunday, so Ella's meeting me at the library. It's a nice change of scenery from the four walls of my dorm room, but part of me is worried that I'm going to see Ryan when I'm out and about.

And if I see him, I don't know what I'll do. Or better yet, I don't know what he'll do.

I even canceled book club this week, and instead of bugging me about it, the girls brought over ice cream and we played a bunch of board games. It was needed, honestly. The girls can always fill my cup back up after it feels like it's been drained.

But today I woke up and I needed to tell my side of the story. I need to say out loud what happened because I can't keep living like this. I can't keep ghosting through life because someone did something I didn't ask them to do.

Ella comes back to the booth with my coffee. "You can start whenever you're ready."

So, I tell her everything. I tell her about Ryan and what he did. I tell her about Grant and everything that happened when I made it outside of the ballroom. I go over every single thing that happened while I try to remain as detached as possible.

By the end of it, she looks like she's ready to kill someone. "You mean to tell me all that happened with Ryan, and then Grant confessed his love for you all in one night?"

"All in one hour, actually."

"Oh my fucking god."

"Yeah." I don't know what else to say. Admitting that out loud has definitely helped the weight off of my shoulders, but now I feel empty.

"Hads, this was not your fault by any means. I need you to know that," she tells me.

"Why does it feel like my fault, though? Why does it feel like I'm the one to blame here?"

"Guilt is a weird thing and you haven't fully healed from what happened in high school. Ryan took advantage of those feelings you have for Grant and he manipulated you because he saw that connection you two share. He's a shitty person who has nothing better to do than to fuck with other people's lives because his is too boring. None of this is on you, babe. Even Grant knows that."

"I know it's not—deep down, I know that. But I wish I could rewind time and make a different decision than I did. If I could, I'd go to Grant right away and maybe things would have turned out differently." That's what I've been struggling with. I made the wrong decision back when Ryan first blackmailed me.

I should have played my cards differently.

"You don't know that, Hads. You don't know if it would have worked out any differently. Don't let those fake scenarios cloud your mind and confuse you."

That's all I've been thinking about for the past few weeks. I don't know how to stop. "But if I did something different, then maybe what Ryan did wouldn't have happened. Maybe I wasn't even in that situation in the first place."

"Don't do that, Hads. It's not healthy." She reaches over and grabs my hand. "What do you think about what Grant said?"

"I couldn't say it back, Ells. Not then." I feel it. I do feel that way towards him, but saying it that night after everything that happened didn't feel right. When I say those three words to him for the first time, I want to be absolutely sure that I'm ready. I want to be absolutely sure I'm not going to run from him and all the possibilities of us because every time I open myself up, I retreat.

But this time, I don't want to do that. Especially not to someone like Grant whose mere presence makes me feel safe, loved, and wanted.

"He didn't need to know that night and he knew that. All he was worried about was you. He only wanted to make sure you were okay."

And that's why I've considered handing over my heart to him completely, but I have to get my mind in order before I can do that. "I know. I feel so broken now—so worthless. I can't wrap my mind around all that's happened in the past few weeks. Part of me wants to hide in my room forever."

Ella scooches closer to me, wraps me in her arms, and wipes my tears. I didn't even notice I was crying, but that's yet another thing that's changed about me in the past few weeks. I can't handle accidental brushes against people in the hallways. I can't stop sulking in my room. I can't stop being sad. I thought I was stronger than this.

"Hads, you could talk to someone about this. You went through something traumatic and it's always better to let it out than let it fester. It doesn't have to be multiple sessions if you don't want it to be—you could do one if you wanted to."

"I don't know, Ells." I could probably benefit from talking to someone about all this, but the thought makes my skin crawl. I've never been good at expressing my emotions, but maybe that's what a therapist could help me with.

"Have you thought about reporting Ryan to campus police?"

"It crossed my mind. I walked into criminology with Paige the other day, and I couldn't even sit there knowing I was in the same room as him. Paige made up this excuse to get us out of there, and we went to an empty classroom so I could cry in peace." It was not my finest moment. I had never left in the middle of a class before, and it embarrassed the hell out of me. "My brother tried to follow us, but Paige yelled at him, and he left. He looked upset, and I felt horrible turning him away. Oliver's a fixer—he likes to fix things. I just don't know how to tell him I don't know if I can be fixed."

Ella smooths my hair back, her touch comforting while we talk about the scariest things I've ever had to talk about. "Hads, I think it's a good idea. He's not someone who should be freely walking around, but I'll support you in whatever you decide."

"Thanks, Ells."

"And in regards to Grant—don't rush your feelings. Take the time to think about everything he's done for you. The girls and I will support you in anything you do, and if you need to skip classes to focus on getting your head on straight, that's okay. Your mental health matters more than your grades and assignments."

I'm crying at the support she's giving me. I know missing a few classes won't make my grades slip, and maybe I should give myself some grace and focus on myself over my grade point average and attendance record.

"Thank you for always being there for me. And thank you for jumping in the car and coming to get me when I needed you."

"Of course. I might have broken a few traffic laws and went way over the speed limit, but I'd do it again in a heartbeat." I laugh because I can absolutely see her doing that. Paige is the slowest driver of the four of us, but give Ella a loud song and put the windows down and she'll almost run her car off of the road.

"I think I love him, Ells."

"You think? You're going to have to do better than that, but I think that boy would wait forever for you if it meant he got you for one day." I smile at that knowing damn well Grant said the same thing to me outside the ballroom.

"I'll think about it. Thank you again, Ells. These chats have saved my fucking life over the past few months. I feel like I've been saying thanks a lot, but I mean it."

"I know, babe. Just let me know what you decide to do about Ryan. I'll go with you to campus police or therapy if you decide that route."

"Thanks. I'm going to sit here for a few and read." She gets out of the booth, and I get up to hug her. It's been nice being out of my room, and I think I can handle a few more minutes outside of those four walls. Baby steps are still steps.

"I love you, Hads. Be patient with yourself, okay?"

I nod at her, and I watch her leave before I sit back down and throw myself into my book.

I know healing is going to take time. It requires a bit of brokenness before it gets better, and I'm in that stage right now. I'm a little broken. I'm like a painting where the frame has been chipped, but the inside remains the same as it's always been.

Except I'm not the same. I'm different. The meaning behind my painting has changed, and that's okay. Sometimes, you can see things as one way when you're younger, but when you grow up it changes because of the things you've experienced.

Everything hurts like hell, and when I'm ready to let it go, I will. I'll let it float off into space and be taken away from me, but there will always be a small piece that stays with me—a piece to remind me of how I got through it.

I can do this. I'm letting myself feel for once, and that's okay. It doesn't make me weak or vulnerable—it makes me a human.

44

Grant

THE FIRST FEW DAYS after the night of the banquet, all I felt in my body was rage. Rage at Ryan and whatever the hell he did, but I took all of that out on a punching bag instead of his face. Then, after a week, the anger simmered and all I felt was sad.

I couldn't protect her. I couldn't do anything but watch her crumble to pieces in front of me after Ryan did whatever he did to her.

It's been two agonizing weeks of every worst scenario possible running through my mind as to what Ryan could have done. My mind has not been my friend the past few weeks, but Hads' is probably a hundred times worse.

I'm playing the waiting game now. All I do is check my phone a thousand times a day to see if she texted me, but she hasn't yet. Which is fine. I'm giving her time and even though I hate playing the waiting game, I'd do it for however long Hads needs.

And if what she decides she needs in the end isn't me, I'll support her in that decision, too.

Jacks is trying to keep me positive. We have this whiteboard on our door on which he keeps writing inspirational messages. I hate to admit that they make me feel better most days when I get out of bed and feel like shit.

I'm sitting in bed in the same sweatpants I've been wearing for days when Jacks comes in and hops onto my bed. "You look like shit."

"What happened to being nice to me while I'm down?"

"Well, downtime is over. Take a fucking shower, Grant."

"Hey, fuck you. At least you have someone to take a shower for. I'm sitting here dying a slow death. The longer it takes, the worse it's looking for me."

"You don't know that. Don't jump to conclusions." He throws my towel at me.

"Well, what the fuck do I do? What do I do if she realizes I will never be enough for her? What if she gets bored of me in the future? The what-ifs are running through my head and they won't stop!" I'm yelling and pacing around the room. Jacks is sitting and watching me pace back and forth, knowing I need to get it all out.

"Where do I go, Jacks? I feel so lost—like a kite with no strings attached, just floating freely into the atmosphere. The only thing running through my mind has been her since I walked away from her on those goddamn steps the other day! I just— I don't—" He cuts me off by grabbing me and hugging me.

I'm so fucking afraid I gave my all to her only for it to not be enough. She told me she fell for me, but what if falling isn't enough? What if she realizes love isn't worth it and that whatever happened is too much to deal with?

I want her by my side while she heals. I want her next to me so I can help her through this hard time she's clearly facing, but I also don't want to push myself where she doesn't want me.

"What if she never realizes how she feels? What should I do? Am I supposed to let her move on while I watch from a distance? Jacks, what do I do? Please tell me what to do."

"I can't. You just have to hope this works out. I think it will. I've told you she needs time, and that's okay. Whatever happened with Ryan had to have shaken her a lot for this to affect her so much."

I shoot him a glare. "I told you not to say his name around me."

"I know. I'm sorry. I'm just saying that we don't know what happened in that hallway."

I stop and think for a moment. He's right. We don't. "We could maybe find out, couldn't we?"

"Oh, I don't like that face you're making right now. What's going on in your head?"

"We could confront him and make him tell us what happened. A douche like Ry— like him would want to rub it in, and be a dick about it like he is with everything else."

"What should we do then?" Jacks asks me.

"Do you know where he is?"

"It's Saturday. He's probably at the gym or something."

"Let's go find him then."

"Alright, let's go." I grab the keys and am about to head out the door but I stop us before we leave.

"Okay, maybe I should shower first," I say.

"Yeah, that's a good idea."

We go to his dorm, the dining hall, and then the gym. We find him in the gym, and Jacks rubs it in because he suggested we come here first, but I wanted to try his dorm.

He's lifting weights, and Jacks shoves his spotter away and stands behind him. Ryan stalls for a second and realizes that Jacks is over him but I don't think he's seen me yet.

"Are you only benching ninety-five pounds? What the fuck? I could lift that with one hand, but you sure are breaking a sweat," I say to him. What a pathetic little man.

"Grant, come on, let's go easy on him. He needs a spotter for benching that little weight. Let's be nice to the poor fellow," Jacks says to me. When Ryan heard me speak, he faltered a bit, the bar starts to shake a little more as he continues his set.

"I'm on set number four, might I add. What are you two doing here?" He's struggling to put the bar back on the rack, and it's stalled against his chest. Neither of us moves to help him.

"We wanted to ask you about what happened at the banquet. You clearly did something to someone we both care about and I want to know what happened." I've never seen Jacks act like this before. He's actually good at this. Is this interrogating? Are we interrogating?

"Little help here?" Ryan's struggling, and I can't help but laugh. He's struggling with ninety-five pounds. Pathetic.

"You help us first. What did you do to Hadleigh?" I ask, trying to keep my voice as neutral as possible, but my voice cracked when I said her name. The worst has gone through my mind over the past few weeks, so if he says anything I've thought of already, I might explode.

"Yes, and we want details. We'll know if you're lying because you suck at it." Jacks adds.

"Oh yeah?" He says, out of breath and turning red. I don't feel bad. It's kind of fun to watch him struggle.

"Start talking or that bar is going to impale you. I don't have all day," I say as I push it down on his chest.

"Get the bar off me and I'll tell you!" he shouts, and Jacks lifts it off of him using three of his fingers before he gently places it back on the rack. Ryan stands up and goes over to his water bottle. He takes a long sip before he speaks.

"We're listening," I say to him.

"Not only was she my date and making eyes at you all night, but she elbowed me in the face when I tried to take what I deserved. Sure, I manipulated her feelings to piss you off while you watched us at the banquet, but she didn't even let me fuck her! It was a giant waste of my time."

"She elbowed you in the face?" Jacks questions with a chuckle. "She let you off easy."

"Fuck off," Ryan tells him.

All I'm seeing is red because Ryan just admitted to attempted assault. He tried to assault her in that fucking hallway and I was in the next room sulking instead of protecting her.

"So you're admitting you assaulted her? She said no and told you to stop and you continued. I knew you were a prick, but I didn't think you were a fucking rapist, Ryan."

"Woah!" He holds his hands up at us. "I didn't rape her! I didn't do anything she wasn't asking for, okay? She got away before we could get anywhere, but at least I was able to fuck with you, Carter."

"Why do I piss you off so much? Why did you do all of this? For what reason, Ryan?"

He smirks at me. "It's fun playing around with people's lives and emotions. It's like I'm playing with pieces of a chessboard."

"Great, so you're fucking crazy," Jacks says, running a hand down his face. "Why don't you leave every person alone within a one-hundred-dred-mile radius?"

"I should kill you for what you've told us, but instead, I'll educate you. If a girl says no, you fucking stop. If she's hesitant, you fucking stop. If she's stiff as a board and isn't having a good time, you fucking stop. Have you not heard of consent or do you only like having sex when it's illegal?" I'm fuming. I want to grab a dumbbell and beat his face in. How dare he do that to her?

I want to run and find her and hug her tight, never letting her go. But first I have to deal with this stupid fucker in front of me.

"It's not fucking illegal if she was asking for it." He spits at Jacks and me. "I had to keep her in her place somehow."

"That's it—" I swing my fist back ready to hit him, but Jacks beats me to it. Ryan's jaw makes a crack, and Ryan hits the floor with a thump. "Did you just knock him out?"

"It's not knocking him out if he was asking for it." Jacks throws a smile in my direction. "Sorry, he was getting on my nerves. If he were saying this about Claire, I would've let the ninety-five pound bar crack his chest open."

"Thanks, J. You're a good friend."

"I know. Do you feel better?"

"No, actually, I don't." I can't believe he did that. He fucking assaulted her. He should be in prison for what he did.

"Did you get it?" he asks me, shaking his hand out.

I take the recorder out of my pocket and show it to him, the red button recording every single thing Ryan admitted to us, but I know this won't be enough evidence to do anything. We need actual proof.

"Didn't Leo say his sister was good with hacking and shit?" I ask Jacks. Leo is friends with our captain so he always hangs around when we go out, but I've never spoken to him directly.

"Yeah, why?"

"Do you think she can hack the security cameras in the ballroom and get the footage from that hallway?"

He smiles at me. "I like where this is going. Ask him for her number."

I pull my phone out, stopping the voice recording I was taking, and send the text. "I just did. I'm waiting for a response."

"Ah, your favorite game." He laughs as we walk out the door to the gym.

"That's hilarious, J," I say, clearly not laughing.

"Ah, come on. It's all going to work out. Now, I'm going to sit on this comfy chair while you go get me ice for my hand—which really fucking hurts, by the way." I shoot him a stare. "Please?"

"I'll be right back, don't lose any fingers while I'm gone."

"No promises."

I pull my phone back out and make sure the voice-recorded confession I took is still there. It is, and I exhale. I knew recording it could be dicey, but I needed to do it. The more evidence, the better right? Plus, I don't want this all to fall on Hads. She's been through enough.

This is the least I could do for her.

But by the time I get back to where Jacks was sitting, he's gone, and I'm stuck holding a bag of ice that's beginning to melt. There's a metaphor here somewhere, I'm sure of it.

45

 **Hadleigh**

"Okay, since it's the end of April, I brought the printout of all our stats from this semester. It's organized from most to least enjoyed with other categories—" I stop dead in my tracks because when I get into the classroom we normally sit in for book club, the vibe feels completely off.

"Book club tonight is turning into girls' night," Amelia says, grabbing my arm and leading me to an empty chair.

"What's going on?" I set my stuff down next to my chair.

"We're worried about you," Paige says.

Oh. I guess I should have known this was coming. I've been worried about myself, too. "I didn't want to make you guys worry about me."

"Hads, we're your friends. We'll always worry about you." Ella tells me. "And we know it's going to take time, but we're worried you're retreating from everything and that's not healthy. Have you thought about what we talked about?"

I nod. "I have, but I feel like if I start talking to someone about all this that I'm admitting I can't fix myself. I'm used to always patching myself up, but this feels like admitting I'm not strong enough to do that this time." When I say it out loud, it sounds a little crazy, but that's how I feel. I could ask my brother how therapy helped him, but I don't want to talk to him about what happened to me.

He's a great listener but I don't want him getting kicked out of school for doing something stupid to defend my honor, or whatever. And we're not great at talking about the hard stuff. I still don't fully know all of his feelings about Mia, but it's probably going to stay that way.

"That's not what therapy is, Hads," Paige smiles at me as she grabs my hand. "My therapist is someone who knows my brain and is able to untangle all the threads from my head and my past when it feels like I can't. I like to think of her as a professional listener. But talking to someone doesn't mean you're not strong."

"I could argue it makes you stronger being able to admit you might need a little help through this period of your life," Ella says.

"What are you afraid of, Hads? What does it all boil down to?" Amelia asks me.

I take a shaky breath before I speak. "I've been trying so hard to move forward, but I feel stuck. I don't know if I can pick myself up and move on this time, and that scares me. What if I feel like this forever?"

The girls all get up and crouch in front of my chair.

"The dark doesn't last forever, Hads. I thought it did at one point too, but eventually, I got out of the dark and only felt warmth. It takes time to get to that point, and needing a little help with how to find the way out is okay." Paige caresses my hand as what she says sinks in.

I'm not weak for needing a little help to find my way again.

"Will you guys help me?"

They all nod.

"Of course we will," Ella tells me.

A happy and content feeling washes over me. *This is the right decision.* But something still feels... missing. I can't put my finger on it.

The girls sit back in their chairs as I sit here and try to figure out why I feel so odd.

"Do we want to pick a short book to read since next month is the end of the semester?" Amelia asks.

"I'm down for that. There's this really short novella that sounds good. I saw a bunch of people talking about it," Ella says to the room.

I start to stand up, needing to pace out all of the thoughts swirling in my brain. I'm glad I realized I need to talk to someone, but this is a different spiral.

"Can you guys make me a chart or something? I feel weird."

"Weird, how?" Paige asks me.

"I don't know. My stomach feels off."

"Are you going to throw up or something?" Ella asks me.

I shake my head. "No, it's not like that. Am I having a heart attack or something?"

"Does your left arm hurt?" Amelia asks and I touch my arm.

"No."

"Then it's not a heart attack."

"Well, maybe it's a different kind of heart attack," Paige says. "Like a heart attack because you love Grant."

Oh, God, is that what's happening? I have one breakthrough emotionally and now my mind suddenly realizes I want Grant.

No—I need Grant. He's the only other person missing from my side while I get through this. I've never been able to lean on people easily. I didn't have anyone to lean on when Kyle did all the shit to me in high school, but this time around, I do.

I have people willing to be a shoulder for me to cry on, to rest my head on, to lean on. And for once, I want to let them help me, even though asking people for anything scares me. Consider this me running full force into the terrifying unknown.

"I do love him," I whisper under my breath. "I love him," I say as I turn around. "Holy shit, I love him!'

"We know, Hads. We've all known," Amelia says.

"It's about damn time," Paige giggles.

"I mean it was obvious to all of us but we understand why you waited to fully say it out loud." Ella smiles. "What are you going to do with this revelation?"

"Go find him! You need to tell him!" Paige shouts.

"Right now? It's late. I don't even know where he is. Plus, I might need to write on some index cards so that I remember what to say and—"

"Index cards? No. You go find that man and tell him!" Ella exclaims.

"I don't know where he is!" I yell.

Who knew a bunch of romance book lovers would be this passionate about real-life love? I certainly never would've guessed that.

"Try his apartment," Amelia offers. "He's bound to be there this late in the night."

I grab all of my shit and shove it into my bag, wanting to find Grant as quickly as possible.

"Okay, I have to go confess my love or whatever. I love you guys!" I pull them all in for a group hug.

"Good luck," they all say to me, but I don't have time to respond because I'm running out the doors and into the night air towards where Grant hopefully is. I'm severely out of shape but I get to his building in five minutes, swipe in, and run right into Jacks coming down the hallway.

"Woah, Hads, where's the fire?" he asks me.

"There isn't one. Where's Grant? Is he in your apartment?" I move past him, and he catches my arm. When I turn my head, he's smiling at me. "What?"

"Why do you want to know where Grant is?"

"You're really going to make me say it?"

"Oh, absolutely." He's smiling wider now. I know he knows why, but like my friends, he's going to make me say it.

I take a deep breath. "I love him, and I need to tell him. Where is he? This is an urgent situation."

"I knew it. Ugh, this is great news. He's been sulking around our room for what seems like months now."

"Can you just tell me where he is? I'm not against kicking you in exchange for information."

He smirks at me. "I'm not opposed to the ruler if you have that on hand."

"You know, for someone so happy I'm admitting this, you're being very unhelpful." He puts his hand to his chest as if I've offended him. "Tell me where he is, Jacks. Please."

"He's at the rink."

"Isn't the season over?" I ask because I literally went to the banquet.

"He goes there to clear his head. He's been there a lot lately." That hits me right in the chest, but at least I know where he is.

"Thank you, Jacks."

"No problem."

I run out of their building and head straight for the rink. God, why do people run for fun? I should have Paige add running to her list of torture techniques. I feel sweaty, gross, and not presentable, but I don't care.

I need to get to him. I need to see him. I need Grant by my side because he's the only person besides my friends I trust to hold me up while I'm falling.

I almost run straight into the rink doors. I pull the door open and go straight to where we were last time we were in here. I'm going into this conversation unprepared and not knowing what I'm gonna say, and that kind of terrifies me. How do people just declare their love with no preparation or index cards? It's barbaric. I have no idea what's about to come out of my mouth.

It's not hard to spot him since he's the only person here. Granted, it's a Wednesday night, so that doesn't surprise me. I don't even bother putting skates on because that will take too much time, so I open the door to the ice and start shuffling toward him. He's skating with his back to me.

"Grant!" I yell, not wanting to scare him and he turns around, eyes widened in surprise, and caught off guard. I knew he would be.

"Hads, what the hell are you doing? You don't have skates on!" He reaches me in four long strides and steadies me with his hands on my shoulders. He tries to pick me up, but I hold my hand up, and he stops.

"Don't pick me up. I have something to say to you, and I'm not going to say it to your ass when you throw me over your shoulder."

He smiles awkwardly before he motions for me to continue. "Okay. Go ahead."

I take a steadying breath before the words flow from my mouth. "Grant, you drive me insane about fifty percent of the time I'm with you. You're loud, you play a sport I don't understand that well, and you actually enjoy arguing with me. It's weird, and it drives me crazy."

I stop because we both laugh, that statement being way too accurate.

"I'd never want to push anyone else's buttons like I do yours, Hads." He runs a hand through his hair, hope blooming on his face. "What about the other fifty percent?"

"The other half of the time, you make me laugh like I've never laughed before. You make me smile and I've realized I've never really smiled until you came along. They were always fake or forced, but not with you."

"That's absolutely false. I've seen you smile like you do with me when you're with the girls."

"Yes, but it's different with you."

He smiles at me again. "What else?"

"The only other thing I know is that I love you one hundred percent of the time. I don't know when it happened, I don't know how it happened, but I'm in love with you. That's a fact, Grant. I love you and you love me. I love you more than I think I've loved anybody—including charts, and I really do love charts." I'm absolutely rambling right now, so I cut right to my main point.

"My point is, I love—"

He cuts me off by kissing me, and I practically melt into his arms. I'm not only coming off of the high from running all over campus but also the adrenaline of what I admitted. My heart races as he kisses me deeper. He pulls away and touches his forehead to mine. He really likes doing that with me, and I like being able to see right into his eyes when our foreheads are pressed together.

"It took you long enough."

"Hey! I wasn't the one who blurted it out at the worst possible time. That was you!"

"I can't control my mouth sometimes!" He laughs. "It just happened, and I don't regret it one bit. You were the one who said you had feelings for me."

"And I do, Grant! Obviously, I do or else we wouldn't be here," I say to him. "It's all your fault, actually. Your stupid smile and personality reeled me in like a siren luring a pirate to their death."

"Does that make me the mermaid in this scenario? Because I have a mermaid tail back home that—" This time, I cut him off with a kiss. He's shocked for a moment because I've never done that, and then he responds by cupping my face and pulling me closer to him. When we pull away, I can see my cold breath when I breathe in and out.

Before I can say anything else, he scoops me up and brings me off of the ice and onto one of the small benches. He gently sets me down and sits next to me, not leaving an inch of space between us.

"What does loving me feel like?" he asks me.

"What?"

"Oh, come on. I gave you so many metaphors in my big confession, and I didn't hear you give any. That means I beat you." He draws a fake line in the air. "Grant one, Hades zero."

"You cannot beat me at confessing our love for one another. That's not a thing," I say to him.

"All I'm hearing are excuses. You really are a sore loser, aren't you?" he asks me.

"Fine! Fine, my God, leave it to you to infuriate me when I just confessed my love for you."

He shrugs his shoulders. "I'm just saying mine was way better. I compared you to the damn green light from Gatsby which is the entire reason we're here right now."

I take a deep breath, and for the second time tonight, I don't think. I just let the words flow from my mouth.

"Loving you feels like losing myself in my favorite book. It feels like listening to my favorite audiobooks on repeat. It feels like being in an art museum while it's raining and hearing the rain tap on the roof. Loving you feels like realizing I'm not scared of all the tough things with you. I want all of it. As long as you're by my side, I don't feel scared." His eyes are getting teary, and I can feel mine loading up.

"Loving me feels like losing yourself in your favorite book? That's kind of funny, actually." He leans over and reaches for something inside his bag. He pulls out my favorite book from this year and hands it to me, a bunch of tabs sticking out from the sides.

"Did you steal my book? What did you do to it?" I ask him.

"No, I didn't steal it. Of course, that's your first thought," he mumbles under his breath and I smack him with the book. "I bought it, read it, and annotated it for you. I stole some tabs from your room when you were sick and got some pens and shit from Amazon." I flip through it, and sure enough, his handwriting is all over the pages, and one of my favorite quotes is highlighted.

"You did this for me?"

He smiles at me. "Of course I did. I know you love reading, and I wanted to show you how much I was willing to do for you. Actions not just words, you know? Brendan and Jacks helped me come up with the idea. Is it okay? Do you like it?"

"It's perfect," I say as I launch myself onto him. He wobbles a bit as I slip my arms around him and hug him tight. I never want to let him go. "Did you like the book?"

"I really enjoyed it. I was not expecting that one scene, though. I'm pretty sure you know the one."

"I do," I giggle.

"I think I might be into reading, and it's all thanks to you, Hades." His cheeks turn red, and I laugh. I'm still on his lap, the book next to us, and he's rubbing my back. Yet another reason he's shown me he's willing to do anything for me. How could I ever doubt my feelings for him? Of course my heart is safe with this kind, gentle, and loving man.

"I need you to chart your top five favorite moments from the book to discuss this deeper."

"Hads, I'll do anything you want me to. Just say the word."

"Please, can you chart your favorite moments for me?" I ask.

He smiles at me, leans in, and kisses me again. It feels like all the happiness is coming back into my body. I'm feeling things again, and I've never been happier to have so many emotions rushing through me.

He pulls away, and I smile at him again. I can't stop fucking smiling. I want to live in this feeling with him forever.

"Can I skate with you?" I ask.

"Absolutely, baby."

46

It's officially May and finals week is in full swing.

My girlfriend and I have been studying nonstop for my final exam in my literature class, and she even made me flashcards to help get some extra study time in before the test. For the first time ever, I feel overprepared—Hads made sure I knew the last half of this book by the back of my hand.

We've been spending a lot of time in the library working on different assignments together. We even sit in our old tutoring room and I often lose myself in the memories of where we were then and where we are now. It's crazy to think about how much has changed in only one semester.

She still smacks me with the ruler and I still tell her to stop, knowing she won't and secretly loving our little inside jokes.

We've also implemented a weekly date night because when we go home for the summer, we're not going to see one another all the time, and I know we've only been dating for a few weeks, but I'm a clingy motherfucker. At first, I was afraid it was too much, but Hads reassures me that she loves having me by her side.

For our first date, I took her to this old-school printing shop, and we were able to print out a bunch of charts for her. I even have one in my dorm. It's a ranked chart of all the things she loves about me. I hung it over my bed because it's a nice reminder—especially since I'm so worried about failing her in some way.

That's not the only good thing that has happened as the semester starts to wind down. With Hads' permission, campus police were sent an anonymous video and a voice confession of Ryan assaulting Hads in the hallway. It included volume and was clear as day.

You could hear Ryan saying everything he did and even Hads telling him to get off of her. She was called to the Dean's office and was able to tell her side of the story and corroborate the video.

Ryan was then kicked out of school and off of the hockey team instead of the school or Hads pressing charges against him.

When Alissa found the video, she offered to send it to me to watch it, but I didn't want to. I knew when Hads was ready to tell me what happened, she would. She told me everything one night when we stayed up late talking about our feelings. After I threatened to kill him a thousand times, she promised me she was okay.

She also had her first therapy appointment the other day. Ella and I went with her and waited for her in the car. She's been going once a week now since she started, and I couldn't be more proud of her.

I'm walking into my last final exam—the one about Gatsby—and I sit at my desk. I got here early and brought my flashcards to review them one last time before taking the test. I have to write four essays and answer other questions, but I'm not nervous. I just want to get this over with so I can conclude this semester on a high note.

I'm flipping through the flashcards when I see a new one I never noticed. I wonder if Hads added something else last minute, but when I look at it, it's different than the others.

It says 'From Hads' on the front. I turn it over and read what's on the back and fifteen little words are scratched onto the back that mean more to me than anything else on the planet.

You're not a failure as long as you try your best. I believe in you.
— H

I hold the tears back because what did I do to deserve this girl? She continues to amaze me every single day. She understands my fears and loves every part of me—even the ones I don't like.

My professor comes in and the class grows silent. We're all spread out so we don't cheat, although I don't know how you can cheat on essays, but whatever. I shove my flashcards into my bag and grab my pencils. I take a deep breath as I open the test and begin writing.

I can do this.

I HAND MY TEST in two hours later and head out the door. I was one of the last people in there because I was writing so damn much. I may have gone overboard, but I would rather have done too much than not enough.

I think I did well, and I can't wait to tell Hads about how confident I feel after taking this. It's far different from the first quiz I took and failed. I was like a lost puppy during that exam, but this one felt like a breeze.

I grab my phone from my bag to text Hads and meet her somewhere when I see a familiar pair of boots in front of me.

I look up, and there she is standing right in front of me. My beautiful fucking girlfriend. Hads is wearing her signature black skirt and forest green sweater combination, but she has my jacket on—the one I told her to keep from the banquet. It still looks better on her than me, and I can't get over how damn beautiful she is.

She gives me a cute half-wave, and I walk over to her and kiss her. She's startled, mostly because she hates public displays of affection, but she relaxes a bit when I snake my hand around her waist.

"What are you doing here?" We planned to meet back at the library so I could help her write a paper, and by helping her, I mean distracting her while she shoots me glares and threatens me.

"I wanted to see you after your test. I got nervous when you didn't come out until now. Were you the last one in there? How do you think it went? Did you remember the thing I told you last night about—" I cut her off with a kiss again. She tends to ramble when she's feeling nervous, and this is the only way I know how to relax her mind from spiraling.

"You were worried about me?" I ask her.

"No. Shut up. How do you think you did?" I grab her hand, and we walk out of the building. I hold the door for her, and she exits, grabbing my hand again when we get onto the sidewalk. I love when she initiates things like holding hands and kissing because that shows me she's comfortable with me—that she trusts me. And that's all I've ever wanted.

"I think I did really well. Thanks to you and your amazing flashcards and study techniques, I'm sure I passed."

"I'm really proud of you, boyfriend."

"You are?" I stop her where we are and turn her to face me.

"I'm so proud, Grant."

"Thank you, girlfriend." I smile against her lips and feel her smile too.

Part of me wants to replay every moment of how we got here because I still don't believe I got this lucky with her. I know I can't repeat the past, but I sometimes wish I was able to watch it again.

It's been a long journey to get here, but we did it, and I couldn't be happier. Loving her and being loved by her is something I want to do forever, and I never want to be undone from Hads. I grab her hand again, and we start walking toward the library, hoping to lose ourselves in the next chapter of our story.

And I know this next chapter will be full of love, laughter, smacks with rulers, and more happiness than we know what to do with.

47

Hadleigh

It's officially the end of the semester, and summer is right around the corner, but before we all leave campus officially, the group of us will be getting together one last time.

Grant and I are walking into the restaurant where Ella has invited us for her post-graduation dinner. As of this morning, she's now an official graduate of Grand Mountain College with a bachelor's degree in marketing.

We're all so damn proud of her, which is why we all complied when she told us about the dress code for tonight. I'd do anything for Ella, and I'm trying to suppress my emotions about her not being on campus next year, but it's not working. I know we're all going to miss her.

We walk into the outdoor seating area and I immediately spot Alissa and Ella at their table because they both just downed a glass of something. Knowing those two, it was probably tequila.

Ella spots me instantly and runs over to us.

"You look stunning! And Grant, you clean up wonderfully as well." She's got her drunk tone of voice on, and I smile as she sways in front of me. Good for her, honestly. She graduated from college as an honors student while doing an internship and working a job at the same time. She deserves to let loose for an afternoon.

"We went ahead and started the party before everyone got here. I hope nobody minds, but Ells and I are already smashed." She smiles at that, and I bring her in for a hug because it's been way too long since I've seen her. Alissa is now one of Ella's best friends, and in turn, she has become an honorary member of our book club.

"How about we go sit down and wait for Paige and Ames." I motion them back to the table, and Grant's hand on the small of my back guides me over.

While we walk, he leans down and whispers in my ear, "You do look stunning, girlfriend."

"You look wonderful as well," I say as I quickly kiss his cheek.

Grant and I have a lot to celebrate as well since we both passed all of our finals. Grant even passed his literature class with flying colors. He was so excited when his grades came back. I wish I had taken a picture of the smile on his face—it could have lit up an entire room. Every single day, I'm more proud of him than the last. He worked hard this semester and with everything that went down, I'm glad it ended well for the two of us.

We all sit down at the two picnic tables Ella and Alissa pushed together so we could fit everyone. It's just all of us friends here today. Ella's family is going to do something special with her too, but today is for us.

"So, Grant, what are your plans for the summer?" Ella asks him.

I see Alissa wink at me from across the table, a subtle way of letting me know I did well with Grant and she approves.

"I'm not sure yet. Hads and I have some things in the works." He throws his arm around me. "I might spend part of the summer at her house, and she might spend half at mine, but we still have some kinks to work out."

I'm so excited to spend the summer with him. I can't wait for him to meet my family and vice versa. He talks about his mom a lot, and I'm both nervous and excited to meet her. I've never met a boyfriend's parents before, and I told Grant I needed him to make me flashcards so I could study his family. He looked at me like I was insane, but he agreed to do it for me since he knows it will make me more comfortable when meeting them.

"Kinks, you say?" Alissa giggles, and everyone laughs.

"Guys, over here!" Ella yells at Paige and Amelia. The two just walked outside, and they look absolutely stunning—both in dresses and heels. I know Paige stole that from Amelia's closet because I don't think the girl even owns a dress.

We all look adorable in our outfits, and we might be a bit overdressed for this place, but we don't care. Whatever Ella wants today, she will get it. This is a celebration of her, after all.

Paige and Amelia hug everyone, and we all sit back down.

"I can't believe you've graduated, Ella. That's so crazy to me." Paige says, already a bit emotional.

"I still can't wrap my head around the fact that I won't see you around campus. It's weird, and I hate it," Amelia says, her tone serious.

"She'll still be at book club. If not, she can just call when we get together on Wednesdays," I say.

"Alissa, can I ask you a few questions?" Grant asks her.

"Sure, babes. You can buy me a drink," Alissa says to him.

"I'm twenty."

"Oh shit, right. I always forget the drinking age is higher over here than in England." Alissa takes a sip of her drink before she gets up. "Whatever, let's go over here. We can have a chat."

I'm positive he's going to ask her about what happened with Ryan. Grant told me what Alissa did for him—for me—and I'll forever be grateful that she helped how she did. I'm sure if she hadn't found that footage, Ryan would still be roaming around campus causing trouble. But I know Grant still worries about me, my emotions, and Ryan coming back for revenge.

I keep telling him he doesn't need to worry about it, but I'm sure he'll never stop worrying about me and my safety.

I can't believe I was ever worried about him being like Kyle was. He's nothing like that asshole. Grant's love is the only one I ever want to feel. I'm sure of that now.

"So Ella, Ames told me you've had a few interviews. How have those gone?" Paige asks and Ella starts to shake her head.

"I've had interviews but no bites yet. I'm only looking for something entry-level. I know it'll take time to get to my dream job, so I'll take anything at this point." She seems confident, and I don't doubt she'll reach all her goals one day. If someone is going to crawl their way to the top and rightfully earn their spot, it'll be her.

"How does it feel to be seniors in college, you two?" Ella says to Paige and Amelia. "I know I was afraid. It was the beginning of the end."

"It's weird, and I don't want to talk about it because I might cry," Paige says.

"It feels like I'm waiting for another shoe to drop. I just don't know when or where it's going to happen," Amelia says.

"That makes sense, I think," I say to them. I'm sure I'll understand that next year when I'm a senior and the only one left. "It's weird to think that after next year, I'll be the only one left of the four of us. It's going to be weird without you guys being here," I say. The tears are coming now, and I don't even try to push them away. I want to feel these ones.

I used to think the future was scary, and it still is in some ways, but imagining my girls not being around me while I'm here for my senior year makes me never want to grow up. I'm sure we'll still find a way to get together, but I'm going to miss studying in their living rooms while music plays softly in the background. I'm going to miss us all getting distracted and talking for hours about certain topics we've already discussed at length.

Paige gives me a side hug. "We'll always be close. I don't think any of us plan to go that far, and even if we do, we're always one phone call or text away."

"Plus, you're not going to be totally alone." Amelia flicks her head over to where Alissa and Grant are standing. I look at Grant, and he meets my eyes because he can always sense when I'm looking at him. He shoots me a wink and continues with his conversation. My stomach flutters because she's right. I won't be alone. Grant will be by my side, and in turn, so will Jacks and Claire. We've already talked a few times since we shared a few classes together, and I'm excited that we both get to watch the two of them play hockey together for the next two years.

"Yeah, you're right. I won't be alone." I smile at them. For the first time in a long time I feel truly happy. How did I forget I won't be alone now that I have him?

"You okay?" he asks me as he gets back to the table.

"I'm amazing," I say back to him.

"Grant, would you mind taking our picture?" Ella asks as she drags Amelia by the arm so she stands up.

"Just hand me a phone and tell me what angles you want," he says and we all laugh.

We all get up from the table and form a line, our hands overlapping as we all get into our pose. I'm really glad we all take a thousand pictures whenever we get together—I love the memories, but I also love capturing the memories we created so I can look back at them in the future.

This is the last time all of us will be together before we split off for the summer. Hell, it's the last time all of us will be students of Grand Mountain College at the same time.

Paige is going home to New York. Amelia is heading back to her hometown as well. Ella has her job search ahead of her, and Alissa is going back to England with her brother for a bit. Grant and I are heading to either his or my house first.

We're all splitting up for now. I know it won't last forever, but I wish I could stay in this moment forever. In this beautiful moment with my friends beside me and my boyfriend behind the camera—looking at me like I'm the only person in the world he sees.

I desperately want to grasp onto this feeling and never let it go. I want to hold it close to my chest and let it sink into my bones.

I'm excited about the future with Grant, but I'm even more excited knowing our little book club will follow us no matter where we end up. I know these girls will be beside me for the rest of my life—Grant, too. I have a gut feeling it's all going to work out for the group of us.

"Everyone say book club!" Grant says as he clicks the button a bunch of times and changes angles.

None of us says a word. We all know that this moment is too special for them, so instead we take it all in and let the emotions we're feeling linger in the air around us. After the picture is taken, we sit, eat good food, have some drinks, and laugh. We laugh a lot because that's what happens when you find your people—you laugh because one little decision to do something led you to your forever people.

The little moments before the big jumps are often remembered the most, and because we took that picture, we can replay this memory over whenever we want. When we look back on these photos we'll remember how we felt, how we laughed until our stomachs hurt. I know I'll look back and remember the feeling that flows through my body—I've stumbled upon true and real friendship. And no matter what happens in the future, these three girls will be doing it all with me.

I read somewhere once that moments of transition are often the loneliest, but I feel more supported than I've ever been before. These people around me will never make me feel alone in a crowded room—they'll be the ones standing next to me in it.

Grant sticks his tongue out to me as we walk back to his car, our stomachs full of food and our hearts full of love.

"I hate you," I say with a laugh.

"I love you too," he tells me as he opens my door for me. I slide in as I watch the rest of us trickle out of the restaurant. Paige and Amelia are walking with their arms linked together, the two of them laughing about something. Amelia's drunk and Paige is leading her back to the car. Alissa is hugging her brother while Ella shoots invisible lasers out of her eyes at him. Alissa must have called her brother since the two of them were drinking, and Ella gets dragged into the back seat by Alissa.

I cannot wait for the day I find out about Ella and Leo.

Grant slides into the car and kisses me on the cheek. "That was really fun. I always love hanging out with the girls."

"Me too," I say with a smile. My cheeks hurt from smiling and laughing so much tonight.

Grant turns his car on and looks over at me. "Are you ready to go?"

"I'm ready," I say as I grab his hand.

I'm ready to see all the world has to offer me. I'm ready for everything. The good, the bad, and all the love that comes with it.

Epilogue

Hadleigh

I'm SITTING NEXT TO Grant on Amelia's couch as my junior year of college has officially started. Ames invited us over to watch a travel documentary with her. It's been nice seeing her one on one because she and I don't get a lot of time where it's just the two of us.

And one thing I've learned about Grant in the time we've been together is that he enjoys a travel documentary as much as Amelia does. The two of them together can also gossip to their heart's content, and it's been an adjustment seeing Grant with all of them, but I love it.

Today is Saturday and the first week has gone smoothly so far—syllabus week always does. But the real reason I'm over here is to hear about the concert Amelia went to over the summer. I've been wanting to see pictures since we got back to campus, but she's been eerily quiet about it.

Typical Amelia, but I'll get something out of her.

Grant and I had a summer to remember. I'm glad to be back on campus together but we never really were apart. We spent the summer between our two homes—California and Vermont. At first, I was worried about Oliver and Grant interacting, but the first time they saw each other, they shook hands and did some weird dude thing as if they had known each other for years. I was skeptical, and neither of them would tell me about if they've interacted before—since they live in the same building.

Whatever. As long as Oliver doesn't kill him, that's all that matters.

Both of my parents adored him, especially when we showed Grant all of the traditions we do. He was so excited to learn more about my culture. Yet again he proved to me how much he cares about my life and who I am as a person.

Grant and Oliver went to the beach most mornings. Oliver tried to teach him how to surf, which didn't work because Oliver is a terrible teacher, but lots of laughs were shed. Mostly by me as I watched them from the sand. Since then, I've been taking more pictures and printing them out to hang all around my new room on campus.

In Vermont, Grant showed me around his hometown. It was the most perfect small town and I felt like I was dropped into a small-town romance series. He took me on a tour of all his favorite spots—the rink his dad used to practice on with him, his old job at this ice cream place, and he even took me to where his dad was buried to introduce me to him. It was a beautiful moment. He told me his dad would approve of me because as long as Grant was happy, that's all he ever cared about. And Grant told me I make him the happiest person on the planet. I cried a bit after that, and so did he. I don't know how he does it, but he brings out my emotions more than anyone else can.

We even went ice skating at his old rink, and I had a lot of fun with him this summer. Now, we have to go back to reality and start another semester, but this one has already been smoother than last.

Jacks and Grant are still in their same old apartment as last year, but Taylor and I moved into a four bedroom dorm with two other girls. It's been okay so far. The other two are super quiet, so I guess only time will tell with how this living arrangement goes.

It's nice being so close on campus to everyone because we all get together and have dinner, study sessions, and movie nights a lot of the time. Jacks and Claire are still going strong and the four of us do double dates all of the time when our schedules are able to line up. When hockey season starts, all of us are going to be super busy, so we try to hang out as much as we can.

My brother and I have been having dinner a lot lately too. He cooked for Grant and I back home, but since we got back, we've been making some meals together that we didn't get to have at home. It's been a nice bonding experience for us since I wasn't with him all summer like I usually am.

Speaking of Oliver, he's currently with Paige at a meeting this morning. They're both co-chairs of the criminal justice club on campus since the other seniors graduated last semester. I think they're trying to fundraise for something, but I have no idea what. I stopped listening after he grunted at me for the third time. I should know he wasn't going to tell me much.

Life is good so far. It's been nice being back in a routine, and as Amelia hands me the popcorn, I smile. I missed these hangouts while we were apart.

"Thanks for watching this with me. Paige has been so busy she told me to watch this one by myself. But since Grant likes them too, I figured you guys would watch it with me."

"Amelia, I feel like you and I don't get much time together. Plus, I like watching Grant's eyes light up like yours when you watch these. And so you know, I'll always support you and your dreams. I think you could make it to National Geographic one day." I lean over, grab her hand, and squeeze it.

"Okay, it's starting." She turns the volume up and the three of us start to watch it. I'm not as interested in this stuff as the two of them are, so they spend most of the time explaining different things to me.

About thirty minutes into the documentary, Paige and my brother burst through the front door. Immediately, we all notice that Paige has tears streaming down her face, and she doesn't say a word as she goes to the sink and starts scrubbing her hands. I can see her shaking from here. Oliver tries to go to where she is, but Grant stands up and reaches him before he can.

"Dude, back up and give her some space," he says to Oliver, and my brother doesn't say a word. *What the hell is going on?* Oliver nods and steps back while Grant stands beside him. Amelia and I get up and she goes right for Paige while I stand in confusion and stare at my brother.

"What did you do to Paige? She looks scared," I ask, wanting some answers. Amelia motions for Paige to stop scrubbing what looks like ink off her hands, but Paige swats her away. She still hasn't said a word and neither has my brother. It would be super nice if either one of them said something.

"Only took your brother four years to get on Paige's nerves. What did it this time? The grunts or the evil stares?" Amelia says as she shuts off the water. Paige immediately turns it back on again.

"Guys, I didn't do anything. Something happened," Oliver says to the room. Paige pauses when he says that. Tears stream steadily down her face, and her hands are red from all the scrubbing she's been doing.

Grant shuts the front door, and it slams when he does. I see Paige flinch where she stands and then Oliver finally moves from where he is and heads toward her. In a complete twist that nobody could've seen coming, my brother hugs Paige. She relaxes a bit, and I swear the world has flipped on its axis because my brother just hugged someone willingly.

"Cut the bullshit and start talking," Grant says to them. Thank God he said something because I would have been a lot meaner. Someone needs to start talking because I'm tired of seeing Paige cry. Oliver looks a bit off-kilter from how he normally is, and I don't like it. Nothing really rattles him much anymore, so whatever happened to them must have been something bad. That scares me more than it should. Weren't they at a meeting? How bad could it have gone?

"Oliver, what happened to Paige?" I ask, a bit more harsh than usual. I want some fucking answers. I want to know why my friend is crying, shaking, and refusing to speak. Oliver lets go of Paige and looks at me.

"What's to say something didn't happen to me, too?" he asks, speaking a bit louder now.

"Oliver, you have one facial expression—the one you're wearing right now," Grant says. "Just tell us what happened to Paige."

"Guys, I'm right here, and I'm fine, I swear." Paige finally speaks and we all fall quiet. She smiles, but it's not real. She almost looks unrecognizable—like she cut out a smile and pasted it onto her face.

"P, you're not. You're shaking and still crying. Something must have happened," Amelia says. "You don't get like this for no reason. Let's sit down, and we can talk about it."

"Wait, back up. Has Paige been like this before?"

Amelia shakes her head at my question, and I drop it. That conversation is for another time, it seems.

"Oliver, fucking say something," Grant snaps at him. Oliver looks over at Paige, and she looks back at him. There's this weird charged energy in here. Are they not allowed to talk about whatever happened? How serious was it? A thousand possibilities run through my mind, and none of them are good.

"The dean of students is dead and Paige found the body. He was murdered," Oliver finally says, and we all go silent. "We just came from the police station because as the only witnesses, we had to answer questions, and they fingerprinted us." I look down at Ol's hands, and sure enough, his fingers are inked like Paige's are.

Nobody speaks for a solid few minutes. We all just stand there. Sure, Paige likes true crime and has seen pictures of dead bodies all the time, but seeing someone dead? That must've been terrifying for the two of them.

"Do you guys need anything?" Grant asks, looking between them both. The two of them are still staring at one another having some sort of telepathic conversation.

"Paige, no," is all Oliver says to her.

"Why not?"

"It's dangerous," he tells her.

"Fine."

"Okay, that was a wonderful conversation none of us had the context to. I'm going to call Ella. This is an emergency, and we need everyone here," Amelia says as she exits the room to grab her phone.

"The school sent out an email. A shelter-in-place. Holy shit," Grant says, looking down at his phone.

I guess junior year is going to be more hectic than I thought.

Extended Epilogue

Grant

A Few Years Later

"Did you really need to blindfold me for this? I thought we were going to dinner?"

My beautiful girlfriend asks me that as I escort her to her surprise. Today is our anniversary and I've spent the past few years loving her and creating a beautiful life alongside her.

We recently bought an apartment in Virginia near the school I'm coaching at, and right down the road from where Hads works as a super smart scientist for a pharmaceutical company.

After graduation, we moved in together, and it's been nothing but love and stupid little arguments that always end with us being on the same team and her smacking me with whatever she can find. Every time, it ends with a kiss and we hold one another until we forget what we were even arguing about in the first place.

Hads has become more comfortable with her emotions and less tense over the years. She tells me it's because of me, but I think she's genuinely happy for the first time ever, that everything else melts away. Those walls she built up for all those years have officially been knocked down, never to be put up again.

"The blindfold was necessary since you keep asking me questions about the surprise. It's bad enough you can tell from my face when I'm lying, but for this I want you to be completely shocked. I want to see that look of surprise on your face."

"Grant, if you're pregnant just tell me now. I can handle it," she says to me.

"Don't spoil it, baby. How did you guess that so easily?" I feign heartbreak, and she giggles at me, still blindfolded.

Little does she know I'm leading her into a building we know very well. It's a Saturday afternoon in the middle of May and nobody is in here because school is officially out for the summer. It took me forever to put all of this together—with the girl's help, of course—and I paid a security guard to keep people still on campus away from this building.

The girls made sure it was perfect, and I'm so thankful all of us still talk and are as close as we are. All of us have created our own little family with one other. We get together on holidays, and the girls still have book club once a week. Every Wednesday night, just like always.

I asked Oliver to help me pick out a ring for Hads after I asked for his and her father's blessings. Thankfully, they both gave it to me. I thought I'd have to convince Oliver a bit more, but he was on board.

The ring box in my jacket pocket has been burning a hole in my body. I've had the ring for a year, but life got in the way, and I never found the right time to do this.

Not anymore. My girl deserves the best proposal on the planet.

Hads and I are twenty-three this year, and I knew it was time. I knew from the moment she confessed her love to me on that ice rink I was going to spend the rest of my life with her, and I couldn't wait any longer to live that life officially with her.

"Okay, I'm opening the door in front of you, and there are three steps up after this." I guide her into the building.

"Grant, where are we? It's chilly in here."

I wouldn't know what it feels like because I've been sweaty and itchy all day. I didn't think I would be this nervous, but I am. I don't think she's going to say no, but she could. That thought alone is terrifying.

"I finally brought you back to the Underworld, sorry."

"Very funny, boyfriend."

I open the second door and lead her to the spot I marked on the floor. "Okay, stand there and don't move." I shuffle a few steps over and get in my spot. "You can take the blindfold off now."

She takes it off, and her face looks as shocked as ever. We're back in the exact place where I ran into her for the first time when I only knew her as someone who got an A in the class I was failing. Back then, she was just my tutor.

Now? Now, she's everything to me—my life, my girl, my future. *Everything.*

Surrounding us, all my favorite pictures are hanging from strings from the ceiling. Pictures from hockey games during senior year, our dates throughout the years, her wearing my jersey. All of my favorite moments I've spent with her surround us and hang from the ceiling. Some strings are blank, signifying that we have more memories to create together in the future.

"Wh-what is this?"

"The spot where I first laid my eyes on you. The spot where it all started—you and me."

"I know, but what are we doing here?" She's looking around at the pictures that hang, and tears start to fill her eyes. She starts to walk toward me, but I stop her.

"Hold up. You're not allowed to move from that spot," I say as I start to walk toward her.

"When have I ever listened to you before?"

"True, but please, just this once?"

She smiles at me. "Okay. Only because you said please."

I reach her, and I take a deep breath as I grab both of her hands. I drop to one knee and look up at her. Tears are brimming in her eyes, and I know she's trying her best not to start crying. I open the ring box and start talking.

"Hadleigh Baker, you are the most extraordinary person I have had the chance to love these past few years. I've known for a while I've wanted to spend the rest of my life with you, but I wanted this planned to perfection because you deserve nothing less. I hope these pictures remind you of how beautiful and chaotic our life has been so far, and I cannot wait to create so many more memories with you in the future. Will you marry me?" I'm crying at this point, and I don't know why I'm still afraid she might say no. And then she says one word that changes everything.

"Yes." Tears are spilling from her eyes.

I place the ring on her finger—it fits perfectly—and I wrap her up in my arms. I kiss her, pick her up, and spin her around, needing her closer but knowing she can't crawl inside of my skin. The strings with the photos get caught in our happiness that spins around the room.

"I love you so much, Hads."

"I love you too, fiancé," she says back to me, a new nickname for me.

We kiss a bit longer in the same spot we first met, and this moment feels full circle from how we originally started—me falling for her as soon as I saw her.

I reach behind me and hand her a small gift I prepared for this moment—another full-circle metaphor for this special occasion.

"What's this?"

"Open it," I say to her.

She does, and a few more tears fall after she realizes what it is. *The Great Gatsby* is annotated and tabbed just for her. It felt fitting since this book is the reason we met and got closer.

"This is perfect," she says as she flips through the pages. I drew a bunch of annotations—including the famous green light I once compared her to. I was able to step up my annotated book game, finally. I've come a long way since I gave her that very first book I tabbed and highlighted.

Little does she know there's one more surprise at the restaurant. All the girls and her whole family are waiting for her. I flew them all in from California as a surprise, so I'm really glad she said yes.

As we walk out of the building we first met in, our hands intertwined, I stop to think about how much of a turning point this is for our life and future.

Unlike Gatsby, I was able to reach my green light, and I'm never going to let her go.

Acknowledgements

First off, thank you to Lexi and Hannah for not laughing in my face when I said I wanted to rewrite this book. I can't believe how far our team has come since we published this story the first time. Now, almost two years later, here we are still doing this thing together from three different states. I love you guys more than words! Thank you for sticking by me throughout this insane process.

Hannah—Your covers are always so beautiful but this new one is stunning. I am so deeply grateful that your art is wrapped around my art. I can't wait to see what we do together in the future.

Lexi—Thank you for everything you have done to help me when I had to rewrite this story in one month. Your tireless effort in making sure my stories are perfect does not go unnoticed. I love how you love my characters, but I love even more that I get to collaborate with you on these books. Let's say we do this forever, huh?

Cassidy Hudspeth—You always make my books shine, and I absolutely adore working with you. You're the freaking best!

Amy & Maine—My original beta readers. Thank you for the continuous support for these characters. It truly means the world to me.

Alyssa Williams—I've known you since we were two but I don't have the words to describe what your friendship means to me! You are one of the reasons I believe platonic love is as important as romantic. But getting to watch one another fall in love is peak girlhood, and I love you so much. Bookstore trips and loud music forever, okay?

Josh—Thank you for keeping me afloat during this rewrite. I know I spend a lot of time in romance novels, but trust me, ours will forever be my favorite.

Andrew—Thank you for your help with some of the dialogue that stayed from the original. One of these day I'll write that ghost book you keep bugging me about.

Mom—For being confused as to why I was rewriting. All of your questions make me giggle because I know you have no clue what I'm talking about, but you listen anyway.

My brother—Thanks for helping with some of the hockey language. You will probably never read this, but thanks for all the support from afar.

Jan Boswell—For inspiring me to rewrite this novel to be the best it could be. Your inspiration, voice notes, and support means the world. We may not be authors in every universe, but I'm absolutely sure we're friends in every single one.

My readers—I truly have the best ones in the world. Thank you for welcoming this new version of Hads and Grant's story into your hearts. It means to world that you love them as much as I do. I couldn't do any of this without you, so thank you for helping to make my dreams come true.

Finally, to my younger self, who always dreamed of holding her book in her hands. We did it! I wish you could see us now and see who we have become. I'm so proud of us.

Also By Emily Tudor

The Hart Sisters
The Road Not Taken
The Road Less Traveled By

About the Author

Emily Tudor creates characters and stories about platonic and romantic love for anyone and everyone. She lives in the state of New York and loves listening to music and creating stories. She loves Marvel movies, the song *mirrorball* by Taylor Swift and buying too many books when she already has many to be read at home.

You can find her on Instagram at:
@authoremilytudor
www.authoremilytudor.com